# The
# Midwife's Tale

# The Midwife's Tale

SAM THOMAS

MINOTAUR BOOKS ✼ NEW YORK

This is a work of fiction. All of the characters, organizations, and events portrayed in this novel are either products of the author's imagination or are used fictitiously.

www.minotaurbooks.com

ISBN 978-1-250-01076-6 (hardcover)
ISBN 978-1-250-01077-3 (e-book)

First Edition: January 2013

10 9 8 7 6 5 4 3 2 1

*For Spencer and Oliver*

# Acknowledgments

The idea that writing is a solitary endeavor is both a cliché and manifestly untrue. If this book has any redeeming qualities, it is thanks to the efforts of the following people who read early drafts: Benj Thomas, Susan Baird, Carol Pal, Brooke Newman, Sandra Shattuck, and, most of all, Laura Gaines. Thanks also to the staff—both past and present—at the Borthwick Institute for the Archives, where I first met the historical Bridget Hodgson, as well as my agent, Josh Getzler, and all my book-writing friends and cobloggers at *Book Pregnant*. I am also grateful to the Occidental University Library for the map of York. Finally, thank you to my wife, Nikki Marzano, for believing that lying on the couch reading a novel can be "work."

And moreover there is another manner of treason, that is to say, when a servant slays his master, or a wife her husband, or when a man secular or religious slays his prelate, to whom he owes faith and obedience.

— Statute of Treasons

The blood of man when violently shed doth cry out as far as from Earth to Heaven for vengeance. How much louder doth that blood cry when the crime is not merely murder, but treason also? Just as bloody-minded rebels have risen against our divinely appointed sovereign King Charles, servants, women, and children throughout England have harkened to the demands of that first rebel Satan and risen against their lords and masters. Through the workings of these home-rebels, families are torn asunder, all order is lost—truly England is a world turn'd upside-down. And such was the case in the royal city of York, when a citizen of that city was barbarously slain by she who owed him reverence above all.

—from *Bloody Newes from York: A true relation of the horrid instance of petty treason committed on the body of a citizen of the said city*

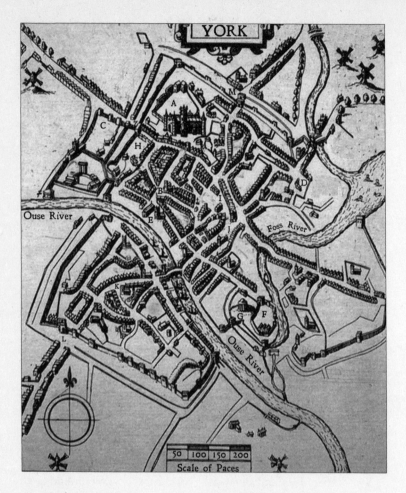

A. York Minster

B. St. Helen Stonegate Church

C. The King's Manor

D. The Black Swan

E. St. Martin Coney Street Church

F. York Castle

G. Clifford's Tower

H. Bootham Bar

I. The Shambles

J. All Saints, Pavement

K. St. Martin Micklegate Church

L. Micklegate Bar

M. Monkgate Bar

# June 1644

YORK, ENGLAND

# Chapter 1

On the night I delivered Mercy Harris of a bastard child, the King's soldiers burned the city's suburbs and fell back within its walls to await the rebel assault.

It was evening when the Overseer of the Poor arrived to summon me to the birth and my servant, Hannah, ushered him into the parlor.

"Lady Hodgson," he said when I joined him, "I am sorry to bother you on such a terrible day, but one of the parish's maidservants is in travail with a bastard. The churchwardens have sent me for a midwife."

"What parish are you from?" I asked. I knew he was not from St. Helen's, and most parishes handled their own bastard births.

"St. Savior's, my lady."

"Surely you have midwives in St. Savior's."

"They are unwilling to venture out, what with the fires, the smoke, and so many soldiers running about. They think it too dangerous."

I shook my head in despair—some women did not know the meaning of an oath. "I will come. What is the mother's name?"

"Mercy Harris, my lady. She lives on an alley off St. Andrewgate."

"Has she named the father yet?"

"She refuses. That is why we need a midwife."

"God save us from obstinate mothers." I sighed. "Wait here while I get my bag. You'll have to take me to her."

"Yes, my lady."

I sent Hannah upstairs for my tools and quickly changed into an apron fit for the work that lay ahead. The Overseer and I walked past the Minster's towering spires, toward the warren of streets, alleys, and courtyards that make up St. Savior's parish. In one hand the Overseer carried the small valise containing my tools and in the other a lantern to aid me in my work. The streets around us thronged with townspeople racing home, carrying whatever food they had found for sale in the shops or markets. A young woman with frightened eyes hurried past us, trying to manage the squalling infant in one arm and her day's purchases in the other. She turned off St. Andrewgate and disappeared down an alley.

We reached Mercy's door and I gazed up at the Minster, now silhouetted by the smoke pouring into the summer sky. *May the Lord affect our hearts with the sad fruits of wasting wars.*

"Go home," I told the Overseer. "The fire will unsettle your wife and children. They'll feel safer with you there."

"Are you sure, my lady?" he asked. "It won't be safe for you to return alone on a night such as this."

"I won't return before daylight," I assured him. "It's her first child, and she has refused to name the father. It will be a long night for both of us." He nodded and hurried back toward the relative safety of St. Andrewgate. I steeled myself for the night to come and entered the house without knocking.

I glanced around the room in which I would do my night's work. It would have been dim even at noon, and the setting sun provided only the slightest light through the horn windows. Mercy lay on the bed, staring at me with a surly expression. She was perhaps twenty-three years old and no great beauty. Obviously, I was not her first choice for a midwife. But to be fair, I hadn't chosen her for my client. A girl of perhaps fifteen years, with hair as dark as Mercy's, stood in the corner. She shrank from my gaze, apparently hoping to disappear entirely.

"By the look of you, you're Mercy's sister," I said gently. "You'll be my deputy tonight. What's your name?" My voice startled her, and she looked at Mercy, who nodded grudgingly.

"Sairy, my lady."

"Hello, Sairy," I said. "Do exactly what I tell you, exactly when I tell you, and everything will be fine. Do you understand?"

"Yes, m-my lady," she stammered.

"Good. Now, let's see what we've got here," I said, surveying the room. The watery light afforded by the small windows made it hard to tell where the shadows ended and the dirt began, so I counted the late hour as something of a blessing. Mercy lay on the straw mattress that she and Sairy undoubtedly shared. She wore only her shift, and without her skirts and apron, her pregnancy could hardly be missed. The canvas sheet and a single rough wool coverlet completed the picture of a family on the edge of poverty. Adjacent to the bed were the only other furnishings—two rough stools, an unsteady trestle table, and a clothes chest that had seen better days. Through a low door, I could see a small kitchen but held out little hope that it would provide much in the way of sustenance during the long night ahead. I turned back to Mercy.

"Look at me, Mercy. Look at me." She did. "You know I cannot help you unless you father the child aright. Tell me who the child's father is. If you tell the truth, I will help you through the pain and danger. Tell me the truth and I can testify before the Justice of the Peace. He will make the father pay for the child's upkeep." She looked away without responding. "Did he offer you money to keep silent?" I continued. "A shilling or two? Perhaps even a pound? Is he already married, and trying not to upset his wife?" I looked at Sairy, hoping for a clue, but she quickly looked away. Mercy suddenly tensed and cried out through clenched teeth. Her travail had begun in earnest. I sat on the stool farthest from the bed and leaned back against the wall. My valise remained conspicuously closed. "If you don't tell me who the father is, Mercy, I can't help you, and no one else will. You'll do this alone." She remained resolutely silent.

"Sairy, is there a fire in the kitchen?" I asked.

"We've no wood." The girl looked as if she would cry.

We would need food after the birth, but it was more important we have fire to heat water, so I gave Sairy a few pennies to purchase wood from a neighbor. She returned and built a small fire in the kitchen hearth. She then produced a smoky tallow candle, which, combined with my lantern, lit the room tolerably well. With any luck the child would wait until morning to be born so I could have a bit more light, but women like Mercy weren't lucky very often.

The Minster bells marked the hours of the horrid contest that followed. When the labor pains struck, Sairy's eyes begged me to tell her what to do. I hardened my heart and avoided her gaze as resolutely as Mercy avoided mine. I longed to assist the poor girl and could not help wondering how she had come to this point. Where were her parents? Was Sairy the only family that she had? At eleven o'clock, Mercy's waters broke. With shaking hands, Sairy tried to soak up the mess using just a soiled rag from the kitchen. Poor girl. Around two o'clock, Mercy's final travail started.

"Mercy, I'll ask one more time. Who is the father?" She clenched her teeth and stared at me, her eyes blazing. She had bitten through her bottom lip, and in the flickering candlelight the blood ran black down her chin. Her chest heaved as she breathed, but still she said nothing. I turned to Sairy. "You can try to find another midwife if you like, but few will venture out on a night like this, especially for a woman such as your sister. And even if you find someone, she will ask the same questions." Her eyes widened with fear, and I continued. "The neighbors might help, but they've no love for a fatherless bastard. The two of you will be on your own tonight." I picked up my valise and lantern and opened the door. "Be careful when you cut the navel string," I added. "If you do it badly, the baby will die, and so might your sister." I walked out, closing the door behind me.

Once outside, I stepped into a neighbor's doorway to hide, only to find it occupied by one of the pigs that roamed York's streets. I gave the animal a swift kick in the side, and it raced off with an indignant squeal. I slipped into the shadows to wait. As I expected, Mercy's door burst open, and Sairy raced pell-mell past me, holding up her skirts as high as she could. I called out, startling her, and she nearly skidded into the urine-filled gutter. She hurried over and grasped my arm to pull me back to her house. Once again I fought the urge to put my arms around the girl and help her in any way I could. It was not in my nature to withhold aid, but in this situation I had no choice. I pulled my arm free and she fell to her knees, sobbing.

"Why won't you help her?" she cried out. "She'll die without you! The baby will die, too. You said so."

At the sound of her pitiful cries, my heart melted and I reached down to help her to her feet. I felt for the poor girl—it was Mercy who had sinned, after all. "If she doesn't name the father, the city will have to support the child for years to come," I explained as gently as I could. "The law forbids me to help her so long as she refuses. It is also for the good of the child. If I tell the Justices who the father is, they will order him to support the baby. You all will benefit from that."

"What should I do?"

"Tell her to name the father," I said, cupping her face in my hands. "If she promises to do so, I will come back and all will be well, both tonight and in the future."

Sairy nodded and disappeared into the house. Moments later, she emerged. "Mercy said she will tell you who the father is. Now will you help?" I nodded and followed her back into the room.

I crossed the room and squatted between Mercy's legs. I paused before touching her. "Mercy, you must name the father of your child, or I will leave again. Your life is in peril—do not make the last words you speak a lie, for you will answer for it on Judgment Day."

"Peter Clark," she said between breaths. "The father is Peter Clark."

"I know no Peter Clark," I replied. "And it is a common name. Which Peter Clark is the father of your child?"

"He's apprentice to William Dolben. He is a butcher in the Shambles. He is the father, I swear. We were betrothed when he got me with child, and to be married in the spring. His master would not give him leave to marry until the end of the summer."

I would have to ask her again, of course, but Peter Clark was a good place to start and I could begin my work. "Thank you, Mercy," I said. "You did the right thing, both for you and for the child."

I opened my valise and laid out the oils and medicines I would need. I said a prayer as I slipped a small knife for the navel string into my apron. The small satchel of cutting tools remained at the bottom of the bag, and I hoped they would remain there. I opened a vial of oil and, muttering another prayer under my breath, anointed my hands and the neck of Mercy's womb. I slipped my hand inside to see how the child lay and to judge how best I could smooth his journey into the world. I could feel the child's head and knew that he would be born soon. I looked up at Mercy. The skin was drawn tight across her cheeks and her eyes shone with pain, giving her the look of a demon. She should have eaten to sustain her strength, and I wished I'd brought some food for her.

I turned to Sairy. "The baby will be born shortly. Do you have linens prepared?" She looked at me blankly. "For swaddling the child?" I added.

"In the chest," said Mercy. "I purchased them last week." I nodded at Sairy, and she sprang into action, pulling a small packet out of the chest and laying it on the table.

"Now take some water and put it on the fire," I said. Sairy hesitated again. A sweet girl and good sister, but not what I would want in an assistant. "We'll need to wash the baby. Not too hot, just warm enough to clean him." Sairy disappeared into the kitchen, and I turned back to Mercy.

"Here, let me help you up—you'll do better squatting on

your haunches than lying down. The child will struggle to be born, and it's better to give him a downhill road." She hesitated, unsure if walking around while in travail was a good idea. "It will also mean you don't have to burn your mattress afterwards." She grasped my hands and with some effort hauled herself off the bed and to her feet.

We walked in small circles around the room, Mercy's arm over my shoulders, mine around her waist. From time to time she rested her head on my shoulder, and I saw her wipe tears on my collar. It seemed to me that these were tears not of pain but of regret. She had sinned, of course, and deserved some measure of her fate, but I wondered what possible future Peter Clark had stolen from her when he got her with child. Would she ever live as a respectable housewife? Would she raise her children in a home with more than one bed, two stools, and a table? Or was this a final step into dire poverty? Would she end her life as one of the city's whores, her child an urchin destined for a similar life?

"You'll be fine," I said, squeezing her shoulders. I also added a silent prayer that I spoke the truth. "Your travail is going well, and the baby's head is at the neck of your matrix. Who knows? It may not even hurt." At this, even though fear and exhaustion threatened to overtake her, she smiled a little. "It will probably hurt," I conceded, and we continued to walk.

As the height of Mercy's labor approached, I called to Sairy. "You'll have to support her while I deliver the child. Sit on the edge of the bed and put your arms under hers, holding her up." I renewed my questioning.

"Mercy, tell the truth, who is the father of your child?"

"He is Peter Clark."

"Swear, Mercy."

"If the father is any man other than Peter Clark, may this child and I never part!"

But a short time later they did part, and by the grace of God I ushered a lusty baby girl into the world. If healthy lungs guaranteed a long life, this child would outlive her own grandchildren. I cut and bound the navel string.

"Bring the water and a clean cloth," I told Sairy. She went to the kitchen and returned with a pot, which she set on the table. With no great optimism she began to root in the chest for a cloth. "Never mind," I said. I unclipped my collar and tested the water's temperature. Miraculously, it was just right. I dipped my collar-turned-washcloth into the water and began to clean the squalling infant. Once that task was accomplished, I took the linen bands from the package Mercy had bought and swaddled the girl. Mercy now sat on one of the stools, leaning against the bed, looking dazed. I placed the infant in her arms and held my lantern so mother and child could gaze upon each other.

"If the afterbirth does not come on its own, in a moment I'll have to fetch it out myself," I told her. She nodded. But luck was on her side, and a few minutes later the afterbirth was delivered of its own accord. After dressing Mercy's privities, I helped her into bed. Exhausted, she lay back and closed her eyes.

"No sleep yet," I told her. "You should nurse the child and then you can both sleep." Her nipples were well suited for nursing, and the child sucked greedily. I turned to Sairy and saw that she had dozed off in the corner. Only the Lord knew how long she had been awake. I glanced at the window and noticed that morning had come. I heard the Minster bell toll once—half-five, I guessed. I went into the kitchen to see what food they had but found only a stale bread crust and pot of weak ale. I returned to the parlor and saw that all three of the house's inhabitants slept. I shook Sairy awake. She looked up at me, still half-asleep.

"Do you and Mercy have any money?" I asked.

A look of horror spread across her face. "We can't...we don't...the Overseer of the Poor said...," she stammered.

"Not for me, Sairy, for food. Your sister will awake with the appetite of two men."

"We have nothing at all. She spent the last of our money on the linen for the baby."

I fetched some more coins from my valise. "Here. If you find meat you can afford, boil it rather than roast it. She should also have broth and eggs, but no mutton. It will give her a fever. I imagine Peter Clark can get you some beef or a chicken. It would be the least he could do." White wine would have helped her regain her strength, but it was clearly more than they could afford, so I suggested barley water. "And almond milk if you can find it." She thanked me profusely, helped me gather my belongings, and accompanied me to St. Andrewgate.

"Everything should be fine for now," I said. "The nearest midwife is Elizabeth Halliday, over in St. Cuthbert's parish, around the corner from the church." Sairy nodded. "She is a good midwife and nurse, and can help. Tell her I sent you, and that I will repay the courtesy. If you need me, go to St. Helen Stonegate. Ask any of the shopkeepers there, and they will tell you where I live. I am Lady Bridget Hodgson."

She nodded again. "Yes, my lady."

"Good. You did well last night. Your sister is lucky to have you. Now, go find some food for the both of you."

"Thank you, my lady."

I watched the girl disappear around the corner, and then I started for my home.

# Chapter 2

As I walked home in the early morning light, I looked toward Bootham Bar and said a prayer of thanks that the previous night's fires had burned themselves out. A smoky haze drifted into the sky as the ashes smoldered, but the worst had passed. I hoped that the King's men had succeeded in denying the rebels cover should they attempt to storm the walls. Only the Lord knew what slaughter would follow if the rebels took the city by force. When I turned onto Stonegate, a group of soldiers came into view, marching toward the barbican for their turn walking the city's walls. The sergeant saluted me, and I wished him Godspeed.

As the soldiers passed out of sight, I reflected on York's journey from a free and prosperous city to these desperate straits. Curiously, England's road to civil war began in Ireland, when the Papists took up arms against their Protestant masters and slaughtered them by the thousands, giving quarter to neither women nor children. Fantastic rumors soon spread that the Irish had acted with the King's approval and that he intended to bring them to England to continue their bloody work. Parliament raised an army to defend England against the Irish, and King Charles raised an army to defend himself against Parliament; within weeks war had begun.

The Parliament-men said that the King meant to put down the Protestant religion and return England to the shackles of Popery. Some even warned that the King hoped to bring in an Irish army to slaughter English Protestants in their beds. Others charged that the King meant to do away with all Parliaments and rule as a tyrant. They said he would put himself up as a new Pharaoh, lay waste to ancient English liberties, and claim for himself the right to take any man's property.

For his part, the King branded the Parliament-men traitors, bent on destroying every kind of order. If the rebels succeeded in bringing down the monarchy, he declared, they would pull down the Church soon after, and then the authority of fathers and masters. They would not stop until they had destroyed all order, even that which God Himself created. Their goal, he said, was anarchy. For my part, I chose order over chaos and favored the King, but most of all I lamented the passing of a time when King, Church, and people lived and breathed as one body.

The war came to York in December 1642, when the Marquess of Newcastle—then but an Earl—entered the city and established a Royalist garrison. A few months later, the Queen brought weapons and money to help defend the city, but (praise be to God) no enemy showed himself. For over a year, we had the luxury of watching our nation's civil war from a distance, as other towns were taken and retaken and other men's sons bore the brunt of the fighting. All of this ended in the spring, when the Scots joined with the rebels and marched to the city's walls and began to tighten the rope around York's neck. Food had not yet begun to run short, but the siege could last for months, and what would we do then? In the meantime, the Parliament-men shot their artillery into the city, unconcerned with what they hit. God ordained that most fell into the river Foss, but the devil had his say as well. Houses were destroyed, innocents killed, and the church tower of St. Denys was shot through with a cannonball, making a mockery of Parliament's pretensions to defend true religion.

As I approached the narrow street that would take me home, a few of the trained bands approached. They were local boys and doffed their caps when they recognized me.

"Returning from a birth, Lady Hodgson?" their sergeant enquired.

"Indeed." I fumbled for his first name—I knew I had delivered two of his children, and while I never forgot a mother, the fathers were a different matter. "How are Barbara and your girls, Sergeant Smith?" Better to stick with the rank.

"The girls are well, praise God. Bridget is nearly two now and running all about the house." He knew I would remember Bridget's birth. His wife's travail lasted for days. Another midwife said the child was dead and had wanted to call in the surgeon with his cutting tools. The husband came to my door in a panic and begged my help. In the end it turned out that there were twins. I could not save the boy child, but the girl lived, and her father consented to name her in my honor. I resolved to have Hannah bake a pie and send it over to them when I got home.

After taking my leave of the sergeant, I completed the last few steps of my journey. Like those around it, my home stood three stories tall, with each one extending a bit farther over the street than the one below it. On narrower streets it was nearly possible to climb out the window of one building and in the window of the neighbor across the street. As my home came into view, I realized how tired I was. I only hoped that the women I had promised to assist in their travail would wait until the evening, or better yet until the next morning, to go into labor. And if the Overseer of the Poor called again? Well, York had half a dozen midwives, and one of them would have to suffice.

When I entered, Hannah rushed into the parlor and began fussing over me. She was perhaps twenty-five years my senior and had been my maidservant for as long as I could remember. She had helped to raise me, then left her family in Hereford to accompany me to York. She had seen me married twice, widowed twice, and I think she still held out fond hope she would see a third wedding and perhaps another child or two. She insisted that she felt as young as ever, but I wondered how much longer she would be able to do the housework by herself. She took my cloak and ushered me into the dining room, clucking all the while.

"So," she asked, "who was the father of the baby?" Among the benefits of living with a midwife was being the first to hear local gossip.

"Nobody of note," I said. "He's just a butcher's apprentice."

She could not hide her disappointment. A debauched Alderman would have made for much better gossip in the city's markets and shops. She went to the kitchen, returning a moment later with a steaming bowl of pottage. She placed it on the table before me and disappeared upstairs to continue her work. I was famished and began to eat, but the clink of my spoon against the bowl echoed through the empty room. I wished that Hannah had stayed with me, or at least busied herself in the kitchen, so I would not be so alone. Such melancholy feelings robbed me of my appetite. I pushed my bowl aside and started upstairs to my chamber.

On my way through the parlor I gazed at the portrait of my second husband, Phineas, the man who had brought me to York. Despite having looked upon the picture every day since his death,

I was struck once again by the artist's inability to portray him as any less pathetic than he had been in life. In truth, it was a peculiar kind of masterpiece. As in life, my husband's eyes were somehow both sunken and bulging, and his uniquely weak chin became his most remarkable feature. His ears were perfect for a man twice his size, and his nose seemed to be recoiling from the prospect of smelling his own fetid breath. More than once I had considered remarriage if only to rid my home of so perfect a picture of so ridiculous a man.

From Phineas's portrait, my eyes slid to the much smaller drawing of my first husband, Luke. While Phineas lived, I had kept the picture in a drawer, of course, but after his death I placed it on the small table in the parlor. Phineas compared unfavorably to most men, but he suffered in particular when I contrasted him with Luke. I had met Luke only after our marriage had been arranged: Our families' lands in Hereford lay near each other, and our parents made the match without consulting either of us. While such marriages sometimes ended in disaster, Luke and I had similar temperaments and we soon fell deeply in love. But just two years after we married, my joy turned to mourning when Luke died of an ague during a trip to London. The abject sorrow I felt after his death left me little time to think about anything else, but my parents immediately began their search for a new husband. A few weeks into my widowhood, my father came to me and announced he had arranged my marriage to Phineas Hodgson, the second son of the Lord Mayor of York. I could hardly blame him for his decision. A twenty-four-year-old widow with no children brought no benefit to the family. A few months later, still numb from the loss of my beloved husband, I climbed into a carriage and, with Hannah at my side, set out for a new life in York.

Seen from Hereford, my father's second match appeared as

good as the first: The Hodgsons were among the most powerful families in the city, and both Phineas's father and his brother cut impressive figures. I discovered too late that Phineas came from some lesser branch of the family. His unappealing visage was matched by a singular weakness of mind and character. He had squandered his patrimony long before I arrived in York, and after we married he spent most of his waking hours trying to coax me out of my estates in Hereford. When that failed, he would settle for a visit to our bed but made it clear he would have preferred my land to my body. To this day, I wonder if my father knew what kind of man he had chosen for me. When Phineas succumbed to a fever in 1642, I counted myself among the luckiest of women in England. I had my youth, my fortune, my freedom, and my beautiful daughter, Birdy. But now Birdy's picture sat on the table next to Luke's.

The sound of Hannah clattering down the stairs, her arms full of laundry, startled me out of my reverie. "I'll to bed, Hannah. Come help me undress." In my room, Hannah unlaced my stays and took my soiled clothes. I put on a clean shift and knelt by the side of the bed to pray. Afterward I sank into bed and let my mind wander. I wondered what fate awaited Mercy and her bastard child. I feared she would turn to the parish for relief soon enough. With luck, she might find employment in one of the city's workhouses, which would keep her and her child from starving, but not much more than that. I wished I could do more to help her, but she had made her choices, and they could not be undone. Perhaps the baby's father would marry her, I thought. With hard work he could gain his freedom and give Mercy a better life than she could rightly hope for. I preferred to think of that fate.

I heard the thump of cannon in the distance and wondered what future awaited our nation. English and Scottish armies ransacked the countryside, and an Irish horde threatened from abroad. Eventually sleep came, but I found no rest. In my troubled dreams, I was standing on the Ouse Bridge next to Mercy Harris, who was holding her newborn daughter. Mercy looked out over the water, tears coursing down her cheeks. I watched helplessly as she stepped to the edge of the bridge, kissed her baby tenderly, and let her fall into the river. As the water swallowed the child, I saw that she was no longer Mercy's daughter, but my own lost son, Michael. I clapped my hands over my face, and my nails raked my eyes in anguish. Mercy fell to her knees next to me, and we both cried uncontrollably.

I awoke with a start and tried to control my sobs before Hannah heard them and came to see what the matter was. As I quieted my breathing, I prayed that Mercy would never know the sorrow of losing a child. Her daughter had been born healthy, but I knew all too well that was no guarantee. Michael was a picture of health when he was born, but he sickened and died just a few days after his christening. Birdy had lived long enough to see her brother and her father buried, but the Lord had claimed her as well. On a Sunday morning she sang the Psalms at the top of her lungs. That afternoon she had a cough. That night she died in my arms, feverish and shaking, leaving me alone.

Once I'd stopped my tears and dried my cheeks, I summoned Hannah and had her bring me a glass of milk to cool my blood. I then sent her away with a warning not to disturb me until supper. I dared not close my eyes for fear that the dreams would return, so I resolved to put my household accounts in order. We still had some of the provisions I set aside when a siege seemed likely, but the prices commanded by necessities such as butter and eggs disturbed me all the same. I still had plenty of money locked in my trunk, as well as hundreds of pounds out on loan to wealthy friends and to the goldsmiths, but if the siege dragged on and food could not be had at any price, access to ready cash could be the least of my problems. As I finished my accounts, I prayed that it would not come to that.

After the previous night's events and that morning's dreams, I decided to dedicate what was left of the afternoon to reflection. I began reading some of Mr. Herbert's sacred poems. Naturally enough, within minutes Hannah appeared in the doorway.

"Sweet peace, where dost thou dwell?" I asked aloud. She looked puzzled but said nothing. "What is it, Hannah?"

"My lady, a maid is here with a letter for you. I don't know who she is, and she is not from the city."

"Well, take the letter, give her a penny, and send her on her way," I said. "I told you not to disturb me."

"I tried, madam. She insists on staying while you read it." She clearly did not relish giving me the news. I considered chasing the girl away, but her persistence piqued my curiosity.

"Very well," I said. "Bring me the letter, but keep her in the kitchen. Who knows who she is?"

Hannah returned with the letter and slipped back downstairs. The wax seal on the envelope coupled with the elaborate script on the outside indicated that it had been written by a professional scribe. I opened it and found that the letter inside was written in the same hand as the envelope. It was from my cousin, who had passed away a few months earlier. She was one of the godly sort, and it came through even in such a brief letter.

*Written at my home in Hereford, the xi of March, 1644*
*My Dearest Cousin,*

*As I write this, my body is failing. By now I'm sure that you have heard the news of my death. Weep not, for I am at the Right Hand of God. As I settle my earthly accounts and prepare to approach the*

*Heavenly Throne, I am working to ensure that my faithful servants are well-settled. Martha Hawkins, the maid who brought you this letter, has been in my household for two years and has proved one of the most diligent servants I have. She is modest, honest, and hardworking. She can even read and write. The times we live in are dangerous to maidens without employment. With armies roaming the land, who knows what could become of her? If you cannot bring her into your home, I beg of you to find her a place with a godly family in the city. I will next see you at the Right Hand of God, but until then I am*

> *Your ever-loving sister in Christ,*
> *Elizabeth*

The letter was clear enough but left many questions unanswered. I considered for a moment whether God might have brought this girl to my house to help Hannah with her labors, even as old age weakened her body.

"Hannah! Take the girl to the parlor and come back. I will see her, but need to dress first."

A few minutes later, Hannah returned. She helped me into one of my richest set of clothes, one that I knew would impress a country girl from Hereford: a fine linen skirt, silk bodice, and linen jacket embroidered with blood-red silk. Finally, I added a coif of French lace and went downstairs.

Before entering, I paused before my gilt mirror. At thirty years, I was probably not much older than the girl waiting in the parlor. My darling Luke had called me beautiful, and I supposed he told the truth—after Phineas died I was beset by suitors who lusted after more than my wealth. I looked closely at my face, trying to remember how it had appeared before I lost my little ones. I wondered if strangers could discern in my face the scars that sorrow had left on my soul. Had the crease on my forehead been so deep when Birdy was born? Were the lines around my eyes always so pronounced? I did not know.

I turned my back on such dark and fruitless thoughts, drew myself up, and went to meet the girl. When I entered, I found a young woman of perhaps twenty years waiting for me. She was standing at the window, looking onto the street. She turned and curtsied deeply. I dismissed Hannah more sharply than necessary, for I wanted the girl to understand that I was her judge and no one else. She wore a simple skirt and bodice over a high-necked shift. The shift and her coif were pure white and likely new—she had come prepared. The girl tried to keep her eyes lowered, but I caught a flash of blue as she glanced up at me. In that moment, I felt my stomach lurch, for her eyes seemed to be the same shade of blue as Birdy's. I composed myself before addressing her.

"My cousin speaks very highly of you, Martha. How long were you in her service?"

"Two years, my lady. I came to her from another household in the parish when I was twenty-one." She paused and I nodded for her to continue. "She hired me when she started to suffer from a palsy. That is why she had a scribe write the letter." Her Midlands accent with its touch of Welsh confirmed much of her story—I had no doubt she came from Hereford's lower orders.

"Who was your master before my cousin? I'm from Hereford, you know."

"Samuel Quarels. I served him before he died, and then I served his widow. When she remarried, her new husband took her to Lincolnshire. Your cousin was kind enough to take me in. I can only pray that you will see fit to do the same."

Martha's story made sense. I had known Samuel and had heard of his death and his widow's remarriage. I looked the girl over, and I noticed that her hands shook. For a moment I thought

22

she might have a palsy of some sort, but I realized that my efforts to impress my authority had worked too well—the poor girl was frightened. I decided I couldn't simply cast her onto the street— I would take her on as a servant, at least for the time being.

"Hereford is a long journey, and York is under siege," I said in a gentler voice. "How did you get to the city and then evade the armies surrounding it?"

"When your cousin died, my lady, she was kind enough to leave me a bequest of forty shillings. With that I made my way up here. It was a dangerous journey—I had to be careful of my traveling companions and avoid soldiers." There was no denying that point. Whether they were Royalist or Cavalier, too many of the men fighting our war were rogues at best and murderers at worst. She went on: "I did not know of the siege until I was nearly here. By then I hadn't enough money to return. As I approached the city, I learned that the north was lightly patrolled. I slipped in on Monday, and found you yesterday."

"Have you any money left?"

"No, my lady. I spent most of it on the journey, and the rest to buy these clothes. I wanted to present myself properly. The journey from Hereford reduced my skirts to rags. I still have them, though," she added, indicating a small bag in the corner. "I'm not a spendthrift." Good, I thought. After sauciness and thievery, there were few things I could abide less than a profligate servant.

"I will employ you for a fortnight. If you do well, I will keep you on at fifty shillings per year. You will sleep in the attic with Hannah."

A look of relief spread across her face. "Thank you, my lady."

"Hannah will show you to your room and get you a chest for your clothes. You will start after supper. She will set you to work."

In the days that followed, Martha lived up to my cousin's

praise. She was as hardworking as any servant I'd had, following my instructions and Hannah's without a moment's hesitation. Hannah acquainted her with the household routine and introduced her to the city, showing her which grocers held back their finest goods for wealthy clients and which bakers sold the largest loaves. After a few days in service, I accompanied her to the market to see how she matched up against York's grocers, who drove a notoriously hard bargain. After the apprentice measured out the grain that Martha had ordered, she spoke up.

"Why are you stopping?" she asked. The edge in her voice caught the youth unawares. He looked at her in complete confusion. "Are you trying to cozen me?" she demanded. It was less a question than a challenge.

"No, madam," he said reflexively. Her status was no higher than his, but she demanded his respect and received it. "That is the amount you asked for." To my eye it seemed a fair measure. I considered reining her in, but I was curious what her game might be.

"It certainly is not, you Scotch rogue!" Martha cried out. "Has your master ordered you to cheat your customers in this way? I find that hard to believe. Or are you cheating your master, too? That's it! You intend to keep my money for yourself! Is he here? He'll pull your ears off, I imagine." She peered over his shoulder in search of his master and then turned to scan the street. "If he's not here, I shall have to summon the constable." By the look on the boy's face, she had him completely fuddled.

"Wait," he said. Looking around nervously, he added another scoop of grain to her bag. "There's no need for that. For any of it. I just started with my master and I don't need trouble." He handed over the grain and looked imploringly into her eyes. Her performance was remarkable.

"Thank you," she said, smiling warmly and then lowering her eyes briefly before looking up again. "I'm sorry if I seemed harsh. These are difficult times, and I would hate to disappoint my mistress."

"It's quite all right," he said. I saw the blood rushing to his face, and his ears turned bright crimson. "Come back any time." I think that by the time we left the shop, the poor boy would remember the look she gave him rather than the grain she took.

"The original measure seemed right to me," I commented as we made our way back to my house.

She stopped and looked at me, her face the very soul of innocence. "Oh, no, my lady," she said. "He was trying to give me a short measure. I'm quite sure of it." She sounded genuine, but I thought I caught a mischievous glint in her eyes. I wondered if she had fooled the boy for her own amusement or because she knew I was watching.

"Well, whatever the case, you shall take over some of the shopping duties from Hannah." I couldn't openly countenance such behavior but had to admit I enjoyed the performance, and if food became scarce, her "negotiating" skills could come in useful.

As we stepped through the front door, Hannah met us carrying my valise and the case containing the parts of my birthing stool. "Martha, you'll have to prepare supper for yourself," Hannah said. "Lady Hodgson and I will be with Patience Askew." She turned to me. "One of her gossips was just here. She said the child is coming soon. You must hurry."

# Chapter 3

I took the valise from Hannah and the two of us set out for Patience's home in St. Crux parish. Patience and her husband lived in two rooms above a small blacksmith's shop not far from the parish church. When we arrived, we found Patience sitting on the edge of the bed with her arms over the shoulders of two of her gossips. I was pleased to see that Esther Cooper had taken the lead in caring for Patience. Esther had assisted me in many deliveries and acquitted herself well on every occasion. She knelt between Patience's legs, examining the child to learn how he lay in the womb. I waited until she had finished with her work before I approached. Esther smiled when she saw me.

"How is she?" I asked as we embraced.

"She is well enough, and the child is coming soon. My only fear is that her waters have not yet broken and she is already tired."

I examined Patience and saw that Esther was right. Her shift was soaked with sweat, and her face had the haggard look of a woman twice her age. For her sake and the child's, we needed to hasten her labor. "Hannah," I said, "fetch some featherfew from my bag and boil it in white wine. Esther, I need you to help me with the birth."

I talked briefly with Patience as I anointed my hands, but she was already too fatigued to tell me much. Hannah returned with the wine and held it to Patience's lips as she drank. I was loath to break her water before nature saw fit, but I knew that we hadn't time to wait. I told Patience what I needed to do and then reached inside her to rend the afterbirth with my thumbnail. I said a prayer that Patience's waters would ease the child's way into the world. For the next hour, Esther and I worked together to help Patience in her travail, and around noon we delivered her of a baby girl, thanks be to God.

After we swaddled the child and settled Patience in her bed, Esther and I sat together and talked of our friends and neighbors. I had met Esther soon after I had arrived in York, and we became fast friends. I attended her wedding to Stephen Cooper and offered her advice and medicines when she had trouble becoming pregnant. With my help and God's, she finally could conceive, but she'd not yet had a child who lived. In three years she had four miscarriages, each one more painful to bear than the last. Despite these repeated blows, Esther never stopped attending her gossips in their travail; she rejoiced with them when their children lived and mourned with them when they died. If a more generous soul lived in York, I had not met her.

I knew less about Stephen's reaction to Esther's miscarriages, except that he saw divine providence in it and sought remedy more in prayer than in my decoctions and poultices. In the few conversations we did have, it became clear that he disliked me and did not approve of my friendship with Esther. In my more charitable moments, I told myself that he worried that I would gossip about his failure to beget a child or that I blamed him for the miscarriages. But I also knew that he held a low opinion of all women and did not approve of young widows who refused to re-marry; women, he thought, needed a man's guiding hand. What-ever Stephen's judgment on women, I knew that Esther loved him and I made my peace with her choice. I continued to help them as best I could—the previous month I recommended Esther eat sa-tryion or ragwort flowers soon after the end of her terms.

"Has my prescription had good effect?" I asked.

"It is too soon to tell, but at least there is pleasure in the try-ing." She laughed. "If God sees fit, He will answer our prayers." I thought about Michael and Birdy and wondered at some of the things that God saw as fit. I pushed away such blasphemous thoughts as best I could.

"If you do become pregnant, remember my advice," I said.

"I know, I know, 'pomegranate seeds boiled in oil of lilies,'" she said with a laugh. She mimicked my Herefordshire accent with alarming accuracy. "Sometimes I think you want me to have a child as much as I do, if only so you have one to indulge." She must have seen the sadness that welled up inside me. "My lady, I did not mean that as it sounded."

"Do not worry," I said, patting her knee. "You may well be right." I changed the subject as quickly as I could. "You did well with Patience today. Are you quite sure you won't let me take you on as my deputy? You have a gift for working with women in tra-vail."

"Thank you, my lady, but I cannot. Someday I will, but Ste-phen does not think it meet for me to do so before I have chil-dren."

"I think he fears that you'll spend even more time with your gossips, and leave him unattended," I said. "Or that you'll have money of your own."

28

"Stephen is a good man," Esther said with a laugh. She knew I did not approve of how he treated her. "When I give him children, I'm quite sure he will relent. Then I will be happy to learn from you."

Esther and I gossiped a bit more, but soon enough it was time to leave. We embraced again and went our separate ways.

That evening, clouds swept in from the west and rain began to fall. As I warmed myself by the fire, I found myself hoping that the rain would soak the rebels to the bone. I should not have had such uncharitable thoughts, and in His wisdom, God punished me for my vindictive spirit. As Hannah helped prepare me for bed, Martha came in and announced that Elizabeth Asquith's manservant was at the door.

"He says that his mistress had been in labor for some time, and will soon need a midwife." Without my saying a word, Hannah began retying my bodice.

"Tell him I'll be there shortly," I said. "Do you feel up to assisting me tonight?" I asked Hannah.

She looked uncomfortable. "Honestly, I am not well, my lady," she said. "I've been in and out of the jakes since the afternoon. I fear I'll be there for much of the night. My guts are pinching me . . ." She trailed off. I considered my options. Any of Elizabeth's gossips could assist me in the delivery, but I felt uneasy at the prospect of walking the city alone at night.

"Very well," I said. "Show Martha where my bag is, and tell her we'll be leaving shortly." Hannah nodded and left. "Make sure she gets the birthing stool as well," I called after her. The stool had been a bequest from my mother-in-law, who had trained me in that art. Except for my house, the stool was the oldest thing I owned. I finished dressing and went down to the parlor, where

Martha waited. Martha picked up the stool and lantern while I carried my valise, and the two of us stepped into the night.

As we left my house, Martha slipped on pig dung left by one of the scores of animals that roamed the city. She landed hard on her rear and uttered a string of oaths more fit for a sailor than a maidservant. "I'm sorry, my lady," she said. "I'll mind my tongue." It was not an auspicious start to our night's work.

We walked down Stonegate and turned onto a narrower side street that would take us directly to Elizabeth's. I knew the way but still felt a bit nervous—thanks to the rain, the light from our lantern seemed to extend only a few feet in front of us, and the street's broken paving stones made for treacherous footing. The city had ordered householders to set out lamps to provide light to passersby, but even at times of peace the order had always been more honored in the breach. Now, with Parliament's forces overlooking the city, even fewer people put out lanterns for fear of catching the eye of a bored artilleryman. A few blocks farther on, the street narrowed, and the sky was reduced to a narrow sliver as the buildings' eaves nearly met overhead.

"I feel as if we're walking into a cave," said Martha.

"It's the shortest way," I explained, but at the same time I regretted that we hadn't brought an extra lamp and, for that matter, that I hadn't asked Elizabeth's manservant to accompany us. Few respectable city residents would be out on such a night, and the discipline among the Royalist soldiers was breaking down. The week before, a maid had been raped and left for dead by a foreign mercenary from the King's garrison. The soldier had been hanged, but I had no illusions that the city was much safer. I silently prayed that the rain would keep people in-doors and allow us to pass unmolested. Unfortunately, as with so many prayers, God answered this plea in the negative.

As we approached a darkened alley, a soldier stepped from the shadows and barred our way. He towered over the two of us, and from the smell of him he'd spent the evening soaking himself in liquor. Even in the dim light offered by Martha's lantern he recognized my rank, and he offered a false smile that revealed broken and rotting teeth.

"Good evening, m'lady," he slurred with an exaggerated bow. "And what brings you into such a dangerous part of the city at this hour? Surely you will allow me to escort you to your final destination." The glint in his eye made clear that this was a threat, not a request. He was a predator, and the scent of weakness would only embolden him further, so I saw no use in playing his game. I stepped between Martha and this rogue.

"I am a midwife and a gentlewoman of the city. Unless you wish to spend tonight in the city gaol, step aside." This was an empty threat, of course, and the question was whether he recognized it as such. Upon hearing my words, he straightened up, and his lupine features hardened. A moment later the smile returned, but with a crueler edge than before.

"Ah, I see I was mistaken. Yours are not the clothes of a gentlewoman, but of a bawd, and this must be your whore. No wonder you are abroad at this hour. Now, bawd, is that how you should speak to a gentleman such as myself? I think I should show you and your whore your proper place. Perhaps I shall make the two of you *my* whores."

Without warning, he lashed out with his foot and knocked my legs out from under me. I landed hard on the stone street, my breath knocked out of me. Try as I might, I could not call for help. As I struggled to regain my breath, I looked up and saw that the soldier now held a knife. My heart racing, I scrambled to my feet, desperate to find a way to protect Martha from whatever horrors this monster had in mind. He seized Martha's collar and held the knife against her neck. When she felt the blade, Martha froze, though I could see her eyes darting left and right in search of some escape.

"Unless you wish to bathe in her blood, hold your tongue," he hissed at me. He pressed the knife to her throat to underline his threat. A drop of blood, black in the moonlight, slid down her neck before pooling in the notch of her collarbone. "I'll take my pleasure with your whore now. If she pleases me, I'll send you on your way. If not, perhaps I'll see if you are more to my liking. If you move before I have finished with her, I will cut her throat."

Panic welled up inside me as he dragged Martha toward the mouth of the alley. I could not cry out or run for help, for he would undoubtedly kill Martha and flee. But neither could I stand by as he raped my maidservant. Martha's fate lay in my hands, and I resolved to save her life, even if it meant losing my own. If I could surprise this rogue and knock the knife from his hand, we might be able to escape. I took a deep breath and braced myself for the coming battle.

I charged into the alley, but before I had taken more than a few steps, the lamp slipped from Martha's hands and shattered on the cobblestones. As the candle sputtered out, I saw the soldier struggling to keep his grip on Martha's cloak as she twisted away. As to what happened next, I had only my ears to guide me. From the shadows, I heard a man's voice shout in surprise. This cry was followed by the sounds of desperate combat and a moan that ended in blood. I knew I had just heard someone's last breath. I peered desperately into the darkness, knowing I should flee but unable to leave Martha behind.

"Martha!" I cried. "Are you there?" When she didn't respond, I shouted for help: "Murder! Murder!" At that moment the full moon broke through the clouds, illuminating the street. To my surprise Martha strode from the alley, her bodice and apron shining black.

"Hush!" she whispered. "You'll wake the whole town."

"My God, you're covered in blood!" I cried, and pulled desperately at her cloak, sure I would find a fatal wound. She grabbed my arms firmly and looked into my eyes.

"It's his blood, my lady. We'd best be going. Mrs. Asquith needs you, and neither of us wants to spend the evening answering the constable's questions." She reached down, picked up my valise, and handed it to me. I still could not comprehend her words or what she must have done.

"Martha, what happened? Where is that man? Did he run off?"

"No, he's there," she said, indicating the alley. "We must go."

"But we need to summon the trained bands and have him arrested," I said.

"He's beyond arresting," she said with a hint of irritation. "You can either spend the rest of the night explaining why your maidservant killed one of the King's soldiers, or you can come with me and deliver Mrs. Asquith." I hesitated. "Trust me," she added. "For both our sakes, we should go." I nodded and gripped the handle of my valise. She picked up the birthing stool and held my arm as we hurried away from the alley and the bloody work its shadows concealed.

For a time I paid no attention to which streets we took as we walked—all I saw were Martha's blood-soaked clothes, and all I heard were the echoes of our attacker's final breath. Martha's path twisted and turned as she put as much distance as she could between us and the soldier's body. I did not object until I realized that Martha had led us onto a street that would eventually return us to the very alley we were trying to flee.

"Martha, stop."

"My lady, we cannot. We must get as far as we can."

"Martha, this is the wrong way."

She looked around, trying to get her bearings. She cursed softly and shook her head. "These shitting streets and alleys. It's as if the city were built by a lunatic."

"Never mind that," I said. "We need to think before we find ourselves in even more trouble." The shock of the attack had worn off, and I took a deep breath and examined our circumstances just as I would a perilous birth. From a practical perspective, the problem was not that my maidservant had just slashed a soldier's throat—from ear to ear, by the look of her dress—but that she was walking through the center of York covered in blood. In that light, the solution was obvious. We had to get her off the street and into a new set of clothes.

"Martha, we've got to go home." I stopped. "Do you have the knife?" I asked.

"I'm no fool. I left it by the body."

"Good. Let's see what we can do about your clothes until we get home." I pulled her into a doorway, untied her apron, and rolled it into a ball. It wouldn't do to simply drop it—naturally, the authorities would suspect a man had done the killing and I saw no reason to dispel that illusion. I then turned her cloak inside out, hiding the worst of the blood. "This way," I said. I led her down a small side street. The overhanging buildings made the street darker and thus more dangerous, but it also meant that anyone we met would be less likely to notice the blood on Martha's clothing. For the time being, the trained bands were as much a threat as another brigand.

We wound our way back toward St. Helen's, avoiding the larger streets when we could, and arrived without incident at the stables behind my house where I kept my horses. Before the siege, Hannah and I rode them to births in the suburbs or to visit friends in the country, but with the city closed they were trapped and restless. The smell of blood unnerved them all the more—they began to nicker and neigh loudly enough that I feared they might rouse my neighbors. I quickly gave them a measure of grain each, which quieted them. I helped Martha strip down to her shift, and then we looked up at my house. All the windows were dark, and while the back door would be padlocked, Hannah had left the kitchen window open a few inches. The hard part would be reaching the window, for it was six feet above ground level.

I can only imagine how the scene that followed would have appeared to my neighbors, had they cared to open their shutters and peer into my yard. Martha and I tried to keep to the shadows as we slunk across the yard to my window. She wore nothing but her shift, while I carried her blood-soaked skirts wrapped in her equally bloody cloak. Martha crouched below the window and helped me up so that I could clamber through. I stood quietly in the kitchen, hoping that Hannah would not burst in and start screaming for the local watch. When she didn't, I retrieved the key to the padlock and opened the door for Martha. She stepped into the kitchen and slipped into the shadows. Without a word I opened the oven door and stoked the fire that Hannah had banked a few hours earlier. I added a few coals and followed them with Martha's bloody clothes. I gestured for Martha to wait there and slipped into the buttery, where I knew we had stored some older clothes. Since Martha could not parade through York dressed like a gentlewoman, I had to choose carefully, but with a little digging I found clothes appropriate to her station. It was possible that Hannah would recognize the pieces, but it was not her place to ask questions. I went out the back door, and Martha locked it

35

behind me. With surprising grace, she perched on the windowsill, closed the window behind her, and dropped to the ground. Once back in the stable she dressed quickly, and we departed once again for Elizabeth Asquith's house, giving the scene of our earlier adventure as wide a birth as possible.

"Won't they wonder where we've been?" Martha asked as we walked.

"They'll wonder, and they may talk among themselves, but they're unlikely to say anything." I smiled faintly. "It's one of the benefits of rank." You can get away with murder, I thought to myself.

Mercifully, we arrived at Elizabeth Asquith's home without further incident. A servant met us at the door and ushered us into Elizabeth's chamber. The room glowed with the light of beeswax candles, and a half dozen women from the neighborhood surrounded Elizabeth. Many of them were my clients, and they offered Martha and me a warm welcome. Some women sipped small cups of wine, and Elizabeth's servants had laid out a plate of bread and cheese on a table near the door. I made my way over to Elizabeth.

"How is your labor?" I asked. This was her sixth child, and she had attended the deliveries of many of her friends, so by this time she would know the signs if the birth was close.

"Tolerably well," she said. "The child is beginning to push his way down, but there is time yet."

I nodded and turned to tell Martha to bring me the birthing stool so I could show her how the parts fit together. To my surprise, I found it sitting next to the bed, fully assembled. I looked for Martha and saw her across the room, pointing at the half-empty bottles of wine and giving instructions to one of the servants. She turned around and scanned the chamber, apparently looking for anything else that might be amiss.

Elizabeth looked at me with one eyebrow raised. "She is new to your household, isn't she? Has she done this before?" she asked.

I shook my head as I led her over to the bed and eased her onto her back. "She is full of surprises. If I told you what else she can do, you wouldn't believe me." I oiled my hand and checked the child. His head was down, praise God, but his mother was right in saying he would not enter the world for some time.

"Martha," I called out. She came over immediately, carrying herself more like the midwife in charge of the proceedings than a servant in an unfamiliar situation. I could not help seeing some of myself in her ability to take control of the delivery room and wondered if God had sent me a deputy as well as a maidservant. "Have the servants bring Mrs. Asquith some chicken and a poached egg. Then fetch her a glass of wine."

"Yes, my lady," she said, and slipped out of the room.

"Your new servant is holding up well, then?" Elizabeth asked. "At least you haven't scared her off like the last girl you hired."

The image of Martha stripping a soldier of his knife and then killing him with it sprang to mind. "She doesn't frighten easily. You should have seen the dressing-down she gave a grocer's apprentice in the market. He was nearly in tears." We laughed at the thought.

I helped Elizabeth back to her feet, and we resumed the merry business of gossiping. As usual, the chief topic of discussion was the lives of our neighbors. We discussed Anna Thompson's husband, who had been seen pawing a serving-wench at an alehouse. It wasn't the first time he'd behaved so badly, and the anger toward him was palpable. A few days later, I heard that one of Anna's neighbors had "accidentally" emptied a chamber pot on his head as he walked down Coneystreet, and I imagine that another in our company had some hard words for the serving-wench.

When husbands could not be trusted, respectable women turned to their gossips.

As morning approached, Elizabeth's pains came closer together. Elizabeth preferred the birthing stool, so Martha and I helped her there, and I applied oil of lilies and a beaten egg to her privy passage to smooth the child's journey.

I checked the child and found his head was entering the neck of her womb. "The next time he pushes," I reminded Elizabeth, "you must hold your breath." She nodded. On that day God blessed Elizabeth with a strong bairn, who entered the world just a few minutes later. I told Martha to look in my valise for my commonplace book that contained recipes useful to laboring women and new mothers.

"Near the back is my recipe for caudle. If the kitchen has a red wine, use that instead of the ale. If they have cinnamon, make sure to add that as well."

She nodded, found the book, and dashed off to the kitchen. A few minutes later, she reappeared with the mixture of spiced wine and havermeal. I washed and swaddled the baby, and as Elizabeth sipped the caudle, I helped myself to a cup of sack. I was about to direct Martha to clean and disassemble the birthing stool when Faith Bray burst into the room.

"Stephen Cooper is dead!" she announced. The women began to chatter, but Faith recaptured their attention when she added, "They say he was murdered."

# Chapter 4

With that, Faith became the center of our attention. Despite her fatigue, Elizabeth waved Faith to her bedside so she could join in the questioning. The child was asleep and we all knew Esther—we could hardly ignore the murder of her husband. It soon became clear that these few words had largely exhausted Faith's knowledge on the subject. She didn't know when he had died or where his body had been found. How he had died remained a mystery, as did the question of whether anyone had been arrested. The group became exasperated with Faith's inability to offer more detail, so the women began to fill it in on their own. Esther was distraught, or at least everyone imagined she must be. Did anyone else think that he must have been killed by a business rival? Or had the siege so disrupted his trade that he took his own life? Soon the theories became so fantastical that I could not bear to hear another, so I packed my valise while Martha disassembled my birthing stool. We said our good-byes, wished Elizabeth well, and started for home.

As Martha and I walked home in the dawn light, I realized

that the awful events of the previous night had forged a bond between us. Martha asked me questions about Elizabeth's travail and all the things I had done to ease her labor. I explained a few of midwifery's mysteries. While a stranger might not have noticed the difference, I think we both knew that from that day forward we would be not just mistress and servant, but friends as well.

"Did you know the man who was murdered?" Martha asked.

"Stephen Cooper? Not as well as I knew his wife. Esther is a dear friend. She often assists me when I attend her neighbors in travail. She was with me yesterday morning. I have tried to convince her to become my deputy so I could teach her more about the art of midwifery, but Stephen insisted she become a mother before a midwife. She was desperate for children; this will be a terrible blow for her." I shook my head, unable to believe that Esther had become a widow in the few hours since we last saw each other. I paused for a moment. "Martha, we need to talk about what happened before we arrived at Elizabeth's."

"My lady, I had no choice!" she cried. "You saw what he intended to do."

"I know, I know," I assured her. "He met an end no worse than he deserved, and if necessary I will swear to that before the Justices. I will protect you as I would my own daughter."

"And you won't report his death?"

"It's a bit late for that now," I said. "Justice could not be served any better than it has, and in these uncertain times it might well miscarry. I will talk to my brother, and see what he knows about the case." A look of concern crossed Martha's face. "Don't worry," I continued. "Midwives trade in gossip the way he does in wool. My questions won't seem unusual. I'll also find out what he knows about Stephen Cooper's death."

We arrived home as the sun appeared over the city's rooftops.

Hannah prepared a small meal for us. While I ate by myself in the dining room, I could hear Martha telling Hannah the details of Elizabeth Asquith's labor and delivery and of Stephen Cooper's possible murder. After eating, I told Hannah to take over Martha's duties for the morning so she could sleep, and then I retired to my chamber. It was the Sabbath, but I did not think the Lord would begrudge our absence from that morning's service. After prayers I fell into a deep sleep, mercifully free of dreams.

I awoke feeling refreshed to the noonday sun streaming in my windows. When Hannah came to help me dress, she brought news of Stephen Cooper's murder, or at least rumors about it. Even in the midst of a siege, the death of a wealthy merchant could capture the city's imagination.

"It's all the neighborhood is talking of," Hannah said. "Mr. Baker said that Mr. Cooper was murdered by the rebels."

"What?" I cried. "That's ridiculous! Why would they do that?"

"Mr. Baker didn't say, but I heard Mr. Lee swear that it was the King's men who killed him. He said Stephen Cooper was a precise fool and a Puritan."

"Well, he was that," I admitted. "But if the King's men killed all the Puritans, we'd bury half the city's Aldermen within the week."

Hannah laughed. "Mrs. Lee disagreed, said Mr. Lee didn't know anything about the case."

"That's unusually sensible for her," I said. Mrs. Lee was a notorious gossip and did little to distinguish truth from lies.

"She said that Mr. Cooper was murdered by Mrs. Cooper and her lover. 'Just like in *Arden of Faversham!*' she said."

"Once idle tongues start wagging, there is no end to the trouble," I said, shaking my head in wonder. "Is Martha awake?"

"Yes, my lady. She's doing laundry."

"Tell her I'm going out shortly, and I'll need her to accompany me." Hannah curtsied and disappeared down the stairs.

With all of the uncertainty surrounding Cooper's death, I decided to visit my brother-in-law, Edward. He was Phineas's elder brother, and in the years since Phineas's death we had remained close. Despite his relative youth, he had risen to become one of the most powerful of the city's Aldermen and doubtless knew where the truth about Stephen's murder ended and the rumors began. Edward was handsome, intelligent, and dedicated to the welfare of York. Unlike my husband's pathetic efforts, Edward's business ventures usually succeeded, and as a result he followed his father up the ladder of civic government.

After Phineas's death, I had been beset by creditors claiming that they had loaned him money for one or another of his disastrous business ventures. Some of their claims may have been true, for nobody had ever accused Phineas of competence, but I had fought long and hard to protect my fortune from his outlandish schemes, and I had no intention of handing it over to these snakes. When it became clear how far in debt Phineas had been, I approached Edward for help. I never asked him how he accomplished his end, but within a few days, lawsuits had been withdrawn, and I even received a letter of apology from one creditor. It was said that in his youth, Edward ordered his sleeves cut an inch longer than was fashionable in order to hide the pommel of his dagger. This seemed right to me.

Like many of the city's ruling families, the Hodgsons were inclined to Puritanism, and while Edward was not as hot as some, he spent large sums of money to bring godly preachers to the city. In 1640, he went so far as to hire a Puritan to be vicar for his parish of St. Gregory's. I had rarely seen Edward so angry as when the Royalists took control of the city and expelled his minister. Once war broke out, he muted his political voice for fear of angering the King's friends, but everyone knew that he supported Parliament. While Edward knew I had little sympathy for the rebels, we remained friends by carefully steering around our political differences.

Martha and I walked down Stonegate toward the Ouse, and with each step the stench of the river grew stronger. By the time we reached Coneystreet, Martha looked positively ill and held a handkerchief to her nose.

"What in Christ's name is that smell?"

"The river brings us goods from abroad, and provides the city with a port forty miles from the sea," I said. "In return we give it our filth."

"It is horrid!"

I laughed. "I thought the entire city reeked when I first arrived. It was the worst part of coming here from Hereford. They say London is worse, but even there you become accustomed to the smell. If it's any relief, this is the foulest part of the city. The currents pass by this spot, and leave the filth behind. Phineas almost bought a house down here, but I refused."

"And for that I am very grateful, my lady."

We turned onto Coneystreet and the smell of the river faded a bit. As we neared the Ouse Bridge, I was reminded of my nightmare from the day before. We passed the spot where I saw Mercy Harris throw her child into the river, and I remembered how her child had become my own lost boy. Martha looked at me strangely when I said a prayer under my breath, but I couldn't find the words to explain.

Crossing the bridge into Micklegate Ward gave one the feeling of entering a different and much more prosperous city. Not coincidentally, over the years most of the city's governors had migrated there. The streets on the south side of the Ouse were much wider than those on the north, and the houses were not built so closely together. Most impressive, while my backyard consisted of a small courtyard and stables, houses in Edward's neighborhood featured large, carefully tended gardens. Edward's house had once belonged to his father, and it was one of the grandest in that part of the city. I could see the surprise on Martha's face as we approached. My house was likely the largest she'd ever been in, but Edward's was on a different scale altogether. We ascended the steps to the front door, and a servant opened it before we could knock; Edward ran an efficient household. The servant ushered us into the front parlor, and I declined his offer of a glass of wine while I waited.

I had not sat there long when Edward's younger son, Will, came in. He smiled when he saw me and, despite walking with the aid of a cane, moved quickly across the room to embrace me. Will's mother had died when he and his brother, Joseph, were just boys, and while Edward remarried soon after, Will had never taken to his step-mother. Instead, he'd become a frequent fixture in my house, knowing that neither Hannah nor I could resist his earnest entreaties for cakes. From the time he was old enough to roam York's streets alone, other children had teased him about his clubfoot, and he'd quickly learned that the best way to stop the taunts was to fight. For years he took more clouts than he gave out, and I spent many afternoons dressing his wounds and drying his tears. Eventually, he'd become skilled enough with his fists that his tormentors sought less dangerous targets for their malicious fun. While his foot hardly made him a cripple, it did keep him out of the war, and his shame at this seemed to have grown each time I saw him. To make matters worse, in recent months word reached York that Joseph had been promoted to captain in Cromwell's cavalry, and Edward took visible pride in his older son's heroics. To make up for his inability to fight on the battlefield, Will became too quick with his fists when another man challenged his honor. Rumor had it that while his father had concealed a dagger in his sleeve, Will hid a sword in his cane. I looked at his face and saw an unusually colorful complement of bruises.

"Oh, Will, now what?" I exclaimed, exasperated. "It is one thing to fight as a boy, but you are a man of twenty-one, and you have no need to prove yourself in an alehouse brawl." He cast his eyes downward and took a step back.

"It was nothing, Aunt Bridget," he said. "Just one insult too many." I was prepared to remonstrate with him further, but Edward's servant entered and announced that he would see me now. I put my hands on Will's cheeks and looked in his eyes.

"Be careful. These days you may be up against a soldier who knows how to kill, not a drunken apprentice." He nodded and slipped out of the room. I had no illusions that I'd changed his mind and could only hope he would outgrow that sort of behavior.

When I entered Edward's study, he came around his massive desk to embrace me. Edward was a voracious reader, and the walls of the room were covered with bookshelves containing works on every subject imaginable. There were books in English and Latin, of course, but also French and what looked like Greek. Massive folios of Shakespeare's plays sat comfortably next to cheap pamphlets detailing a monstrous birth in Sussex, and next to them lay account books from his many financial interests. His desk was a riot of correspondence and commonplace books in which he scrawled notes to himself or his secretary. Despite all this, the room exuded not chaos, but a sort of controlled energy. This was a place where business was done and problems were solved.

Edward's appearance contributed to this aura. He stood a bit shorter than me and was powerfully built. Despite the gray in his carefully trimmed beard, he moved with a quickness that belied his forty-five years. He poured each of us a glass of wine, and we sat down to talk.

"To what good fortune do I owe your visit?" he asked with a smile. "All is well, I hope. Surely another of Phineas's creditors has not crawled out from under a rock."

"No, no . . ." I laughed. "I think I've seen the last of them. I come about the news of the town, the murder of Stephen Cooper."

"The *possible* murder of Stephen Cooper," he corrected. "Until we complete the inquest, we have no idea how he died. But it is not a matter that concerns you, I shouldn't think." I wasn't surprised at his reluctance to discuss the subject. The murder of a citizen could cause a political crisis under the best of circumstances, and in a city under siege it could easily turn the city's factions against each other.

"Of course, of course," I said quickly. "It's just that there are the most remarkable and pernicious rumors being discussed. Some say he was murdered by the King's party. Others say that the killer was a Parliament-man, perhaps even one from within city government."

Edward's eyebrows flew up, and he leapt from his chair, sputtering, "That is absurd—why would we do that? Stephen was on *our* side! He wanted nothing more than to expel the Marquess, the Lord Mayor, and all their Catholic cronies."

"I know, I know," I said, shaking my head in sympathy. "But once rumors start to spread, they are devilishly hard to stop."

"Well, *that* rumor is one that must be put to rest at once. It is far too dangerous at a time like this."

"If I knew the truth, I would certainly do my best to dispel the more fantastic stories."

"Until the coroner completes his inquest, we won't know what happened. Tell *that* to your gossips."

"Very well," I said. There would be no getting anything out of him today. I paused before broaching a more delicate subject. "I also heard that Stephen's was not the only violent death in York last night."

He scowled at me in annoyance. "Trying to keep a secret from a midwife is like trying to keep Ouse from rising in the spring. Yes, there was *one* murder last night, but there's no mystery about it. One of the members of the garrison was stabbed in an alley on your side of the river. He'd been in an alehouse drinking most of the evening, and most likely picked a fight with someone meaner than he was."

"How horrible," I said with as much conviction as I could muster. "What an awful fate."

"It was grisly, to be sure, but in some measure he got what he deserved. He had a reputation as a brawler and plenty of enemies."

"So you don't know who did it?"

"It doesn't appear to have involved any of the city residents, so we're leaving it to the garrison. They can find and punish the offender if they care enough," he said. "But that too is none of your concern." This was good news indeed. I would have liked to know more, but I decided not to push him.

We continued to talk, mostly about city politics. I could never hold office myself, of course, but I found the covert maneuverings fascinating and did what I could to help Edward. As different factions fought for control of the city, secrets and gossip could be more valuable than gold, and soon after my arrival in York,

Edward realized that a well-connected midwife could be a valuable ally. While I never betrayed the women I served, I had no qualms about revealing the names of the men who got their servants or mistresses with child. But today, we talked mostly of the siege. Edward said that for now the city had enough grain to feed the people. Even better, the King's men had begun to negotiate with the rebels, and so long as the talks continued, an assault on the city was unlikely. Edward clearly hoped that they would surrender to Parliament without a fight, while I prayed that the King would relieve the city before the situation became too dire; neither of us said as much, of course. Edward gave me a bottle of claret as a parting gift, and Martha and I began the trip back to St. Helen's.

"There are two pieces of good news about last night," I said to Martha as we crossed the bridge. I kept my voice as low as possible, and the hubbub from the crowd meant only she could hear me. "The army is convinced that the rogue we encountered last night was killed by another of his kind. They will look first among their own ranks, and doubtless give up before long. They know what kind of man he was, and he will not be mourned. Mr. Hodgson also said that Mr. Cooper might not have been murdered at all. They only know that he died suddenly."

"Oh no, my lady, he was murdered," Martha replied. "Poisoned, actually." I stopped and stared at her.

"Why in heaven would you say such a thing?" I asked. "The rumors are awful enough as it is, and I don't need you adding to them!"

"It's not a rumor, my lady. While you were with Mr. Hodgson, I talked with the other servants. They told me everything." I was scandalized that Edward's servants would betray his business, and she knew it. "Well, it's not as if they deliberately eavesdropped. What with all the coming and going, it would have been impossible for them *not* to overhear what was said. The Lord Mayor and his man came, the surgeon was there, and Mr. Hodgson even summoned an apothecary. If Mr. Hodgson wants to keep his secrets, he should raise his voice less often. His servants said he was quite upset by the news." She had a point. I relented.

"Well, what else did you hear?" I asked.

"Mr. Cooper's wife discovered him in the parlor. He died so suddenly, she thought he'd suffered a stroke. Mrs. Cooper summoned servants, neighbors, and the vicar, and they all agreed with her. But a house-cat began to drink the milk from his cup, and within a few minutes it began to yowl fearfully and died shortly after. That's when the neighbors began to suspect poison. They sent the servants for a stray dog, and gave it some of the milk. It died the same way."

"So if the cat hadn't drunk the milk, his wife would have buried him and nobody would have been the wiser."

Martha nodded. "Those fools see the hand of God in it."

I began to reprimand Martha for her blasphemy, but the words died on my lips when I realized the implications of her news. "Whoever poisoned the milk put in just enough to kill Stephen, but not so much that he showed symptoms of poisoning."

Martha immediately saw what I was thinking. "Someone was either very lucky or very good with poison."

I agreed. "Did they say what poison it was?"

"The surgeon said it was ratsbane, but none was found in the kitchen."

"Do they have any idea how the poison got into the milk?"

Martha shook her head. "It must have been someone in the household. His wife? Or perhaps a servant? Nobody else could have put the poison in the milk unobserved."

"Esther would never have done such a thing," I said. "And what maidservant can use poison so precisely? Could you?"

"I have many useful skills, but poisoning is not among them. One servant said she heard someone talking with Mr. Cooper before the body was found. Perhaps a visitor was with him when he died, and slipped something into his drink."

"God save us," I said. "Perhaps the rumors of an assassin are not as fanciful as I thought." I paused. "Be sure that in the future you do not follow the example of my brother's servants. Many women's secrets are made known in the birthing chamber, and neither a midwife nor her servants can reveal them."

"No, my lady," she said. After a moment she asked, "My lady, I have a question about the city. Today we have been in Holy Trinity, Micklegate and St. Martin, Micklegate, but have yet to see a gate or even the city wall."

"At the moment, you are *on* Micklegate," I said. She looked around her, and I could not help laughing at her confusion. "It is one of the peculiarities of the city. The streets are called gates: Micklegate, Walmgate, Petergate, and so on."

"If the streets are called gates, the city gates are . . . what?"

"The gates are called bars, oddly enough. There are four of them in the city. You came in Monk Bar on the north. That's the poorest part of the city, and as you've seen it can be dangerous at night." She smiled ruefully. "There are many others, and it's a bit bewildering, but it will seem familiar soon enough." We continued down Coneystreet, home to York's best inns and shops, before reaching Stonegate, which led to my house. Along the way, Martha studied the churches and shops that would help her find her way in the future.

"The Thursday Market is down that street," she noted when

we reached St. Helen's church. "Hannah told me that a cannon-ball killed a maid there last week."

"Yes, while she bought salt for her mistress. It was a terrible thing." I wondered briefly what profit the rebels had from killing her. She was no political animal, yet the rebels slaughtered her just the same. I pushed such dreadful thoughts from my mind. "Up ahead is Swinegate, which will take you to the Shambles. Most of the city's butchers have their shops there; it is a stinking place."

Soon enough we reached my home, and Hannah let us in. I had a small meal and read in the Bible for a time. Before retiring, I called for Hannah.

"Susan Dobson's churching is tomorrow afternoon, and there will be a supper afterwards. Be sure that one of my best dresses is ready. And tell Martha to make sure that her dress is clean. I'll take her with me." She curtsied and disappeared downstairs.

Churchings occasioned much gossip, and I had no doubt that the chief topic of conversation at the feast would be Stephen Cooper's murder. As I drifted off to sleep, I wondered what new rumors would have appeared by then. I never suspected, of course, that gossip exchanged in Susan's parlor soon would lead me to another murder, this one even more pitiful than Cooper's.

# Chapter 5

I awoke Monday morning to the sound of footsteps in the hall-way and, still half-asleep, I rolled over to make room for Birdy. Even as I moved, I realized the steps could not be Birdy's, and I was overcome by melancholy. Until the day she died, Birdy joined me in my bed every morning as soon as she awoke. For many years, I'd begged her just to lie still and perhaps go back to sleep, but I could not recall her ever doing so. As soon as her eyes opened, Birdy's mind went to work, deciphering the world around her. Such work was neither quiet nor solitary. I prayed for strength, for God to take from me my pain, but on this morning He de-nied me. Reluctantly, I rose and picked up a second drawing of Birdy, one I kept on the table by my bed. In the early morning light, her features were indistinct, but I did not need to see them, for each one, from the shape of her brow, to the curve of her nose, to the line of her mouth, would stay with me until I breathed my last.

After my tears had stopped, I called Hannah. As she dressed me, I heard someone rapping on the front door. I sighed and tried to think which of my regular clients were far enough along to be going into labor. I went down and was happy to find not a servant calling me to a labor, but my nephew Will. I crossed the parlor to embrace him and was struck simultaneously by the richness of his clothes and the distress evident in his face. Whatever the clothes meant, his visage made clear that his visit was not for pleasure.

"Aunt Bridget, I know you came to my father regarding the death of Stephen Cooper, and that you know his wife. I wanted to bring you this news in person." He paused. I almost told him that I knew that Stephen had been murdered, but something in his voice made me hold my tongue. His news went beyond the murder itself.

"The surgeon says that Mr. Cooper was murdered by poison," he continued. "After my father discovered this, he ordered the constable to search his home. I went with him to oversee the search. The maid helped them with the search and she discovered a vial of ratsbane hidden in Esther Cooper's clothes chest. Aunt Bridget, Esther killed him. The constable arrested her, and took her to the Castle."

I sat abruptly and tried to absorb what my nephew had told me. Esther, a murderess? It seemed impossible—for all his faults, I knew that she loved Stephen. My eyes drifted to Phineas's portrait, and I had the most absurd thought: I had lived with Phineas without killing him; surely Esther could have tolerated Stephen.

"How can you be so sure it was her?" I asked.

"The apothecary and surgeon agreed that ratsbane killed Mr. Cooper, and we found the vial in her chest. She had hidden it there."

"Did she confess?"

"Not yet, I don't think. As they took her to gaol, she sobbed and protested her innocence. She might have confessed since. I don't know how hard they've pressed her."

"God save us," I said. I sat in silence, trying to imagine why Esther would poison her husband's milk and then hide the poison in her own chamber. Even if Stephen had driven her to kill, he surely hadn't made her into an idiot.

"Will, is that the only evidence you have? That the poison was in her chamber?"

"The neighbors said that they fought," he said. Before I could object, he continued. "There is more news than this. She'll be tried tomorrow."

"Tomorrow? With that evidence? You must be jesting! And who will oversee the trial? The city is under siege. Has the Lord Mayor smuggled an assize judge into the city?"

"The Aldermen have met and decided to hold a special court just for this purpose. The Lord Mayor will preside, and the rest of the Aldermen will sit as the jury. It's a more learned group than she could hope for in a conventional trial. My father will be there. He will see that justice is done."

"But the Lord Mayor wasn't even elected!" I objected. "He was installed by order of the King, and has been kept there on the King's insistence. This is no court at all. Surely you can see that."

"It is irregular," he conceded. "But the evidence is damning. And what would you have them do? Does the siege suspend the laws of God? The Lord Mayor believes that the presence of rebels at the city gates makes it more necessary than ever to prosecute treason, wherever it takes place. And my father agrees."

"And you? Do you support this court?" I was incensed.

"Aunt Bridget, she murdered her natural lord and master," he insisted. "Whether it is a servant who kills his master, a son his father or a wife her husband, by law it is petty treason." He knew my sympathies lay with the King and hadn't expected this reaction.

"And she deserves a trial. A real trial, not one intended to show how much the Lord Mayor loves the King and hates rebellion."

"Well, it wasn't *my* decision," he said. "It's not even my father's. There's really nothing to be done, not by me, and certainly not by you." I considered his point and relented.

"Ah, Will, I am sorry. You are the bearer of bad tidings, not the cause." He nodded, accepting my apology. "But I will have words with your father, you can be sure of that."

"I will warn him, though I can't imagine it will do him much good," said Will with a smile.

"Will, can you join us for dinner?" I asked. He was never one to turn down Hannah's cooking.

"I'm afraid I cannot. My father has business to which I must attend." As he spoke, Will's voice swelled with pride. With Joseph at war, Edward had begun to give Will some political responsibility. The change pleased Will to no end, but I feared that when Joseph returned to York, Edward would push Will to the side once again.

"Well, that explains the clothes, at least."

His ears turned red at the compliment. "Are they too much?" he asked, suddenly worried. "I just had them made. They cost me a pretty penny."

"And it was money well spent," I assured him. "You cut an authoritative figure. Dare I ask what the mission is?"

"I'm to be one of the city's representatives at today's parley with the rebels. A minor role, I'm sure, but I wanted to look the part." Will seemed to be the only one in the city who believed that the talks were anything more than a delaying tactic by both sides. The King's men hoped to put off an assault on the city until the King could send assistance, and the rebels, I was quite sure, were using the time to tunnel beneath the city's walls. But he was so enthusiastic, I held my tongue.

"God be with you," I said. "As you go," I continued, "would you mind seeing Martha to the Shambles? Capons are so dear, and I was hoping she could find one at a reasonable price for our supper." He agreed, and I saw the two of them off.

Within an hour Martha had returned, capon under her arm, but I could tell that the journey had not gone as planned. The blood had drained from her face and her entire body shook as if she suffered from an ague. Perhaps it was because my mind had been much on Birdy, but Martha's pale and feverish appearance reminded me of nothing so much as my daughter on the day that she died.

"Martha, are you all right?" I exclaimed. "What happened?"

"My lady, it was…" She groped for words. "I thought I saw the man from that night, the soldier," she whispered. "In the Shambles, peering at me from an alley."

I didn't know what to make of this. Obviously she had not seen the same soldier, but it was equally clear that something had given her a terrible fright. I led her to the parlor and asked Hannah to bring a glass of wine. In her fear, Martha suddenly seemed like nothing more than a girl, far from home and afraid for her life. My heart compassioned after her, and I swore to myself that I would do everything in my power to save her.

"You are safe now. Tell me what you saw," I said. She took a deep breath and drank some of the wine. It seemed to calm her nerves.

"It was him," she said, and then paused. "I mean, I know it wasn't, but it looked like him. He had the same broken teeth and the same horrible look in his eyes when he smiled."

"Listen to me, Martha," I said. "The city is full of soldiers like him. It may even have been a brother or cousin, but you know it wasn't him. It can't have been."

"I know," she said, gazing into the bottom of her glass. She seemed to have regained herself. "But he gave me such a fright. I'll be seeing him in my sleep. My lady, could you send Hannah to the market for a few days? I think I'd rather not go back for a while." Her hands still shook. I could not refuse.

"Of course," I said. "I'll let her know, but you'll have to pick up some of her duties. Now why don't you go help her in the kitchen. I'll take her with me to the churching this afternoon, and you can have an evening here." She nodded and went back to work, but I could see that something still weighed heavily on her mind, and I sensed that there was more to the story than she had told me.

After we had dined, I changed into a more elaborate skirt and bodice, and Hannah and I walked to Susan Dobson's house. Susan and Francis had married about a year before, and as we all had hoped, she soon became pregnant, giving birth to a girl in May. Today marked the end of her lying-in, and she would leave her house for the first time since giving birth. We met the rest of the party, about a dozen in all, at the front door. Naturally enough, Susan was the focus of attention, and I joined in. After a few minutes, we all made our way to St. Helen's. Susan wrapped a beautiful veil of French lace around her face and head, proceeded up the aisle, and knelt near the communion table. There, the minister blessed her and read from Psalms, and she made a gift of thanksgiving for surviving the perils of childbirth.

After the ceremony ended, the joyful company returned to Susan's home for the festivities that always followed a churching. There were meat and wine aplenty—clearly Francis was a better merchant than I had thought!—and we were very merry. The servants took care of Susan's daughter and saw to it that no wine-glass went unfilled. Soon enough, the talk turned to the more tawdry doings of our neighbors. Mary Hudson announced in a voice just loud enough for everyone to hear that one of her neighbor's servants was with child. As she'd hoped, the news of an illicit pregnancy drew everyone's attention.

"Well, at first it was nothing I could be sure of," Mary said, feigning reluctance to tell her story. "She wore her skirts in such a way that hid her condition for many months." The women knew what kind of woman tried to hide a pregnancy and shook their heads in disapproval, but they laughed raucously when Mary added, "But like the little bastard himself, the truth will come out eventually!"

"Who is it?" one of the women called out, and many others echoed the cry. "Tell us!" Mary had warmed to the task but coyly refused to answer.

"All I can say is that she is as wanton a wench as I've ever seen. You could tell by the way she looked men in the eye that she was no maiden. I have an eye for that sort of thing, you know. It was only a matter of time before she allowed some apprentice or soldier to get under her skirts."

The company laughed at the girl's foolishness. We all were listening attentively, but I did so not just as a neighbor and gossip, but as a sworn midwife. Once I knew the mother, I could press her for the father's name and at the same time make sure that she had a midwife when she delivered her child. Despite the danger, too many pregnant maids hid their condition and gave birth like wild beasts, in secret and without help. To my surprise, Mary steadfastly refused to name the mother, which made for a poor ending to the story.

"What do you mean, you won't tell?" challenged one woman,

drunk and surly. We all were in our cups by this time, and the women became frustrated with Mary's obstinacy. Gossiping made for good neighbors, but only when done well—one could not promise to reveal secrets and then renege.

"There's no servant at all," called out another guest. "Or perhaps there is, and it's *your* servant who is with child." The women were quite taken with this idea and prepared to make Mary the object of their cruel sport. If the game continued, she would be forced to expel her maidservant just to maintain her own reputation. Luckily for Mary, our hostess intervened, taking her arm and steering her into the kitchen. The company quickly lost interest in Mary's story and set their sights on a neighborhood widow who had just married a younger man. I followed Susan and Mary into the kitchen.

"Susan," I said, "I need to speak with Mary in private." She nodded and slipped back into the parlor with the other women. I crossed the room and put my hands on Mary's shoulders. "Mary, as a midwife, I must know the name of the servant who is with child." To my surprise, her eyes filled with fear. "Mary, *she* is the one who has sinned against God. You are not in trouble—tell me her name."

"I . . . I said too much already," she stammered. "I am not even sure that she is with child. Please."

Now my curiosity was piqued, and I continued to press her. I grasped her wrists, leaned close to look into her eyes. To my surprise, she seemed on the verge of tears. What was going on?

"Of course you can't be sure. But it is my responsibility to investigate rumors such as this. If I am going to do that, I need you to tell me the name." She tried to free herself, but I squeezed her wrists all the harder. "Mary, you must tell me." I squeezed again and she cried out in pain.

"All right," she said at last. "But you must promise never to tell anyone that you heard it from me." I nodded. "It is Anne Goodwin, Margaret Goodwin's daughter." I continued to look at her. I knew Margaret—her husband, Daniel, was a poor cobbler in St. John del Pyke, north of the Minster—but I could sense that it was not the Goodwins who frightened her.

"Go on," I said.

"She is maidservant to Richard Hooke." Ah, I thought, now I see. Richard Hooke was not a man who usually inspired this kind of fear, but his wife, Rebecca, was made of stronger and more vicious stuff than he. Indeed, Rebecca was the most powerful and malevolent woman I'd ever had the misfortune to encounter. If the devil ever chose to take human form, he would do well to study Rebecca Hooke beforehand. Though none would say so aloud, it was whispered that she was the illegitimate child of a maidservant seduced by her master. But thanks to her natural guile and (I must admit) her astonishing beauty, she had overcome this stain and found a rich husband. In many ways, her Richard had much in common with my Phineas. Both men came from wealthy families, and both lacked any inclination to think for themselves. In the end, this reluctance to think was probably for the best, as neither had any brains to speak of. Richard did as Rebecca told him, blissfully unaware that the growth in his political influence and family fortune was entirely her doing. Rebecca ruthlessly pursued power on behalf of both her weakling husband and her even weaker son, James. Rebecca gave birth to James soon—*too* soon, according to some—after she married Richard. Some said she had *wanted* Richard to get her with child so she could coerce him into marrying her. Others went further and said she had bewitched him. Whatever the case, James took after his father in every way. Even as a boy, he'd been accounted little more than a common idiot, and he'd not improved with time.

Given the men with whom she had been saddled, Rebecca had to go to great lengths to advance her family's fortunes. Her favored weapon was gossip, which she sought out with little concern for its veracity and used ruthlessly to destroy those who stood in her path. This was why Mary had been so reluctant to speak. If Rebecca suspected Mary of spreading the rumors about her maidservant, Mary's reputation would be in tatters by morning. I considered how best to proceed when I heard a cry from the parlor followed by the breaking of glass. I hurried in and found the women staring in shock at a late-arriving gossip. Susan Dobson leaned on the edge of a table, surrounded by broken glass and red wine. I turned to the gossip nearest me, seeking an explanation.

"Esther Cooper has been arrested for the murder of her husband," she breathed. "She'll be tried tomorrow and executed within days."

This news transformed the company's spirits. Until now, gossiping about Stephen Cooper's murder entailed flights of fancy. They had imagined a foreign assassin stealing into the house and slipping the poison into his cup. They wondered if a business rivalry had gone too far or if Cooper had been murdered by his highborn mistress. In every case, Esther had been a bystander, grieving at her husband's death but in no way responsible. They had even imagined a future for her—she was young, pretty, and wealthy. She could remarry if she chose or enjoy a long and prosperous widowhood. But now she stood accused of petty treason.

I listened in horror as the company of women turned against her. Within minutes of the news, the women invented much darker explanations for Stephen's death, and with each telling Esther became more villainous. One woman said that *Esther* had taken a younger lover when her husband couldn't satisfy her. Another argued that she had succumbed to the temptations of Satan himself, and a third claimed that she had bewitched Stephen before murdering him. The last struck too close to home by suggesting that Esther blamed Stephen for her miscarriages and wanted to be shut of a husband with such weak seed. But in the minds of these women, the explanation for her actions became secondary to the enormity of her crime. This was not a crime of passion, but deliberate and cold-blooded murder, and one that threatened all order. If wives murdered their husbands, servants would soon kill their masters—or mistresses. The women said she would be lucky to escape with hanging but hoped that she would be burned. When such slander began, I tried to remind the women that Esther was a friend, but I spoke too late. Once they turned on Esther, there was nothing I could do to save her reputation.

Powerless to stop such loose talk, I slipped from the room and started for home.

# Chapter 6

That night I lay in bed for many hours considering the day's events. My mind first went to Esther Cooper's plight, for hers was the most dire. I did not for a moment believe that she had murdered her husband, and the discovery of a vial of poison in her chamber did little to change my mind. Who knew when it had been put there? In a busy household such as the Coopers', any number of guests or servants could have hidden it. But I could not see any way to help her. She was in gaol, and in the morning the Lord Mayor would have his trial. It seemed clear that the only possible result of such a farcical proceeding would be conviction and execution. I prayed to the Lord that Esther would somehow avoid the terrible fate that seemed so near. I also considered how I might address the rumors that Anne Goodwin was with child. Rebecca Hooke would never allow me to question her, for even raising the issue would bring shame on her household. But I knew that Anne's mother, Margaret, lived in the city and resolved to speak to her first. If she knew of her daughter's condition, she might convince Anne to slip away from her mistress and talk to me.

In the morning, I found Martha in better spirits, and with only a little coaxing she agreed to accompany me to meet Margaret Goodwin. The Goodwins lived on the northern edge of the city, in St. John del Pyke, one of York's poorest parishes. Martha and I walked up Stonegate and the Minster towers came into view, bathed in sunlight. Even after years living in the city, I was struck by the majesty of the cathedral, and I said a prayer that the Lord would see it safely through our wars. The so-called godly complained so long and loud about the beauty of churches, I sometimes wondered if they might be of a different, more barbaric stock than most Englishmen. I was no Papist, but I could not see God becoming enraged over a stained-glass window, silver candlesticks, or a brass reading desk. I shuddered to think what fate awaited the Minster and our parish churches if the fever-brained rebels and their schismatic preachers took control of the city. We turned southeast at the Minster and wound our way through the city's narrow streets until we reached the square tower of Holy Trinity Church. I pointed it out to Martha.

"I thought Holy Trinity was on the other side of the Ouse, past your brother's house," she said.

"York has so many churches, they had to share names," I said with a laugh. "This one is Holy Trinity, Goodramgate, the other Holy Trinity, Micklegate." She nodded, and I continued. "There are three parishes called All Saints, two each named after St. Helen, St. Michael, St. Martin, and St. Mary." She shook her head in wonder. "If you pay attention to the neighborhood they are in, you won't get *too* lost."

"Where I grew up, we made do with just the one church." She smiled, and I laughed again, relieved that she had recovered from the previous day's fright. Martha thought for a moment and then became serious. "Hannah said that you had children," she said.

Her directness took me unawares, and I swallowed hard before answering. "I had two children, both from Phineas. I had a baby boy named Michael. He was born just after I buried Phineas. He died soon after."

"And the picture in the hall—is that your daughter?"

I knew the question was coming, but a second a wave of sadness rose up in my breast and I fought to hold back my tears. "That is Bridget. We called her Birdy. She died too." I started to say more but worried that my voice would break. A gentlewoman could hardly be seen sobbing in the middle of a city street.

Martha stopped and turned toward me, taking my hands. "I can't tell you how sorry I am. It is a terrible burden."

"The Lord has His plans," I said. "It is not our place to question His will."

To my surprise, a bark of laughter escaped Martha's lips. "Begging your pardon, but that is so much shit," she said. "The Lord has His plans? My God, what nonsense!"

"Martha!" I cried, aghast at her blasphemy.

"I'm sorry, my lady, but I've seen many things in this world, and God's plan is not among them. God wanted your baby to die? *That* is His plan? If so . . ." Her voice trailed off, leaving even more profane thoughts unsaid. I cannot say that I hadn't had similar ideas and I wondered how Martha had come to such awful conclusions. I knew I should pursue the matter and convince her of God's goodness, but with Birdy's death still hanging in the air, I could not do so. Martha rescued us from the silence. "Is that why you became a midwife?" she asked. "Because of your son?"

"Lord, no," I said. "It takes longer than that to learn the business. I had helped deliver a few women before I came to York, and Phineas's mother took me on as her deputy when I arrived. When she died, many of her patients came to me." I paused for a moment, considering her question. "But it is true that I have taken on more clients since Birdy died. The house is so quiet. I'd rather be among my gossips."

We turned onto the narrow street where Daniel Goodwin had his shop. He greeted us when we entered, surprised that I would come to see him in person. I saw that his apron was torn in places and his trousers were fraying. He was perhaps fifty years old, so the lines on his face were not out of place, but his eyes had a haunted expression more common in beggars than shopkeepers. Clearly the siege had not been good for business. He was located near the Monk Bar and for years had profited from the traffic passing through that gate, but with the siege, that traffic had stopped. At the moment, he was working to repair a laborer's boot, but the bare shelves behind him announced that he would soon be done for the day. It would be a lean month unless the siege ended soon.

"My lady," he said. "It is an honor. Do you require my services?"

"Mr. Goodwin," I replied. "It is good to see you. No business at the moment. I need to speak to your wife." He could not hide his disappointment. I knew he would not accept charity, so I resolved to send Hannah back that afternoon with some of our older shoes and an order for a new pair.

"Of course," he said. "Margaret," he called out. "Lady Hodgson is here, and would like to speak to you." I heard an exclamation and then the clatter of footsteps as she hurried down the stairs and into the shop.

"Lady Hodgson, how are you?" she asked. She was a bit younger than her husband, but her life had been no easier. Her clothes were fading from repeated washing and her plain coif had been mended in many places, but her eyes showed none of the desperation I saw in Daniel's. While I had come to York after

Margaret's childbearing years had ended, I knew her as a gossip from the delivery and churching of other city women.

"I am well, thank you," I said, and got right to the reason for my visit. "I wish this were a social call, but I am here about your daughter." She cast her eyes downward briefly.

"Aye," she said. "When I saw you, I thought that might be the case. Well, come up, then. We should not discuss such matters in the shop."

Martha and I followed her through the kitchen that lay behind the workshop and up the stairs to the small rooms where she and Daniel lived. Their furnishings showed the Goodwins to be poor but dedicated to a respectable lifestyle. Three stools and a single chair sat around the trestle table in the front parlor. They were simple but solidly made, and I did not see a speck of dust in the room.

"I'd send out for something to drink," she said, "but we've no help in the shop anymore. We had to let go our journeyman because of the siege. There is just no work."

"That's quite all right," I said. "We won't be long. Tell me about your daughter." At this, her face fell. I think she had hoped we would spend a few minutes talking about the news of the town. Anything, even the murder of Stephen Cooper, would be better than to dwell on her daughter's misfortune. "They say that she is with child," I continued. "If that's true, I can help her, but only if she cooperates with me. We can obtain an order from the court—the father will have to support the child."

She looked up at me and nodded. "She is with child. Or she was. When I last saw her, she said her time was near, but that was several weeks ago. I pray for her nightly, but . . ." She wiped a tear from her cheek as her voice trailed off.

"Did she tell you who the father is?" I asked.

"She said she couldn't. She said that making a public declaration would bring too much trouble from Mrs. Hooke."

"Do you mean that Mrs. Hooke knows of your daughter's condition?" I asked. Margaret nodded and started to weep. I was surprised Rebecca Hooke knew of the pregnancy, and I did not know what to make of it. Usually, when a maidservant became pregnant, her master or mistress dismissed her, for no respectable householder wanted to be accused of harboring a wanton woman. I put my hand on Margaret's shoulder to comfort her. "All is not lost," I said. "I will see what I can do for her. Perhaps after she has the child, she can return here and help in the shop. Surely the siege will be lifted by then." I looked around their rooms again. There was barely enough for Margaret and her husband; two more mouths to feed could push them onto the poor rolls. I slipped a few coins into Margaret's hand and then made my way down the stairs, with Martha close behind. We bade Daniel farewell and started back to my house.

I looked over at Martha and saw that she had been holding back tears. I was somewhat surprised at this—she didn't seem the type to be moved by so common a story. I considered pressuring her to tell me what was wrong, but at that moment a voice called out from behind us. We turned and saw Margaret Goodwin hurrying to catch up to us.

"If you are going to find Anne, let me go with you," she said as she approached. "She might not talk to you, but if we approach her together, she will tell us who the father is."

"Good," I said, and we continued on our way. "You said she never told you who the father was, but could you hazard a guess? Did she have a suitor?"

"No. A few apprentices tried to court her, but Mrs. Hooke is a hard mistress, and would not allow it. She said it would bring shame on the family."

A harsh laugh escaped my throat. "Given her own family's mottled history, she is hardly in a position to take such a stance. How does she expect her servants to marry?"

"I don't think she cares, my lady." She was probably right.

"If we are to talk to Anne, it will have to be when she is out of the house," I said. "When Mrs. Hooke sends her out, where does she go? Our best chance is to catch her while she is at the market."

Margaret thought for a moment. "I usually see her when I am buying butter and cheese. So we should start with those shops."

Butter and cheese were usually sold in All Saints, Pavement, just beyond the Shambles. As we neared the butcher shops, the stench from the offal littering the gutters struck us with an almost physical force. We passed one shopkeeper who stood knife in hand over a large sow whose throat he had cut moments before. I couldn't help wondering if it had been his animal or just one that had wandered by his shop at the wrong time. The creature jerked as blood spurted from the wound with every beat of its heart, each one weaker than the last. The butcher stared at us, as if daring us to report him to the authorities for fouling the gutters. None too soon, we emerged from the Shambles and stepped into the market.

"Margaret, you know that I cannot leave your daughter until I learn the truth. If I suspect she is with child, I have to press her until she confesses. It is a hard thing for a mother to see."

"I've questioned women before. I know what it is like."

My heart went out to the poor woman. No mother wanted to see her daughter in such a situation.

To my surprise, Martha reached out and put her hand on Margaret's arm. "You are doing the right thing," she said. "If she kept her condition a secret this long, she likely intended to bear the child in private, and that is a dangerous thing. It is better for Anne and her baby if Lady Hodgson knows the truth."

Margaret blinked back tears. "Thank you. I just hope we can find her."

"With God's help we will," I said. "You start on that side of the street. If you see Anne, don't approach her. We should question her together."

Margaret nodded and disappeared into the crowd. We began to work our way through the market, scanning faces in search of Anne. I was ready to give up when I spied Margaret waving at us. Martha and I hurried over, and she pointed to a shop window. Anne was inside, haggling with the shopkeeper.

"Wait until she comes out, and then follow her," I told them. "Once she is away from the crowds we will approach her." They both nodded. I don't know that this is the kind of work Martha had in mind when she came into my service, but my instructions did not seem to trouble her.

We didn't have to wait long before Anne came out of the shop and started back toward the Hookes' home. She carried a basket in front of her belly—no accident that!—so I could not tell whether she was then pregnant or had recently given birth. But I would know soon enough. Martha and I approached Anne from behind and seized her arms, pushing her forward. She let out a surprised cry and struggled briefly. When she saw who I was, her face hardened, but she stopped trying to shake free. I could tell she knew why I had accosted her in such a manner. A few yards ahead lay a small orchard, an ideal place to question her, for there was no exit. Martha and I pulled Anne off the street, and I pushed her against a wall. She looked at me with a mixture of anger and fear.

"What do you want?" she spat. I let her mother speak first.

"Anne, Lady Hodgson knows you're with child," she said. "She can help you. She wants the father to answer for what he's done. Tell her who he is and let her be your midwife." Something in Anne's face changed, and for a moment, I thought that Margaret had convinced her daughter to cooperate. She opened her mouth to speak and then closed it. Margaret was on the verge of tears. "Please, Anne. Let her help you."

"There is no child," Anne replied through clenched teeth.

"Please," she said, grasping her daughter's arms. But the girl pulled away and looked toward the street. I decided that if her mother's tears did not work, I would try hard questioning. I seized her collar, dragged her farther into the orchard, and held her against the wall.

"Listen to me," I hissed. "It is well-known among the respectable people of this town that you have behaved in a sluttish fashion, much to your family's shame. The good people of this city are not going to support your bastard. You will tell me who the father is, and you will confirm it when you are in travail."

"I'll tell you nothing."

"Then I will see for myself," I said, and started to pull at her skirts to expose her belly. Like most maidens in her situation, she had used her clothes to hide her condition, layering and rolling her skirts, and filling her apron's pockets with everyday items—a dusting rag, a spare coif, a small apple—anything that would hide her shape.

To my surprise, my assault did not break her will. Rather, she dropped her basket and fought to keep me from finding the truth. She slapped my hands away and kicked out at my legs. Her impudence infuriated me, and I grabbed her by the neck with one hand and raised the other to strike her. I could only imagine what people would say if they saw me (a gentlewoman!) tussling with a servant. Order must be preserved.

I was shocked when Martha stepped between us, and I struck her back rather than Anne's face. Initially, this only increased my anger, for I could no more have a servant interfere in my work than I could have a maidservant refuse to be examined. If servants were allowed to do as they pleased, soon we would be awash in rebels and bastards both. Before I could strike, Martha grasped Anne's shoulders and, speaking soft words into her ear, guided her away from me and farther into the orchard. I started after them, intent on rejoining the battle, but Martha looked back over her shoulder, imploring me to give her a moment. I stopped. When Martha reached the back corner of the orchard, she forced Anne to look into her eyes. She then spoke to her in earnest tones too soft for me to hear. Anne shook her head, rejecting whatever Martha had said, but Martha continued to talk. After a few moments, Anne looked up at me with a little less suspicion. She nodded, and the two women made their way toward me and Margaret.

"Anne is willing to confess the truth," Martha said. I looked at Anne, and she nodded. But before I could continue to press her, an angry voice broke the silence.

"Anne, you stupid bitch, what are you doing? You were supposed to buy butter, and meet me at St. Crux! Who are you talking to?"

I turned and saw an older maidservant striding toward us. Her cold blue eyes and narrow face left one in mind of nothing so much as the executioner's ax. Unless I missed my guess, she was the head servant in the Hooke household. Ignoring the rest of us, she grabbed Anne's arm and dragged her out of the orchard. Anne looked desperately over her shoulder at her mother, fear in her eyes. We started after them, but as soon as they were free, the older servant hissed in Anne's ear and shoved her ahead. I heard only a part of what she said, but her final words were clear: "Mrs. Hooke will hear of this." Anne looked as if the devil himself had made the threat, and hurried away from us.

The servant turned and barred our way. "She is needed by her mistress, and she is forbidden from speaking to you again." She picked up the basket that Anne had dropped and started after her. Without warning, Martha tried to rush past her, but the servant uttered an oath and lashed out with her foot, catching Martha's heel as she raced by. With a cry, Martha tumbled into the gutter. She scrambled to her feet and charged after Anne, but she had lost precious seconds.

Margaret and I followed as quickly as we could but were hampered by my status and her age: As a gentlewoman I could hardly run pell-mell through the center of the city, and at her age, Margaret could not run at all. As we hurried after Martha, my concern for Anne's fate grew. The maidservant's reaction told me that there must be more to Anne's pregnancy than sluttish behavior with a neighborhood apprentice; she seemed no less afraid than Mary Hudson had when I interrogated her about the rumors. Whatever secret Anne kept touched on Rebecca Hooke or someone close to her. I could not help worrying what Rebecca would do when she learned that Anne had spoken to us, and I said a quick prayer that I could find a way to help her.

Martha was the only one in our party who could have caught her, but we soon found her standing at the corner of Petergate, unsure which way Anne had gone. Martha walked toward us, looking disgusted with herself.

"She escaped," she said.

"No matter," I said. "We know she was going to the Hookes' house, so we'll meet her there. Come, let us hurry. Perhaps we can find her alone and finish this sordid business."

# Chapter 7

The Hookes' residence stood out from its neighbors on the street. It was no larger than my own house—Rebecca had driven her husband far, but not as far as she'd like—but remarkable attention had been paid to its appearance. The plaster wall reflected the noon-day sun like glass, and even the paving stones outside the house had been scrubbed of dirt. A footman stood outside the front door, prepared to announce any guests, but his main task seemed to be shooing pedestrians away from the door and keeping the entryway clean. A footman was hardly necessary—Edward was far more powerful and did without one—but it sent a message to neighbors and guests: This was a family to be reckoned with, one that had so many visitors they needed a guard, and so much money they could spare a servant to do nothing but stand outside.

As Margaret, Martha, and I approached the door, the manservant saw us coming, but rather than attempting to stop us, he disappeared into the house. Unfazed, we approached the door, and I raised my fist to knock. Before I could, the door flew open, revealing not the footman but Rebecca Hooke herself.

"Ah, *Lady* Hodgson, how nice of you to visit." She sneered as she said "Lady," making clear that she no more considered me a lady than she was glad to see me. I swallowed my anger as best I could, for sharp words would not open any doors. "And who do you have here?" Rebecca continued. "From their clothes, I'd guess a pair of beggars. Shall I have my servant get you a crust of bread?"

Margaret blushed but stood her ground. "We're here to see my daughter," she said through clenched teeth.

"I'm sorry, I don't know who you are, and I have several servants. Perhaps you could be more specific." Rebecca's tone made very clear that she knew exactly whom Margaret meant.

"We're here for Anne Goodwin," I said. "I spoke to her at the market, and I must have another word with her."

"Ah, yes, Anne. She is a silly girl," said Rebecca, ignoring me to stare at Margaret. "She is working at the moment, so you cannot see her. What is the nature of your business?"

"I have heard that she is with child," I said. "I am here to find out the truth."

"Surely you are not accusing me of harboring a bastard-bearer." Her voice was as cold as a tomb. "That would be a grave insult, and not one I would easily forget."

"I will speak to her, and I will search her body," I insisted. I tried to sound calm, but I could feel my heart pounding in my chest.

Rebecca drew herself to her full height and stared down at us, her eyes blazing. "Let us see who will be so bold as to view my maid's body without my permission!" she hissed.

We stood, staring malevolently at each other. Rebecca was unwilling to stand aside, and I refused to retreat when I was so close to finding the truth about Anne's pregnancy. The standoff was broken by the arrival of Rebecca's son, James. He was about Will's age and a handsome boy. If not for his well-earned reputation for stupidity and laziness, Rebecca would have found a wife for him without any trouble. As it stood, York's leading families would leave their daughters unmarried before they tied them to such a wretch. By the smell of him, he'd come from an alehouse.

"Hello, Mother!" he cried jovially, somehow unaware of the situation into which he had wandered. "Hello, Lady Hodgson," he said, pronouncing it *Hodgshun*. "What brings you here?"

I turned to face him, trying to stay between the boy and his mother. "James," I said sharply. "We're here because Anne Goodwin is rumored to be with child. Is it true?" The blood drained from James's face, and his mouth opened and closed like that of a fresh-caught fish. He couldn't even think of a lie, let alone tell one convincingly. "Tell me the truth, James."

Without warning, Rebecca pushed me aside and threw herself at her son. Martha caught me before I fell to the ground, and behind me I heard a screech of pain. I turned to see Rebecca dragging her wailing son toward the front door by his ear. She shoved him into the house, then turned back to me.

"Stay away from my house and from my family," she said. Her eyes were wild with anger and her breath ragged. "I do not need your help to maintain order in my household. If I see you again, you will regret it."

"I *will* search Anne's body," I said. "I will find out who is the father of her child." I turned and strode off, hoping that Margaret and Martha would have the good sense to follow. When I was safely away, I turned and found that they had indeed stayed close behind.

Margaret looked at me helplessly. "Now what do we do, my lady?"

I didn't have a good answer. "We hope for another chance," I said. "Anne will have to leave the house at some point. Perhaps she will come to you." I knew, of course, that Rebecca Hooke was capable of keeping Anne prisoner, but I had to offer her some hope. "For now, go home. If I learn anything, I will send word." She nodded and set out for home.

After Margaret disappeared into the crowd, Martha and I started down Petergate. "That Rebecca Hooke is one stone-hard bitch," she said. I smiled despite myself.

"I would not have put it quite that way, but I cannot disagree."

"She has a special hatred for you—can I ask why?"

"It's widely known, so I suppose there's no harm in telling you. Before I arrived in York, Rebecca was the best-known midwife in the city. She was far from the most capable, but in every conversation she would trumpet her mastery of the mysteries of childbirth, and list the lives she had saved."

"*She* was a midwife?" Martha asked, arching an eyebrow in disbelief.

"Hard to believe, isn't it? In truth she cared not for mother or child. But she loved the power that came with the office. Midwives are privy to the secrets of women, and she used her knowledge to destroy her enemies and advance her friends."

"What happened?"

"I started to take away from her business. My mother-in-law trained me well, and the women of the town began to call me instead of Rebecca. You can imagine her reaction."

"She hates you for taking some of her clients?"

"No, but that was the seed. Then a few years ago, I was called to the labor of a singlewoman in Fossgate. When I arrived, I found Rebecca sitting idly by as the child died in the mother's womb. What was worse, Rebecca had told the poor girl that there was no hope to save her *or* her child. The mother lay there, waiting to die, and Rebecca just watched."

"My God!" Martha cried.

"In the end, Rebecca was half-right. The child died, but I was able to save the mother. The girl's family petitioned the Church to take Rebecca's license. I was called as a witness, and told the court that a child died as a result of her poor work. They banned her from ever practicing again."

"And she hates you for it."

"She swore she would have her revenge, and while she's not yet gotten it, I am careful to keep my affairs separate from hers whenever I can."

"Then why would you pursue Anne Goodwin's case? Surely that can only make things worse between you two."

"I imagine it will. But I've sworn an oath. If I do not try to discover the child's father, I am no better than Rebecca. Besides, Anne is in a great deal of trouble now. If I can save her, I must."

"Is there really nothing more we can do?"

"Not for the moment. Rebecca has Anne, and soon she will have the baby. But unless she kills them both and buries their bodies in her garden, she can't keep them secret forever."

By that time we had reached my house, and Hannah met us at the door.

"My lady, there is a letter for you!" she exclaimed. "A boy brought it from the Castle this morning."

Puzzled, I took the letter from Hannah and opened it. To my surprise, it was from Esther. I read it aloud to Martha.

*Lady Bridget,*
*As I'm sure you know, I have been arrested for Stephen's murder. I*
*should hope that I do not need to tell you this, but I swear that I am*

*innocent. I have tried to convince the Lord Mayor and Aldermen of this, but they would rather see a rebel die than uncover the truth. Once they convict me they will try to hasten my death, so time is short. None of Stephen's friends would dare to help me, even if they believed in my innocence, so I turn to you. If anyone can find out who killed Stephen and save me from the gallows, it is you. As your friend, I beg you to help me. We will discuss this matter soon, but until then you must believe that I remain your loving friend, Esther.*

"What does she mean that you will discuss this matter soon?" asked Martha. "Are you going to visit her?"

"No, I'm not," I said, shaking my head in confusion. "At least I have no plans to. Moreover, the Castle guard would never let me through the gate, even if I tried. I have no idea what she means."

I stood there for a few moments more, thinking about the letter, when suddenly my house started to shake and a dull roar filled the air. Hannah, Martha, and I raced to the front door and ventured out into the street. A huge cloud of smoke filled the sky to the north of us, in the direction of the King's Manor. As the rumble subsided, we heard the dull thump of cannon and the crack of pistols.

"What has happened?" asked Hannah.

"It appears the negotiations have broken down," I said. "Quick. Get inside and bar the door. The rebels are attacking the city."

For a few uneasy hours, Martha, Hannah, and I waited inside. We dared not venture out for news—if the rebels had breached the wall, ours would be among the first parishes to be overrun. I told Hannah to cook supper, joking that if the rebels came we might as well be well fed, but in truth I just wanted to keep her busy. My own mind dwelled on the horrible fate that awaited the city and my household if the rebels won the day. Would the city be burned or simply looted? I wondered if I would be able to protect Martha—her youth and beauty would inspire envy in many women, but if soldiers rampaged through the city, it could cost her dearly. I spent nearly an hour in prayer before a boy came to our street crying the news that the attack had been defeated and the city was saved. I gave thanks to the Lord and told Hannah to serve supper.

In the hours that followed, the news of what had happened gradually spread. As we'd feared, even as they negotiated with the King's men, the rebels dug under our walls, and the explosion was the fruit of their efforts. Once they had blasted a hole in the wall, the question became who would control the breach. The rebel soldiers who clambered through the wall found themselves in the King's Manor, on the same tennis courts and bowling greens where Edward and Phineas used to play. Blessedly, the King's soldiers rushed to the breach and defeated the assault. Later, Edward told me that upward of forty rebels died in the attack and over two hundred more were captured.

After dinner, I retired to my chamber and reviewed the month's rental receipts from some of my estates in Hereford. In the midst of this work, Hannah announced that my brother-in-law, Edward, was downstairs. I was surprised and more than a bit worried—a man of his stature did not often call upon others, preferring to do business on his own terms and in his own home. I closed my account book and descended to the parlor, a thousand possibilities racing through my head. Was the city in greater peril than it seemed? Had the Lord Mayor decided to surrender to the rebels? The loss of York would be a blow to the King's cause, but the city would fare far better if it was handed over peacefully than taken by force.

Edward stood in the middle of the room, resplendent in a fine silk doublet. He gazed out the window at the city over which he wielded so much power. I wondered what he thought of the day's events. I knew that his sympathies lay with the rebels, but he certainly would not want to see the city sacked. I did not envy his position between Scylla and Charybdis. When I entered the room, Edward turned and embraced me. We talked briefly of the attack before he changed the subject.

"Bridget, I need to speak to you in confidence." I nodded. "Early this morning the Aldermen and Lord Mayor met at the Castle and tried Esther Cooper for murder." I started to object, but he held up his hand. "There was nothing else to be done. The Lord Mayor and several Aldermen—Aldermen who are partial to the King, if you must know—demanded a trial. It was too vicious a crime to delay, particularly in the midst of a rebellion. I assure you that the proceedings were scrupulously fair."

"And the verdict?" I asked, though I already knew. The politics of the moment meant that only one verdict was possible.

"I'm sure Will told you that the constable found a vial containing the same poison that killed Stephen in Esther's cupboard. The evidence is clear. She is guilty, and she will die for her crime." I felt anger rising within me, but I controlled the urge to lash out at Edward.

"How did she explain the ratsbane?"

"What do you mean?" His refusal to meet my gaze told me something was amiss.

"At her trial the constable must have testified about finding the ratsbane. It was the only evidence against her. How did she respond?"

He coughed softly and looked at his feet. He was as embarrassed as I'd ever seen him. "She did not appear at her trial. The evidence was so clear that the Lord Mayor deemed it unnecessary."

At this I could no longer contain my fury. "Surely you are joking!" I shouted. "You establish a court with no legal basis, you leave Esther in gaol during her own trial, and then you sentence her to death?"

"What would you have had me do?" he protested. "And what difference would her presence have made? There was only one possible outcome."

"And that excuses this charade?" I cried. "Edward, you know Esther. Surely you cannot believe she killed Stephen."

Edward looked away before answering. "I know that St. Paul says we are by our nature children of wrath. It is only by the grace of God that each of us does not commit such a wicked act." Such sophistry enraged me all the more.

"Answer the question, Edward! Do you really believe that Esther killed her husband?"

Edward sighed heavily. "What I think is immaterial. The court heard the evidence against her, convicted her of petty treason, and sentenced her to die. That is all that matters." He took me by the arms and looked in my eyes. "Bridget, I am sorry. There was nothing I could do."

I believed him. "How long will they wait to hang her? I should like to visit her."

Edward exhaled slowly and once again looked away from me. "The Lord Mayor refused to hang her. She will be burned."

I felt the strength leave my body, and I sat down on the sofa. Burning? Witches and heretics—those rebels against God—often died by burning, and deservedly so. And while I knew the law prescribed burning for servants or wives convicted of petty treason, I had never heard of such an awful sentence being carried out.

"Is the Lord Mayor so vindictive?" I whispered.

"These are difficult times," Edward replied. "The Lord Mayor wishes to uphold the divine order as best he can."

"And since he cannot defeat the rebels outside the walls, he wishes to burn one within them?"

"That is the sum of it, yes."

"So she has confessed?" I asked.

At this, he looked distinctly uncomfortable. "Erm, no, not yet. The ministers are still talking with her, trying to convince her to do so. I do hope she does. She should acknowledge her sins before her execution. This actually brings me to the reason for my visit. The city requires your services. After she was sentenced, Esther Cooper claimed to be with child. She is pleading the belly."

At this I nearly laughed out loud, for I realized what Esther meant when she said we would discuss her case soon. I quickly turned away so Edward wouldn't see the smile that flitted across my lips.

"And why have you come to me for this service?"

"She insisted that you are her midwife. The Lord Mayor wanted to send a woman of his own choosing, but I prevailed upon him to grant Esther this one request. In any event, you must examine her to see if she truly is pregnant. The Lord Mayor believes she is merely trying to delay her execution. He is quite furious but cannot risk the death of an innocent child."

"Very well," I said. "When should I visit her?"

"The Lord Mayor would like justice to run its course as swiftly as possible. He asks that you visit her today, if you can."

"I take it she is being kept at the Castle?"

He nodded curtly. "I have already sent word to the Castle guard to expect you, and I brought you a letter from the Lord Mayor." He handed me a sheet of paper with an ornate wax seal on it. "The jailor should give you free access to her." I took the letter and read it over. Everything seemed to be in order.

"I'll examine her on one condition," I said.

"What is it?"

"You must promise that nobody will question my verdict in this matter. If I say she is with child, she is with child."

"I give you my word." He paused. "Incidentally, he will pay you fifteen pounds after you complete your work." I looked at Edward in shock. Fifteen pounds was an outrageous sum for a single visit. "He also asked me to emphasize that he appreciates your efficient service."

I did not have to ask what the Lord Mayor meant by "efficient." The money was a bribe and a threat; and he would have his burning, or I would feel his wrath.

# Chapter 8

After Edward left, I summoned Martha. "I need you to accompany me to the Castle to visit Esther Cooper," I said.

Martha raised her eyebrows in surprise. "How did she manage that?"

"By pleading the belly. They cannot execute her if a midwife confirms that she is with child. She requested that I come to the Castle and examine her."

"Nicely done," Martha said with an admiring smile. "I wouldn't have thought a wealthy woman like her would think to play that card."

"When we get to the Castle the two of you can discuss criminal strategies," I joked. "If we prove her innocent, you can become brigands together." Martha smiled thinly. "For now, fetch my valise. I'll need it for my examination."

While Martha gathered my tools, I told Hannah to pack a meal of pork, bread, and cheese for us to take to the gaol. I could not imagine her jailor made a point of feeding her well, so she would rely on her friends for necessities. We also brought a pot of ale and a small ham as "gifts" in case her jailor proved uncooperative.

As Martha and I left the house, a group of soldiers marched along Petergate on their way from Bootham Bar back to their quarters. They looked exhausted and a few appeared to have suffered minor wounds in the fighting. I wondered how many of their company had died to save the city and how many more would have to do so. And what if the next assault succeeded? Or the one after that? The longer the siege lasted, the more brutal the treatment the city's residents could expect once it fell. As we walked, I looked at Martha, wondering what would become of her if the rebels sacked the city. As a member of my household, she would be safer than most people, but that was hardly a guarantee that she would survive unscathed. The lot of young women, especially poor ones, in wartime was a hard one. I swore to myself that I would protect Martha from whatever danger the future might bring.

From my house we went down Stonegate before turning toward the Castle. I don't think either one of us relished another walk through the Shambles. As we neared the Ouse Bridge, Clifford's Tower came into view. It sat on a hill overlooking the city and the rest of York Castle. The keep was as old as any building in the city—some said it had been built by William of Normandy. Before the civil war, the Castle had fallen into disrepair, but after the King's men entered the city it became a hive of activity as they strengthened the walls and dug ditches to fortify the defenses.

"Is that where they are keeping her?" Martha asked, gazing up at the keep.

"No," I said. "That's Clifford's Tower. It's the part of the Castle closest to the city, and the one everyone sees first, but there is much more to the Castle on the other side of the hill. You'll see the rest presently."

We crossed the drawbridge and the smell of the moat assaulted us. The river always had a stink about it, but the moat was truly noxious, for the soldiers used it to dispose of their waste. I made the mistake of looking down and saw the corpse of a large dog, half-submerged in the water. On the far end of the bridge, two posterns loomed above us, guards peering down as if we were the vanguard of another assault. Another group of soldiers stood outside the gate. They wore heavy breastplates and helmets and kept their weapons at the ready. The contingent was on edge after the day's attack and did not know what to make of me and Martha. The sergeant approached us, clearly hoping that there was some sort of mistake and we would go away.

"My lady," he said. "What brings you to the Castle at such a troubled time?" If I had not been a gentlewoman, I'm quite sure he would have chased us off with a few choice words; but he knew his place.

"I am a midwife of the city, and we are here to see a prisoner," I announced, handing him the letter with the Lord Mayor's seal. He looked dumbly at the letter, and I realized that he could not read. "It is from the Lord Mayor," I explained. "It instructs you to take me to see the prisoner in question." He continued to stare at the letter as if the writing would suddenly become clear and tell him what to do. I sighed. "Call the officer who is in charge of the guard. I am quite sure that he can help us." The sergeant seemed almost grateful that I'd given him some direction. If the hopes of the King rested on men such as this, England's future looked dark indeed. The sergeant retreated to the gate and spoke through a small window. A few minutes later he returned.

"I'll take you to the tower where the prisoner is being kept," he said as if it were his idea. He handed me the Lord Mayor's letter. "From there you can talk to the jailor."

He barked a command, and the gate slowly opened. Martha and I followed the sergeant into the Castle just as a cannon at the far end of the compound roared. Instinctively I ducked, then waited as smoke washed over us. As we passed the emplacement, artillery-men worked to reload the piece. Tents were scattered throughout, and I could see soldiers scurrying about, preparing for battle. We reached a tower built into the Castle's wall, and the sergeant pounded on the heavy door. A window opened and a small, heavily lined face appeared.

"What do you want?" the jailor barked.

"We are here by order of the Lord Mayor to see a prisoner," I announced. There was no sense in letting the sergeant mumble through his mission, and I wanted to make clear that I was in charge.

The jailor looked at me, cannily assessing my appearance and no doubt calculating how much of a bribe he could extract. Once he'd arrived at a figure, he nodded curtly and snapped the window shut. A few moments later, the bolt drew back and the door swung slowly inward. We entered a small room and discovered that the gatekeeper stood only as high as my waist. Briefly confused, I turned and saw that a small ladder had been fastened to the in-side of the door, allowing the dwarf to use the window. He wore a short leather coat appropriate for a child, and his heavy belt held an ugly club and a set of iron keys.

"Let me see your letter," he demanded. Unlike the sergeant, the dwarf could read, and he quickly took in the contents.

"The Lord Mayor's writ doesn't run to the Castle," he said with a sly smile. "You'll need a letter from the Marquess of Newcastle himself. He commands the garrison and the Castle." He knew, of course, that Newcastle had more on his mind than a local murderess and it would take days or even weeks to obtain such a letter. On the other hand, I also knew that he wanted a bribe, not a nobleman's signature.

"How are the rations they give you these days?" I asked, knowing full well that a dwarf-jailor might receive only bread and gruel for his daily meal.

"I've done better," he said. "What concern is it of yours? You need to worry about getting a letter from the Marquess."

"I ask because I've got a lovely ham that you might like." He looked eagerly at Martha's basket. I reached in and removed the ham. It was as large as the dwarf's head. He eyed it lovingly. "As it happens, I also have a pot of ale that would accompany it quite nicely. But only if you honor the letter and take us to the prisoner."

He nodded, took the food, and scurried into a nearby room to put it up. When he returned he led us down a set of steps to a cell that was partially underground. It was said that when the Ouse flooded, prisoners would sometimes drown in their cells, and I wondered how many men had died in Esther's cell. The dwarf opened the door and allowed us to enter.

"I'll be at the top of the stairs. Knock when you're done." We entered Esther's cell and he locked the door behind us.

Esther Cooper wore a gray skirt and bodice, an outfit appropriate for a woman of much lower rank and one that even Martha would hesitate to wear. She turned when we entered and a wan smile crossed her face. "I was worried the Lord Mayor would send some old crone to do his bidding," she said as she walked over to embrace me.

I looked around the cell. A thin sunbeam came through a narrow window high on one wall. The moat was out of sight, but the smell wafted through the window, giving everything the odor of death and decay. The only piece of furniture was a rough wooden bed with a straw mattress and moth-eaten wool blanket on it. Dirty rushes covered the floor. The comfort of a murderess was of little concern to the warden, no matter her rank.

"I'm here for the city," I said. "I've been sent to examine you."

A look of puzzlement crossed her face at my deliberate formality. "Lady Bridget—," she started.

"If you are going to avoid execution in the morning, I have to certify to the Lord Mayor that you are with child." She nodded, still confused by my tone. I inclined my head to the door and raised an eyebrow. The dwarf said he would wait upstairs, but I worried that he could eavesdrop on our meeting.

She gazed at the door for a moment before realizing what I meant. "Yes, of course."

"How long has it been since your monthly courses?" I asked.

"Ten weeks," Esther said. "And as you well know, I did lie with my husband before they stopped."

"I need to examine your breasts," I said. She nodded and without a trace of embarrassment unlaced her bodice. I looked closely at her nipples before cupping her breasts and squeezing them gently. As she retied her bodice, I reached into my valise for a small glass, which I handed to Esther.

"Make water in this if you can," I told her. She slipped the glass under her skirts. After, she handed it back, and I dropped a needle in the glass and held it up to the window. The light could have been better, but it was good enough. After I poured the glass into her chamber pot, I saw that Martha had removed a small mirror from my valise and gone to the cell door. She put the mirror through the window, gazing into it as she moved it back and forth. She nodded to herself and turned back to me.

"He's gone," she said. I looked at her a bit longer, wondering where she had learned such a trick. Before I could ask, Esther spoke.

"Thank God you came," she said. "You *do* believe that I am innocent, don't you?"

"Tell me what happened."

Esther looked sad, but not surprised. "I suppose even you must have your suspicions."

"The evidence against you seems thin," I said. "But I do not want to judge your case too hastily. I want to hear from you."

"Yes, I suppose I owe you that," she said. "Since coming to the Castle, I have had a lot of time to think about my husband's murder. Does it strike you as odd that whoever poisoned my husband nearly escaped undetected?"

"Martha and I discussed it, yes. That's part of the reason I came."

"If the cat hadn't drunk the milk, we would have buried him and nobody would have been the wiser."

"And you would not be here," I said.

She smiled and shook her head in disbelief. "Don't think that hasn't crossed my mind—damned cat. With many hours and no books, the mind has time to wander."

"If you did not kill your husband, who did?"

"I wish I could tell you. My husband had many dealings he kept from me. And with these came enemies."

"What do you mean?" I asked.

"I don't know much. He spoke of his enemies, but never by name. Ever since the siege began strangers called on him without warning. They always met in his study, so I do not know what they discussed, but they had a hard look about them, and were not from the city. I fear they were with the rebels."

I knew that Stephen had favored Parliament in the wars but had not realized he'd been actively helping their armies. "Do you think he was conspiring to help the rebels to take the city?"

Esther shook her head. "I don't know. I didn't want to know. But there is more. I know he was involved in a suit at law with a great deal of money at stake. That took up much of his time."

"Was the suit with someone in the city?"

"I don't know that either. Stephen loved me, but did not think it appropriate to include me in his business."

I shook my head in wonder. My first husband was a gentleman rather than a merchant, but we talked of his affairs regularly. When he went from Hereford to London, the management of his lands fell to me. If he'd not taught me well, he would have been much the poorer for it. Even Phineas told me of his plans—his fault was not that he didn't talk to me, it was that he didn't take my counsel.

"What happened the night Stephen died? When did you last see him?"

"I spoke to him before I went to bed at eight. He told me he would come to bed late because he expected a visitor."

"He met with someone the night he was murdered?" I exclaimed. "Surely you told the constable this."

"Of course," she said. "But by then the Lord Mayor had made his wishes known, and nobody was going to listen to me."

"Whom did he meet with?"

"I don't know." Esther sighed. "I asked him. He said it was business that didn't concern me, and would say no more. So I retired to my chamber and he went to his study to work. I was asleep when I heard Ellen scream. She found Stephen's body."

"Who is Ellen?"

"One of our maidservants. I went downstairs and found him on the floor. I summoned the vicar and our neighbors. We were going to lay him out when the cat started to howl. I think you know the rest."

"Is there anyone he talked to about his business? Someone who might know about these late night visits, or might even have been the visitor the night he died?"

"My uncle Charles Yeoman might know," she said. "Stephen and Charles dined together constantly. Stephen confided in him on many matters. Tell him I sent you, and he might be willing to help."

"Your uncle is Charles Yeoman, the Member of Parliament?" I asked.

Esther nodded. "When the war started he retired to York to avoid the conflict. He said he just didn't have the stomach for it."

"He was a powerful man in his time."

"In truth, he frightens me a little. He has ever since I was a girl. We are not close, but he is family."

"I will speak to him as soon as I can. Is there anything else?" I asked. "You say you are innocent, but how can I prove it to the Lord Mayor?"

She nodded. "Look in Stephen's study, on the top story of our house. He kept a diary, and made notes of all his important dealings. The diary and his letters are in a large chest chained to a pillar in the center of the room. It is secured with iron bands and a heavy lock. It's where Stephen keeps ... kept ... his most important papers, as well as ready money. When a siege seemed likely, he gathered as much money as he could. I saw it a few weeks ago. It was more than I've ever seen in my life. That chest is where Stephen kept the things that mattered to him."

I paused for a moment, considering the path that lay before me. I knew that whoever had murdered Stephen Cooper was vicious enough to kill in cold blood and expert enough to do it well. If he could slip ratsbane into Stephen's milk, what would keep him from poisoning my wine? If I took up Esther's cause, I would put myself between a killer and his freedom.

"How can we get into that chest?" I asked.

Esther strode across her cell to the bed and stuck her hand in the mattress. She withdrew a chain with two keys on it and handed it to me. "This key"—indicating the larger of the two—"is to the door of my husband's study. The other should unlock the chest. He never took this chain off his neck. Ellen is still in the house, and she will let you in. I told her she should look for another household, but she refused to abandon me. She is convinced I'll be home soon. You and Ellen are the only ones in York who have shown yourselves to be true friends."

"I don't know what I would do without my Hannah," I said. "But the truth is that even if we find evidence that Stephen had enemies, you are the one who has been convicted of his murder. The Lord Mayor will not reverse the verdict simply because someone else might have been happy to see your husband dead."

"What other choice do I have?"

I had no answer to that, so I gave her the food that Hannah had prepared, bade her good-bye, and pounded on the cell door. The dwarf shuffled down the stairs, unlocked the door, and let us out. I paused to talk to him.

"You've seen more than a few murderers in your time," I said. "What do you make of Mrs. Cooper? Is she guilty?" At this he stopped abruptly. I could only imagine the scorn with which the soldiers must have treated him, and he wasn't used to being asked his opinion. He looked up at me, his eyes sharp.

"In my opinion, she's no guiltier of murdering her husband than I am. Anyone can kill, if they get angry or drunk enough. But this ain't that kind of murder. This one was cold and careful, very deliberate. She hasn't got it in her." He shrugged, as if her innocence were of mild interest but not anything he could concern himself with.

"Do you know who I am?" I asked.

"I saw the letter," he said. Apparently he took his diminutive stature as license to speak insolently to his betters.

"Then you know I have power in the city," I said. He nodded. "If you see to it that Mrs. Cooper is well treated, I would count it as a favor to me. And if you hear anything about the murder that I might find of interest, send me word right away. What is your name?"

"Samuel Short," he said with a laugh. "But they call me Short Samuel, of course. Whatever the case, you have a deal."

He opened the tower door and ushered us out. We passed through the Castle grounds, crossed the bridge, and reentered the city. By now the summer sun had begun to set, and with the shops closed, we were among the only people on the street.

"Do you believe her?" Martha asked.

"I take it that you do not?"

Martha shrugged. "If I have to choose between an assassin who slipped into Mr. Cooper's house, poisoned his milk, and then escaped—all without being seen—or a wife who grew sick of her husband's wandering eye, heavy hand, or inability to get her with child, I'll look to the wife. That she stumbled on the right amount of poison is nothing more than the devil's own luck."

"Stephen would never mistreat Esther, nor would he take a mistress, any more than Edward would!"

"Was he not a man?" Martha asked, arching one eyebrow.

"And even if he did beat her," I continued, "Esther was telling the truth."

"How do you know?"

"Unmarried mothers will often lie to me about the father of their bastards, so I know a lie when I hear one."

"It is possible that frightened girls in pain do not make the best liars," Martha replied. "And to my eye she was not telling us the truth about something. I promise you that."

"Perhaps," I said. "But I believe her. And now it is my duty to discover the guilty party."

"Your duty?" she asked, puzzled. "As a gentlewoman?"

"As Esther's midwife. She is my friend and I am her midwife, so I cannot abandon her. I am the only chance she has to escape burning for a crime she says she did not commit."

"And if we find evidence that she is guilty?"

"I believe she is innocent."

"But what if you are wrong?"

"Then I will see her burn," I said. "Justice, however tardy, will be done. *That* is my duty as well." By now we had turned onto Stonegate. "But those are concerns for another day. Tomorrow you will take a letter directly to the Lord Mayor informing him that Mrs. Cooper is with child. The execution will have to wait."

# Chapter 9

The next morning I wrote a letter to the Lord Mayor informing him that Esther's execution would have to wait for some months. I imagined that my verdict would bring an angry letter from Edward or even from the Lord Mayor himself, but there was little that they could do. Men might claim knowledge of the law, government, and the Word of God, but secrets of pregnancy and childbirth remained in women's hands. I then wrote a more careful missive to Charles Yeoman, asking if he would meet with me that day. I left the letter as vague as I could, for I could not know if he lamented Esther's fate or might resent my role in putting off her execution. I sent Hannah to Yeoman's and told her to wait for his reply. Not half an hour later, Hannah returned—Charles Yeoman would see me right away.

Not wanting to keep a man like Yeoman waiting, Martha and I left immediately. We walked up Stonegate toward Yeoman's house near the church of St. Michael-le-Belfrey. Contrary to its name, St. Michael's had neither bells nor belfry, but it impressed just the same. It was the largest parish church in the city and lay just across the street from the Minster itself, basking in the cathedral's glory. When Charles Yeoman came to York, he had chosen a parish appropriate for a man of great wealth, and his home was no less impressive. They said that Yeoman had come to the city to escape the wars, and his choice of homes also spoke to his retirement from political life, for it lay on one of the city's winding side streets that led nowhere in particular. I couldn't help wondering if the war might have been avoided if moderate men such as Yeoman had seen fit to fight as courageously for peace as the partisans had fought for war.

Even though I knew of Yeoman's wealth, the sumptuousness of his home was striking. Elegant paintings in the style of Rubens adorned the walls, and the furniture coverings were of the finest silk. I had only a moment to absorb the luxury of Yeoman's parlor before a servant whisked me to his study and took Martha to the kitchen. Yeoman sat in a large chair behind his desk, a pair of spectacles perched on his long nose. When we entered, he glanced up momentarily from the papers he was reading and held up one finger for me to wait. When he'd finished the page, he set the papers on his desk and looked up. His white hair was cut close to his scalp in the style of the Parliament-men, but I did not think he cleaved to any party. While old age robbed some men of their authority, such was not the case for Yeoman. Everything about him announced that he was a man accustomed to wielding a great deal of power. While I considered myself equal to most men and superior to some, Yeoman overawed me. Esther had told me that he'd left politics, but I now had my doubts. He may have given up his public offices, but I did not believe for a moment that he had forsaken his power.

"Sit, sit, sit," he said. I had the sense not that he wished to rush through our meeting, but that he conducted all his affairs efficiently and expected those around him to keep up. He stared at me intently, and I had the distinct feeling that the judgment he formed in the next few seconds would dictate the nature of our relationship.

"So you are Edward Hodgson's sister, the Lady Bridget. Edward speaks very highly of you. I am happy to talk with you as a courtesy to your brother," Yeoman continued, "but I am not entirely clear what interests we could have in common. What is it that you want? Not a loan, I hope. If you need money, you should marry."

I realized then that the one thing Charles Yeoman and Stephen Cooper shared was a disdain for women. I forced a smile and hoped that my face did not betray the revulsion I felt rising in my throat. I knew that he would end our interview if he thought I was wasting his time, so I got right to the point. "I am here at the behest of your niece, Esther. She says that she has been wrongly convicted of Stephen's murder. I believe her, but too many men have their own reasons to see her burnt for her protests to do any good."

"And how does that concern me?" he asked. "She has been convicted and the law should take its course." What little hope I'd had that his affection for his niece would inspire him to help died a quiet death.

"I cannot believe that you want to see your own niece burned for a crime she did not commit. You know the circumstances of her trial. Surely the law must mean something, even during war."

Yeoman grunted in agreement. "It was . . . an unusual trial, I'll grant you that. But what can *you* do about it?"

"I intend to prove her innocence," I said with as much strength as I could muster.

He smiled at me as he would a youngster declaring her desire to fly. "Of course you do. And what can I do to help you?"

"Esther felt sure that Stephen had many enemies within the city, but did not know whom they might be. Because you have advised him, she suggested I consult you."

Yeoman's expression changed instantly from indulgent to wary, and I knew I had touched a fresh wound. "You will have to be much more specific if I am to help you."

"She told me that Stephen was involved in an enormously expensive lawsuit. If his opponent feared losing the case, he might have had Stephen killed."

"Ah, yes, you mean the lawsuit, of course," he said with ill-disguised relief. "It is safe to say that Richard Hooke is not among those grieving Stephen's death. If he had lost the suit, he would have been ruined."

I looked at Yeoman in shock. "Stephen was suing Richard Hooke?"

"It was the other way around, actually. Richard sued Stephen. Stephen only returned the favor. It is an immensely complicated case."

"Do you *know* Richard Hooke?" I asked skeptically.

"I know him well enough. Do you mean to say that you don't think he was behind the suit?"

"The man is a simpleton," I replied. "He has neither the intelligence nor the strength to pursue an expensive case."

To my surprise, Yeoman laughed out loud. "He is that," he said. "In answer to your question, no, I do not think he is managing the case."

"Rebecca is."

"It seems likely. Stephen certainly thought so. If you are bent on finding someone else who might have killed Stephen, Rebecca would be a good start. From what Stephen said, he was on the verge of winning his suit and ruining the Hookes."

I leapt to my feet, unable to contain my excitement at this news. I had no doubt that Rebecca would resort to murder if she felt her family were on the verge of destruction. I thrilled at the prospect of bringing down Rebecca even as I saved Esther. "Esther also mentioned that Stephen may have thrown in his lot with the rebels," I said, almost as an afterthought. "She said he was receiving visits at odd hours from strangers to the city."

Yeoman's face turned deadly serious and his ice-blue eyes bored into mine. "She told you that."

I was taken aback by his reaction and sat back down. "She—she worried that he might be conspiring with Parliament's armies to take the city," I stammered. What had I said?

"I will tell you right now that he was not involved in any such business," he said with an air of finality.

"But the men who visited him . . . ," I protested.

"Do you know why I'm here in York?" he asked.

"It is said that you became disgusted with the wrangling between the King and Parliament and retired from public life. You came to York to escape the war, but it followed you here."

"Do you believe that?"

"I don't think you would ever give up power willingly."

"No, I would not," he said with a mirthless smile. "And I must profess amazement at the number of people who believe that I did. I came to York at the behest of the city council when it seemed likely that Parliament would attempt to take the city. Because the council is divided between the King's men and Parliamentmen, they worried that under the pressure of a siege, violence might break out within the city itself. Visions of St. Bartholomew's massacre, I suppose."

"And they brought you here to prevent that."

"The council has hired me—at great expense, I might

add—to do two things: to mediate divisions within the city so that they do not become violent; and to prevent the rebel armies from sacking the city. So long as the city survives, I don't care whether the Royalists keep the city or hand it over to the rebels. In that sense I am without political opinion."

"How does this relate to Stephen's murder?" I asked, puzzled.

"Since coming here, I have gained each faction's trust. More importantly, I have spies in each camp, and I would have known if Stephen were involved in any conspiracy. He was not."

"But what about the visitors?" I asked. "Esther seemed quite sure—"

"Lady Bridget, let me be clear. After yesterday's attack on the city, the political balance in York is precarious at best. If in the course of your . . . investigation, you were to spread the rumor that Stephen Cooper had conspired with the rebels in the attack, the repercussions would be disastrous. Such actions would violate the truce I have arranged, and the Royalists would demand retribution. If I could not satisfy them, they would take matters into their own hands, perhaps by killing one of the city's Parliament-men." He paused. "Given your brother's political inclinations, I should be very careful about stirring up this particular hornet's nest. There is no way of knowing what the effect will be. If violence breaks out, I will be unable to protect you or those you care about." The threat was clear. "Now, if you will excuse me, I have other business that demands my attention. I'm sure you understand."

"Why did you tell me about your role in the city?" I asked. "It is not public knowledge."

"I trust a midwife as much as any woman. You keep your clients' secrets, and now you will keep mine." As he said this, his eyes narrowed and he stared at me intensely, and I felt my skin become clammy with fear. While he'd said nothing explicit, he'd made it abundantly clear that if I revealed our conversation, I would suffer dire consequences. "I take it there is nothing else, my lady." It was a statement, not a question.

"No," I mumbled.

"Good. I'm glad I could be of help. Please see yourself out." With that, he returned to his correspondence, and I left the room.

Yeoman's servant escorted me back to the parlor, and a few moments later Martha appeared. As we walked back to my house, I told her what I had learned.

"What do you think?" she asked.

"I think Rebecca Hooke would kill the King himself if she thought it would benefit her family."

"What about Mr. Cooper's involvement with the rebels?"

"I don't know what to make of that. Stephen may have been involved with some dangerous men, but Yeoman seemed quite sure he was not a rebel agent."

"What do we do now?"

"Follow the lead Esther gave us. This afternoon we can go to the Coopers' house and see what Stephen's diary and letters tell us."

I was in the parlor preparing for our trip to Esther's house when I heard someone rapping on my front door, and a few moments later Hannah ushered Will into my parlor. From the look on his face, I knew he'd come about a serious matter. I assumed Edward had sent him to demand an explanation for my failure to provide the desired verdict on Esther Cooper.

"Aunt Bridget, there's something I need to speak to you about concerning your new servant, Martha." Puzzled and more than a little worried, I nodded for him to continue. "Remember when I escorted her to the Shambles on Tuesday? After I left her, I continued on business to the Castle. As I returned, I caught sight of her in an alley talking with a strange man."

"You came to me because you saw my maidservant talking to a man?" I interrupted. "She may talk to whomever she pleases. She is my servant, not my slave."

"No, it's not that," he said. "This was a hard and dangerous man. He seemed to threaten her. I've never seen him before, but I know the type. He was dressed like a soldier, and carried weapons, but he had the air of a criminal about him. I'd certainly hesitate before trifling with him."

Will's story confounded me. Surely this had to be the man that Martha said she had seen, the one who reminded her of the soldier she had killed. But she never said that she had been accosted by him or that they had spoken, just that he had looked at her and she had fled in fear.

"What worries me," Will continued, "is that they seemed to know each other. He grabbed and twisted her arm very hard, but she didn't call for help. She stood there and continued to talk to him. After a few minutes he let her go, but I don't think she's seen the last of him."

Now I was worried, too, on a number of accounts. Martha had never mentioned having a companion in the city, yet it seemed she had one. If she had lied about the encounter in the Shambles, it called into question everything that she had told me since she'd come to my home. If Will was right and this man was dangerous, Hannah and I could be at risk.

I tried to recall every detail of Martha's story, this time with a more suspicious eye. I remembered that the letter had been written by a scribe because, according to Martha, my cousin had a palsy. But except for Martha's word, what evidence did I have that the palsy was real? And once doubt had been cast on the letter, what evidence did I have that *any* of Martha's story was true? She knew my sister could write, but all godly gentlewomen could do so. She knew of Samuel Quarels's death and his wife's decision to remarry, but so did most people in that part of Hereford. I realized that Martha's story hinged on a letter that she could have forged easily. I now had to reconsider much of what I had seen since she'd come to my house. Her ability to disarm and then kill the soldier who attacked us, the ease with which she had sneaked through my kitchen window, and the way she instinctively moved to the shadows—all of these pointed to a woman with a criminal past. In retrospect, even her most innocent actions took on a sinister meaning. While she hadn't robbed me, perhaps she was simply biding her time, trying to gain my trust. Perhaps she intended to admit her accomplice to my home, murder me and Hannah, and then take everything they could carry.

I very nearly asked Will to escort Martha from the house immediately, but the image of Esther sitting alone in her prison cell came to my mind. I had suspicions about Martha, but what evidence had I seen that anything untoward was going on? Will's unheard conversation? Martha's small lie about meeting someone in the Shambles? Perhaps she feared I would reprimand her for talking to a stranger. The only thing I *really* knew about Martha was that she had not been entirely truthful about the man in the Shambles. Such evidence was far less damning than the vial of ratsbane in Esther Cooper's cupboard, yet I had taken on Esther's cause. Surely I owed Martha the benefit of the doubt—after all, she was my servant and relied on me.

"Aunt Bridget, I know what you are thinking, and you must dismiss her immediately," he urged.

"I'm considering my options, Will. I won't make a hasty decision."

He crossed the room and took my arms so he could look me in the face. "Aunt Bridget, since last year you've played the mother to every needy soul in the city. If you insist on extending your hand to strays, you will be bit sooner or later."

What he meant, of course was not "since last year" but "since Birdy died." He was just too kind to speak so bluntly.

Nevertheless, I resolved to give Martha a hearing. Will left and I sent Hannah for Martha.

"She's up to her elbows in washing, my lady," she said. "I'll send her down when she's finished."

"She can leave her elbows there or bring them with her," I snapped. "I don't care which, but I will see her. When did my servants start questioning my instructions?" Hannah stammered out an apology as she curtsied and scurried off. I had no doubt that she would communicate my mood to Martha, and so much the better. I wanted her to be uncertain and unsettled when we met. Martha appeared a few minutes later, hands dry but still wrinkled from the washing. She curtsied deeply and adopted a servile demeanor. Hannah had prepared her.

"You wished to see me, my lady?"

"Martha, the one thing I expect from my servants is honesty. It is even more necessary if you are to assist me at women's travail, for women's lives and my reputation depend on you. If I cannot trust you, I will turn you out of my house. And if I even suspect that you have stolen from me, I will see you whipped from the Castle gates to the Thursday Market. Do you understand?" I stared into her eyes and waited for her to start to cry, protesting that she'd told no lies and that she would never even consider stealing from me. Instead she nodded, apparently in agreement.

"You want to know about the man who accosted me in the Shambles," she said. A look of surprise crossed my face. "Will isn't very good at spying," she said. "He should concern himself with business. It suits him better." If you think that, you would be surprised at the sword in his cane, I thought, but let her continue. "As you've guessed, my lady, there is much that I haven't told you, and some of what I have said is untrue. I will start there, so you know the worst about me. Then, if you want to hear the rest of my story, I will tell it. If you wish to dismiss me, I will go right away." I motioned for her to continue.

"My first lie concerned my service to your cousin. In truth I was never in her household. I served instead in Samuel Holdsworth's house, not far from your cousin. Lady Elizabeth talked constantly of your success in York. She told all who would listen about your fine marriage and said that you were the best midwife in the city. I wanted to start anew, so I decided to try my luck here. The Lord knows I had no luck in Hereford. I found a scrivener who would write whatever I pleased if I paid him enough. After that I came here and entered your service. So I have lied to you and forged a letter from a dead woman. But I pray you believe me, my lady, since that first lie I have never betrayed your trust."

I gazed at her, considering her confession. It fit with what Will had told me, though by now I knew that she was an adept liar. As I'm sure she intended, her story piqued my curiosity rather than satisfying it. Why had she left her former master? Why had she wanted to leave Hereford so badly? A maiden traveling alone across England in the midst of a civil war took on a dangerous mission. And where had she gotten the money to pay the scrivener and for her journey to York?

"Tell me your story," I said. "But tell me the truth."

Martha nodded and took a deep breath. She smoothed the front of her apron before she began to speak. "The best place to start is with my brother, Tom. My first memories are of him giving an older boy a thrashing he'd never forget. Even now, most of my memories of childhood involve Tom fighting. The violence frightened me, but I worshipped him. By the time he was a young man, he was known and feared in our village and beyond. I lost count of how many times he was taken by the constables. But he never changed. We all thought he would finish his days at the end of a rope, probably sooner rather than later.

"Around the time I turned sixteen, he nearly killed a gentleman's son and fled to the German wars. Before he left, he said he was going to defend Protestantism against Antichrist, but we knew better. He wanted to save his own neck and fight without fearing the law. I shudder to think what freedom he found there."

"And Tom is the man Will saw in the market?"

Martha nodded. "He said he's come here to kill me. And that he might kill you, too, while he's at it."

"He knows you are in my house?" I gasped.

"I don't know how he found me," Martha replied. "But if he somehow discovered that I am living with you, we are both in danger." Instinctively I looked out the window onto the street.

"He wouldn't come yet," Martha said.

"How can you be so sure?" I asked, not reassured in the least. "Will said he seemed ready to kill you in the market."

"And he was. But he prefers to commit his crimes under cover of dark," she said.

"How can you know this?"

"Because before I came here, I was his accomplice."

I looked at Martha in surprise. "I think you should tell me the rest."

# Chapter 10

"Soon after Tom left," Martha began, "my father placed me in service with Mr. Holdsworth, a yeoman from a parish near ours. At first, I thought I was lucky. He was prosperous enough and lived in a fine stone house. He seemed kind. But all that was a lie. In truth he was a grasping, malicious man. While he was rich, he refused all charity for the parish poor. Even at times of great need, he never let a groat out of his hands except at interest. The blackguard treated his own wife no better, dressing her in worn and faded clothes, sewn in a dozen places. In all my time in his household, he never tired of telling Mrs. Holdsworth how much my help cost him, and that she was lucky to have me."

"He sounds like an awful master."

"He was a tyrant if ever one lived," Martha said. "But he got his," she added with a small smile that sent a chill down my spine.

"What do you mean?" I asked, not at all sure I wanted an answer.

Martha glanced at me but ignored the question. "He worked me very hard, of course, and on winter nights I wished for a second blanket. But I never complained—I thought it was my lot. But in my second year things turned much worse. Mrs. Holdsworth became pregnant, and when her time came, Mr. Holdsworth refused to call a midwife. He said that his animals did without one, and he'd be Goddamned if he would pay for a woman to deliver his wife."

"What?" I cried.

Martha nodded. "He was an awful man. When she was in travail, I attended her at first, but knowing nothing of childbirth, I could only comfort her. After three days, Mr. Holdsworth relented and called a midwife. She could do nothing to help. Two days after that the midwife called a surgeon."

"Oh, no," I said softly, knowing what had to happen next.

"I held Mrs. Holdsworth's hand as the surgeon removed a girl in pieces," Martha continued, her eyes filling with tears. "It was the most horrible thing I've ever seen. I dreamed of it for weeks after. I still do sometimes."

I put my hand on Martha's arm, guided her to the sofa, and sat beside her. I'd seen the aftermath of a surgeon's work in the delivery room and knew from experience the kinds of dreams she'd had.

"Mrs. Holdsworth lived, but the surgeon's tools wrecked her body. She could hardly leave her bed, and could never have another child.

"After this, Mr. Holdsworth began to trouble me. It began with compliments. 'You're looking very pretty this morning, Martha.' 'That dress flatters you, Martha.'" Martha spat the words as if they were poison. "He was a beast . . . as if I owned more than one dress! I ignored him as best I could, but soon he began to steal up to me as I worked and try to stroke my privities. I protested, but he just laughed. I didn't like it, but what could I do? And it was no worse than many servants suffer from their groping and grabbing masters." I knew that to be true, for I'd delivered many servants of their master's bastards. It pained me to think of Martha in such desperate straits, and my mind returned to her cold smile when she recalled his ultimate fate.

"Did you flee?" I asked, though I knew that she could not have done so.

"No. I was too young and too frightened to leave." Her tears had dried and now she spoke with an anger I'd never seen in her. "One night as I slept, Mr. Holdsworth came into my room and threw himself on top of me. He used me horribly that night, and many nights after. I think that Mrs. Holdsworth knew what her husband was doing, and it hurt her in a way that the surgeon never did. She slowly shrank in her bed, dying of shame for her husband's actions and her failure to protect me. When she died, I laid the blame at Mr. Holdsworth's feet.

"After we buried Mrs. Holdsworth, my courses stopped. I told myself it was an excess of wind or water, and that my body would be right soon enough. But I knew that I was with child. The prospect was so terrible I hid it as best I could. I started bundling up my skirts and wearing a cloak even when the weather did not require it. Nobody suspected."

"What did Mr. Holdsworth say?"

"I never told the swine," she said. "I knew he would call me a whore and turn me out of his house. I would have wandered from parish to parish, and soon enough I would have been reduced to the whore he had tried to make me. When my time approached, I slipped into the woods not far from Mr. Holdsworth's house. There I gave birth to a boy, dead.

"Ah, how I cried," she continued. "He never drew a breath or

saw my face, but I loved that child. But you know this pain, too."
Here, Martha's mask slipped, and I saw the grief she still felt for
her lost child, a grief I knew all too well. I nodded, fighting my own
tears. "I wrapped him in a piece of linen I stole from Mr. Holdsworth, blessed my boy, and then buried him deep so the animals
couldn't get him.

"Do you know what I did the afternoon after I buried my
baby? I went back to work washing and mending Mr. Holdsworth's
breeches. Such was my lot. The next day was the Sabbath, and
Mr. Holdsworth took me to divine service. The minister said
servants should obey their masters as they would God Himself.
When we got home, Mr. Holdsworth repeated the sermon and
then troubled me again. After that I lost interest in what the
priests had to say about God. If God wanted Mr. Holdsworth to
rape me, then I've no interest in Him or His plans."

At that moment, my mind returned to the conversation we'd
had as we'd walked to Margaret Goodwin's house. I remembered
her reaction when I told her of losing Michael and Birdy and her
scorn at my suggestion that the death of my babies had been a
part of God's plan. Now I understood both her sympathy for me
and her wrath toward God. I also knew that she was telling me the
truth. The look in her eyes as she told me of her son's death was
the same one she'd had when we'd talked of my lost children.
While she might be an accomplished dissembler, no woman could
lie so convincingly about the death of her own child.

Martha took a breath, and her face hardened. I did not yet
know what had happened to her master, but I knew that fate had
not been kind. "That day Mr. Holdsworth must have realized I
had a child, and for a time he left me in peace. But he never asked
what happened, and I hated him for it. It was during this respite

that I found my escape from Mr. Holdsworth. One afternoon, he sent me to deliver five pounds he was loaning to a neighbor. As I passed a hedgerow I heard a familiar voice call my name."

"Tom," I said.

"He'd returned from the wars the very picture of health—another part of God's plan, I suppose," she said with a sneer. "He told me that he'd done his best for God, and now he would do his worst for himself. Without warning, he tore the coins from my hands. 'Well, you've done it now,' he said. 'You've become a thief just like me.'

"I protested that I had done no such thing, but even then I knew the truth didn't matter. Mr. Holdsworth would beat me within an inch of my life for losing such a sum no matter what happened. Tom had made sure I could never go back even if I wanted to. Then he offered to take me with him on the road. He said he needed an assistant to replace the pocky wench they'd hanged in London."

"You went with him willingly?" I asked, aghast.

"I promised to tell the truth, and I will." Her voice took on a harder edge. "But tell me, my lady, if I had come to you then and asked you what I should do, what would you have said? Would you have sent me back to Mr. Holdsworth to tell him that I'd been robbed by my own brother? The *best* I could hope for would be a whipping. Would you have told me to return to that goat and his lechery? He'd have raped me again and again, and soon enough I'd have become pregnant. Would you have asked me to do that? Would you have asked me to lose another child, or be turned out of his house as a whore?" To my relief she did not wait for me to answer, for none presented itself. "No, my lady," she continued, "it was far better to go with Tom than to suffer for Mr. Holdsworth's sins. I know many would say my decision was wrong, that I should have gone back. And I know that I could still hang for my crimes. But I had no choice, and I have no regrets." I nodded. While I could not condone her decision to become her brother's accomplice, I could understand it.

"As we walked away from my former life, Tom sang the praises of life as an outlaw: 'I'll show you how to rob a man blind without him knowing it, and how to kill him if he finds out. When I'm done with you, you'll be able to pick locks and pockets. You will follow a man without being seen, and break into his house without making a sound. Ah, Martha, there are great and terrible things ahead of you, and I will make them possible.'

"Whatever his faults," Martha continued, "when it came to teaching thievery, Tom was as good as his word, and soon I surpassed him in all his crimes. At the time, it seemed like a grand adventure, for there is nothing quite as exciting as sneaking about a man's home when he is asleep. Tom took great pride in stealing from the rich, and I told myself that we had greater need of money than the people we robbed. For a time we were fortunate, too, and nobody got hurt. My sin was far less than Mr. Holdsworth's."

I took a deep breath. "Martha, I have to ask you this, though I fear the answer more than you can know."

"You want to know if I ever killed anyone." I nodded. "No, my lady, I never did. At the time I thought it was because we were careful, that Tom tried to avoid situations that could lead to murder. But soon enough I saw that it was simple luck that kept my hands free from blood."

"Soon enough?" I asked with trepidation. "Do you mean Mr. Holdsworth?"

She nodded. "But even before that awful night, I began to search for a way to escape from Tom. We had tested our luck too many times. I knew that soon it would run out, and we would hang. But I did not know where I would escape to. I realized that my only hope was to take the money that Tom and I had stolen together and strike out on my own. I made a plan that would get me my money, my freedom, and, best of all, revenge on Mr. Holdsworth. But with Tom, even the best plans end in blood.

"My plan was simple. I convinced Tom to rob Mr. Holdsworth. Once we had his store of coins, I would knock Tom on the head to then take the money for myself. The loss of his money would hurt Mr. Holdsworth more than anything, and I was determined to deal that blow. Tom is a greedy soul, and readily agreed to the plan. We returned to Hereford, and while I remained in a nearby town, Tom watched Mr. Holdsworth's house to make sure that everything was as I'd said. A few days later he returned, and I could tell from the look in his eye that it was.

"That night, Tom and I walked quickly through the fields and forests to Mr. Holdsworth's house. From my time in service, I knew the surest paths and which ones would be deserted at night. When we arrived, the house was dark and the doors locked tight. But I knew that he had refused to replace the broken lock on a narrow kitchen window. I would squeeze through the window and let Tom in the front door. The money was on the first floor in a small room protected by heavy oak door. It was made to withstand hours of battering, but our plan did not involve breaking it down.

"I waited for clouds to pass over the moon and raced from the woods to the house. I eased open the broken window and slipped in. As always, the keys to the back door hung on a nail in the buttery. I opened the door, and Tom, moving more like a shadow than a man, crossed to the door that stood between us and our prize. He took his tools from his pocket and went to work on the lock. He was as good a burglar as you'd want to meet, but this lock was more than his match. After a half an hour he looked at me, his eyes ablaze. I could tell he was ready to charge upstairs and demand the key from Mr. Holdsworth at knifepoint. I did my best to calm him, and took the tools from his hands. The lock was tough, but after ten minutes' work, it clicked open. Tom was first through the door. He stopped short with a soft cry, and I pushed past him. The room was completely empty. The only sign of its former use was an iron ring in the wall to which his cash box had once been chained.

"Tom turned to me, and demanded where the money had gone. His fury was something to behold. I could do nothing except shake my head, for I had no idea what had gone wrong. Tom drew his dagger and charged up the stairs. I knew that Mr. Holdsworth wouldn't be any match for Tom, so I waited below. I could imagine the scene: Mr. Holdsworth would awake to the tip of Tom's knife pressing into his throat, perhaps drawing a little blood. Tom would ask him if he preferred his life or his wealth. I hoped Mr. Holdsworth would have the good sense to tell Tom where the money was. A few minutes later I heard Tom shouting and I knew that Mr. Holdsworth had refused. Then I heard a pistol shot from upstairs. I started up the stairs and froze. Tom wasn't carrying a pistol that night. I heard bodies crashing about the room, a strangled cry, and the sound of a body falling to the floor. It had to be Tom. I had always known he'd meet a violent end, but never thought it would be at the hands of a man three times his age."

"It wasn't Tom's body," I said, my heart sinking. "Your brother killed Mr. Holdsworth."

"When I thought Tom had been shot, I ran for the door. Mr. Holdsworth had no idea that I was in the house, and I thought I could escape. Tom's voice stopped me, and he called me upstairs. Even before I entered Mr. Holdsworth's chamber the smell of blood told me all I needed to know. I tried to prepare myself for the scene within, but it was far worse than I imagined. Mr. Holdsworth lay in the corner, his throat slashed so wide his head seemed barely attached. His eyes were still open—he looked surprised. Blood soaked his nightshirt from neck to waist. A pistol lay next to his body, and I saw a hole in the wall. Tom stood at the foot of the bed, surveying the horrible scene and cursing the most horrible oaths. Mr. Holdsworth's blood soaked his tunic and pants.

" 'The lying rogue said that the money was in his cupboard, and then he turned on me with the pistol,' he said, kicking Mr. Holdsworth's corpse in the chest. A thin stream of blood burst from the neck, and landed on Tom's shoe. He paid it no mind. 'You shitting fool!' he shouted at the body.

"I then realized that Tom's time in Germany had turned him from a ruffian into a murderer, that killing was *always* part of the plan. I cannot say I was sorry for what happened to Mr. Holdsworth—he deserved his death. But at that moment I knew that Tom's next victim would likely be an innocent, a child who had the misfortune to wake up when Tom was in his room, or perhaps his mother. I knew what I had to do.

"Tom and I searched the house but found no sign of the money. We returned to the hall, and I saw my opportunity to escape. While Tom peered out the window, I picked up the iron poker from the fireplace and called Tom's name. As he turned, I swung the poker, striking him just above the ear. He fell without a sound, and for better or worse my fate was sealed.

"I used my dagger to cut away his purse. It wasn't the fortune I'd dreamed of, but it would have to do. I stepped over his body, out the front door, and ran for the forest. Within moments I disappeared into the safety of the woods. I knew the area far better than Tom, and when he awoke covered in Mr. Holdsworth's blood he would have more immediate concerns than hunting for me. By the time morning came, I had nearly reached Worcester, and had devised the plan that brought me to your door. I found the scrivener who wrote the letter I gave you. The rest is as I told you when I arrived. I came to York, sneaked into the city, and found you here."

I took a deep breath, trying to absorb all that Martha had told me. But one question remained. "How did Tom find you?"

"I don't know. Perhaps someone I knew saw me in Worcester and told Tom. But it doesn't matter now. In the Shambles that day he threatened to kill me for my treachery, but said that I could buy my life if I helped him rob you. I don't believe him, though. He sees me as a traitor, and will not rest until he kills me himself. I could see the wrath in his eyes."

"You know that I should call the constable and have him arrest you," I said.

"That would be the wisest course," she admitted. "And while I am sorry for many of the things I did, I will not apologize for misleading you. Had I told you the truth on the day I arrived, you would have turned me out in an instant. Then where would I have been? A single woman without protection in the midst of a war? I might as well have walked straight to a brothel and raised my skirts. But the lies I told were without malice. I have never hurt you, and never will. You have been more loyal to me than anyone I've known. You protected me when I needed your help, and I am in your debt. If you give me the chance, I will repay you."

"I must think more about this," I said. "Go to your chamber and wait there." She curtsied and left without another word.

I sat for a time, considering what Martha had said, and what I should do about her. Obviously the prudent course would be to summon the constable or at the very least to send her away immediately. By her own admission, she was a confessed felon, complicit in a murder. And what if she was lying? She could be scheming against me at that very moment. What proof did I have that *she* was not the killer and Tom her dupe? But I could not believe that. It seemed impossible that she invented the story of her son's death and burial, and I could not imagine that she had turned so quickly from a serving-maid raped by her master into a cold-hearted murderess.

Martha's story drew my mind to mistakes I had made when I was her age. I knew from the first time I met him that Phineas was a wastrel and an embarrassment to his family, and I knew that I would regret marrying him. But I did so anyway, simply because I was too young and frightened to refuse the match. I had received the gift of a second widowhood not through my own doing, but through the grace of God. Martha had none of my advantages of birth or wealth and had suffered grievously at the hands of the man who was supposed to protect her. What would I have done in her place? The Lord had used Tom to take His vengeance on Samuel Holdsworth. Perhaps He had chosen me to redeem Martha. I would bring her into my home.

"Hannah! Tell Martha I will see her now."

# Chapter 11

Martha entered the parlor and looked at me nervously. I saw no point in drawing things out. "Martha, I am going to keep you on as my servant." As soon as the words passed from my lips, she looked up in relief, and I knew I had made the right decision. She wiped away nascent tears and struggled to speak.

"Thank you, my lady," she said once she had gained control of herself. "I know that this is not an easy choice, and that you must harbor some doubts. I will not disappoint you."

"I know you won't," I said. "But there is still one problem we must address."

"My brother."

"Yes. Do you think he knows where you are living now?"

"I don't know. I made sure I wasn't followed when I left the market, but that's no guarantee. Even if he doesn't know where you live, he's sure to make enquiries. He's a resourceful rogue."

"We have to plan as if he knows you are here and is intent on doing us both harm. You know him best—what do you think he will do?"

"There is no chance we've seen the last of him. He knows of your wealth, so his first priority will be to rob you. If he kills me in the process, that would be all the better." She took the prospect of being murdered by her own brother with more aplomb than I would have. "The house is busy enough that he won't bother waiting until it is empty to burgle it. He will either try to break in at night, as we did with Mr. Holdsworth, or . . ." She paused, putting herself in her brother's place. "No. He will bide his time to see what happens with the siege. If the city is taken, he will use the chaos and lawlessness to rob you in broad daylight. I imagine he'd have little trouble finding a few accomplices—he probably already has. They could break in, ransack the house, kill everyone they find, and then disappear. It would just be a particularly bloody episode from the pillaging of the town. He will break in on his own only if the rebels abandon the siege. He's a violent man in the heat of battle, but when he is planning a robbery he can be patient."

I considered this. If she was right, the soldiers who had repelled the rebel assault also delayed Tom's attack on my house. "Of course, knowing what Tom is likely to do is only half the battle," I said. "We have to figure out how to protect ourselves." I thought for a moment. "I assume that if Tom is captured, he will tell the Justices about your history together?"

"The truth would be bad enough, but by the time he finished his story, I'd be hanged three times over."

"Then we'll have to be discreet," I said. "I know men in the trained bands who could be of help." I felt sure that with the cost of food so high, Sergeant Smith and a few of his men would be happy to earn a few shillings by guarding my house. I quickly wrote a letter explaining my situation and dispatched Hannah to deliver it.

# The Midwife's Tale

Not long after, a stone-faced bailiff appeared at my door with the summons I'd been expecting ever since my visit to the Castle. "Lady Hodgson, the Lord Mayor requires your presence immediately," he said as he handed me the letter. "I will accompany you."

My heart sank at his announcement, for I'd hoped to spend the afternoon searching Stephen Cooper's study. I considered protesting, but I knew the Lord Mayor would not accept any excuses. I called Martha and told her where I would be going. "Hannah will be home shortly, and I shouldn't be long." I glanced at the bailiff, hoping to confirm that my visit would be a short one, but his face remained impassive.

I followed the bailiff across the Ouse into Micklegate, where the Lord Mayor kept his residence. I noted with a smile that while he and Edward were miles apart in their political outlook, they lived just a stone's throw from each other. When we approached the Lord Mayor's home, the two guards in front snapped to attention. The bailiff did not bother knocking as he led me in. Perhaps half a dozen men sat in the Lord Mayor's parlor, waiting, I imagined, to petition the Lord Mayor for some favor or another. The bailiff did not even pause but led me straight through to the rear of the house, where the Lord Mayor conducted business.

"Wait here," he said, then knocked on a heavy door and slipped inside. A few seconds later, he emerged and held the door open for me. "The Lord Mayor will see you." I took a deep breath to steady myself and entered.

The first thing I noticed was the outsized portrait of King Charles hanging above the Lord Mayor's desk. It sent an unambiguous message that the Lord Mayor was the King's man and no one else's. The Lord Mayor himself sat directly beneath the portrait behind a large desk piled high with papers. Ruling a city such as York was no easy task in peacetime—I could only imagine

123

how difficult the siege had made the job. He stood when I entered, and I could tell by his aspect that my finding that Esther was with child had infuriated him to no end. He was a tall man and took full advantage of his height by crossing the room to look down at me.

"Lady Bridget," he said through clenched teeth. "How good of you to come." I knew better than to reply. He returned to his desk and picked up a sheet of paper with my handwriting on it. "You say that Esther Cooper is with child?"

"That is what my examination revealed," I said with as much authority as I could muster.

A voice from behind startled me so badly that I had to suppress a scream. "You have no idea if she is pregnant or not. You know as much about Esther Cooper's condition as a virgin knows about fucking."

I spun around to see who had spoken, for I'd not noticed anyone when I entered the room. A small, wiry man hovered behind me, his black eyes boring into mine. He wore a brightly colored silk doublet cut in the Italian style, and a jagged scar ran from his forehead across his left eye and down his cheek. The scar caused his eye to droop in a most unnerving fashion, giving him a look of perpetual sadness.

"This is Lorenzo Bacca," said the Lord Mayor. "He came to York with the Marquess of Newcastle, and before that he was with His Majesty. He helps me with . . . delicate matters." Bacca smiled at the Lord Mayor's words, but there was no mirth in it, and his eyes remained hard as stones. "I do not need to tell you how disappointed I was with your letter. I shall have to speak to your brother about this." I felt my stomach sink. I had not thought that my allegiance to Esther would affect Edward. What trouble had I begun?

"I know a bit about women's bodies," Bacca said with a leer at mine. "I saw Mrs. Cooper's before her trial. She is a beautiful woman, but in no way is she with child. Why would you lie about that?"

"That was no lawful trial," I said to the Lord Mayor, doing my best to ignore the Italian. "There was no judge, no real jury, no evidence. You did not even allow her to appear in her own defense!"

"Lawful trial?" the Lord Mayor shouted, his eyes blazing. "Who are you to judge what is lawful? Your own brother had no such scruples when Parliament took up arms against their *lawful* sovereign. The city is surrounded by rebels and foreigners, who very nearly breached its walls, and you are concerned about the trial of a murderess? *I* will decide what is lawful, and I will see justice done on every rebel I can find. The lawyers can take their laws to the devil for all I care. Your friend rose up against her husband, and I'll be damned before I let a woman such as you keep her from her fate."

"And *I'll* be damned before I let any man render judgment on the secrets of women," I growled. "I say she is with child, and until I say otherwise you will not have your execution."

The Lord Mayor's chest heaved as he struggled to regain control of himself. "You will change your judgment on Esther Cooper's condition. If you fail to do so, I will do everything in my power to destroy you and those you love. I will have the Church take your license. I will destroy your brother's business and drive him from politics. I may even ask Lorenzo to play a role in humbling you." The Italian smiled at the prospect, and I felt my skin crawl.

"Why don't I accompany Lady Hodgson back to her house?" Bacca said. "Evening is close, and I should feel very sad if anything were to happen to such a beautiful woman. It also would be good if we got to know each other before she makes such an important decision."

The Lord Mayor nodded and looked at me. "You have two days, Lady Hodgson. With or without your cooperation, I will see Esther Cooper burned. The question you must answer is whether you wish to be destroyed along with her. You may go."

I turned and left the office, with the Italian close behind. One of the Lord Mayor's servants opened the front door and saw us onto the street. As soon as we stepped out the door, I tried to escape Bacca, but before I'd taken more than a few steps he grasped my wrist and wrapped my arm around his, as if we were simply strolling together through the city. "Not so fast, my lady, I am far from done with you. I shall see you home. Do not worry; I know exactly where you live." I tried to pull my arm free, but his thin frame belied remarkable strength, and he held me fast. "I want to make sure that you understand the trouble you have caused, and how important it is that you find a solution as soon as possible."

"I stand by my opinion," I said. "You cannot execute Esther if there is even a chance that she is with child."

"Surely you do not believe that this is about your friend, do you? I am told that for a woman you are surprisingly well versed in politics. The Lord Mayor is simply trying to maintain order. If he is to keep the rebels outside the city walls, surely he cannot suffer a rebel to live inside them."

"Do you mean Esther Cooper, or Stephen?" I asked suddenly. "In my investigation I have heard things about Stephen that certainly would have drawn the Lord Mayor's ire, that he conspired with the rebels."

Bacca smiled broadly at me, and I felt the hair on my neck stand on end, for he looked like nothing so much as a wolf about to feast on a lamb. "That is funny. I have heard such rumors as well. I do enjoy the irony of a rebel against the King being struck down by his own wife. I think we can both agree that the Lord works in strange and wondrous ways. It is even possible that Mrs. Cooper helped save the city by killing her husband just before the rebels launched their attack. You might suggest that Mrs. Cooper beg the Lord Mayor for clemency on those grounds." He laughed softly, as if the thought of clemency for a murderess amused him.

"I cannot help wondering if the Lord Mayor might have seen fit to execute Mr. Cooper without the trouble of an arrest and trial," I said. "He has little enough respect for the law. And I imagine he would be able to find an assassin without too much trouble."

Bacca abruptly stopped walking and began to laugh. "Oh, Lady Hodgson, I believe you are trying to flatter me," he said, wiping a tear from the corner of his scarred eye. "I do not lament the death of such a man as Stephen Cooper, and I salute the skill of whoever did kill him. But I assure you I played no role in his death." With astonishing speed, Bacca pushed me into an alley, drew his dagger, and held it to my throat. He leaned in as if he intended to kiss me. I recoiled from the sour smell of red wine on his breath. "If I had decided to kill Mr. Cooper, I would not have gone to the trouble of poisoning him. It would have been far easier to cut his throat while he slept. Or approach him on the street and find this spot, here, between his ribs." He dropped the knife from my throat, and I felt its tip in my left side.

"Let go of me," I breathed. "The Lord Mayor shall hear of this."

Bacca laughed again and stepped back. The knife had vanished from his hand as quickly as it had appeared. We stepped out of the alley and resumed our journey. "Tell me, Lady Hodgson," he said playfully as we walked, "if you became . . . unavailable to serve as Mrs. Cooper's midwife, what do you suppose would happen?" He continued without waiting for a response. "I imagine the Lord Mayor would find her a new midwife who would be more agreeable than you have been. It is just a thought you might want to keep in mind. The Lord Mayor becomes quite irate when his will is thwarted. I can only imagine how angry he will be if a woman prevents Mrs. Cooper's execution. Who knows what he will do?

"Ah, I see we have come to your street," he continued. "I'm sure you will be safe from here. Think about the Lord Mayor's demands, but do not take too long. I think you should heed him." With that, Bacca sauntered back the way we had come, his brightly colored silks shimmering in the evening sun.

Once he was gone, I felt the tension run out of my body, and only then did I realize how frightened I'd been. I stepped into a nearby doorway and leaned against the wall in hope of regaining my strength. My hands shook and I could hear my heart thundering in my ears. I told myself that he would not have hurt me—not on the street in the middle of the city, certainly not before the Lord Mayor's ultimatum had passed. But I also knew that the danger I faced was very real, and unless I acceded to the Lord Mayor's demands, it would continue to grow. Though I knew Bacca had gone back to the Lord Mayor—no doubt to describe his threats in detail—I peered into the street before leaving my shelter. I saw no sign of Bacca in the crowd, so I hurried the last few steps to my door and slipped inside, locking the door behind me.

When Martha heard me enter, she came to meet me. "My God, my lady, you look as if you've the ague! What has happened?"

"It's no fever," I said, trying to calm her fears. "Get me some small beer to cool me. I'll tell you in the parlor." Once Martha returned, I settled myself on the sofa and described my visit to the Lord Mayor and Lorenzo Bacca's threats on the way home.

"Why is that son of a whore so eager to see Mrs. Cooper to the stake?"

I shook my head. "At first I thought it was simply that he believes she killed Stephen and wants to see justice done. He has no patience for rebels, and in his mind she's no different than the Parliament-men—the quicker she's executed the better."

"But now you're not so sure?"

"We still have no explanation for Stephen's mysterious visitors. If Esther is right, and Stephen *was* in league with the rebels, the Lord Mayor would have liked nothing more than to see him hanged for treason."

"But if the Lord Mayor couldn't try him, he might have simply had him killed."

"Precisely," I said. "We've already seen he has no respect for the law if it cannot be bent to his will. I also can't help wondering if Stephen might have had a role in the attack on the city. If he were in league with the rebels, it is quite the coincidence that his killer struck just days before the assault."

"And with that Italian in his pay, he has someone who knows poisons. Tom was always going on about Papists and poisons, and whenever he met an Italian he'd ask for lessons. He swore they learned it in the nursery."

With Bacca in his pay, the Lord Mayor has someone to do the killing for him. He said he prefers the knife, but I expect that he knows his poisons as well."

"What are you going to do about the Lord Mayor's demand?" Martha asked. "And where does that leave us with the Hookes?"

"I've no idea—I had no idea Stephen had made so many

enemies. If Rebecca Hooke saw Stephen as a threat to her family's fortune, she might have resorted to murder. As for the Lord Mayor, we'll see what we can do with the two days he gave us. Tomorrow we'll search Stephen's study, and see what we can learn from his letters and diary. If we can find the truth before the Sabbath, perhaps we can save Esther and ourselves." I paused. "Does this mean that you have changed your mind about Esther's guilt?"

Martha thought for a moment and shook her head. "I'll grant you that Mr. Cooper had more than his share of enemies, but she's still the one who would have had the easiest time giving him the poison. I'll wager you a week's wages that there is more to their marriage than Mrs. Cooper said."

I could not help smiling. "A week's wages it is."

# Chapter 12

I woke early the next morning and went to prayer, but my mind wandered to Stephen's death and the growing number of people with a motive for killing him. I could only hope that his letters would help me figure out who had actually accomplished their goal. Once I heard Hannah rise, I went downstairs and read in the Gospels while she prepared breakfast. Before she had finished, a girl appeared at the door, summoning me to the labor of Elizabeth Wood. Elizabeth lived south of the Ouse and was one of my regular clients. I knew her time was near, so the call came as no surprise.

"Her labor started late last night," the servant said. "It began in earnest this morning."

"How is she?" I asked.

"Mrs. Wood is well, but—" The girl broke off, uncomfortable with the rest of her message. "It's the gossips. They have been there drinking wine all night. Mr. Wood is at a loss."

I thanked the girl and gave her a penny for her trouble. I called for Martha, and together we wolfed down a cold breakfast of bread and cheese. "Never arrive at a labor hungry," I told her as we ate. "Elizabeth's husband is wealthy, but she may be far enough along that I'll need to get right to work. It also sounds like the gossips may have already emptied the larder." Without being told, Martha gathered the case that contained my birthing stool as well as my valise, and the two of us set out for Micklegate.

We crossed the bridge and followed Skeldergate along the river until we came to the Woods' home. It was not as large as my own, but comfortable enough. When we arrived, Elizabeth's harried and helpless husband met us at the door. "Please help," he said in a nervous whisper, though Martha and I were the only people within earshot. "The women have drunk all my wine, and are calling for more. I told them I had none, and they beat me with their hats and sent me out to buy some. And they want a suckling pig. What should I do?" I knew he was a good husband, but at that moment his demeanor reminded me too much of Phineas's.

"I'd get the wine and pig," I said. "You should always do what the women tell you, particularly if they are drunk." I was quite sure that my voice dripped with sarcasm, but he proved incapable of hearing it. He gave me a despairing look and scurried off. I shook my head in wonder. "Lord knows I have no love for overbearing husbands, but a man should at least control his own house."

With Elizabeth's husband gone, Martha and I went in search of the delivery room. It wasn't hard to find—even from the front door, we could hear the drunken laughter of Elizabeth's gossips. I opened the chamber door and thought that we had found a drinking rather than a birthing. The gossips gave Martha and me a warm welcome and pushed glasses of wine into our hands. ("We told that dolt we were out of wine, and sent him out for more," cackled one woman.) My first concern, of course, was for Elizabeth, but the room was so full of company that it took me a few moments to find her. She lay on her bed, clearly miserable. The gossips had lost interest in her travail, and she was attended only by a nervous servant, too young to know anything of childbirth. To my dismay, one of the gossips lay next to Elizabeth, very drunk and snoring loudly.

"This is not like most labors," I said to Martha. "But sometimes the gossips can be as much a hindrance as a help. Help me get them under control. Let's start with this one." I indicated the sleeping woman on the bed. She had rolled onto her side and thrown one arm over Elizabeth's chest.

"What niceties must we observe?" Martha asked warily.

"I can rely on my rank, but if you want anyone to obey you, you will have to make them," I said. "So long as it's for the benefit of the mother, none will complain."

Martha nodded and without another word reached down and seized the sleeping woman by her ears. As Martha hauled to her feet, the woman let out a squeal loud enough to shake the windows. "Time for you to be on your way, madam," Martha announced, as much for the other gossips as for the woman whose ears she held tight. Martha dragged her hapless victim across the room, opened the door, and fairly hurled her out. I was relieved not to hear a body tumbling downstairs; few mothers wanted a midwife to kill her gossips, however unruly they became.

Martha turned to the rest of the group and announced loudly, "Now, if you are here to assist Mrs. Wood in her travail, and are sober enough to do so, you may stay. If not, please be on your way. Now."

The women looked dumbly at the maid who had just taken over their gathering. When none moved, Martha marched around the room, snatching glasses from the women's hands and emptying them into the chamber pot. One woman tried to protect her glass, but Martha was having none of it. She wrestled it away none too gently, saying, "Now, now, give it to me, madam. You've had your fun. It's time to leave poor Mrs. Wood. She must have her baby in peace." Once she'd confiscated the glasses, Martha herded the women toward the door and shooed them down the stairs. She later told me that Elizabeth's husband had the misfortune to return as the women were leaving. "They plundered him of his new-bought wine, and left him quivering in their wake," she said. Watching Martha take over the delivery room, I felt a certain amount of pride—it took a strong woman to handle a gaggle such as this.

With the gossips taken care of, I began my examination of Elizabeth. I could feel the child's head. "It won't be long now," I told her, but after six children she already knew that. In the quiet of the room, I gossiped with Elizabeth about the news of the town, carefully avoiding the topic of Stephen Cooper's murder. Martha asked a few questions about childbirth and how a woman's first travail differed from her second and her sixth. She was a quick study and asked good questions. Soon it was time for the child to be born, and since it promised to be an easy delivery, I let Martha receive the child. She gently cradled the infant as he was born, and the look on her face reminded me of the first time I'd delivered a child. A midwife's work was never easy, but few things brought more joy than welcoming a new soul into the world.

I turned my attention to the child, and my heart sank. His complexion was pallid and his cries weak. "The child is sickly," I said quietly. "We must help him."

While Martha held the child, I put my hand into Elizabeth to deliver the placenta. I usually preferred to let it fall naturally, but we had no time. Once I had the placenta out, I put the dull edge of my knife to the cord and used it to force what blood was still in it back into him—a sickly child needed every drop. After I cut his cord and tied it tight, Martha and I gave him a bath of warm wine, being sure to rub his limbs to give them strength. "Swaddle him well," I told her. "I'll talk to Elizabeth." Martha looked at me blankly, and I remembered that she'd never served in a household with children. I quickly showed her the best way to wrap a newborn. "Now he must be put to the breast. He will turn the milk to blood, which will give him strength." I handed the infant to Elizabeth, and he began to nurse, but with less vigor than I would have liked. Elizabeth looked at me nervously. Her other children had been lusty eaters, and she was worried. I gave her what I hoped was an encouraging smile. "Good." Soon the child slept, but it was too soon for my liking. I told Elizabeth to give him suck as often as he would take it, and when she fell asleep, Martha and I left.

"Will he live?" she asked when we reached the street.

I didn't know what to tell her. The joy of welcoming a child into the world was matched only by the sorrow of seeing one out. "He is in God's hands," I said. It was the only response I could think of. Martha snorted rudely, so I tried another explanation. "It is not good that he was born in such a state, but I have seen weaker children thrive, and lusty ones waste away within days. He is lucky to have Elizabeth as his mother, for she has raised her share of healthy children." Martha only nodded. "You could say a prayer," I added. She cast me a sideways glance, silently dismissing the idea.

We crossed back over the Ouse, and when we didn't turn toward my house, Martha looked at me curiously. "It won't get dark for several hours," I said. "I thought we might go to Esther Cooper's house and see if we can get that box of letters she is so keen for us to read." My plan seemed to give Martha some cheer.

While she would likely remain melancholy until Elizabeth's son gained strength, this would at least keep her mind on other things.

When we reached the Coopers' house, I knocked on the door. We heard someone moving about inside, but nobody opened the door. After a few moments, I knocked again, this time more forcefully. Whoever was inside must have decided we were not going away, for we heard the lock click, and the door opened slightly. A young woman peered out at us. "Yes?" she said.

"We are here at the behest of your mistress," I announced. "She sent you a letter about us. Open the door." The maid hesitated. Disobeying a gentlewoman would not come naturally, but she clearly did not relish the prospect of admitting strangers to her mistress's home.

"How do I know you are the ones in her letter?" she asked.

"I am the Lady Bridget Hodgson. I assume she mentioned my name in the letter."

The maid hesitated again. "How do I know you're really her?" she asked. I took a breath and tried to control my temper. The girl was scared, an idiot, or both. If I pushed too hard, she would slam the door in our faces. Martha stepped in.

"Have any other women claiming to be Lady Hodgson tried to enter?" she asked with more kindness than I could have mustered. The maid shook her head, as if this were a reasonable question. "This is Lady Hodgson. I give you my word." To my surprise the door swung open, and the maidservant motioned for us to enter. Martha was proving more valuable an assistant than I'd dared hope, first clearing out the drunken gossips, now persuading a frightened maid to let us into her house.

Once we were inside, I allowed Martha to continue doing the talking for us. She asked the servant her name, which would not have occurred to me, but the question seemed to put the girl at ease.

"Ellen Hutton," she said. She was a handsome young woman around Martha's age, pleasingly plump, and ready for marriage. She still seemed nervous, but I could not fault her for that. With her master dead and her mistress condemned for his murder, her future was uncertain. Good servants rarely went without employment, but her background would work against her, to say the least.

"Mrs. Cooper asked us to come to her house and retrieve some items from Mr. Cooper's study," Martha said gently.

"You've seen her?" the girl asked. "What did she say?"

"We visited her Tuesday," Martha said. "She said that you've been much on her mind. She's worried about you."

"She is too kind," she said, the blood rising in her cheeks. Too kind by half, I thought impatiently, Esther barely mentioned her at all.

"Where is Mr. Cooper's study?" I asked, wearying of the small talk.

"It is on the third floor," Ellen said, suddenly nervous again.

Martha took Ellen by the arm and turned her away from me. "Before we go up could I ask you some questions about Mr. and Mrs. Cooper?"

"What do you mean?"

"What kind of master was Mr. Cooper? Was he unkind? I've had unkind masters before."

"Oh, no," Ellen said quickly. "He was a godly man and this was a godly home. We rose every morning at half-past four for family prayer."

"What were your duties?"

"Prayer ended at five and I made oatmeal for breakfast. Every breakfast was oatmeal and every supper was a boiled chicken with carrots."

"You had the same food every day?" Martha asked in disbelief.

"Once, Mrs. Cooper suggested roasting the chicken. For her insolence, Mr. Cooper whipped her bare back ten times with a rod." I tried to hide my surprise at this. I had no great love for Stephen, but I'd no idea he could be so zealous in his search for order.

"Did he beat her often?" Martha asked. I thought I detected a note of hope in her voice.

"Not often. She learned quickly. But sometimes she was willful."

Martha looked over at me and raised an eyebrow. She clearly thought she'd just won an extra week's wages.

"Did he beat you?" Martha asked. "Sometimes masters can be cruel."

"No, never," she exclaimed. "I was very careful. He only became angry once when he found out I was courting a boy. I told Mr. Cooper that he was respectable—an apprentice and would be free soon. I said he would make a good husband. But Mr. Cooper wouldn't listen. Said he wouldn't let my 'lewd carriage' bring shame on his home. But he never struck me."

"We have heard that Mr. Cooper sometimes received strangers in his office," I said. "Do you remember any of them?"

"Some men from the city gave their names. Mr. Yeoman and Alderman Hodgson visited a lot." Hearing Edward's name gave me a start, but I didn't think Ellen noticed my reaction. "The strangers just told me to take them to Mr. Cooper."

"Do you remember who visited him in the days before he died?"

"Mr. Yeoman came here twice," she said with a shrug. "But he came here often."

"Do you know if Richard Hooke ever visited your master?" I asked without much hope.

"Maybe," she said, but without much confidence. "I don't know Mr. Hooke...." She thought for a moment. "There was an Italian here last week," she offered. "Said he came from the Lord Mayor."

I looked at her in astonishment. "A small man with bright clothes?" I asked. She nodded. "Did he have a scar?"

"Yes, my lady, running down his face like this." She drew her finger across her face along the same line as Bacca's scar.

"Did you hear anything of what they said?" I asked, barely concealing my excitement.

Ellen nodded vigorously. "Mr. Cooper saw him in his study. He sent me away, but even from the second story I could hear Mr. Cooper shouting."

"What did he say?"

"He called the Italian a Papist wretch, that the King should not surround himself with such devilish company. He said that God would have His revenge on him for his Popery."

"Did the Italian say anything?"

"Not that I could hear. When he left, he almost seemed in higher spirits than when he arrived. I don't think Mr. Cooper frightened him. On his way out, he said I should mind my master before he got in trouble. What did he mean by that?"

I ignored the question. "Ellen," I said, "what happened the night Mr. Cooper died?"

"I was already in bed when it happened. I heard a crash. It must have been when he fell. I came to see what was the matter. By the time I came downstairs he was dead. It was a horrible sight."

"Did anyone visit him that night?"

"I don't think so. But I retired early that night because . . ." She suddenly grew apprehensive and seemed to swallow the rest of the sentence.

"Why did you retire early?" Tears filled the girl's eyes and she looked away from me, desperate not to answer. "Ellen, you must answer."

"Because Mr. and Mrs. Cooper fought that night," she cried out at last. "It was horrible. He screamed that she must submit to him, that it was God's law. She struck him on the arm with a ladle, and he punched her in the breast. That was when I fled to my room. I never saw Mr. Cooper again until I saw his body."

I felt a coldness gripping my heart. Could Esther have killed Stephen after all? I pushed the thought away—married couples fought. It was the way of the world.

"They say a servant found the ratsbane in Mrs. Cooper's cupboard," I continued.

"I found it," she said, weeping. "Why did she kill him? Mr. Cooper could be a hard man, but he loved her." I waited with ill-disguised impatience while Ellen dried her eyes. "Why are you here, my lady? What is your business?"

"We told you that," I said. "We are here at Mrs. Cooper's behest."

"Yes, but she is my mistress. Before I help you, I must know why." There was an edge to her voice as she came to Esther's defense. I could not help admiring her resolve.

"Lady Hodgson believes Mrs. Cooper is innocent," Martha blurted out. "She is here to find the guilty party."

"Innocent? But the constable seemed so sure! Mr. and Mrs. Cooper fought that night, and I found the poison in her cabinet myself," Ellen said. She looked at me, her eyes alight. "Do you really think someone else killed Mr. Cooper? Can you prove it?" Tears filled Ellen's eyes once again, this time in relief that someone else had taken up her mistress's cause.

"I will never believe that Mrs. Cooper killed your master. And I promised her that I would find out who did. I intend to keep that promise."

Martha crossed the room and took Ellen's arm. "Can you take Lady Hodgson to Mr. Cooper's study?" she asked.

Ellen wiped her nose on her sleeve and nodded. She led me up two flights of stairs and stopped at a heavy door. "I don't have a key," she said apologetically.

"Lady Hodgson has one from Mrs. Cooper," Martha said. "Lady Hodgson, why don't you take care of our business, and I'll visit with Ellen a bit more. I don't imagine she's had much company of late." Ellen looked grateful, and I nodded. The two of them went down the stairs, and I inserted the larger key in the door's lock. It turned easily, and despite its weight the door swung open without a sound.

The sense of order that pervaded Stephen Cooper's study bordered on the fanatical. His massive desk lay directly across from the door, so that anyone who entered would find the man hard at work. I surveyed the office. Behind the desk on a shelf were perhaps a dozen large, leather-bound books, presumably where he kept his accounts. The walls were lined with hundreds of books that appeared to have been organized by height; folios, quartos, and octavos all stood together with no intermixing at all. The spine of each one was flush with the edge of the shelf. Four quills sat on the desk, lying perfectly parallel with the front edge, and an ink pot with a fifth quill still in it sat next to them. I looked more closely and found that the pot still was nearly full of dried ink.

The wasted ink seemed out of place with the prevailing order of the rest of the office, and I took it to mean that Stephen had mixed a batch of ink just before he died. But if that was the case, what had he planned to write? There were no papers or books on his desk.

Two cabinets flanked the door through which I'd entered. Presumably this was where Stephen had kept his business papers. They were secured with small locks, better for discouraging snooping servants than resisting determined thieves. My eyes fell upon the chest Esther had described. I crossed the room and knelt by the chest but immediately realized that the key Esther had given me was far too large for the flimsy lock that secured the strongbox. I considered the situation, for it raised a number of vexing questions, the most immediate of which was how I would open the chest. After a moment, I realized that I didn't need a key.

"Martha," I called down the stairs, "may I speak to you for a moment?"

"Yes, my lady," she said as she climbed to the third floor. I closed the door behind her and explained the situation.

"The key and the lock don't match?" she asked, no less confused than I.

"We'll talk about that later. But right now I need you to open the lock."

She brightened at my request and without hesitating removed a leather pouch from her apron. She selected two delicate tools from the pouch and began to probe the lock. After a few minutes, I heard the lock snap open. She turned and handed me the lock with a flourish. "My lady," she said, and started for the door.

I put my hand on her arm to stop her. "That didn't take long. Was it a simple lock to pick, or are you that expert?" I asked.

"Well, I am an expert," she said with a modest smile, "but it was dead easy. That lock is better suited for protecting your linen than . . ." She stopped and gazed at the chest. "Why would someone put so weak a lock on that kind of chest?"

"Why indeed?" I asked. "We'll worry about that anon. It's open now, and you should get back to Ellen." Martha slipped out of the room and started down the stairs. I closed the study door and briefly pondered the meaning of the lock I held in my hand. No answers presented themselves, so I turned my attention to the contents of the chest.

The lid of the chest opened as silently as the door, revealing several large bundles of letters, each tied carefully with a silk ribbon. I leafed through them and saw that Stephen had made copies of every letter he sent and matched it with the reply, then grouped them by the subject of the exchange. I carefully placed each bundle in my valise. To my surprise, there was a single loose letter lying at the bottom of the chest. I slipped it into my bag with the rest and looked in confusion at the empty chest. Esther had been very clear that Stephen kept his diary in the chest—but where was it? I searched the room, but everything seemed to be in its place. The desk drawers were all unlocked and contained a few account books along with a well-thumbed Bible, but no diary. I scanned the room one last time but could find nothing more of interest, so I took my bag and descended the stairs.

I followed the sound of voices to the kitchen, but when Ellen and Martha heard me coming, the conversation stopped. As I entered the room, Ellen began to scrub the table furiously, though it seemed clean enough to me. I considered her situation and felt the same sympathy for her that I had for Martha the day she came to my door. She seemed a hardworking and conscientious girl, but her life had been blown off course by winds far more powerful than she. With Martha now in my household, I could not take on another servant, but I thought I could find a place for her.

"Ellen," I said, "have you thought about where you will go?"

"Go? I won't go anywhere. I'll wait here for Mrs. Cooper to return."

"What if she doesn't?" prodded Martha. "She has been convicted of petty treason." Ellen seemed unsettled by the question but said nothing.

"Ellen, I have many friends who might be in need of a maidservant as diligent as you," I said. "If you like, I can try to find you a place."

Ellen looked at me in astonishment, trying to find words of thanks. "My lady, I—I do not know what to say. That is very generous of you," she stammered. "But I can't. I . . . I don't know what I will do."

"You might need a new position," I persisted. "Let me help you."

Ellen agonized over my offer before curtsying deeply. "I would be very grateful, my lady."

With that, Martha and I bade Ellen good-bye. She saw us to the front door, and we began the walk back to my house.

"What a strange girl," I said. "She might soon be out of employment, and she wasn't sure she wanted my help finding a position? It will be no easy thing for her to find a new household, not if her master has been murdered and mistress burned."

"If I came from that household, I'd be in no hurry to find a new master. Mr. Cooper was different than Mr. Holdsworth, but not much better. Chicken for dinner every day?"

"I had no idea Stephen could be so rigid. How did Esther live with it for so many years?" I wondered aloud.

"Maybe she chose not to," Martha said with an impish grin. I ignored the comment, and she did not pursue it. "What did you find in the chest?" she asked.

"It's not what I found, but what I didn't find," I said. "His letters were exactly as you'd expect." I opened my valise and showed her the beautifully wrapped packets. "But the diary is missing."

Martha raised her eyebrows in surprise. "It wasn't in the chest?"

"Nor the desk, nor anywhere else. It's gone."

"I don't have the sense that Mr. Cooper is the sort of man to misplace his diary. Could he have hidden it before he was murdered?"

"He could have, but why would he? He didn't know he was going to be murdered. No, it must have been taken after he died."

"What about the money? Did someone take that, too?" She said it in a joking tone, but it wasn't until that moment I realized that there had been no money in the chest. I stopped on the spot, trying to put the pieces together.

"There was no money," I said. "There was no money, no diary, and Esther gave us the wrong key. What is going on?"

"That's easy enough to explain," Martha said tartly. "She lied to us about the money and the diary—if there ever *was* a diary— and then she gave us the wrong key. She never told us that Mr. Cooper beat her, or about the fight the night Mr. Cooper died. She's sending you on a wild goose chase. And by convincing you of her innocence, she gained another six months to play her game. And *I* have gained an extra week's wages." Martha looked at me triumphantly, fairly exulting in the evidence against Esther.

"We don't know anything yet, and she is still my friend," I said peevishly. "I trust you'll remember that."

"Yes, my lady," she said. "I am sorry."

"And the business with the strongbox explains neither his quarrel with Lorenzo Bacca nor the suit with the Hookes. And who was Stephen's late night visitor? Whoever it was, he was likely the last one to see him alive. No, there's too much other business for this to be something as simple as a wife killing her husband." Even to my own ears, my words rang hollow. I still believed in Esther's innocence and would fight to prove it, but I could not deny that what I'd learned had only hurt her cause.

"We should go to the jail and confront her," Martha suggested.

"We can't just walk in whenever we please," I pointed out. "As far as the Lord Mayor is concerned, we've done our job, however badly. We'll need another letter to get us through the gate." I looked at my valise. "Perhaps there is something in the letters that will help."

"Or confuse things even further," Martha added helpfully.

I smiled despite myself. "Yes, or that."

We arrived at my house, and I was pleased to find a member of the trained bands standing guard at the door. He was one of Sergeant Smith's men, and as we approached he bowed and stepped aside. While Martha and Hannah prepared dinner, I went upstairs to read Stephen Cooper's letters. I'd just laid them on my desk when there came a loud knock at the front door. I wondered if it was another birth or if Elizabeth's son had weakened further. Hannah appeared at my door a moment later.

"My lady, a boy just brought this for you." I recognized Edward's handwriting and opened the letter, expecting an overdue reprimand for my testimony on Esther Cooper. But it was far too short for that.

# The Midwife's Tale

*The body of an infant has been discovered in a privy at the end of Co-neystreet nearest St. Martin's Church. Please come as quickly as you can.*

I sighed heavily. Enquiring into the death of an infant was an awful business. I called Martha and told her we were going back out.

# Chapter 13

"There are few things more horrible than investigating the murder of an infant," I said as we neared Coneystreet. "And sometimes finding the culprit only makes matters worse." I didn't have to tell her that most infanticides were committed by servants, pregnant by their masters and desperate for escape. Sometimes the infant's body was carefully wrapped and left at a church door in the hope that he would receive a Christian burial. Other times the body was thrown away like so much trash. I could not decide which case was more heartrending. We turned onto Coneystreet and immediately saw where the child's body had been found. A crowd gathered around the entrance to a courtyard, and I could see a footman holding Edward's horse. As we approached, Edward emerged from an alley and waved us over.

"One of the neighborhood children heard crying from inside the privy," he said. "By the time they got the baby out, he was nearly dead. He was a boy."

"Someone threw the child in the privy while it was alive?" Martha asked in horror. Edward glanced at her and nodded.

"I need to see the body," I said.

Edward led us through the crowd and into a courtyard. A distraught woman stood by herself, holding a small bundle that could only be the child's body. I motioned for Martha to wait. I went to the woman and held out my arms. Sobbing, she handed me the child. The boy's eyes were closed as if he were sleeping, but his skin had a waxy texture that bespoke death. Taking the child's body into my arms made me think of my Michael, but I pushed that memory away. I could grieve for him later, but right now this child needed me. The swaddling clothes were clean, and one of the neighborhood women had washed him after he had been retrieved from the privy. I gently unwrapped him and examined his body. Whoever had cut the cord did a poor job of it, hacking rather than slicing, and it was clumsily tied. I looked at his fingernails and found them long—he was born on time. I wrapped him and handed him back to the woman.

"Did you retrieve the body?" I murmured. She nodded, tears coursing down her face. "How was he wrapped when you found him?"

"He'd been swaddled in fine linen." She pointed to a soiled cloth lying next to the privy. As she spoke, she realized the significance of this. No mother would wrap her child in expensive cloth and then cast him away. "This was someone's bairn," she whispered in horror. "Someone took him from his poor mother and killed him."

"You might be right," I said, "but you should keep such thoughts to yourself. If we are going to find whoever did this, we must keep our knowledge secret." I went in search of Edward to tell him what I'd found.

"He was newly born, and not delivered by a midwife. His color was such that he had taken a breath." Edward nodded—we knew all this. "I don't think he was killed by his mother; more likely it was his father." At this, Edward looked at me sharply. Infanticides rarely involved fathers, and it raised the prospect of a scandal touching on a citizen. "The child had been well tended until he was murdered. He was wrapped in expensive linen, and I believe he had fed at his mother's breast."

"No doubt it was a servant got with child by some apprentice or another," Edward said. He was eager to turn my attention to one of the city's meaner sort. After the murder of Stephen Cooper, he would be loath to see another respectable man pulled down.

"Few servants or apprentices could afford the linen that the child was swaddled in. This child came from a wealthy home."

"The linen proves nothing. A woman who would murder her own child would not hesitate to steal from her master."

"In recent days you've shown yourself ready to credit flimsier evidence than this," I noted testily. "A poor woman would not steal expensive linen so that she could then throw it away with her child. If the child was born to a maidservant, the father was a wealthy man, and *he* was the one who killed the child."

Edward pursed his lips in annoyance. "Whatever the case, it will be easiest to find the mother. I'll send word to all the midwives in the city," he said. "They will enquire if any servants or other singlewomen have been pregnant or given birth of late." Martha and I exchanged a glance, each of us thinking of Anne Goodwin. The look was not lost on Edward.

"Lady Bridget," he warned, "if you know whose child this is, you must tell me. The Lord Mayor and I have had enough surprises from you for the week."

"I do not know anything yet," I said. "I will make enquiries as I always do."

"All right," he said. My years of work for the city had earned his trust. "So long as we are speaking of enquiries," he continued, "I must say that the Lord Mayor was quite furious with your letter regarding Mrs. Cooper." I could tell that he enjoyed tweaking the nose of an unelected Lord Mayor, but he still considered Stephen Cooper's murder a serious matter. "Are you *sure* that she is pregnant?"

"I have examined her body, and told you what I found," I said. Anger rose within me at this challenge to my authority. "Judging a woman's body is no easy task, for it is a deceitful thing, but in this *I* will be the judge. You may rest easy, though. If she is not pregnant, you will still have the pleasure of burning her—perhaps for Christmas." I considered telling him about Lorenzo Bacca's threats, but I knew that if Bacca chose to strike, Edward could not protect me.

"Lady Bridget, you do me an injustice—," he protested, but I cut him off.

"Let us go," I said to Martha. "We can make some enquiries into the present matter before nightfall." As we walked away I could hear Edward calling after us, but I ignored him.

"Do you think it is Anne Goodwin's child?" Martha asked.

"The timing is right," I said. "But they say there are ten thousand people in the city, and it is possible that the child belonged to another maid. Let us go to Rebecca Hooke's and we will know the truth soon enough."

"Why would she let us see Anne now when she refused us before?"

"Before there was no body," I said. "Thanks to Edward's order to search out pregnant servants, we can demand to see Anne."

We walked quickly in anticipation of the conflict that would surely come. I considered summoning some of the neighborhood women to assist me in my enquiry—few people could withstand the pressure brought by a dozen angry matrons bent on finding a murderess. While that tactic would convince most women to yield their servant for interrogation, I feared that such an approach would only further antagonize Rebecca. She was so sensitive about her own birth, any public scandal touching on an illegitimate child would send her into a fury. It would be better to keep things quiet for now—I could always return with more women. We approached the Hookes' front door, and this time the footman stood his ground.

"We are here to see Anne Goodwin," I demanded. "We have orders from Alderman Hodgson to search for pregnant servants."

The footman looked at me with undisguised insolence. "Anne has been discharged from Mrs. Hooke's service. She left this morning. Or perhaps it was last night, I cannot recall."

"What?" I sputtered. "Where has she gone?"

A broad smile crossed the footman's face as he enjoyed my reaction. "Where she went was none of my affair, and it is none of yours. I cannot help you." He turned and went into the house, slamming the door behind him. I imagined Rebecca Hooke's glee when her footman recounted our conversation, and it enraged me further.

I looked up and saw Rebecca staring down at me from a second-story window, a thin smile on her face. She had bested me again, and she knew it.

"Come," I said to Martha. "I can't bear to have her staring at me."

"What can we do now?" Martha asked as we started toward my house. "We can't just go home and hope for the best."

"We can go back to her parents' house," I said after a moment's thought. "If she was discharged, she'd have few options other than going home."

We turned toward St. John del Pyke. As we passed the Minster, the bells tolled the hour. This put me in mind of the child we'd left on Coneystreet—no bells would toll for that poor creature, and he would have justice only if Martha and I found it for him.

As soon as we reached Daniel Goodwin's shop, I knew that Anne had not returned home. Margaret was sweeping out the shop as if nothing unusual had happened. I tried to escape unseen, but Margaret saw me and rushed out to meet us. When she was close enough to see our faces, she stopped.

"I take it you don't have any news," she said.

"Not yet," I said.

"Then why have you come?" she asked desperately. "Something has happened, hasn't it? What has happened to my daughter?" Margaret was a tough, perceptive woman, and I wouldn't be able to fool her even if I tried.

"We don't know anything," I said. "We went to Rebecca Hooke's today, and they said she had been dismissed from service. We came here to see if she'd come home."

"Rebecca Hooke is a lying whore if she says she dismissed Anne. She would have come straight here, and she hasn't even sent a message. She is still in that house, and they'll keep her there as long as they can. Until the baby is born if it hasn't been already."

"That seems likely," I replied. I couldn't tell her that her grandson had probably died earlier in the day after being cast into a privy, not until I knew it to be true.

"Well, I'd better get back to my work. My husband needs me." She turned and walked back into the shop. From behind, her gait resembled that of a woman twice her age. The loss of a child carries a terrible weight.

Martha and I walked back to my house, talking over the facts of the case and in the process becoming increasingly dispirited. An infant had been murdered, his mother had vanished. While Rebecca Hooke seemed the most likely suspect, we had no evidence to bring before the Justice of the Peace.

"Perhaps one of the servants knows something," Martha said. "We could question one of them the way we did Anne."

"You saw the footman and that witch who snatched Anne from under our noses. They've already joined in Rebecca's black-hearted ways."

"I could use a drink," she said, and without waiting for a response she turned in to an alehouse. I followed her and we sat at a rough wooden table. Neither of us spoke until the barmaid brought us cups of ale.

Martha drank most of hers in one gulp. "I would say we're back where we started," she said, staring into her drink. "Except that yesterday the child was alive and we knew where Anne was. Now we have a child's body and no idea where to find Anne." She paused. "My lady, do you think we will find justice for that child?"

"Under the best of circumstances, most crimes such as this one go unsolved, especially here in the city," I said. "There are simply too many people to be sure who the child belonged to. And in this case, if Rebecca is behind the murder, our chances are far worse."

"So you've done this before?" she asked. "Investigated a child's murder?"

"A few times. The death of the child is horrible, but often-times finding the killer is worse. In your heart you want the murderer to be someone you can hate, someone you can rejoice to see hanged. But in most cases it's a poor serving-maid, who was scared out of her senses." I shuddered involuntarily. "If a child dies after being born in secret, the mother must prove her innocence or be hanged for murder. Even if we found Anne, she would face a trial for killing her son. And unless she could prove that someone else threw the child in the privy, she would be executed." Martha grew visibly pale, and I realized that I had very nearly described what had happened to her. If someone had discovered her son's body and traced the child to her, Martha would have been hanged for his murder. We finished our drinks and went home.

When we arrived, I sent her to her quarters, and I retired to my chamber, intending to write to friends in the city who might be willing to hire Ellen as a maidservant. When I reached my desk I found my valise where I had left it—in all our running about, I had forgotten that I had a bag full of letters that might tell us who had murdered Stephen Cooper. I put aside my plan to write for Ellen and sat down to read. While I did not envy Esther's marriage to so exacting a husband, I do admit that his precise ways made reading his correspondence much easier. The first packet included copies of letters to and from his various business associates, as he bargained with merchants in London and Hull, with the shipowners responsible for transporting goods, and even with overseas contacts as far away as Venice. From these I learned much about Stephen's business practice—he drove a hard bargain and sought any opportunity to reduce his payment due to delays— but I gained no insight into his murder. While some of his partners complained about his hard dealings with them, nothing pointed to violence.

I opened the second packet of Stephen's letters and found that it concerned his lawsuit with Richard Hooke. Stephen's letters to his representatives at court confirmed what Charles Yeoman had said about the financial stakes. Over ten thousand pounds were at risk—whoever lost the suit would be destroyed. As I read, however, the picture became less clear. Yeoman had said that Stephen had nearly beaten the Hookes in court, but Stephen's letters painted a rather different picture. While the suit seemed to be running in Stephen's favor, in no way had the Hookes been defeated. Either Stephen had lied to Charles Yeoman about the suit, or Charles Yeoman had lied to me. But why would he want to implicate the Hookes in Stephen's murder?

I found a part of my answer in the final set of letters, which detailed a heated battle among York's leaders concerning the fate of the city. Though they maintained a unified face in public, Stephen's letters made clear that, much like the rest of the nation, the council had divided their loyalties between the King and Parliament, and Stephen was among the most violent supporters of the rebels. To my surprise, I found that my brother-in-law Edward's name loomed large in the correspondence as he and Stephen argued over where the city's best interests lay. Stephen had clearly begun a campaign to convince the godly members of York's city council—including Edward—to take up arms against the Lord Mayor and the Royalist garrison and expel them from the city. While Edward had no love for the Lord Mayor or the King, he wrote against Stephen's plan, saying it was too risky. In his opinion, the most likely end to such a rebellion would be execution for the conspirators and suffering for the city. Edward had won that debate, but more recent correspondence made clear that Stephen had not given up. In a letter Stephen sent to Edward the week before he died, Stephen claimed to have made contact with the besieging armies and told Edward of their plans to assault the city. He begged Edward to help him gather men and arms so that he could lead an attack on the King's men from inside the city at the precise moment the rebels attacked the city walls. In the final letter between them, Edward sounded much like Charles Yeoman, arguing that the city would suffer far more from a rebel assault than it did under Royalist rule. He urged Stephen to give up his plotting and warned of dire consequences if he did not. The letter was dated two days before Stephen was murdered.

I sat back in my chair, stunned by what I'd found. Charles Yeoman had sworn to me that Stephen was not conspiring with the rebels, yet the letters before me, written in Stephen's own hand, proved the contrary. This lie paled in comparison with his exaggeration about Stephen's suit with the Hookes, but it raised the same question. Why would he mislead me in such a way? Why did he want me to focus on the Hookes but ignore Stephen's ties to the rebels? But my puzzlement at Yeoman's lies was more than matched by my anger at Edward. He knew that Stephen had planned a rising within the city and had hatched a conspiracy against the Lord Mayor but had said nothing about it. If Stephen had become involved in the dangerous business of treason, and had made deadly enemies among the King's party, how could Edward allow Esther to be burned for the crime? He would answer for his deception when I next saw him.

I retied the bundles, though not so neatly as Stephen would have wanted, and placed them in my own secure chest. As I went to put away my valise, I noticed one last letter in it, the one that I had found beneath all the others in Stephen's strongbox. I opened it and was first struck by the hand in which it was written. Unlike the rest of the letters, which clearly came from the desks of educated men, this one had been written by someone who rarely picked up a pen. The letters were out of proportion, and some were made incorrectly—it seemed to me a woman's hand, but I could not be sure. More remarkable than the handwriting, however, was what the letter said.

*Mr. Cooper,*

*I know what you have done and what kind of man you are. If you do not give me ten pounds, I will tell everyone what you have done. I will have the money in one week's time. I will tell you when to deliver it.*

It was unsigned, of course, but also undated, so I had no idea whether it was relevant to his murder. If it had been lying at the bottom of his strongbox for ten years, it told us little except that he had his secrets. In light of this letter, it seemed even more important that I see Esther Cooper, though I knew my next visit would be far more delicate than my first. I would have to ask about her husband's violent outbursts, of course, but also the changed lock on the strongbox, the money missing from inside, and now the extortion letter. With every new piece of information I found, the facts of the case became ever cloudier. As I said my prayers that night, I asked God to protect Anne Goodwin, to give life to Elizabeth Wood's son, and to provide me guidance in speaking to my brother-in-law.

That night I was visited once again by foul dreams. This time I was outside the city walls, part of a joyous throng awaiting Esther's execution. When the sledge approached, I could see Esther wearing nothing except a white shift and holding a bundle of faggots. She was praying fervently. Then I saw her tied to the stake, up to her knees in wood. I looked down and saw that I had a torch in my hand and realized I was to be her executioner. Blessedly, I awoke before I started the blaze. I lay in bed for a time, wondering if I would be the one who sent my friend to the stake.

# Chapter 14

After a dream such as that, I was not surprised when I awoke feeling no less tired than when I went to sleep. After my morning prayers I wrote letters to friends on Ellen's behalf, praising her diligence and loyalty, and then considered the day that lay before me. My first order of business would be to confront Edward about the half-truths he'd told me regarding Stephen Cooper's political activities and business rivalries. I was furious and would let him know in no uncertain terms. But I also knew that by confronting him with his deception, I could obtain a letter allowing me to visit Esther again. Then Martha and I could question her about her relationship with Stephen and all that I'd found in his correspondence.

After breakfast, Martha and I crossed the Ouse Bridge toward Edward's house. A wind blew from the east, bringing with it the sound of the rebel artillery firing into the city and the King's guns firing back. As we walked, I told her what I had discovered in Stephen Cooper's letters.

"Even if Mr. Cooper was working that closely with the rebels," Martha said, "would the Lord Mayor murder him? Certainly he could have just had him arrested."

"I don't know. If he knew that Mr. Cooper planned a rebellion within the city, he might have feared that arresting him would inspire his friends to rise up. On the other hand, if he murdered Mr. Cooper, he could eliminate a rebel and prevent the rising with one blow. That could be why the murderer tried to hide his crime."

"And it would explain Bacca's visits to Mr. Cooper as well."

"Aye," I said. "He might have been questioning him or warning him against conspiring with the rebels."

"Where does that leave the Hookes?" Martha asked. "Do you think that they would kill a man over a lawsuit when the outcome was still in doubt?"

"If you told me that Rebecca Hooke had eaten her own child for supper, I would believe it." I considered this image for a moment. "Of course, she hates James so deeply that it's not so outlandish an idea." Martha looked at me quizzically. "You met James at Rebecca's door. He was the one she dragged in by his ear." Martha smiled at the memory. "James reminds me of no one so much as Phineas. He is among the weakest of men that you will meet, a fault particularly grievous in one of his rank. There are worse men, to be sure—James can't even manage to choose a vice—but none so ineffective. His parents tried to groom him for a life in trade, but he has no head for figures, and no heart for business. They sent him to London to purchase some fine silk, and he came back with neither the silk nor the money. Even the servants who went with him could not give any account of how he had lost such a fortune. He may have been cozened, but if so he does not know it."

Martha smiled broadly, enjoying the Hookes' misfortune. "And Mrs. Hooke hoped for more in her son?"

I could not help laughing. "She sees weakness as a vice worse than lechery or sloth, and feels only contempt for men who suffer from it. A man with her strength, intellect, and ruthlessness would be formidable indeed, but James takes after his father, and outshines him in every one of his deficiencies. I wonder sometimes if Rebecca would be less cruel if any of the men in her household could match her. It is a hard thing for a woman to rule her family, but given the limitations of her men, she has little choice." I paused. "If Phineas had lived a long life, we might not be so different, she and I." There was a thought.

"So the Lord Mayor had his reasons for killing Mr. Cooper, and the Hookes had theirs. Your friends certainly lead interesting lives."

"Then there is the extortion letter," I said. "My hope is that Esther will be able to offer some idea of when he received it. Until we know that, we cannot know whether it is connected to his death. Of course, if he paid the money, she might have no knowledge of the matter."

"It is also unlikely someone extorting money would murder him," Martha pointed out. "If he paid once, he would pay again. Success at extortion is just a matter of knowing how much a man will pay to keep his secrets." I looked at her sharply. "Tom trafficked in information as well as stolen goods," she explained without apology. "But he wished those victims long and healthy lives. It never occurred to him to harm them—that would be killing the golden goose."

Just as we reached the south side of the bridge, a terrifying shriek tore through the morning air, and a cart coming toward us exploded in a cloud of dust and blood. Martha and I ran to see if there was anything we could do. As we approached, we could hear the shrieks of the horse that had been drawing the cart. He was trying to regain his feet, but even from a distance I could see that his hindquarters had been wrecked by the cannonball—his rear legs were naught but a twisted, bloody mess. The horse continued to bellow, his eyes wide and rolling. Mercifully, one of the shop-keepers raced out of his store with a mattock and felled the horse with a single blow, bringing a sudden and eerie silence to the street. Martha stared wide-eyed at the carnage, pale and shaking.

Ahead, I saw that the door to St. John's church was open, so I took Martha's arm and steered her toward it. She offered no resistance when I led her inside and helped her into one of the pews. Once safely in the darkness and quiet of the church, I felt tremors race through my body, and my heart began to hammer as never before. Without meaning to, I fell to my knees and with tears coursing down my cheeks I gave thanks to God for our survival. Martha remained seated, apparently unmoved by our deliverance, but I didn't care. After I had regained control of myself, I sat down next to Martha.

"My God," she said. "If we'd left the house a few seconds earlier, that cannonball could have found us."

"God was with us," I said.

"Or He really disliked that horse," Martha said, and began to laugh.

Though I would never have predicted it, Martha's blasphemy—spoken in a church!—made me laugh harder than I had in many weeks, and once I started, there was little I could do to stop. Despite all that we had seen, or perhaps because of it, Martha and I roared until tears rolled down our cheeks, and the vicar rushed into the chancel, demanding what was the matter. Without answering—

indeed, we could hardly breathe—Martha and I stumbled back to the street and continued on to Edward's house.

By the time we arrived, we had regained our breath and except for a little extra pink in our cheeks, we looked none the worse for our brush with death. Edward's servant led us into the parlor before disappearing into Edward's study. Moments later, he emerged and told me that Alderman Hodgson would see me presently. When he left us alone, I had the opening I needed. I strode across the parlor and, without pausing to knock, burst into the study. Edward sat at his desk and looked up quickly, shocked at the interruption. Before he could gain his feet, I crossed to his desk and stood over him while I had my say.

"How dare you make me complicit in the murder of Esther Cooper!" The look on his face told me I had succeeded in putting him on the defensive. "You sent me into York Castle to hasten Esther Cooper's execution, when you knew that Stephen's enemies were competing for the privilege of killing him. Did you investigate anyone other than Esther?"

"Lady Bridget, I assure you . . . ," he sputtered.

"Can you assure me you did not know he was conspiring with the rebels? Can you assure me that you did not know that he and Richard Hooke were each bent on the other's destruction?" Edward looked harried but said nothing. He could say nothing.

"Well?" I demanded. "Have you no explanation?"

"Lady Bridget," he started, and then stopped. "The evidence marked her as guilty, and the Lord Mayor demanded a trial for petty treason; as you well know, he had his reasons. By the time I involved you, her guilt had been established in court."

"That was no trial, and you know it. If I had known the true circumstances, you would have had to find another midwife to do your bidding."

"If the Lord Mayor had found a more malleable midwife, Esther would have burned yesterday," he pointed out. It was a fair point, but I had no interest in being fair.

"Is this a comedy to you? As her midwife, I will need to see Mrs. Cooper regularly. She requires special care if the child is to live until birth. I will not leave your office until I have a letter granting me access whenever I please."

As I hoped, he leapt at the opportunity to mollify me. "Yes, of course. I will send word to the Castle, and write a letter for you immediately." He fumbled for a piece of paper and scrawled his instructions. As he placed a wax seal on the letter, he glanced up to see if my anger had abated. "Now, you must tell me how you found out about Stephen's enemies, and whom else you suspect," he said. "I doubt he told Esther. He was of the opinion that knowledge of such matters ought to be reserved for men."

"Esther insists on her innocence and has asked me to find out who might have murdered her husband. She said I should look at Stephen's private correspondence for clues."

Edward looked at me in shock, the blood draining from his face. "You have read his correspondence? Where is it?"

I could not help smiling at his reaction. "It is secure in my house," I said. "I take it you know the danger you'd be in if the Lord Mayor read the letters. Corresponding with a rebel such as Stephen Cooper? You'd be in irons before the day was out."

Edward sighed in relief that the letters were safe. "I simply did my best to save York. Stephen was willing to see the city sacked if that was the only way to deliver it to Parliament. How could I support that?"

At that moment, a realization struck me like a pistol shot.

"*You* have Stephen's diary!" I cried. "That is what he was writing in the night he was killed. You knew that it would implicate you in his schemes, and you took it so the Lord Mayor would not find it! I must see it immediately."

Edward's eyebrows flew up in surprise. He gibbered a denial but quickly became too flustered to continue the ruse. Without further protests, he opened his desk and removed a leather-bound octavo. "You may read it here, but it may not leave my house. I am quite sure you will find plenty of fuel to fire your suspicions. The biggest mystery surrounding Stephen's death is why it took so long for someone to kill him." I reached for the book, but he held tight and looked into my eyes. "I have no illusions about persuading you from your mission, but remember that Esther has been tried and convicted. Merely raising questions about the verdict will do no good. All you will do is anger some very powerful and dangerous men."

"I have to find the truth," I said. "I cannot let them burn Esther if she did not murder Stephen."

Edward nodded and let go of the book. "I have business to attend to at the Merchant Adventurer's Hall. I'll leave you here to read. Again, do not take the book with you. It is far too dangerous."

"Thank you, Edward," I said. "You are a good brother."

"We'll see," he said with a shrug. "If I end my days on the gibbet, or if the Lord Mayor sends his men after you, things might look a bit different." He left his office, closing the door behind him.

I opened Stephen's diary and began to read. The first entries were from early in the year and chronicled the daily life of a merchant and his growing anxiety about the war. He made no secret of his leaning toward Parliament and his disgust with the Royalist occupation of the city. Unlike most residents, Stephen exulted when the rebels laid siege to the city, and he unashamedly described his efforts both to foment a rebellion within the city and to contact the rebel generals outside. He summarily dismissed efforts by Edward and by Charles Yeoman to convince him to be more discreet in his activity, saying there was no half-way position between God and Satan. Stephen also wrote at length about his suit with the Hookes and the enormous sums he spent in order to secure victory. He claimed that the Hookes had matched him pound for pound, suborning witnesses and lining the pockets of any government official they thought could help their cause. Naturally, he saw God's hand in every victory, however small, and believed that it proved his own righteousness rather than his lawyer's skill.

As I neared the end of the diary, I began to see what Edward had meant about Stephen courting death in the final weeks before his murder. In the last few days before he died, Stephen's conspiracy with the rebels had become widely known among the city's leaders. Stephen wrote of Charles Yeoman's desperate efforts to forestall the uprising out of fear it would lead to the destruction of the city. He described a series of increasingly acrimonious arguments as Yeoman argued for moderation and Stephen insisted he was doing the Lord's work. I felt a shiver run through my body when I read the entry from June 8, the day after the suburbs were burned:

*Uncle Yeoman visited again today with harsh and uncharitable words about the siege and my recent actions, urged me to hold my tongue. I told him I could not hide my lantern under a bushel, said he had sided with Antichrist against the Lord. He said, "I came to York to save the city from destruction, and I have come as a friend and kinsman to warn you. If you will not stop your conspiracy, then for the sake of the city I will. If you will not promise to forbear, you must take what falls. God have mercy on your soul." I told him I was sure of my salvation and God would protect me from his schemes.*

I reread the passage several times, trying to make sense of what Stephen had written. Charles Yeoman had been clear that his first priority was to save the city from pillaging. It never occurred to me that he might have been willing to murder his own nephew in the process. And if Yeoman was behind Stephen's murder, it would explain his deception; he wanted nothing more than to shift my attention from him to the Hookes.

I continued to read, wondering who else might have had reason to kill Stephen. I did not have far to go, for in the next day's entry, Stephen noted the visit by Lorenzo Bacca that Ellen had described:

*An Italian came to me today, saying he was the Lord Mayor's creature. He said he knew of my plans for York, and would not allow me to succeed. I told the Papist that God would decide the outcome of the coming battle. He went away unpleased, with many harsh threats. I know that the Lord has placed these men before me to test my faithfulness to Him.*

The last few entries focused on Stephen's unsuccessful efforts to convince others within the city to rise up against the King's men. If Yeoman or Bacca returned to renew their threats, Stephen made no mention of it.

I returned the book to the desk and found Martha waiting in the front parlor. "How did your meeting go?" she asked with a slight smile. Apparently my voice had carried into the parlor.

"I have the letter that will open the Castle's gates to us," I said. "But that was not all." Martha looked at me quizzically. "Edward had Stephen Cooper's diary. He took it from his office the day after he was killed."

"And he let you see it?" Martha asked, her face radiating excitement. "What did it say?"

"It appears that Charles Yeoman's lies go beyond exaggerating Stephen's impending victory over the Hookes." I told Martha about the fight between Yeoman and Stephen.

"Mr. Cooper had more enemies than the King himself."

"He did at that. We'll talk to Esther now. Perhaps she can help us unravel all this."

"Perhaps," Martha said skeptically. I knew that despite my discoveries, she still believed Esther had killed Stephen. I said a prayer that she was wrong.

When we reached the Castle gate, we found a different sergeant on duty, so we went through the same inspection as at our last visit. Samuel, the dwarf-jailor, was more welcoming, chatting gregariously about the news of the city. He took us down the stairs to Esther's cell and opened the door. In the days since we'd last visited, he had treated Esther well indeed. The wood bed was still present, but she now had a second mattress along with a linen sheet and thick wool blanket. There also was now a chair next to the bed—roughly made, of course, but a chair all the same. Surprised by these improvements, I looked at Samuel.

"Her servant sent the bedding," he said. "The chair belonged to another prisoner, but he doesn't need it anymore, if you catch my meaning." He expertly mimed the snap of a hanged man's neck.

"And I assume she paid handsomely for all of this?"

"Of course she did! You said to make sure she is treated well, and I have. If I'd thought a woman such as yourself was asking me for charity, I'd have told you to piss off."

I conceded his point, and he locked us in the cell with Esther. Given her circumstances, she looked well. I can't say pregnancy became her—she did not yet show any signs of her condition—but her confinement had not yet begun to take its toll. That would change come winter, if she lived that long.

Without preamble Esther crossed the room and grasped my arms. "Did you find the letters and diary, my lady?"

"We did," I said. "But all was not as you said."

"What do you mean?" she asked.

"The key you gave to us did not fit the lock on the chest."

This seemed to deepen her confusion. "Perhaps it was stuck," she suggested.

"What did the lock look like?" I asked.

She closed her eyes to picture it. "It was iron, of course, and square . . . I don't know, it looked like a padlock," she said with obvious frustration.

"Did it have any engravings on it?"

"No, none. Stephen was always one for simplicity."

I looked over at Martha—she had recognized the significance of this. The lock that she had picked had an ornate cross engraved on its face. Someone had indeed changed the lock. The question then became what this meant.

"Esther, someone took the lock off of Stephen's chest and replaced it with another. Can you think why someone would try to keep us from reading his letters or diary?"

"I don't know," she said. "And I don't know how they could have done so. There was only one key, and he always kept it on his body."

"Most padlocks can be picked without much trouble," Martha volunteered.

"Also," I continued, "there was no money in the chest, only the letters." I decided not to tell her that Edward had pilfered the diary even as her husband's body lay downstairs.

"I saw the money a few weeks ago—perhaps he spent it, or loaned it out."

"You said it was a lot of money," I said patiently, "more than you'd ever seen." She nodded. "And you said that he had gathered it because of the siege."

"That's what he told me."

"Then he wouldn't have spent it or loaned it, would he?"

This gave her pause. "Whoever changed the lock must have taken the money," she said, mostly to herself, I think. "But only Stephen had the key. Where could the money have gone?"

"Might he have given it to a business partner for safekeeping?" I asked.

"I told you before that Stephen told me nothing of his business," she said. "I only knew if things were going well or badly from family prayers in the morning. He saw God's hand in all things. If a venture proved profitable, he took it as a sign of divine favor and gave thanks. If he failed, it was because he had displeased God, so he begged forgiveness, and attempted to mend his ways."

It became clear to me that Esther knew nothing of the missing money, so I pushed on.

"Did Stephen ever talk to you of politics?" I asked without much hope.

"Not directly. He prayed about it quite a lot. He constantly begged God to show the King his errors so he would make peace with Parliament, and Popery would be defeated."

"What were his prayers for the city?"

"He prayed for its safety. He'd heard rumors that the Lord Mayor swore he would burn the city before he surrendered it to the rebels. He said we would be better off if Parliament took it."

"Is that all?" I asked.

"I wish I knew more," she said. "Stephen preferred to talk of God rather than trade or politics."

"What were his prayers like before he died? Did they change at all?"

"They *always* changed," she said. "He was always worried about some sin or another: pride, vanity, ingratitude for God's blessings. He went on and on about secret sins, but that was not new." Nor is it very helpful, I thought.

"Did he tell you what those sins were?" Martha asked.

"No. Why do you ask?" Her eyes widened as she considered Martha's question. "You don't think he might have been murdered for his sins, do you?" I felt a pang of regret at the damage I was doing to her memory of her husband.

"We found a note sent by someone trying to extort money from your husband. Whoever wrote it said they knew of his sins, and promised to keep it a secret if he paid ten pounds."

Her eyes bulged. "Ten pounds! For what? What did they say he had done?"

"We were hoping you could tell us that," I said. "Whoever wrote the note seemed to think he'd know."

"No, I know of no sin!" She was aghast at the thought. "He was the godliest of men."

"Someone didn't think so," Martha interjected. I glared at her. This was not what Esther wanted to hear.

"It must have been a mistake. He could be a hard man, but he loved the Lord."

"There is another matter I must enquire about." Esther looked at me warily. "We have heard that Stephen would sometimes whip you."

"Oh, thank goodness!" she cried out. "You frightened me for a moment, my lady. I was worried you had discovered some terrible secret."

Now I was confused. "So, Stephen didn't beat you?" I asked uncertainly.

"After we married he corrected me when I required it, but once I learned his ways he did not have to do so very often," Esther said. "And he never whipped me excessively or marked my face." I gazed at her in disbelief. Of course I knew men who beat their wives often, and I knew wives who did not object. I simply had never imagined that Esther was such a sheep. She had further convinced me of her innocence, but I thought less of her as a friend.

"We also heard that Stephen beat you on the night he died."

Esther's face turned more serious. "Ellen told you that. Yes, we fought that night, and it was one of our worst. I hit him and he replied in kind."

"Esther," I cried in exasperation. "Why didn't you tell me this?"

"Because I needed you to believe me! I had already been convicted and sentenced to death. If I told you that I had attacked my husband on the night he died, you would have abandoned me just as everyone else has. I cannot even remember what we quarreled about. It was some small matter that got out of control. I loved Stephen and will have to live the rest of my days knowing that my last words with him were peevish and hateful. Lady Hodgson, I did not kill my husband."

I gazed at Esther, trying to find some indication of whether she was lying. To my eyes, she seemed to be telling the truth, and if I'd learned nothing else that day, it was that plenty of people wished to see Stephen dead. But I could not ignore her earlier deception or the ease with which Martha had misled me about her own past. I wanted to believe Esther, but I could not stomach the thought of being a murderess's dupe.

I looked at Martha, unsure where our questions had gotten us. Esther knew Stephen better than anyone, but even if she was telling the truth, she had given us little useful information. Martha and I said our good-byes and asked Esther if she needed anything. She said she wanted for nothing except her husband. I had a hard time believing her, but she seemed sincere. There are some women who want that sort of husband, I suppose. God help them. I knocked on the door and Samuel let us out.

# Chapter 15

"I hear you've ruffled the feathers of some very powerful birds," Samuel Short said cheerfully as he escorted us to the Castle yard. "The Lord Mayor was very unhappy when he heard you'd found Esther to be with child." He used Esther's first name deliberately, to rob her of her status, and it rankled. Esther had been born into money and married a prosperous merchant, but now she depended on Samuel as much as she ever had her husband. I didn't think he was cruel or that he treated her badly—but the inversion pleased him. Like so many of the meaner sort, he enjoyed it when the mighty fell.

"Remember our deal," I said. "If you hear anything useful about her case, you'll send word." He nodded and closed the door behind us.

As we crossed the bridge to the city, Martha and I talked about what we had learned during our visit.

"Do you believe her?" she asked.

"About what? That Stephen did not talk to her of his business or politics? To be sure. That she knew nothing of the extortion? That she did not know about the missing money? That he didn't beat her excessively? That the fight on the night he died means nothing? I don't know. She seems to be telling the truth, but . . ."

"She's lying about something or she's stupid as a shit-eating goat," Martha said dismissively. "No woman worth her salt could be so blind to what was happening in her own house." She paused. "Is it possible she murdered him and then took the money, but was arrested before she could make good her escape?"

"You're thinking like a thief, not a merchant's wife," I chided her. "She could no more steal the money and escape than I could. Where would she go? What would she do? She cannot simply appear at a stranger's door and ask to be put into service." She smiled slightly. "If we want to find out what happened to Stephen, we will have to discover the truth ourselves. When the subject is Stephen Cooper's death, everyone lies."

"What now, then?"

"We return to Charles Yeoman's," I said. "I want to see his reaction when I tell him what I read in Stephen's journal. But before that, I need to see a client up in St. Savior's."

"How can you know a client needs you? Did a message come to you at the Castle?"

I laughed. "A midwife's work doesn't end when she cuts the cord. Some mothers need more assistance than others, especially if it is their first child and they don't have a family or proper gossips."

"The client is an unwed mother?" she asked.

"It's a girl named Mercy Harris. I delivered her the day the soldiers burned the suburbs. Mercy's sister is just a child herself, and she has no family here in York. I'll do my best to care for Mercy in her mother's stead."

We wound our way through the alleys and side streets to Mercy's home and found the front door open to let in some air and light. Mercy sat on the bed, holding the sleeping child. When we entered, she looked up and smiled.

"Look," she whispered, pride evident in her voice. The baby was a pleasant pink and seemed to be taking milk tolerably well. A young man stood next to the bed, shifting nervously from foot to foot. I looked at him sternly, and his ears turned a lovely shade of crimson.

"I take it you are the baby's father?" I asked.

"Yes, m-my lady," he stammered.

"It is good that you're here," I said. "Make a habit of it."

"Yes, my lady. I pleaded with my master, and he will allow me to marry after Mercy's lying-in," he said.

"Good lad," I said with a smile. "I don't know where you were the night she was delivered, but better late than never. Now run along, I need to examine Mercy." He bade farewell to Mercy, bowed to me, and slipped out the door. I turned to Mercy. "If you hold him to the marriage, you may escape whipping," I said.

The prospect of punishment sobered her. I had no desire to see Mercy whipped. It pained me to think of a new mother subjected to such brutal treatment, particularly when the father had agreed to marry her. She had not been wanton in her behavior, just unlucky. I would do my best to help her avoid such a humiliation, but some men believed that if the spectacle of one maid's whipping caused another maid to remain chaste, then it was well done. But those concerns were for another day.

While Martha held the baby, I examined Mercy's privities and found that with God's help she was healing very well. I undressed the baby and saw that she too was in excellent health, though displeased at being unwrapped. My mind wandered to

Elizabeth Wood's sickly child, and I wondered at God's providence—why would He give Elizabeth a sickly child and Mercy a healthy one? My mind then asked why He would take Michael and Birdy from me, and I pushed that question away as I had so many times before. Finding God's plan in the life and death of infants was a difficult task, and one I preferred not to dwell upon.

"Your sister and the child's father seem to be taking good care of you," I said. "Have you made arrangements for baptism?"

"We should like to do it on Sunday. Will you be there to name her?" she asked hopefully. At that I was torn. Sunday also would be the christening of a child I had delivered just before Mercy's, and I had already agreed to attend that one.

"Mercy, it pains me to say this, but I cannot be there," I said gently, and explained the conflict. "But as is my practice, I can send Martha in my stead. She has assisted me in many births." Mercy looked at Martha, who nodded encouragingly and then glanced at me, uncertain of what she had just agreed to do.

Before leaving, I slipped ten shillings into Mercy's hand. She looked at me in shock—it was more than she could have hoped to earn in two months. As she stammered her thanks, I swaddled the child and gave her back. With that, I embraced both Mercy and Sairy and bade them farewell, and then Martha and I started toward my home. When we arrived, we found the guard in place, no crisis brewing, and dinner almost ready. Compared with past days, this seemed like no small victory.

A few minutes after we had dined, Will appeared at the door, and I met him in the parlor. As he entered, he looked at me with concern. "An armed guard at your front door, Aunt Bridget?" he said. "Surely your maid wasn't so dangerous as that, or so fool-hardy as to return after you dismissed her."

"Martha is still in my household," I said. Will's mouth gaped in surprise, and he started to speak, but I continued. "The guard *is* here on her account, but not for the reason you think. The man you saw her with in the market is as dangerous as you thought. He is a thief and murderer from Hereford. But he is her brother, not her accomplice. She came to York in hope of escaping from him, and he followed."

"How do you know all this?" he asked worriedly.

"She told me."

"Aunt Bridget, you can't be serious! You are inviting danger into your home. Who knows what she has planned."

I crossed the room and took Will's hand. "I appreciate your concern," I said. "But I believe her, and unless she gives me a reason to rethink my decision, it is final. You will see that she is a good and trustworthy servant."

"I hope you are right. But why has he followed her here? He does not seem to be the kind of man driven by a brother's love for his sister."

"That is an understatement," I said with a grim smile. "She betrayed him and he won't rest until he has his revenge. If he can rob me in the process, so much the better. It is a long story. Perhaps she will tell you one day. The guards are here until I am sure that we are safe from Tom."

I don't think I convinced him my decision to keep Martha was a wise one, and I was thankful when he changed the subject. "I heard from my father that you are investigating Stephen Cooper's death. Have you found anything of interest?"

"I learned that the city officials were more interested in convicting Esther than catching the real murderer," I said, and told him everything I had found in Stephen's letters. "Stephen had many enemies in the city, and any one of them might have had him killed."

"And you are hoping Rebecca Hooke had him killed over the lawsuit? It *would* be lovely to see her brought low. . . ."

"I am hoping for nothing," I objected. "I am only trying to find out who killed Stephen Cooper. If it was the Hookes, so be it, but they are not the only ones who might have done so."

"What is your next step?" he asked. "You could visit Richard and ask if he murdered Stephen." He paused, considering the idea. "In truth, that might work. If he did do it, he is just fool enough to tell you. You'd have to find a way past Rebecca, though."

"No, I'm taking a less direct route first," I said with a laugh. I then told him about Stephen's troubled relationship with Charles Yeoman and my intention to visit him that afternoon.

"Charles Yeoman!" he said with a low whistle. "The Member of Parliament? I heard that he'd retired to York in order to avoid involvement in the wars. He was a powerful man in his time."

"I don't care about his politics. I just hope he can help me with this case. Would you like to accompany us?"

"Of course," he said. "There is no harm in making connections with such a man."

At that moment, Martha came from the kitchen and began to clean the dining room. While she worked, Will kept a close eye on her, as if he expected to catch her in the act of stealing my silver plate. I saw that Martha had been right: Will was terrible at spying. I couldn't tell if she was more annoyed by his suspicion or his lack of subtlety. Eventually her patience ran out.

"My lady, I wonder if I could ask you a question."

"Of course," I said.

"I've only been here in York a short time, but I think that a young man wishes to court me." I tried to suppress a smile as I caught on to Martha's game.

"Really? How exciting! But you are not sure? Have you spoken to him?"

"He's hardly said a word to me, but when we are together, he stares at me constantly. When I look at him, he looks away and pretends to stare at the wall. It's quite obvious what has happened."

"He has fallen in love with you," I said.

"Yes, I'm afraid so. And that's the tragedy of it, for it is a match that cannot be."

"How sad!" I exclaimed with only a little too much enthusiasm. "Why is that? Is there anything I can do to help?"

"I don't think there is. The first problem is that I am not inclined to marry yet. But even if I were, it is impossible. He is far above my station. His family would never allow him to marry a servant." I risked a glance over at Will. He had picked up a book and was staring at it intently.

"Do you know his family?"

"They are merchants here in the city. His father is an Alderman. I know his aunt very well." That last comment was too obvious by half, and I saw Will furrow his brow as he realized that Martha and I were having a jest at his expense.

"That sounds serious," I said. "Does he know that you are aware of his love for you?"

She turned to stare at Will. "I think he is beginning to figure it out."

With that, Will slammed the book shut and leapt to his feet, sputtering with indignation. He was not accustomed to being teased by servants, even with the connivance of a gentlewoman. I burst out laughing even as I tried to mollify him. Martha smiled sweetly, curtsied (whether to me or to Will I could not tell), and wisely retreated to the kitchen. By this time Will's face had become quite red, and he turned his anger and embarrassment in my direction.

"How could you let your servant mock me in such a fashion? I like her less and less."

"And I like her more and more," I replied, still laughing. "You were far too obvious. She could hardly ignore your stares." I squeezed his arm, and he began to regain control of himself. "Will, I cannot tell you the details, but I have good reason to trust her. It is true that she brought trouble in her wake, but it was not entirely of her own making. Except for her murderous brother, she has no family in Yorkshire. If I cast her out, I would lose a valuable servant, and she would be killed by Tom. She also has a number of skills that I think you will appreciate, and perhaps ask her to teach you."

"Aunt Bridget, really. She is a servant. I don't think I have a future in cooking or cleaning."

"Very well," I said lightly, quite sure that he would change his mind if he saw her use a knife or a lock-pick. "Now, shall we go see Charles Yeoman?"

During the journey, Will looked everywhere except at Martha, a fact that amused her nearly as much as his earlier surveillance, and she had little success hiding her pleasure at his discomfort. I was less pleased, however, for the many years of ridicule Will had suffered on account of his clubfoot meant that he took seriously every insult to his honor. What seemed like good-natured teasing to Martha might seem like a deliberate provocation to Will. Moreover, since Will could hardly respond to this offense in his customary fashion by beating her senseless, he retreated within himself and refused to speak at all. By the time we reached

Petergate, I'd had my fill of the silence and regretted my role in Martha's performance.

"Martha, we should apologize to my nephew for our behavior a few minutes ago," I said. She looked surprised and opened her mouth to speak, but I continued. "Will has only my best interests at heart, and he does not know you as well as I do. Regardless of how out of place his concerns may seem, they are born of love, and should not be mocked." I turned to Will, looking him in the eyes. "Will, I was wrong and I am sorry. I ask your forgiveness."

"Sir, I ask your forgiveness as well," Martha echoed, bowing her head, suddenly the very picture of contrition.

Will looked uncomfortable at having to admit that Martha's little play had cut him so deeply and tried to dispense with our apologies as quickly as possible. "No, no, it is quite all right," he said. "It is not just that you made sport of me. I've been thinking about the events of recent days, and the times in which we live. Parliament accuses the King of tyranny, the King calls Parliament rebels. Wives are murdering their husbands and mothers discarding their infants into privies—the world is on its head." He paused before continuing. "I read in my grandfather's commonplace book yesterday. He copied part of a poem that struck me.

*The sun is lost, and the earth, and no man's wit*
*Can well direct him where to look for it.*
*'Tis all in pieces, all coherence gone;*
*All just supply, and all relation:*
*Prince, subject, Father, Son, are things forgot.*

"Do you know who wrote it?" he asked. I shook my head. "He didn't note the author. I wish I knew." With that, Will robbed us of our good cheer, but not unjustly so, for we had bought it at his expense.

"Come," I said in a subdued tone. "We should go." We turned onto Low Petergate and walked the rest of the way in silence.

When we arrived, I told Yeoman's servant we would like to meet with his master. He led us to the parlor and disappeared into Yeoman's study.

"I'm afraid Mr. Yeoman is far too busy to meet with you at the moment," the servant announced upon his return. "He suggests you send him a letter. He assures you that he will try to find time to meet with you."

I hadn't thought Yeoman would confess to murdering his nephew immediately upon my arrival, but neither had I expected this degree of intransigence. The servant took Martha by the arm and started leading her to the front door.

"Tell Mr. Yeoman that I would like to discuss Stephen Cooper's diary with him," I said.

"I will certainly give him the message, my lady. Now, as I said, Mr. Yeoman is attending to important business. You should go."

As Martha struggled to free her arm, I strode across the room and seized the servant's ear and pulled with all my strength. With a cry of surprise and pain, he let go of Martha and followed me across the room toward Yeoman's study. "Nay, sirrah, you will remember your place and give him my message right now." I pushed him down the hall. "Tell him I eagerly await his reply." The servant scarcely paused to knock before scampering through Yeoman's door. I turned back to the room and found Will and Martha both shaking with suppressed laughter.

"My Lord, Aunt Bridget," Will said, wiping away a tear. "I've never seen that side of you before."

"Something I learned from Martha. I told you she had more than a few useful skills."

"Mr. Yeoman will see you, my lady." The servant had returned.

"That is very kind of you," I said as Will and I followed him to Yeoman's office.

Yeoman sat behind his desk, but this time he gave me his full attention as soon as I entered. I wondered if he might reprimand me for abusing his servant, but he chose to ignore my offense. "Have you really read Stephen's diary?" he asked angrily. "If you're lying, you've made a terrible mistake." Only then did he notice that Will had followed me in. "Who is this?" He looked Will over, his eyes lingering on his cane, though what he made of it I could not tell. "You must be Lady Hodgson's nephew. I hear your brother Joseph is serving with Cromwell. It is good that one of you can fight. I imagine that he will inherit your father's power, too. That's probably for the best." He glanced again at Will's cane, and a cruel smile touched the corners of his mouth. I wondered if, in his youth, Yeoman had tormented lame boys the same way that Will had been. If so, I hoped he received a beating or two for his trouble. I could tell from Will's face that he recognized Yeoman's scorn. Tears of anger came to Will's eyes, and my heart ached for the pain I knew he felt. "Mr. Hodgson," Yeoman said suddenly, "please leave the room." Will looked shocked by the order and found himself caught between the obedience demanded by Yeoman's voice and his own wounded pride. "Go," Yeoman repeated. Without a word, Will left.

"Will knows what I've found," I said. "There was no reason for you to do that."

"I don't care what you've told him," Yeoman said with a sneer. "He is weak in body. I cannot trust him. He can wait with your servant. Now, you said that you saw Stephen's diary. I don't know what you think it tells you, but I will answer a few of your questions."

"I want to know why you lied to me."

Yeoman burst into harsh laughter. "Why I lied to you? Do you hear yourself, woman? The better question would be why I ever stooped so low as to meet with you. I could have saved us both time and trouble by sending you away from the first." I tried to speak, but he did not give me the chance. "I lied to you for the sake of the city. I lied to you because you are a woman meddling in matters that do not pertain to you. I lied to you so that you would not put yourself in any greater danger than you already have."

"Danger from Lorenzo Bacca?"

He looked at me in surprise. "So you've met our Italian friend? Yes, he is the reason I urged you to keep your nose out of political matters. He certainly might have killed Stephen, and he would not hesitate to kill you if he came to see you as a threat. The Lord Mayor is desperate and dangerous—you should be very careful not to anger him."

"And I suppose that is why you told me that Stephen had nearly won his suit against the Hookes? You hoped I would miss his political entanglements entirely."

"Believe it or not, I had your best interests at heart. I still believe that Rebecca is behind Stephen's death, and however cruel she is, Rebecca is far less likely to kill you than Lorenzo Bacca. If you find proof that the Hookes were not involved, come back to see me. We can then discuss the best course of action." I realized that Yeoman was not only pushing me back toward the Hookes, but trying to take control of the investigation altogether. I decided to turn the tables on him.

"And whose interests did you have in mind when you threatened to kill Stephen?" I asked innocently.

Yeoman froze and stared at me in silence. I could see him trying to figure out how much I knew and what game I might be playing. "He wrote that in his diary, did he? He would. Even when they are on the verge of victory, the Puritans see persecution and martyrdom at every turn."

"He wrote it, but others in the household heard it as well," I lied. "If the Lord Mayor had seen fit to ask Esther, she could have told him, too. In our first meeting you told me that you came to York to prevent the sacking of the city. We both know that Stephen was trying to aid the rebels in doing just that. I think you would have killed Stephen to stop his plans. What is one man's life compared to the hundreds or thousands who would perish if the city were taken by force of arms?"

"If I thought that killing Stephen would save the city, I would have done so without hesitation," he said bluntly. "But I did not."

"It is interesting that you say that because Lorenzo Bacca made the same claim. And while I've not asked her, I imagine that Rebecca Hooke would give a similar answer."

"You may go."

I stood and started for the door. Before opening it, I turned back and found Yeoman staring at me balefully. "Mr. Yeoman, I will find out who murdered Stephen Cooper, whether it was Bacca and the Lord Mayor, Rebecca Hooke, or you yourself."

"You can play at constable all you want," Yeoman snarled. "But you should realize that it is a dangerous game. I will *not* be brought down by a mere woman."

## The Midwife's Tale

"We will see," I said, and left the room. I could feel my heart pounding as I made my way back to the parlor. I knew I had made an enemy of a very powerful man. The only question was how far he would go in order to protect himself.

# Chapter 16

I found Will in the parlor, staring blankly at the wall. I could see the muscles in his jaw working as he clenched his teeth, trying to contain his fury over his treatment at Yeoman's hands. He knew better than to vent his anger before we had left the premises. Moments later, Martha joined us and we started home. When Martha and I turned off of Stonegate onto my street, Will stopped.

"I have other business to attend to," he said. "I will call on you tomorrow."

"Martha, go on ahead. I need to talk to Will for a moment." Sensing the tension, she curtsied and went without a word. "Will, please," I said. "Come inside, at least for a while." From the look in his eyes, I knew that if he left now, he would seek redemption in an alehouse brawl.

"No," he said, shaking his head. "I'll be all right. I just need to . . ." His voice trailed off. He didn't know what he needed.

"You can't allow men like Yeoman to hurt you so."

"Men like Mr. Yeomen rule England," he said. He spoke with the bitterness of a man robbed of his birthright. "They always have and always will. They think that because I am weak in body, I must be weak in mind. I even see it in my father's eyes some-times."

"Will!" I cried. "Your father loves you!"

"Of course he does," Will spat. "But Yeoman is right—Joseph is his favorite, and when he comes back from the wars, my father will push me back into the shadows. He will make sure Joseph becomes an Alderman, Lord Mayor, and perhaps even a Member of Parliament. I will stay here in York, take up the wool trade, living and dying as a man of no consequence. No matter what my father says, I am a disappointment and he is ashamed of himself for fathering a cripple."

"Will, don't say such things," I begged.

"Why ever not?" he cried. "You and Uncle Phineas were the only ones who never seemed embarrassed by me. But Uncle Phineas is dead, and you're just . . ." He stopped himself too late.

I drew myself up and stared into his eyes. "I'm what, Will? I'm just a woman?" I could feel the blood rising in my face.

"Aunt Bridget, you know what I mean," he protested.

"Yes, I think I do," I said. "A few moments ago, I had almost the same conversation with Charles Yeoman, so I know exactly what you mean—he feels the same way." Will tried to interrupt, but I would not let him. "Perhaps the two of you are more alike than either of you realizes. It is a shame that *this* is the lesson you learned from a lifetime of abuse by men like Yeoman."

I turned on my heel and strode away. Will called after me, apologizing, but anger deafened me to his entreaties. I tried to compose myself, for however much Will's words hurt me, I knew that he had lashed out in pain rather than malice. None could deny Yeoman's cruelty, but he had not so much opened a new wound as ripped up an old one; Edward had been the first to cut into Will's flesh. However much I denied it, Joseph *was* Edward's favorite and always would be. Joseph had the richer clothes, the finer horses, and Edward gave him ever more responsibility in both business and politics. The fact that Joseph fought while Will stayed home would only make matters worse in the future. I could never say anything to Edward or even admit the truth to Will; Edward would deny it, and Will would be crushed. All I could do was care for Will as best I could and help him become a good man in a world dominated by bad ones.

Martha met me at the door. I asked her to pour a glass of wine for each of us and join me in the parlor. When she returned, she gave me a glass and looked at me expectantly.

"What did Mr. Yeoman have to say?" she asked.

"Nothing that made things any clearer. He admits that he lied to us about Stephen's connection to the rebels, but warned us against pursuing that line of inquiry."

"And what did he say when you asked him about Mr. Cooper's diary? I can't imagine he was happy that we know about his threats."

"He warned me off again. He said he would not be brought down by a woman," I said. "I don't think he's as dangerous as Lorenzo Bacca, but I would hate to be proven wrong."

Martha sat back and gazed up at the ceiling. "Everyone connected to the case has lied to us or threatened to kill you," she said. "Mr. Yeoman, the Lord Mayor's man, even Mrs. Cooper."

"How do you find the truth when nobody will speak it?" I asked. We sat in silence, each seeking a new approach to the case.

Martha's eyes suddenly lit up and she jumped to her feet. "The ratsbane!" she cried.

"What do you mean?"

"Rather than focusing on the suspects, we can focus on the

evidence." I shook my head, still not following her thinking. "We start with the ratsbane. With York under siege, it likely came from inside the city. If we find the apothecary who sold the ratsbane, all the lies in the world won't hide the truth."

"There are only a handful of apothecaries in York," I said. "We can enquire who bought ratsbane in the days before the murder. By itself, it wouldn't prove Esther's innocence, but it might tell us which of our other suspects to investigate."

"Of course, we could discover that *she* bought ratsbane just before her husband's death," Martha pointed out.

I paused and considered the prospect of proving Esther's guilt even as I worked on her behalf. "I still do not believe she is guilty."

"And if she is?"

"Then she should die," I replied, unsure if I really meant it. I knew that blood cried out for blood, but I could not envision Esther's execution. I pushed the thought aside and reminded myself that the Esther I knew was no murderess. "Whatever the case, tomorrow I shall send letters to the apothecaries I know and see what they can tell us."

"We can use the bottle," Martha said. "The officers found the ratsbane in a glass vial, which probably came from the apothecary who sold it. If we take the bottle from shop to shop, someone might recognize it. Do you think your brother has it?"

"If he doesn't, he will know who does," I said. "I'll send for it immediately, and in the morning we can begin our search."

I sent Hannah to Edward with a letter explaining our plan. I knew he would not be happy with my request, since it could only complicate matters. I could only hope that he'd not yet expiated his guilt for concealing so much information about Stephen's murder. Apparently he had not, for an hour later Hannah returned carrying a small cloth bag containing a bottle of fine powder. I called for Martha, and together we examined it.

"There are no marks on it," I said in disappointment, "nothing to help us identify the seller."

"Do all apothecaries use bottles such as this one?" she asked.

"No. Different sellers use different vials for their poisons, so if we find an apothecary who uses these bottles, we'll be one step closer to finding the killer. We'll set out tomorrow morning."

That night I prayed for the nation, city, my household, and especially for Will. But my prayers put me in mind of Will's lament for England's present state, and I found myself overcome with sadness. What were his words? "'Tis all in pieces, all coherence gone"? I hoped his dark vision would not come to pass, but I could see no happy resolution to the troubles we had created.

To my surprise, I awoke Saturday morning to a knock on my door. Hannah stood in the doorway.

"What is it, Hannah? Is everything all right?"

"My lady, a servant is here with a message from Elizabeth Wood."

I felt my stomach sink, for this could only mean that her boy had died. He had been so sickly that I was not surprised, but I had held out hope. My heart ached for her, for I knew all too well the pain she now felt.

"Please have her wait in the parlor, and then come help me dress." She curtsied and left. I lay in bed a while longer, saying prayers for the dead child, for Elizabeth, and for her husband. This was the first infant I had lost since Michael died, and I knew that the day would be full of sad mementos of his death and burial.

Hannah returned to help me wash and dress, and then I went downstairs. Before going to the parlor to see Elizabeth's maid, I called for Martha. She had been part of the child's delivery and would be a part of his burial. We found Elizabeth's maidservant standing in the parlor, shifting uncomfortably from foot to foot. When she saw me, she curtsied and kept her eyes lowered when she spoke.

"My mistress sent me," she said quietly. "Her baby died last night." From the corner of my eye, I saw Martha's face crumple, which only compounded my own grief.

I took a shallow breath, worried that I would start to cry. "When will they bury him?" I asked.

"This afternoon. Mr. Wood just sent word to the priest."

"Thank you," I said. "Please return to your mistress, and tell her we will be there soon."

"Did she give him a name?" asked Martha.

"Benjamin, after his father. Mrs. Wood called him Ben." Martha nodded, fighting back tears.

The maidservant curtsied, and I saw her to the front door. I returned to the parlor and found Martha gazing out the window. I could see the tears on her cheeks. I went over and put my arm around her shoulders. She took a deep breath and clumsily wiped at the tears with her apron.

"Will you go and see the child?" she asked.

"Elizabeth needs me. And because you had a hand in the child's birth, you should come as well. We brought the child into the world, so we will dress him for his burial and see him out. Ask Hannah to find some linen. Then have her help you tear some strips to wrap the child." Within the hour Hannah and Martha finished with the linen, and we departed for Elizabeth's house.

All midwives lost infants in childbirth or soon after—it was God's will and a midwife's lot—and a good midwife felt every death in her bones. But the pain I felt on this day was especially sharp. In part it was because it reminded me of Michael, of course, but also because I could see that Martha suffered as much as I did.

"What will you do when you get there?" she asked.

"It depends on Elizabeth's state. Some women fall into melancholy and require constant attention. Others accept it as the will of God and require little help. It is hardest for women who lose their first child."

"I know," she said softly.

"I'm sorry," I said, and I put my arm around her shoulders to comfort her. "I hadn't forgotten about your son."

Just as we reached Elizabeth's door, one of the women who had been present for Elizabeth's delivery opened it and came out into the street. If she remembered Martha or the rough treatment she had received at her hands, she gave no sign of it.

"How is she?" I asked.

"It is not the first child she has lost, but she still feels it deeply." Her red-rimmed eyes and pale complexion told me that she felt it, too. However badly she had acted at the birth, she remained a good gossip. Martha and I stepped through the open door and the Woods' maidservant greeted us.

"Is Mr. Wood here?" I asked. While we would spend most of our time with Elizabeth, sometimes the fathers needed comfort and reassurance as much as the mothers.

"Yes, my lady. He is in the parlor. This way."

Benjamin Wood sat in the parlor, his face taut with grief. One of the older children sat on his lap. "Thank you for coming to see her," he said. "Elizabeth is upstairs. She is melancholy and has asked for you."

"You should be with her," I urged him.

He smiled weakly. "I'm helping to mind the children. They want her, but she does not need the burden."

"Let them go to her," I suggested. "They might take her away from her grief for a time." He nodded. Birdy had done this for me when I lost Michael, but when she died I had nobody.

"I'll take you upstairs," he said. "The baby is there, too."

Martha and I followed him up to Elizabeth's bedchamber. The same room where she had given birth was now her lying-in room, and it was here that Martha and I would prepare the child's body for burial. We entered the room and found Elizabeth sitting on the edge of the bed, talking softly with one of her neighbors. When she saw us, she smiled slightly and stood to greet us. The lines on her face had deepened in the two days since the birth, and her eyes were watery and bloodshot. She embraced me and Martha and began to cry again. I fought back tears, and I saw Martha doing the same. Elizabeth reached out and took Martha's hands, and it struck me that the two women were comforting each other.

"Ben was never long for this world," Elizabeth said. Martha nodded, clenching her jaw to keep from bursting into tears. I looked around for the child and saw that he had been loosely wrapped and laid in the crib that should have been his bed. Two women sat with him and would do so until his burial.

I crossed the room to the crib and picked up the child's body. I found myself unable to breathe as I was hurled back to the day Michael died, and I recalled how my own midwife had prepared his body for burial. That too had been a sunny day, only much colder. I remembered the murmuring of my gossips as they comforted me and how I had tried to find a way to tell Birdy what had happened to her brother. Losing her father had taught her much about death, but she had so loved Michael, I wondered if his death might pitch her into a deeper melancholy than it did me. At first she hadn't understood or at least refused to admit what had happened. She screamed the most horrible curses at me and at God for taking him away. Then, when she saw his body and held it in her arms, she wailed long and loud, as if to raise the dead. It was a wonder that her heart, and mine, too, did not break from the crying.

Like Michael, Ben seemed to weigh nothing at all with his breath stopped. I asked Elizabeth's maidservant for a towel and basin of warm water. When she returned, I spread the towel in the crib, laid the child on it, and motioned for Martha. She looked down at the tiny body as I carefully loosened the swaddling clothes and showed her how to wash an infant's corpse. Unbidden, Martha produced the strips that she had torn, and with shaking hands we wrapped the child. After we finished, we left the body with the women and returned to Elizabeth.

One of Elizabeth's other children, a boy of perhaps four years, lay in the crook of her arm, gazing blankly at his dead brother's body. I sat next to her and took her hand, but I could think of nothing to say. Soon it was time to go to the church. I picked up Ben and brought him to Elizabeth so she could hold him for the last time. A low moan escaped her chest as she took him in her arms, and tears fell from her cheeks onto his. The sound of her sobs wrenched my heart, and I wondered at the God who would do this.

Elizabeth kissed her boy, gave him to me, and bade us farewell. Accompanied by Benjamin and a dozen neighborhood women, we walked slowly to St. Martin's church as the bell tolled softly. The summer sun blazed down from a brilliant blue sky, making our party's grief seem small and out of place. I wondered what the Lord meant by this. The priest met us at the entrance to the church and sang out, "I am the resurrection and the life, saith the Lord: he that believeth in Me, though he were dead, yet shall he live: and whosoever liveth and believeth in Me shall never die." We entered and took our seats. Because it was not the Sabbath, the service would be a short one. I closed my ears to the priest's words and sought refuge in prayer. I begged God to comfort Elizabeth and Benjamin in their grief and asked Him to heal me, to make me whole.

After he finished his reading, the priest led us to the churchyard. Ben's grave seemed terribly small. I saw that the digger had laid a bed of straw at the bottom and hoped that the same had been done for Michael. We said the Lord's Prayer, and with shaking hands Benjamin lowered his son into the ground. Then, as gently as he could, he shoveled in the grave. I thought then of the cold earth that covered Michael first and then Birdy, but my heart was so sore that I could feel nothing more. I heard some snuffling from the mourners but few sobs. I think by then we had all cried enough. As we walked back to his house, I put my arm through Benjamin's and told him of my prayers. He looked at me with red and haggard eyes and offered his thanks. The maid met us at the door and whispered in Benjamin's ear.

"Elizabeth is asleep," he said. "She's not slept more than a few hours since Ben was born. Now that he's gone . . ." His voice trailed off.

"Please tell Elizabeth we came back," I said. "And that we will be here when she is churched."

"I will."

Then Martha and I started for home, and the other women went their own ways. We walked in silence for a while. As we crossed the Ouse, she looked out over the water and asked, "How do you do this year after year? How do you bury the same babies that you deliver?"

"With God's help, and the knowledge that death comes to us all. If Ben hadn't died today, it would have been tomorrow, or some other tomorrow in five, fifty, or a hundred years. We cannot stop death, only slow his march."

"And that is enough?" she asked doubtfully.

"I also remind myself that I am a good midwife. I could not save Ben, but as surely as God created the world, I have saved babies that would have died under another midwife's care. There are the mothers, too. Sometimes they die in travail, but if I am at a woman's bedside, she is more likely to live." Martha nodded and wiped her eyes.

When Martha and I neared my home, the guard at the door raised his hand in greeting. Before I could respond, the door belonging to my next-door neighbor burst open, and George Chapman spilled out into the street, his bulging belly straining at his doublet's buttons. To my dismay, he planted himself squarely in front of us, with his hands on his ample hips.

"Lady Hodgson," he said, "I must have a word with you."

"I imagine you must," I said archly. I wondered what complaint he might have this time. Because I was a young widow who had not remarried, a lady who worked with her hands, and a woman with power, my very existence challenged his carefully ordered world. He respected my rank enough not to confront me directly, but he took advantage of every opportunity to reprimand members of my household for any failing, real or imagined. "May I guess? Was Martha singing too loudly in my courtyard? Or did she not treat you with the reverence you deserve?"

Chapman looked at me closely, trying to determine if I spoke in jest—a difficult task for so humorless a man. "No," he said slowly, apparently convinced of my sincerity. "It is not that. . . ."

"Well, that is certainly a relief. If you will excuse me, I have urgent business."

"My lady, what is the meaning of posting an armed man at your door? If you have brought trouble to this neighborhood, you must warn the rest of us."

I looked at him incredulously. "Mr. Chapman," I began, "the city is besieged by three armies. The King's soldiers have proven themselves rogues at best, and murderers at worst." A look of alarm crossed his face. "You *did* hear that on Sunday night one of the garrison was killed not far from here, didn't you?" He started to respond, but I held up my hand to silence him. "We have marauding rebels outside the city and equally dangerous men inside, and you accuse *me* of bringing trouble to the neighborhood? Are you suggesting I remain in my home with my maidservants with no man to protect us? What, will you do us that service?" I glanced significantly at his massive stomach, daring him to assert his martial prowess. Before he could reply, I grasped Martha firmly by the arm, steered her around Chapman, and hurried the last few steps to my door. As we passed the guard, I whispered, "If he tries to follow, you may run him through." The guard laughed loudly, and I glanced over my shoulder. Chapman still stared at me, trying to think of a response. "Good day, Mr. Chapman," I called as I closed the door behind me.

Once safely inside, I set Martha to work on her household duties, and I retired to my chamber to rest, leaving word that I was not to be disturbed. Just as I was drifting to sleep, Hannah appeared in the doorway.

"My lady," she said, "Mrs. Emerson is here to see you. She says she has found the mother of the infant murdered in Coneystreet."

# Chapter 17

The prospect of finding the mother of the murdered child pulled me from my listless state. "Tell her I'll be right down."

Susan Emerson lived in St. Wilfred's parish, not far from my house. I hadn't delivered any of her children—she was too old for that—but she'd assisted me on occasion and even delivered a few on her own when a midwife arrived late. She was one of the most formidable matrons in her neighborhood and kept a sharp eye on local maidens. She reprimanded them if they behaved lewdly and reported them to the minister if they failed to heed her warnings.

"Mrs. Emerson, how are you?" I asked as I entered the parlor. She was a stout woman and powerfully built. A few years earlier, an unruly youth had attempted to steal from her husband's shop. She chased him half-way to the Minster and thrashed him vigorously when she caught him.

"Very well, Lady Hodgson, it is good to see you."

"Hannah says you have found the mother of the murdered child."

"Perhaps. I have made some enquiries. There is a barmaid

who was rumored to be with child some months ago, but her neighbors never heard of a birth. She lives near the river, not far from where they found the baby." My pulse quickened at the prospect of confronting the woman who could tell us who had murdered the infant.

"Do you know where she is?"

"I just saw her at the alehouse where she works."

"Good. We can go there now."

I considered bringing Martha but knew that my interrogation of this maiden would not be pleasant, and she'd already had a difficult day. As Susan and I walked toward the river, I wondered what this discovery might mean for Anne Goodwin and her child. From the first I had assumed the child in the privy was hers, and I had to admit I relished the thought of laying a murder at Rebecca Hooke's doorstep. But I was no longer so sure. If the murdered child belonged to this barmaid, what had become of Anne's baby? Had he even been born yet? Where was Anne? I said a prayer that Anne and her child might escape from the Hookes and silently cursed Rebecca for abusing Anne so mercilessly. Between my praying and cursing, I became so lost in thought that I walked right into Susan when she stopped outside a small alehouse.

"This is it," she said. "We can take her to the kitchen." I nodded in agreement, and we ducked through the low door. As my eyes adjusted to the dim interior, I found the woman we'd come for.

"Hello, what can I get for you?" she asked when we entered. Without answering, Susan and I crossed the room, grasped her arms, and dragged the squawking girl through the doorway into the back room that served as both a pantry and a kitchen.

"Shut your gob," Susan commanded sharply, and the girl's

mouth snapped closed. "We found the child you threw in the privy, and we'll see you hanged for what you've done."

Disbelief and fear crossed her face when she heard Susan's accusation. "What? I did no such thing!" the girl cried.

I recalled the lifeless body of the child we'd found in the privy and thought of Elizabeth Wood's grief at losing Ben. My hand shot up, clamped on the girl's throat, and squeezed. "You're famous for your lewd carriage, and your neighbors say you were with child this winter. You had the child and you threw him away."

Desperate, the girl clawed my hand away. "There is no baby, I swear!" she cried.

Susan stepped between me and the girl. "Then you'll not mind if Lady Hodgson searches your body, will you?" At this, the girl froze. "If you don't allow her," Susan continued, "we'll return with more women to help, and I'll give Lady Hodgson a free hand. If you have any secrets, we *will* find them out." The girl's fear turned to resignation, and the fight left her body.

"I've done nothing wrong," she said defensively.

"Show me your breasts," I said. She loosened her bodice and I pulled it aside to reveal her nipples. I squeezed them, but no milk came. I squeezed them harder, and she cried out, but they still produced no milk. "Lift your skirts," I said. She hesitated a moment and then hiked them up to her waist. She was no maiden—I could tell she had the French pox on her—but I also could see that she had not given birth recently. I bade her lower her skirts. "Let's go," I said to Susan.

"It's not her child," Susan said as we left the alehouse.

"No," I said. "She may well have given birth, but not recently."

"Have you heard of any other pregnant maids?" she asked. "Surely a woman couldn't have carried and then borne a child without anyone noticing, not in the city. Might it have been a wench from the garrison? Or one of the whores?" She clearly was not going to give up her search for the murderer.

"I have my suspicions, but cannot say."

Susan stopped and stared at me. "If you know something, you must tell me and the other women," she insisted. Gossip of this sort was not meant to be kept, for it was the key to finding the mother.

"I cannot, at least not yet. My suspicions touch on a powerful family. If I make them public and am proven wrong, it would destroy me."

"And if you are right?"

"It will be a scandal that sets the town alight."

"Then I'll wait," she said. "But if you need my help, do not hesitate to call for me. I will do whatever I can."

I thanked Susan and started for home. I had just turned off Stonegate when I heard a lilting voice from behind me. "Lady Hodgson, I would like a word with you." I felt my stomach sink, for I knew from the accent that Lorenzo Bacca had come for me. I spun around as he stepped out of the doorway in which he'd been standing. He had chosen the location well—I had rounded the bend from Stonegate, and my own house was not yet in sight. We were as alone as we could be at midday in York. I considered screaming in hope that a neighbor or the guard from my house would hear me, but if Bacca had come to kill me, any help would arrive too late.

"Mr. Bacca," I said. "What a surprise to see you on this side of the river."

"I go wherever the Lord Mayor needs me," he said with a shrug.

"And he sent you here today?" I peered in the direction of

Stonegate, hoping that a passerby might appear and give me the chance to escape from Bacca, but none did.

"He is worried. He knows that you visited Mrs. Cooper again, and the time he gave you has nearly passed. He wonders why he has not yet received a letter from you. I believe he genuinely hoped that you would see the error in your examination." He must have seen me looking toward Stonegate, for he laughed softly. "Do not worry, Lady Hodgson, I am not here to punish you for failing to obey his commands. Not yet. If that were the Lord Mayor's intention, I would not waste time with idle conversation. You would be dead already." The casualness with which he discussed my murder chilled my blood, but I resolved that I would not be intimidated.

"Mr. Bacca, I have been a midwife for many years now, and you may tell the Lord Mayor that I did not make a mistake."

"For your sake, I do not think that I should tell him that," he said. "I take no pleasure in threatening a woman such as yourself, but the truth of the matter is that you are putting yourself in considerable danger."

"Is that what you told Stephen Cooper?" I asked.

Bacca raised an eyebrow. "I wonder how you heard about that. I don't imagine he told his wife." He snapped his fingers. "He kept a diary, didn't he? You Puritans are so predictable. With no priests to hear your confession, you tell an empty book. In truth, I find it quite pathetic."

"You can deny your role in Stephen's death, but I will find out who killed him."

"I do not doubt your intention," he said. "But the Lord Mayor insists that the murderess has been convicted and sentenced. He will not look kindly on your attempts to undermine Mrs. Cooper's trial."

"Tell him that my verdict will not change."

A wistful look crossed Bacca's face. "I told him that you would say that. He does not understand women, I do not think. I will give him the message, but I warn you that his reaction could be quite violent indeed. And I will tell you now that the guard at your door will do you no good."

"I will be careful of myself."

"I am afraid that it would not be enough. Mr. Cooper was careful, and look at what happened to him."

"Good-bye, Mr. Bacca."

"Good-bye, Lady Hodgson. I do hope you come to your senses. I should hate to become your enemy. But that may happen before long. This is your last warning."

Somehow Bacca's farewell struck me as both sincere and terrifying. With hands shaking, I turned away from Bacca and took the final few steps to my home. When I arrived, the guard at the door doffed his cap and bade me good day, as if nothing out of the ordinary had happened. I supposed, from his perspective, nothing had. I could hardly reprimand him for not knowing about Bacca, but I made a note not to walk alone if I could possibly help it.

When I entered the house, I found Martha waiting for me at the front door.

"Hannah said you had gone in search of the murdered infant's mother," she said. I could not be sure, but I thought I heard a tone of reproach in her voice. I explained what had happened and that we still had no clues as to the mother's identity. I decided not to tell her about my encounter with Bacca. It would do nothing but worry her, and he did not seem to know about her role in the investigation. "Do you still think the child in Coneystreet belonged to Anne Goodwin?" Martha asked.

"I don't know. It certainly could be, but unless we find Anne, we will never know for sure. The midwives and matrons will continue to look."

"If we are going to the apothecaries, we should leave soon."

I agreed, and after a quick meal we set out for the parish of All Saints, Pavement. A number of apothecaries kept their shops there, and they were the ones closest to the Coopers' house. The trip to All Saints also took us nearer the rebel guns, and in the distance we could hear the thump as they lobbed cannonballs into the city. The first apothecaries we visited had not sold any ratsbane in at least two weeks, and neither recognized the bottle we showed them.

We reached the third shop on the street, which, according to the neatly painted sign hanging above the door, belonged to Thomas Penrose. As I reached for the handle, the door swung open to reveal Ellen Hutton, the Coopers' maidservant.

"Ellen," I exclaimed. "It is good to see you again. How are you?"

"Very well, my lady," she said, bowing her head.

"What brings you here?" I asked. "I hope you are not unwell."

She shook her head and held up two small envelopes. "I came for some herbs from Mr. Penrose. The nearness to the river has given Mrs. Cooper a cough, and the apothecary recommended I send her these."

"You are a faithful girl, Ellen," I said. "Have you given any more thought to your future?"

"Yes, my lady. I have found a family in St. Gregory that will take me in if I need a position. They seem very kind. If Mrs. Cooper allows me, I will start in a fortnight." I congratulated Ellen on her new position, and we parted ways. Unless our search for whoever had purchased the ratsbane led us to the killer, I could not imagine Esther coming home before Ellen left.

We entered the shop, and to my surprise I found a familiar figure behind the counter. It was not the apothecary, but his apprentice, Richard Baker. I had met Richard a few years before, when he had been apprentice to an apothecary I frequented. Unfortunately for Richard, his master died the previous winter, less than a year before he would have gained his freedom. I was happy to see that he had found a new home. He glanced up when we entered and nodded curtly to me but continued to carefully measure herbs into a mortar for crushing. If the jars before him were any indication, the medicine he made was complex indeed, including cinnamon, thyme, hyssop, dittany, mugwort, and burdock. I looked more closely and saw that Richard and his new master must have had their differences, for his face was covered with bruises. While some had begun to fade, others were quite recent—they were the result of a series of beatings, not a single fight.

The small shop was impeccably clean, and it seemed clear to me that Penrose was lucky to have found such a hardworking and careful lad. I could not help wondering why he treated Richard so harshly. Once Richard had measured out the herbs to his satisfaction, he set the mortar aside. I realized with a start that the bottles that lined the shelf behind him were identical to the one that contained the ratsbane. I glanced over at Martha and could tell from her face that she'd seen them, too. Well, I thought, at least we have solved that part of the mystery.

"Lady Hodgson!" Richard said with genuine enthusiasm when he turned to us. "What a pleasant surprise. Are the apothecaries on your side of the city no longer meeting your needs? I'm quite sure that Mr. Penrose and I can help."

"Richard, how are you? I'm pleased that you found another master after Mr. Samuels's death. How are things here?"

Richard's face clouded for a moment and I saw a flash of anger in his eyes, but he regained himself. "I'm nearly finished with my apprenticeship," he said with a shrug. "Then I shall have freedom, and all will be well. I do hope you will consider bringing me your business when I have a shop of my own."

"Of course," I said, meaning it. "At the moment, though, I am looking for your master. I have some questions for him."

"He is not in right now," he said. "Perhaps I can help you."

"Perhaps," I said. "Tell me, Richard, how much time do you spend minding the shop?" He was confident and competent, and I had a feeling that the shop was more his than Penrose's. It was all too common for an unscrupulous master to abandon the education of his apprentice and let the poor lad run the shop on his behalf.

"Mr. Penrose has many concerns outside of his shop," he said, trying not to meet my eyes. "I help his customers as best I can." He was a terrible liar, and his response only confirmed my suspicions.

"I am curious whether Charles Yeoman has ever come to the shop."

"If he has, I don't know him. But some customers choose not to give their name, and York has many strangers."

"I understand. Do you know Rebecca Hooke?"

"Yes, my lady, from her days as a midwife." If he knew my role in driving her from the profession, he gave no indication. "But I've not seen her in months."

"What about an Italian?" Martha asked. "He goes by the name of Bacca?"

At this Richard perked up. "I don't know his name, but an

Italian came in last week, looking for Mr. Penrose. He had a scar on his face, like this." He drew a line along the left side of his face.

"Did he buy any ratsbane?" I asked. I was quite sure my face betrayed my excitement.

"Not from me, my lady." He seemed surprised at the question. "But as I said, he wanted to speak to Mr. Penrose in person. It would be irregular, but he may have bought some outside the shop." We would have to find Penrose, then, and the sooner the better.

"Has anyone else purchased ratsbane in the days since the suburbs burned?"

"Nobody, my lady. We have not sold any ratsbane in some weeks. Or at least I haven't."

"Do you have any?" I asked.

"Of course," he said. "However, we keep it locked in the back. When I first came to Mr. Penrose there were some . . . unfortunate errors." I looked at him in shock. A mistake with ratsbane could be dangerous indeed. "Nobody was hurt," he added quickly. "Not seriously. *I* saw to that. One of the soldiers just got a bit worse before he got better. I moved the ratsbane and other dangerous powders so it could not happen again. When Mr. Penrose returns, may I tell him what the matter is?"

"Thank you, Richard, no. But can you tell me where I might find him? I need to speak to him in person."

"You might try the Black Swan on Peasholme Green," he said. "It is across the street from St. Anthony's Hall. He is frequently there." The Black Swan was an alehouse, not far from the shop. St. Anthony's had been a workhouse for the poor but now was occupied by the King's forces, who used it as a hospital, armory, and prison. I imagined that the garrison provided the Black Swan with plenty of customers and wondered why an apothecary would spend his time in such a disreputable house. Whatever the reason, I lamented Richard's misfortune to find himself with so dissolute and cruel a master. I looked again at the bruises that covered Richard's face and realized that I could help him just as I had offered to help Ellen.

"Richard, when will you earn your freedom?" I asked.

"Just after Michaelmas in October," he said. "Why do you ask?"

"Have you the money to start up your own shop yet?"

"I have saved some," he said. "I can only hope that Mr. Penrose will find it in his heart to loan me the rest." I looked again at his bruises. I think we both knew this was a fond dream.

"Richard," I said, "if you need a loan, I will give it to you."

"My lady!" he cried. "I . . . I don't know what to say. I cannot . . ."

"Don't decline just yet," I said, enjoying his reaction. "It would be better to take a loan from me than to put off opening your shop. You *do* intend to stay in York, don't you?"

He struggled briefly for an answer. "Yes, of course," he said at last.

"Excellent," I said. "The city needs good apothecaries."

I thanked Richard again, and Martha and I left the shop and began to walk toward Peasholme.

"What do you make of that?" Martha asked excitedly as soon as we exited the shop.

"If the bottle came from the shop," I said, "the ratsbane probably did as well. We're that much closer to finding the murderer."

"You know the apprentice. Could he have forgotten selling it? Or could he be lying?"

"I don't think so," I said. "He is too conscientious to forget such a thing, and you saw him try to lie on behalf of his master. He's a good lad. Besides, there's no crime in selling ratsbane, so he has no reason to lie. That leaves only Mr. Penrose—with any luck we can find him at the Black Swan."

We passed the entrance to the Shambles and continued toward Peasholme. As we neared the northeast wall of the city, we saw fewer city residents and more soldiers. The occasional thump of rebel guns grew louder, and we saw more and more houses that had been hit. I don't know what the rebels hoped to achieve by this—destroying citizens' homes would not bring the siege to an end any sooner.

Within a few minutes, St. Anthony's Hall and the Black Swan came into view. The Black Swan ranked among the oldest alehouses in the city, and while its half-timbered frame was solid enough, the cracks in the plaster walls showed that it had enjoyed better days. As we neared the entrance, we stepped over a soldier who lay in a stupor against the side of the building. Suddenly the alehouse door flew open and yet another drunken soldier stumbled out, shocked by the bright sun. He bumped into Martha and drew himself up, ready for a fight. He stopped short when he saw two women and that I was a woman of quality.

"I think you're in the wrong place, my lady," he said before weaving across the street toward the gate into St. Anthony's. I glanced at Martha, and even she looked nervous at her surroundings. Steeling ourselves for the worst, we stepped into the alehouse.

The smell of the place struck me like a fist in the stomach.

The rooms reeked of sweat, spoiled ale, and rotting food. We found ourselves in a short hallway, with doorways leading to four large rooms where the patrons did their drinking. A narrow staircase led to a second floor where, I had to imagine, even less savory business went on. In their drunken revels, nobody seemed to notice that we'd entered. Despite the fact that night would not fall for several hours, the alehouse's interior was dim, as filth-covered windows kept out most of the daylight. Rough tables and stools lay scattered around the drinking rooms, which resonated with the rough laughter of drunken soldiers. Mixed in with the soldiers were a handful of tired-looking whores, perhaps the only city residents profiting from the siege.

"How will we find Penrose?" I muttered once my stomach had settled.

Martha and I peered through the first doorway we came to, but nobody inside appeared old enough to be our apothecary. The second room contained only soldiers and whores, but in the third we spied a likely candidate. A man who clearly was not a soldier sat on a bench, slumped against the wall with a flagon in front of him. He was in his forties, and while his clothes were filthy, their quality marked him as a man of some means.

"That's probably him," I said, and Martha and I started across the room. Out of the corner of my eye, I saw a soldier rise to his feet and advance toward us, followed by four of his compatriots. Martha let out a frightened gasp and took a step back. The soldier leading the group was a young man wearing the rank of sergeant. He ignored me entirely, staring instead at Martha. He had one hand on his sword, the other on the handle of his dagger. Even in the dim light of the alehouse, I could see the anger in his eyes, and I realized that they were the same color blue as Martha's. The resemblance and Martha's reaction told me that this could only be her brother, Tom. My heart began to race, for I also knew that if even half of what Martha had said about him was true, we had just walked into very deep trouble.

The man crossed the room in a few purposeful strides and stopped when his face was just a few inches from Martha's. He looked down at her with a cruel smile on his face.

"Hello, Martha," he said, and I felt my stomach lurch. His accent echoed Martha's, confirming my guess as to his identity. "If I judged you by your clothes, I would ask what a respectable maid like you is doing in such a disreputable establishment. But I know far too much about you to think of you as respectable." Martha stared back at him, trying to remain impassive, but I could see a flicker of fear in her eyes. Tom Hawkins glanced at me. "I don't imagine your mistress here knows as much as I do . . . shall I tell of our most recent adventure?" The soldiers formed a circle around us—now we could not simply back out of the room. I looked again at the stripes on Tom's shoulders and realized how we might escape the alehouse with our lives.

"Sergeant!" I said in as sharp a voice as I could muster. Even as I spoke, I realized that my hands had begun to shake, so I gripped my apron to stop them before Tom noticed. I could only pray that my voice did not betray my fear, for once I challenged Tom's authority over his men, there would be no going back. "I am a gentlewoman of this city, and this is my maidservant. We have come here by the command of the Lord Mayor. I don't know who you think my servant is, but you are mistaken. You *will* step back." He looked at me, surprised but not yet angry. By the expression on his face, I think he welcomed the prospect of shaming a gentlewoman. Before he could speak, I turned to his soldiers and picked out the youngest. "Private! Summon your lieutenant immediately." He looked to Tom for direction, but I stepped between them, looking the private in the eye. "Private, do you make a habit of disobeying your superiors?"

"No, m-my lady," he stammered.

"I thought not. Go now." I turned on my heel to face Tom, hoping that the boy would obey. "Sergeant, while we await your lieutenant, why don't you explain to me, and to your soldiers, what exactly you mean by meddling with a gentlewoman on the Lord Mayor's business."

Tom and I locked eyes, and I saw his surprise and anger at losing control of the situation. He may have expected trouble from Martha, but certainly not from a gentlewoman so far out of her element. What authority could I have in an alehouse filled with soldiers, drunkards, and whores? A look of rage flashed across his face, and I saw the knuckles whiten as he gripped his dagger. My breath stopped as I wondered if I might meet a bloody end on the ale-soaked floor of the Black Swan. To my surprise, he regained his composure without drawing his dagger or even raising his hand. He may have been of the meaner sort, but he knew when he had been beaten. He recognized that no good could come from assaulting a gentlewoman in public, so he retreated.

"You are quite right, my lady," he said with a bow. "I mistook your servant for someone else. This is no place for respectable women, so I did not see you as such. I don't know how I could have been mistaken."

I took Martha's arm and began to guide her toward the door. I knew Tom was trying to find a way to regain the upper hand in the confrontation, and this would be our best chance to escape. I saw Martha look back, not at her brother, but at the figure in the corner whom we took to be Thomas Penrose. I nudged her forward. Penrose could wait until we returned with more weapons than just my wits. As we neared the door, Tom's voice followed us.

"It's a small city, my lady. I'm quite sure we will see each other again . . . soon."

At his words, the hairs on the back of my neck stood up; I knew that he spoke the truth.

# Chapter 18

Once we reached the street, Martha and I walked quickly, re-tracing our steps toward the Pavement. Neither of us spoke, but we each cast hurried glances over our shoulders, fearful that we might be followed. When we reached the relative safety of the crowds in the Pavement, we slowed our pace but kept moving toward Coneystreet, which would take us home. As we passed the Angel, one of York's finest inns, I grasped Martha's arm and stopped.

"A glass of sack would suit me quite nicely right now," I said. "Would you care for one?" She gulped and nodded her assent.

As soon as we entered the inn, the hostess ushered us into the dining room. She took us to a table at the window looking out on the street, but as soon as we sat, I regretted it. Sitting in front of the large window, I felt exposed and worried that Tom might catch sight of us. I knew such fears were groundless—he could never attack us in so public a place—but I nevertheless asked the hostess to seat us away from the window. She brought us our drinks and asked if we would be dining. At that moment I realized that I was famished and asked her to bring us whatever was hot and ready. She disappeared into the kitchen, and Martha and I could finally speak in private.

"My God," she said, exhaling heavily. "That was an unwelcome surprise. How did he insinuate himself into the garrison, and as a noncommissioned officer, no less?"

I nodded and swallowed half my sack in a single draught. "We were lucky to escape. The question is where this leaves us. I think it gives us an advantage at least for the moment. So long as he's in uniform and surrounded by his men, he'll have to play the sergeant's part. The last thing he'd want is to be imprisoned for abandoning his post, so he will have to spend most of his time doing the work of a soldier."

"Not Tom. He won't let that stop him for long. He can change his clothes and disappear into the city easily enough. I've seen him do it."

"Then I'll alert Sergeant Smith immediately, and ask him to double the guard on the house. I don't know what else we can do."

"You could tell your brother about Tom," she said evenly. "Now that we know where to look, he'll be easier to find. It would be safer for you. I saw the look in his eyes—he'll not forget what happened. He means to kill us both."

"And I saw the look he gave you. I won't have you tried alongside that rogue just to save myself from danger. The guards can protect us until we figure out a better plan."

"Thank you, my lady," she murmured. Though she tried to hide it by clearing her throat and looking away, for a moment I thought Martha might cry tears of gratitude, and it warmed my heart.

"But I'm afraid that this complicates efforts to question

Penrose," I said. "Even if we bring Will or one of the guards, I don't relish the thought of another row with Tom. Next time we might not escape without violence."

"We can avoid the Black Swan entirely by coming to the shop first thing tomorrow morning," she said. "If we arrive early enough, we can catch him before he goes out. Men like him are not early risers."

"We'll do that, but it will have to wait until Monday. His shop will be closed tomorrow, and after Sunday's service we've each got a christening to attend. You'll be with Mercy Harris, and I'll be at Abigail Stoppard's."

"Surely we could go after the christenings," she protested. "He lives above the shop, we could see him even though it's closed. He might be out again, but we could get lucky. It's worth a try."

I laughed. "After the baptism, you will join in the drinking," I said. "I'll be at Abigail's all night, and while Mercy's poor, you might be surprised what her friends will do on her behalf."

"Do you attend all your clients' revels?" she asked.

"It compensates in some measure for the funerals," I said. "Though the headaches the morning after are no treat. You'll see tomorrow."

As Martha and I walked home in the fading light, I explained her place in the christening of Mercy's baby. She would carry the baby to the font, tell the priest what to name her, and then return to Mercy's.

"How long will the drinking last?" she asked. "I'd rather not wander around the city at night."

"No, I don't think either of us has that luxury anymore. I'll send one of the guards with you, and ask Will to accompany me to Abigail Stoppard's house." I was relieved to see that Sergeant Smith himself was standing at my door when we arrived. Martha went inside and I explained my desire to double the guard.

"I can have a second man here starting tomorrow morning," he said, but a note of concern crept into his voice. "Is there anything we should worry about, my lady?"

"I am afraid so. We have learned that the man who threatens me is well armed, and has disguised himself as a noncommissioned officer with the garrison."

Sergeant Smith grimaced. "I'll have to pay my men more. It's one thing to face down a lone ruffian, but if he's armed and in uniform, things are much more difficult."

"Of course," I said, and described Tom in as much detail as I could.

"I'll tell my men to watch for him," he said. "And arm them with pistols. That should give him pause if he shows his face around here."

I began to close the door when I heard the sound of someone running toward my house and a woman's voice crying, "Lady Hodgson!" A few seconds later, Margaret Goodwin arrived at my door. I led her inside and took her to the parlor as she tried to catch her breath.

"Margaret, what is it?" I asked. I knew it had to do with Anne and that it must be important. I felt a sinking in my stomach. Had something happened to her? Martha heard the commotion and appeared at the door.

"I just saw Anne," Margaret said between breaths. "She came to the shop a few minutes ago."

Questions tumbled out. Did she say where has she been? How was she? Where is she now? Was she still pregnant? Did she say what had happened to her child? Margaret tried to answer, but in her excitement her story tumbled over itself.

"Slow down, Margaret. Tell me exactly what she said."

Margaret took a deep breath and gathered herself. "She came to the shop and called to us from the street. She refused to come inside, for fear of being trapped. She said that Rebecca Hooke is a murderer. She heard her confess as much to James."

"Did she say what she meant? Who did she kill? Was it Stephen Cooper?"

"No, my lady, she didn't say," she said, as she began to weep. "I asked about the baby, and she refused to tell me anything."

"Is she still at the shop?" I asked, my heart racing. If Anne was right about the Hookes, she would need as much help as she could get.

"No," she said, looking even more miserable. "She heard voices from down the street and before I could stop her, she ran off. She was so scared. I didn't know where to turn except you. What can we do?" I looked at Martha, and she shook her head. I had no answers, either.

"Where might she have gone?"

"I don't know. She only said a few words before she fled. What am I going to do?" Tears coursed down her cheeks, and my heart ached on her behalf. The fear of losing your only child endured even after she had grown.

"You should go home," I said. "If she came to you once, she might come back. If she does, hide her there, and send for me immediately. Tell her that I can protect her from the Hookes. And if we learn anything, we will tell you right away."

Margaret wiped at her tears and nodded. I knew it was not a satisfying answer, but given the situation, it was the only one I had.

I embraced Margaret at the door and returned to the parlor, where Martha waited.

"Rebecca Hooke is a murderer?" Martha said. "Could she have murdered Stephen Cooper?"

"Stephen Cooper, or the infant in Coneystreet. I have no idea. The Lord knows she's vicious enough to kill Stephen and the child both."

"Now what do we do?" she asked.

I looked out the window at the lengthening shadows. It would do no good to go in search of Anne tonight. "There is little we can do except wait and pray that we find Anne before the Hookes do."

I awoke the next morning to the church bells calling the city's residents to worship. With one of Sergeant Smith's guards in the lead, Martha, Hannah, and I walked down Stonegate toward St. Helen's for the morning service. I am ashamed to admit that I let my mind wander from the service. I stood, sat, and knelt with the rest of the congregation, but I paid no attention to the priest's words. Soon enough, he dismissed us for the morning, and we filed out of the church.

I stopped at the corner of Stonegate and pulled Hannah aside. "I need you to go to Micklegate and find Will. He will probably be at his father's. Tell him I need his assistance this afternoon and evening."

"If he asks why, what shall I say?"

"Tell him I need his protection." I knew this would please him and perhaps repair some of the damage done by our argument. "Martha and I will attend christenings this afternoon. One of the guards will accompany Martha, and I'd like Will to escort me." She nodded and disappeared into the crowd.

When we arrived at my home, Martha went to her work, and I retired to the parlor. My eyes fell on a box of checkstones sitting on the shelf. I picked up the box and slid my fingers along its edges as tears slid down my cheeks. When Birdy was alive, we had played every Sunday after the morning service. Our last game was less than a week before she died. I bested her, but not by much, and I knew that soon she would beat me handily. Or at least that had been my hope. I was saying a prayer of thanks when Will's appearance at the door pulled me from my melancholy.

"You have two guards now!" he said as he strode into the parlor. "Has something happened, or are you recruiting an army of your own?" I knew he was using the joke to avoid talking about our quarrel, but I would not let him.

"Will, I'm sorry for what I said after we left Mr. Yeoman's."

Will abandoned his pretense, and tears welled in his eyes. "I am sorry, too, Aunt Bridget. You know I love you."

"And I love you as my own son. But you cannot judge yourself through the eyes of men like Charles Yeoman, and I would account you much less a man if you did so."

"I know, Aunt Bridget."

"And just because someone is a woman, that does not mean she cannot be your match in many ways. You'd be better off marrying a spirited woman like . . . like Martha, than a sheep like Esther."

"Like Martha?" he asked. "You want me to marry your servant?"

"You know what I mean," I said. "Someone *like* her. She'll tell you when you are wrong, but you'll be better for it."

"What about Uncle Phineas?" he asked, knowing full well that Phineas and I had fought like cats, and in all our years he'd never been better for it.

"Never you mind Phineas," I said. "But remember that no matter what I said, I do not think you are like Charles Yeoman, Will. He is a hard, bad man, and you've none of his cruelty. That is why I love you." Will crossed the room to embrace me, and I knew we'd made our peace.

"You still haven't explained the guards out front," he said. Now his worry came to the surface. I tried to describe our adventures in the Black Swan in terms that would not disturb him and failed miserably.

"My God, Aunt Bridget, what have you gotten yourself into? You go out in search of one killer and stumble upon another?"

"Will, it's not as bad as it sounds," I protested. "Tom wouldn't dare come here."

"Then why did you hire a second guard?"

"Just for safety's sake," I said. "It is unlikely he'll show his face, but I don't want to take chances."

"You have to tell my father about this," he insisted. "He can have the constables start a search for him."

"If I did that, I might as well send Martha to the gallows myself. Tom would happily perjure himself just to see Martha hanged alongside him."

"We can worry about that after he's caught. You can't risk your life for a maidservant!"

"Be careful, Will," I said coolly. "She is a member of my household, and has more than earned my loyalty and protection. Whether she is a maidservant or the Queen herself is of no import. This is my household, and I will govern it as I see fit. When the time is right, I will inform your father of the situation, but not yet. You must trust me."

Will's face made clear that he did not approve of my decision, but I knew I could trust him not to betray me to his father. "All right," he said. "But if you've already got two men guarding your door, why do you need me?"

"Abigail Stoppard's son will be christened this afternoon, and I must attend. The gathering afterwards will last late into the night, and I would rather not walk alone. There is an alehouse not far from their home, and you will be able to amuse yourself there, I should think. Come on. We should go now."

Will and I chatted amiably during the walk to St. Mary, Castlegate. The Stoppards' home sat just north of Clifford's Tower, only a few houses away from St. Mary's church. Abigail's husband, Abraham, invited me in, and Will disappeared to the alehouse. Inside, three servants worked feverishly to prepare the house for the gathering that would follow the ceremony. I saw them putting up meat pies, roasted fowl, and many bottles of wine. Abraham was an attorney in service to the Crown and had done well for himself in recent years. Today he would christen his firstborn son, and he planned to use the occasion to announce his wealth to all in attendance. I followed him to the lying-in room, where Abigail lay in bed, holding the squalling baby boy, surrounded by five or six of her friends. I had delivered her three weeks earlier and was pleased that both she and the child were in good health.

"Lady Bridget," Abigail called out, "come see the baby!"

I crossed the room and took the boy into my arms. He continued to wail, so I reached into my pocket for the silver rattle I had brought as a christening present and slipped it into his tiny hand. He gave it a vigorous shake and so surprised himself with the noise that he stopped crying. "Ah, the best present yet," said Abigail. "He's been crabby for the better part of the afternoon. All the coming and going woke him early from his nap." I rocked the baby for a bit while the other women continued to talk. Soon enough, a serving-maid entered and announced that it was time to go to church.

"Where is the christening sheet?" I asked Abigail.

"I'll get it," she said as she climbed out of bed and opened an elegant wooden chest. She produced a pure white gown made of the finest silk and lace I'd seen in some months. Together we laid the boy in the gown and buttoned it up the front before handing him to one of the other gossips.

"What name do you want me to give him?" I asked.

"We've decided to name him Charles," she said. In the midst of a war such as ours, a baby's name could signal the parents' political opinions. The year before, a family announced their support for the Puritanical religion and Parliamentary government by asking me to name their son The-Lord-Is-Near. To this day I wonder what the poor boy's friends call him. In naming their son Charles, the Stoppards made a public show of their support for the King.

"Who are the other godparents?"

"We've chosen Abraham's brother and his wife—they should arrive shortly. The other godfather is going to be your brother, Edward." I raised an eyebrow. Securing Edward as a godfather would bind the Stoppards to the Hodgsons for years to come; it was quite an accomplishment. "I know, I know," she continued, amazed at their good fortune. "I wasn't sure Abraham should even ask, but he did, and Alderman Hodgson agreed. We're quite excited."

"You know he supports Parliament, don't you?" I asked. It seemed odd that they would name their son after the King and at the same time ask Edward to serve as godparent.

"Abraham thought it best to make as many friends as possible.

Only the Lord knows how the war will end. Someday Mr. Hodgson might be able to help us, or we might be able to help him." I couldn't argue with Abraham's thinking. While I favored the King, it did not diminish my love for Edward.

As the company prepared to depart, I embraced Abigail, took the child in my arms, and stepped into the street. I walked at the front of the procession, holding young Charles high so that all passersby could see him. We reached the church as the rest of the congregation filed in, and Abraham led us to the pew reserved for the christening party. Edward had arrived already and smiled broadly when he saw me. Abraham's brother and sister-in-law followed me into the pew. I held the child and did my best to keep him quiet during the main part of the service. After the final prayer, the priest called us forward, and using a gilt dipper, he baptized Charles and bade us return to our seats.

When I neared the pew the baby started to wail, so I retreated down the aisle and out of the church. Once on the street, I stopped and looked up into the clear afternoon sky. In the distance I heard the rebel cannons firing and the Castle's guns firing back. The beauty of the day mocked our human cruelties, and I wondered what role Charles would play in future dramas.

I heard footsteps and turned to find two of the other gossips who had followed me out of the church. They came over to see the baby, who had quieted a bit. "He probably would like to get back to his mother," volunteered one of the women. I agreed, and the three of us started back to the Stoppards'. When we arrived, Abigail was in the front parlor directing the servants as they made the final preparations for the army of guests who would soon arrive. As soon as we entered, she scooped Charles out of my arms and held him close. It was the longest the two had ever been apart, so I could hardly blame her.

"How was the service?" she asked. "He didn't cry, did he?"

"He did fine," I said with a smile. "He was done with the service before the priest was."

She laughed. "Mr. Addison does love the sound of his own voice. The service will be done soon. I should feed him before the guests arrive." We followed her into her lying-in room, and she sat on the bed and put the child to her breast.

A few minutes later, we heard the front door open, followed by the cheerful voices of the Stoppards' guests. The door to the lying-in room burst open, and Abigail's gossips flooded in, chattering enthusiastically. Some came over to greet Abigail or see the baby, others made their way straight for the food and drink. I saw no reason to wait and helped myself to a plate of roast goose, venison, cheese, and a custard, all accompanied by a glass of strong red wine. After she finished feeding Charles, Abigail passed him along to a serving-maid, who took him upstairs to a quieter bedchamber.

It was a good decision, for as the women became heated with wine, the conversation grew louder and the laughter many times more raucous. As always, the talk at a christening party turned to childbirth, and the company soon called upon me to tell the story of how Martha had emptied Elizabeth Wood's bedroom of drunken gossips. The crowd scolded the unruly women who would disturb a woman in travail and laughed uproariously as I told of Martha dragging their ringleader from the room by her ears. As more guests arrived, they demanded I tell the story again, and I must admit that with each telling, the women became more unruly and Martha's actions more violent and valiant. I was grateful that nobody mentioned the health of the child.

As the hours passed and we drank our way through the Stoppards' excellent wine, other women told their own tales, each one with its heroines and villains. I found myself more than a little pleased when the talk turned to Rebecca and Richard Hooke. "Tell us, Lady Hodgson," urged Abigail, "how is it that such a womanish man could get such a mannish woman with child? Or did Rebecca sire the child on Richard?" The women roared, and I joined them. Without warning, the image of Anne Goodwin, alone and frightened somewhere in the city, leapt to my mind. The laughter died in my throat. I summoned a servant and replenished my wine.

"Lady Hodgson," called Mary Horton, rescuing me from my own dark thoughts, "tell me—is there a sworn midwife in All Saints, Pavement?"

"Dorothy Mann is licensed," I said after a moment. "Why do you ask, Mary? Are you with child? Your husband must be . . . surprised." We women laughed long and loud at the prospect, and Mary joined us. She had two grown daughters and three grandchildren—her childbearing days had ended long ago.

"No, it is not me, but not for lack of trying," she fairly shouted, while at the same time making an astonishingly lewd gesture with a sausage. I can only imagine what the men in the next room must have thought at the laughter that followed. "In truth," she said, wiping a tear from her cheek, "I have heard that one of the parish's maidens is pregnant, a poor, silly serving-maid. After what happened in Coneystreet, I want to make sure that women are there to witness the birth and ensure no harm comes to the child."

"Tell Dorothy," I said. "She will look into it and search her body. If the maid is indeed with child, Dorothy will inform the churchwardens."

The prospect of a bastard birth and the thought of an infanticide soured the mood for a time, but the good cheer returned when Ann Young joined the crowd. I didn't know her, but Abigail told me that she had been married just the week before, and this was her first time among the matrons. The guests promptly began to interrogate her about the wedding night. "How many times? How long?" they called out. Ann blushed a bright crimson and refused to answer but was clearly happy to be counted among the neighborhood's respectable women.

"How long, you ask?" cried Mary Horton. "Her Harry's a tall one, so I'd say about this long." She held her hands an unlikely distance apart, and once again we descended into fits of laughter. At that moment, one of the husbands had the misfortune to poke his head into our parlor in search of his wife. We greeted his appearance with catcalls and quickly chased him from the room. His young wife started unsteadily for the door. In the few seconds it took her to cross the room, she replaced Ann as the center of attention. She'd not yet borne a child, and we encouraged her to take full advantage of the evening.

As she closed the door behind her, I said to Mary, "When these women find their husbands, this one christening will beget a thousand more."

"It is a good night," she said, laughing. I could not have agreed more. As more husbands came in search of their wives and wives went to find their husbands, the crowd in Abigail's room slowly thinned. The wine continued to flow, but at a more leisurely pace, and the conversation quieted. I found myself sitting on a couch with Abigail as we watched another couple depart for home.

"Will you marry again?" she asked.

I was not surprised at the question. I was young enough to have at least a few more children, and still handsome, to some eyes, at least. I also knew that my name and my wealth would counterbalance any deficiencies a gentleman might find in my body or mind. As I considered the question, I became aware of the exquisite warmth that the wine had brought to me. I thought of my gossips throughout the city: rich and poor, sinners and saints, Royalists and Parliament-men. All the women of York called on me when they were in need. I eased new mothers' fears when they became pregnant, swearing to them that with God's help I would deliver them safely. How many mothers had I helped in their travail? How many times had I done all I could to ensure that a mother and her child would survive? How often had I rejoiced with mothers like Abigail? Three hundred? Five hundred? But in his wisdom, the Lord took more children and mothers than I cared to remember. Some babies, like little Ben Wood, were born weak and never seemed long for this world. Some, like Birdy, seemed full of life from the day they were born, but God struck them down all the same. As a midwife, I helped the women when I could and comforted them when I could not.

But as surely as the women needed me, I needed them. Without my work, who would I be? A wealthy widow and nothing more. I would fill my days with visits to other gentlewomen and discuss my options for marriage. I could buy one house in Hereford and another in London and divide each year between city and country. Over time, I could create a household known for its exquisite manners and taste, and women of quality would clamor for the chance to dine at my table. The thought of such an uneventful and powerless existence filled me with dread, for my work as a midwife mattered in a way that mere housewifery never could. I ensured that men who fathered bastards had to pay for their children and that the women who bore them were whipped. If a maiden was raped, who but a midwife would stand with her against her assailant? Who better than a midwife could recognize the signs of bewitchment and find the witch's mark? Without midwives, lust would reign, and order would turn to chaos. I looked at Abigail and thought of how many of the women I had delivered later became my dear friends. No, I would never give up my work. But what of marriage? Some part of me longed for the happiness I had enjoyed with my first husband. But Phineas taught me the hard lesson that contentment in marriage could not be taken for granted. I preferred the certainty of my work to the unknowns of married life.

"No," I said. "I don't think I will." She nodded and seemed to understand.

When the time came for me to go, I took my leave of Abigail and found Will waiting for me in the parlor. As I crossed the room, he began to laugh.

"My God, Aunt Bridget, how much wine did you have?"

"It is unseemly to mock your elders, Will," I scolded.

"Here, take my arm. It's raining and the streets are slick."

I started to reject his offer, but a look at the steady rain convinced me of its wisdom. With one hand holding his cane and his other supporting me, Will could not even hold his cloak over us, so he draped it over my head and shoulders. Nevertheless, within minutes we both were drenched. I knew my clothes would be soaked by the time we got home, but the cool rain did much to bring me back to my senses.

Just as I began to feel myself again, Will froze and pulled his arm free.

"What is it?" I asked. "Did you see something?" Instead of answering, he twisted the handle of his cane and drew the sword hidden inside.

"Stay behind me," he whispered. "Somebody's laying in wait for us in that alleyway." I began to pray as he raised his sword and stepped toward the shadows of the alley.

# Chapter 19

With an unnerving shriek, a dark figure raced toward us. I cried out and stepped backward in hope of avoiding its charge. Will stood his ground, and moments before he was knocked to the ground he lashed out with his sword, and I saw it find its mark. Will sat up and started to scramble to his feet before he noticed that he had just killed a sow. I could not help laughing.

"Well done, Will! The Lord Mayor will be very pleased that *someone* is taking seriously his injunctions against keeping pigs in the city."

He smiled ruefully and wiped his sword on the pig's carcass. He started to speak when I heard the sound of footsteps racing up behind me. My heart leapt in my throat, for I knew this was no pig. I spun around to face our attacker but slipped on the cobblestones and fell to my hands and knees. Will's sodden cloak fell over my head, and the world went dark. My heart raced as I tried to fight my way out from under the cloak. I heard the bright crash of metal on metal and a shout of pain. A body fell on top of me and pressed me into whatever filth lay in the street. Chest heaving, I clawed my way out from under the cloak and found Will sitting next to me, sword still in hand. He pointed wordlessly, and I saw a figure disappear around a distant corner. Will scrambled to his feet and helped me up, all the while keeping his eyes on the street.

"Aunt Bridget, are you all right?"

"Just a little wet," I said. "And I cut my hand when I fell. It's all right. Are you hurt? Your sleeve is covered in blood."

I checked him for wounds but found none. "It could be the pig's," he said. "And I think I cut him before I fell."

"Did you see who it was?"

Will shook his head. "He covered his face. But he knew how to use a sword."

"You saved my life, Will. Thank you."

"Don't thank me yet. We need to get home. We can talk when we're safe."

We hurried the rest of the way to my house, trying to steer clear of narrower streets and alleys. Will supported me with one hand while keeping his sword in the other. He constantly looked back over his shoulder for fear our attacker would try again. When the guards in front of my house saw our condition, they raced toward us, their pistols drawn.

"We're fine," Will called to them. "Help me get Lady Hodgson inside."

Martha met us at the door and cried out in shock at my appearance. I caught a glimpse of myself in a mirror and understood her reaction, for I looked as if the attempt on my life had succeeded. Mud and blood covered my clothes, my hat was gone, and my hair hung down in strands around my face. Hannah heard the commotion and raced down the stairs, still in her shift. She paled when she saw me and raced back upstairs for towels. Martha took me by the arm and led me to the parlor.

"What happened?" she asked urgently.

"Lady Hodgson was attacked," Will said. "She's fine, but it was close."

Before we could say any more, Hannah returned with the towels. Will retreated to the front entry hall as she helped me out of my clothes and dried me off. Hannah told Martha to fetch me a glass of wine and went upstairs for a clean shift and bandages for my hand.

"Martha, I'd rather have barley water. I think I've had enough wine for tonight."

Once Hannah had finished binding my hand and getting me dressed, she allowed Will back into the room. He had dried off as well, and Hannah had found him a change of clothes that had belonged to Phineas. He sat on the sofa next to Martha, and the three of us tried to make sense of the evening's events.

"Did you see who it was?" Martha asked.

"He attacked us from behind, and between the rain and dark, it could have been the devil himself and I'd not have recognized him. As I told Lady Bridget, he could handle a sword tolerably well."

"Do you think you hurt him?" she asked.

"Maybe," he said. "My sword had some blood on it, but thanks to the damned pig I don't know whose it was. Whoever it was could be dead already or in an alehouse plotting against us."

"And even if you wounded him seriously, we might not be any safer," I said. Will looked at me in confusion. "It could also have been a paid assassin. Between Charles Yeoman, the Lord Mayor, and Rebecca Hooke, there are plenty of people who might be behind this attack, and all of them have the means to hire a killer."

"What are you talking about, Aunt Bridget?" Will cried. "Charles Yeoman? The Lord Mayor? Why would they want to kill you?"

As quickly as I could, I explained the course of our investigation into Stephen Cooper's death and the variety of suspects we'd found. "Mr. Yeoman admitted that he would not have hesitated to kill Stephen if he thought it would save the city. Lorenzo Bacca said that the Lord Mayor would be furious if I did not agree to change my judgment on Esther, and he as much as told me he'd attack me away from my house. And with the garrison overflowing with mercenaries, the Lord knows that neither Mr. Yeoman nor Rebecca Hooke would have to look very hard to find a murderer for hire."

"We also need to ask if it might have been Tom," Martha said.

"Why would he want to kill me?" I asked. "He came to York for you."

"You humiliated him, and he needs no reason beyond that. Also, if he killed you, I would have no protection and would be an easy target. Perhaps he thinks that if you died at his hands, I might rejoin him, and the two of us could loot your estate. He has several reasons and needs only one."

"It might not have been any of these people," Will said.

"Surely you don't think it was a common robbery," Martha objected.

"Of course not. But how many people know you are looking for the apothecary who sold the ratsbane that killed Stephen Cooper?"

"We spoke to a few of apothecaries but then asked them to

tell others of our search," I said. "Richard Baker is smart enough, so he likely knows. By the time everyone finished talking, half the town would have known." I sat back, dismayed. "Whoever killed Stephen Cooper now knows we are close to finding him. We spent the afternoon tying nooses around our own necks."

"And it won't get better soon. If Stephen Cooper's murderer is willing to attack you on a city street, he must be desperate. They can't hang him twice, so he has nothing to lose. He'll try again," Will said.

"Then the best thing we can do is see him hanged as quickly as possible. Will, you should stay here tonight. Tomorrow morning we'll return to Penrose's shop and catch him when he is still abed."

I awoke early the next morning and went downstairs. Hannah and Martha had already begun their day's work, and I slipped into the parlor to read in my Bible without disturbing them. I heard heavy footsteps and a man's voice and knew that Will had risen. I finished my portion and found Will in the kitchen, wolfing down oatmeal and bread with butter.

"How are you, Aunt Bridget?"

"Alive," I said with a wan smile. "After last night, I could not ask for much more. Thank you again." Will nodded, and his ears turned a bit pink. It seemed that playing the hero embarrassed him. "Dare I ask if you are prepared to rejoin the fray? We'll go to Penrose's shop immediately."

He stood up, pleased at the prospect. "Of course. The sooner we find the killer, the safer you'll be."

By the time we arrived in the Pavement, all of the neighboring shops had opened for business, but we found Penrose's locked up tight. I rapped loudly on the door but received no answer. Will stepped forward and pounded on the door with nearly enough force to shake it from its hinges. While neither Penrose nor Richard Baker appeared, he did get the attention of the tailor in the shop next door.

"If you're looking for Mr. Penrose, your man will have to pound even harder than that." He was a thin, nervous man, with the disconcerting habit of constantly looking back over his shoulder, as if someone might attack at any moment.

"Why is that?" I asked.

"I've not seen him in days. He's hardly ever around. He lets his apprentice run things. Then he beats the poor lad for even the slightest mistake. Someone ought to report him to the guild. But it's none of my affair, really. The other apothecaries have said nothing. Quite shameful." He shook his head disapprovingly. He suddenly turned his attention to Will.

"That is a passably fine suit of clothes," he said.

Will looked at him blankly for a moment. "Er . . . thank you," he ventured.

"But a gentleman such as yourself certainly deserves better." He took Will by the arm and started pulling him into the shop. "I am George Cawton, and I think that when you see the fabrics I have on hand, you will agree that these clothes are mere rags." Will looked at me helplessly.

"Have you seen his apprentice?" I interrupted. "We are on urgent business."

"Richard?" he asked. "The constable was here. He took him away."

"What?" I cried. "When was this?"

"Not long ago. He was just here."

"Did the constable arrest him?" Will asked, struggling to escape Cawton's grasp. "Where did they go?"

"I don't think Richard was arrested," he said. "He just went. None of my business, really." Undeterred by Will's efforts to escape, Cawton continued to drag him toward his shop. "Now, just a few more steps and we'll be there."

"Where did the constable take Richard?" Will asked.

"I told you. He didn't take him anywhere. He wasn't under arrest." Will's face turned an alarming shade of purple.

"Where did Richard and the constable go?" I interjected, hoping to keep Will from throttling the poor man.

"That way. Towards St. Saviorgate."

I looked at Martha. "The Black Swan?" I asked.

"Yes, that's it," Cawton interjected. "I can't imagine why the constable would want to take Richard there, but that's what he said."

Martha saw the look of concern on my face and answered my question before I could ask. "I'm coming with you. Will is with us, and if the constable is already there, we'll be fine. Tom is violent, not stupid."

Will extricated himself from Cawton's grip and the three of us walked quickly toward Peasholme Green. As soon as the Black Swan came into sight, I knew that something was amiss. As usual, soldiers stood in front, but they were alert and on the lookout for trouble rather than stumbling about in a drunken haze. When we approached the door, a young lieutenant stepped forward to intercept us.

"I'm sorry, my lady, the alehouse is closed."

Before I could answer, Will intervened. "Do you really think that Lady Hodgson is coming to this . . . establishment for pleasure?" Still frustrated by his conversation with the tailor, he made no effort to guard his tongue, and his every word dripped with disdain. The lieutenant did not take kindly to Will's tone.

"Where Lady Hodgson takes her pleasure is none of my concern. You may not enter."

"Lieutenant," I said, drawing him to the side and shooting an angry glance at Will, "we are looking for a friend of mine, a local apothecary, and have reason to think that he may have come here. Can you tell us why all these soldiers are here? Why are you guarding the door?" He looked uncomfortable. "It is important that you tell me," I added.

"There has been some trouble inside," he said at last. "I don't know what it is. My captain ordered me to post my men at all the doors and make sure that nobody entered."

"Did a constable just take a young man inside?"

"Aye. The captain said to let them in."

"Lieutenant, I need to go in there," I said.

"My lady . . . ," he started. "I am under strict orders from my captain."

"And I have my orders from the Lord Mayor of the city." Eventually someone might challenge this claim, but until that time I would continue with my bluff. "It is urgent that I find Mr. Penrose."

"My lady, I cannot."

"Listen—I will go in alone, and if he is not here, I will leave immediately. Nobody will even know I was here." He clearly did not relish saying "no" to a gentlewoman and stood there without speaking. Taking his silence as permission, I darted past him. He sputtered briefly, but I knew he would never dream of laying hands on me. By the time he found his voice—I heard him shouting, "My lady!" behind me—I had made it through the door and pulled it shut behind me.

The rooms downstairs were unnaturally quiet. Most of the stools were tipped on their sides. A cloud of flies buzzed around the plates of uneaten food, and tankards half-full of ale sat on the rough wood tables. A shiver ran up my spine—something awful had happened here. I heard footsteps and voices from above and climbed the stairs. When I reached the top I found myself at the midpoint of a long hallway, with curtained doorways on each side leading into small rooms. I peered through the nearest door and saw a sad and skinny whore asleep on an undersized bed. Down the hall, a small group of men stood outside one of the other rooms. As I approached, I saw Richard Baker standing among them. Under the bruises he had received from his master, Richard's face was deathly pale, and he looked as if he wanted nothing more than to flee the premises. As I neared the group, my stomach lurched as Lorenzo Bacca stepped out of the room. When he saw me, a slight smile touched his lips and he inclined his head in greeting. I did not think anyone else noticed. Immediately behind Bacca came a tall, well-dressed man who looked at me in surprise.

"Why, Lady Bridget, what a pleasure! York feels so small sometimes."

He was Henry Thompson, one of the city's Aldermen and Edward's good friend. I had known Henry for years and respected his intelligence and dedication to the city. He had inherited a fortune from his father and continued to build it as the city's most prominent wine merchant. Henry was the same age as Edward—indeed, the two had grown up together—and like Edward, he was possessed of sufficient wealth and power to give him the authority of a much older man. "I can't imagine what brings you to the Black Swan," he continued, "but it cannot be the unfortunate business that called me to the scene. You should go." He took me gently by the arm and tried to guide me back toward the stairs.

"Mr. Thompson, I am here—"

"On the Lord Mayor's business?" he asked with a small smile. "Yes, Mr. Bacca told me all about your investigation. He and I have no doubt you will find your culprit. But this matter is unrelated, and you really must leave."

"Tell me what has happened. Please."

"Nothing of interest to you," he said firmly. "One of the whores murdered a client, that is all. She fled, but we will find her soon enough."

"Who was killed?" I persisted. "Is it Thomas Penrose?" He stopped short and turned to look at me with renewed interest. I knew I was right.

"And why might you think that?" he asked.

"I know he frequents the Black Swan, and I can't think of any other reason you would have brought his apprentice to a murder scene."

"Ah, it is interesting you should mention the apprentice. He says that you came to Mr. Penrose's shop on Saturday looking for him. Why?"

If Richard had said that much, he surely told Henry that I had asked about the sale of ratsbane. I saw no point in hiding the truth. "I believe that he sold the ratsbane to whoever killed Stephen Cooper."

"What evidence do you have of that?" he asked, raising his eyebrow. At least I'd gotten his full attention.

"The bottle found in Esther Cooper's wardrobe matches the ones used in Thomas Penrose's shop. His apprentice hasn't sold any ratsbane, which left only Penrose."

"And you thought Mr. Penrose might be able to tell you who bought the ratsbane and thus who murdered the unfortunate Mr. Cooper." I nodded. "What if he told you that he sold it to Esther? Where would that leave your investigation?"

"Then we would know the truth. But now Mr. Penrose is dead, and unable to help me find the truth."

"And you think there is a connection between the murders," he said with a condescending sigh. "You want me to believe that Mr. Cooper's murderer somehow discovered your interest in Mr. Penrose, and killed him before you could question him?" I nodded, and he sighed again. I clenched my fists and tried to contain my fury at his arrogance. "It is all very intriguing, but there is no evidence that the crimes are related. In this we should accept the simplest explanation: Esther Cooper bought the ratsbane from Mr. Penrose, and murdered her husband. For that she will burn. Mr. Penrose lived a dissolute life and was robbed and murdered by one of his whores. In both cases justice is done either through the law or by divine providence. Don't you find this a fitting end to Mr. Penrose's sinful life?"

"Fitting, perhaps," I said sharply. "But I also think that when the unwitting accomplice in one murder is the victim of another, God is an unlikely author. I'd like to see the body."

"I don't think that is necessary," he said, and once again tried to guide me to the stairs.

I pulled my arm away and turned to face him. "Mr. Thompson," I said between clenched teeth, "I have done much work for the city, have I not?" He nodded. "And I know many of the city's secrets, do I not?" He nodded again and began to look uncomfortable. "And unless I am mistaken, some of those secrets touch on those close to you."

"You . . . you promised!" he hissed, the color rising in his cheeks. "You said you would never mention my brother's . . . indiscretion so long as he maintained the child."

"And I haven't. I'm simply pointing out that I have given

much and demanded little in return. Now, I am asking. I want to see Mr. Penrose's body."

Henry sighed yet again, this time in resignation, and started back toward the room where the body lay. "It's not much compared to what a cannonball will do to a man, but I think it is bad enough." I followed him down the hall, and the crowd at the door parted to let us through. When I neared Bacca, I felt my stomach drop, for his left hand was heavily bandaged.

"Mr. Bacca," I said, staring into his eyes, "what a terrible wound. Whatever happened to your hand?"

Bacca glanced down as if he had forgotten about the bandages. "Eh? I was bitten by a horse. The bitch nearly took off my finger. But the surgeon says that it will heal soon enough."

I gave him a skeptical look. "Well, you should be careful. If you get close enough, the bitch might have another bite." He looked at me blankly before nodding his head in acknowledgment. I then turned my attention to the room where Penrose had died.

Even before we entered, I could hear the buzz of flies. I prepared myself for the worst, but the scene shocked me all the same. It was Penrose to be sure, but the damage done to his head and face turned my stomach. He sat on the floor, slumped against the bed, with his head lolling back, mouth agape. An explosion of blood radiated from his head like a grotesque sun. The flies swarmed about him, crawling across his bloodied face and glassy eyes. I closed my eyes for a moment and took a deep breath to try to steady myself. Then I stepped forward to look more closely at his wounds. There was one gash on the side of his head from his cheek to his ear, but the most horrific one ran down the middle of his face. It reached from his hairline to his mouth, nearly cleaving his face in two. It was this blow that sent the ropes of blood across the bed.

"Do we know what the weapon was?" I asked Henry.

He nodded to the constable, who produced a heavy iron crowbar. "We found this on the ground below the window," he said. "It had blood on it." I held out my hand and he let me hold it. It was so heavy that I could hardly lift it.

"Surely you don't believe one of the whores committed this crime."

"Given the location of the murder, that seems the most logical conclusion."

"Have you seen the whores who work here? Two of them together couldn't lift this bar over their heads, never mind swing it hard enough to cleave a man's head in two."

"Then she had an accomplice. We'll find them both."

"Do you even know which whore it was?" I asked, trying to hide my exasperation.

"Not yet. The alehouse keeper said she'd never been in before. But he was drunk as a lord, all he can remember is that she had brown hair. Most of the other whores and their customers fled as soon as the alarm was raised. The ones we've found claim not to have seen or heard anything."

I took Henry's arm and pulled him down the hall so I could speak my piece to him alone. "I want to make sure I understand," I said. "You don't know who this whore was, you don't know who helped her, and you have no witnesses who can recognize her? Tell me again why you are so sure that you will find her."

"She's a whore, not a highwayman," he replied peevishly. "She has no experience with murder, and she can't escape the city. We'll have her by sundown."

"No, you won't," I said, shaking my head in despair. "I don't know what happened here, but this was no robbery. And if you have the killer by sundown, I'll send you a fresh-killed deer for Christmas."

I turned and descended the stairs, still furious at Henry's obstinacy. When I reached the alehouse door, I noticed the hem of my skirt had soaked up some of Thomas Penrose's blood. For some reason, this roiled my stomach more than anything I had seen upstairs. Whether I wanted it to or not, his blood would come home with me. I crossed the street to rejoin Martha and Will.

Will asked the question that was on both their minds. "What did you find? Is it Penrose?"

I tried to answer but could find no words to describe the corpse, the way the blood had sprayed across the bed, or the sheer brutality of the killing. I simply nodded and started home.

# Chapter 20

When we arrived at my house I called for Hannah, went to my chamber, and hurriedly took off the bloodied skirts. "Get rid of them," I told her.

"My lady?"

"Take them, throw them away, burn them, use them yourself, I don't care. I won't wear them again."

She looked at the blood, puzzled. She knew perfectly well that I had worn far bloodier clothes home from deliveries and then worn them again after they had been washed. She started to object but must have seen something in my face that told her I was serious.

After she left, I wondered at my reaction. I could not say why Penrose's death disturbed me so much. I knew how he treated his apprentice and how men like him treated the city's whores; I'd seen their bruises and delivered their bastards. What I found so disturbing was the realization that the drops of blood on my skirt would not be the last ones shed in this case. If I completed my investigation, two more people—Penrose's killer and his "whore"—

would join Penrose and Stephen Cooper in the ranks of the unhappy dead; Stephen's death would beget three more. I sat for a while, looking out the window, and my mind kept returning to the girl who led Penrose to his death. I could not imagine her. She must have known what would happen to Penrose when they reached her room, but why would she do it? What was her connection to Stephen Cooper, and who was her murderous accomplice? A knock at the door interrupted my meditations.

"Are you all right?" Martha asked.

"Fine, fine," I said too quickly. "Help me with my bodice, and I'll come down and tell you what I found." Once I had dressed, Martha and I found Will waiting impatiently in the parlor. We all sat, and I told them what I had seen.

"Last night Mr. Penrose was murdered in the Black Swan. The constable had fetched Richard Baker so he could identify him."

"We guessed as much," said Will. "How was he killed?"

I described the scene in all its gore. "The killer was strong and fast. If you come upon him, be on your guard."

"Do they have any idea who might have killed him?" Martha asked.

"Henry Thompson is leading the search. He thinks—wants to think—that a whore and her accomplice tried to rob Mr. Penrose, but killed him instead. He sees it as divine justice for Mr. Penrose's sins."

"That seems a bit far-fetched," said Martha. "Two thieves just happened to kill the man who could tell us who murdered Mr. Cooper? And they do this a few hours after we tried to question him?"

I shrugged. "In troubled times, men like Henry crave clarity. It's much easier to believe that God struck down Penrose for his evil living than to admit that the city council wrongly convicted Esther. Remember, he sat on the jury and voted to burn her. That is not all. Lorenzo Bacca was there."

"Could it have been a coincidence? The Lord Mayor might have sent him. The murder of a second citizen in as many weeks is sure to get his close attention."

"I don't know why he was there. If he killed Penrose to keep him quiet, he would likely want to steer the investigation in another direction. But there is more. Sometime between yesterday afternoon and this morning, he suffered a wound to his hand that demanded bandaging. Will, do you think you might have stabbed our assailant in the hand?"

"It is possible. But between the dark and the rain, I don't know."

"Could the Hookes have killed Penrose?" asked Martha. "Or someone hired by Charles Yeoman?"

"I wouldn't want to rule anyone out. Either Yeoman or the Hookes could have hired a killer without undue trouble."

"Have they found the whore?" Martha asked.

"There was no whore." I sighed.

"What do you mean?"

"The killer had an accomplice, and she lured Penrose upstairs, but she was no whore. Nobody had seen her before, and what whore murders her first client?"

"Then who was she?"

"I have no idea, and that's what troubles me. We nearly found out who was behind Stephen Cooper's death, but still know almost nothing about the case. We don't know who his killers are, or why they killed him. We don't even have a suspect. And thanks to Penrose's death, the search seems near its end. Once the siege is lifted, the killers can simply flee the city and disappear forever."

Martha cleared her throat. "I think we have to consider whether my brother might have done this. He's killed before, and he saw us looking at Penrose."

"But that is hardly a reason to murder," objected Will. "Surely he doesn't hate you enough to kill a complete stranger out of spite."

"Lady Hodgson bested him once. If he was the one who attacked you last night, his fury at a second humiliation would know no bounds. He would have killed Penrose for the pleasure of it. The fact that it made our lives more difficult would have made it all the more enjoyable."

"So where are we?" Will asked gloomily.

"We still have no idea who killed Stephen Cooper, or why they did so," I said.

"And while the same people might have killed Thomas Penrose," continued Martha, "it also might have been my brother."

"Perhaps we need to speak with Richard Baker again," Will suggested. "He lived with Penrose, and we could convince him to let us search the house. Who knows what we will find?"

I did not believe that going back to Penrose's shop would yield any new information, but I didn't have any better ideas. "Very well," I said. "You will join us for dinner, and then we will return to the shop to talk to Richard."

"We should bring a guard with us," said Martha.

To my surprise, Will nodded in agreement. "She is right," he said. "I am happy to defend you against one killer, but it now seems you have two men stalking you—Martha's brother and whoever attacked us last night. What is more, we know that whoever killed Penrose was not alone."

"Very well," I said. "Sergeant Smith is on duty. We'll ask him to accompany us."

* * *

After we'd eaten I explained the circumstances to Sergeant Smith, and he agreed to accompany us. The four of us set out for Penrose's shop, but when we arrived we found it locked. I peered through the windows and saw no sign of activity inside. Had Richard returned to the shop? Or had he simply disappeared after the death of his master? Will pounded on the door, and once again the tailor from next door popped his head out of his shop.

"Hello again!" he chirped. "Did you find Mr. Penrose?"

"Er, no not yet," said Will. "I don't suppose you have seen him or Richard since we were last here, have you?"

"No, no, not Mr. Penrose. Miss Helen came around looking for Richard. But I haven't seen him either."

"Who is Helen?" Will asked.

"A serving-maid. Quiet girl. Richard's been courting her, I think." He paused and turned to Sergeant Smith. "My, that is a handsome coat." Smith looked bewildered and stammered out thanks. "But," the tailor continued, "I think you can do better, and I know you'll like what I can offer. I'm George Cawton. Come in. I'll show you my wares." Before Sergeant Smith could react, Cawton had his arm and pulled him into his shop. The poor sergeant looked over his shoulder at us, wondering just how this had happened.

"The tailor may not be the most observant man," Will said with a laugh, "but I'll wager Sergeant Smith will have a new suit of clothes before he escapes." He took a more serious tone. "Now what do we do? Stand here until the apprentice comes back? With his master dead, he may be gone for good."

Will's question was a good one, and I didn't have a ready answer.

"We only wanted to find Richard so he could let us into the

shop," said Martha. "Perhaps we can find another way in." She peered at me hopefully. Will looked confused, but I understood well enough.

"Do you have your tools?" I asked.

She smiled and nodded. "I thought we might need them once inside, but they'll work on the front door as well."

"Will," I said, "stand over here next to me, in front of the door." Still unsure what was happening, Will moved in front of the door, and Martha stooped to peer at the lock.

"What are you doing?" he whispered.

"Standing here waiting for Richard Baker to return," I said. "And don't whisper. It will make passersby suspicious."

"Suspicious of what?"

"Mr. Hodgson," Martha said, "may I borrow your dagger? One good turn ought to do it."

Will looked behind him, still unsure exactly what was happening. Nevertheless, he slipped his dagger out of his belt and handed it to Martha. A moment later, Martha proved as good as her word, and the door to Penrose's shop swung open. Martha entered first, enjoying the puzzled look on Will's face. Will and I followed, closing the door behind us. Will drew the curtains lest Cawton or any of Penrose's other neighbors saw us inside, and we began our search.

Will went into the back room, while Martha and I searched the shop itself. Richard's neat work made our search mercifully quick. He had carefully labeled every drawer, shelf, bottle, and envelope. We found everything in exactly the right place. Will finished his search and returned, shaking his head.

"What did you find?" I asked.

"The cleanest workshop you'll ever see. Nothing is out of place, and nothing to help us find out who bought the ratsbane. I did find a locked cabinet—did you say that's where Penrose kept the poisons?"

"That's what Richard told us. Martha, could you have a look?"

"Yes, my lady."

She disappeared into the back room, and we followed her. Martha made short work of the lock on the cabinet, and we crowded around as she opened the doors. Not surprisingly, the poisons were as organized as the more benign substances. I noticed mercury, henbane, ratsbane, arsenic, and opium, but there was no book of sales that might tell us who had bought the poison.

"Shall we look upstairs?" Will asked.

"We're already felons for breaking in." I sighed. "We've no reason to stop now."

We climbed the stairs to the living quarters and found ourselves in a hallway that ran from the front of the house to the back. Through one door we found a room that had to be Penrose's bedchamber. Clothes were strewn across the room, clearly left wherever he had dropped them after a long night at the Black Swan. The sheets themselves stank of sweat, and the smell emanating from one corner of the room told me that he had vomited into one of his chamber pots.

We looked in the second bedchamber and knew in a moment it was Richard's. The room was as orderly as the shop and completely spotless. Richard had attached a small shelf to the wall and begun to fill it with books. The two largest were the Bible and a collection of recipes for making medicines called *The Charitable Physician with the Charitable Apothecary*. I opened the book and found that he had made notes in the margins, changing the amounts of different ingredients and even substituting some recipes of his own invention. Alongside these books, Richard kept a mix of cheaper pamphlets, including a book of prayers and a jest book called *The Friar and the Boy*. However modest it might have been, Richard was assembling a library. He seemed to be the ideal apprentice, and I lamented the suffering he had endured at Penrose's hands. I hoped that Richard would take me up on my offer for a loan. I would happily bring my business to him in the future.

Will's voice pulled me back to the present. "I've found something. It looks like the apprentice kept records of the shop's stock." He was leaning over a small table, peering at a ledger.

I crossed the room and looked over his shoulder. Richard had laid the book out in neat columns, the first listing all the ingredients in the shop and other columns tracking how much of each item he had bought, sold, or used. As Will scanned the ledger, I picked up a commonplace book that lay on the table. On the book's first pages, Richard had written down more recipes for medicines and, as he had in the printed book, noted changes as he learned what worked best. I continued leafing through the book and found that in fact it was two books. At one end of the book he wrote his recipes and at the other he made more private entries. The first date was January 1st, and I was not surprised that his main concerns were the difficulty of his apprenticeship. His description of Penrose's beatings broke my heart, and I wondered at his patience in the face of such abuse.

"I found it," announced Will. I closed the commonplace book and looked up. "He purchased ratsbane a few months ago, but doesn't appear to have used any since. If Penrose sold the ratsbane, he did it without Richard's knowledge."

"Well, that's that." I sighed. "Put things where you found them, and let's go."

We went downstairs and peered into the street. Sergeant Smith had not yet escaped from the tailor's shop. "The street is clear,"

Will said, and the three of us slipped out the door and closed it behind us.

"Martha, how are you at locking doors?" I asked.

"In truth, I've never tried it, but why not?" she said. With Will and me once again shielding her from view, Martha went to work on the lock. A few minutes later, we heard a click and she stood up, proud as could be. "It's not so different," she said with a self-satisfied smile. Will ducked into George Cawton's shop and emerged a moment later with a visibly relieved Sergeant Smith.

"He sold me two new suits," he said. "If you'd not intervened, I have no idea how many more I would have bought."

When we turned onto my street, the guard saw us and called out, "Lady Hodgson, you have a visitor. He says he has a message from the Castle."

A small figure stood next to him, though from the distance I could not tell who it was. We drew closer, and two things became clear. First, my visitor was a small boy who had not had a bath in some months, and second, the guard held him tightly by the neck. Despite the pain he must have suffered, the only trace of discomfort on the boy's face was the slow clenching and unclenching of his jaw.

"Let him go!" I cried out. The guard looked surprised but complied. I looked at the boy's neck and saw marks from the guard's fingers that would become bruises the next day. I turned angrily to the guard. "Did you consider the boy dangerous?" He seemed taken aback by my concern for the boy. "Were you afraid he might overcome you and storm my house?"

"No, my lady," he said. "But he's just an urchin."

I squatted next to the boy and cupped his face in my hands. His brown eyes were flecked with green and shone with intelligence, not unlike Birdy's. "Who sent you to me?" I asked.

"Samuel Short, the jailor." He showed no deference at all. Clearly he'd learned his ill manners from Short.

"Are you his boy?"

He thought about the question before answering. "He's not my father, but he cares for me," he said. "My mother died in the jail and he took me in."

"What is your name?"

"Samuel calls me Tree, because I'm already taller than he is."

"All right, Tree, come inside. Give me your message, and I'll see what food we have for you." At the prospect of a meal—from a gentlewoman's larder, no less—his eyes lit up. As we passed the guard, I glared at him and he lowered his eyes. I whispered to Martha, "Take the boy to the kitchen, feed him well, and keep an eye on him. He's not a danger, but he is poor enough that he might not be above pilfering."

"Follow me, Tree," she sang out, and we trooped to the back of the house.

Hannah set a plate of cheese and bread and a mug of small beer before the boy, and he told us his story.

"Samuel sent me with a message. He says that the soldiers captured a lady trying to flee the city last night. They brought her to the Castle, and when Samuel locked her up, she asked him to send for you." Martha and I exchanged confused looks. We had assumed the message would be about Esther.

"Tree," I said, "when you say that the soldiers captured a lady, do you mean a gentlewoman, like me?"

"No. Like her," he said, indicating Martha. "She weren't dressed so nice as you."

"Do you know her name?" I asked.

"She wouldn't tell anyone. That's why they locked her up."

"How strange," I murmured. "What did she look like?"

Tree looked at me blankly. "She looked like a lady. Could I have some more cheese? It is . . ." He paused, searching for a word to describe his meal. I nodded and Hannah began to refill his plate. While he ate, Martha, Will, and I withdrew to the parlor.

"Who could it be?" Martha asked.

"I don't know," I said. "But it might not be related to Cooper's murder. It could be one of my clients, or a friend's maidservant." Martha looked disappointed.

"I suppose you'll want company on a visit to the Castle?" asked Will.

"That would be lovely, thank you," I said with a smile. "Have some food before we go. We'll walk back with Tree."

# Chapter 21

Tree chattered incessantly during the walk to the Castle, asking the most impertinent questions about life in my house. Did I really have servants to empty the chamber pots? What good did wearing such rich clothes do me? Did my children mind having to go to church? What happened to my children? Why, with so much food in the house, were we not fat? Was Will my husband? My son? My suitor? Why did *he* wear such uncomfortable clothes? Will and I did our best to answer and educate him, but it soon became clear that for Tree, the joy lay more in devising the queries than waiting for an explanation. After a few minutes, I realized that in this he reminded me of no one so much as Birdy. To my surprise, this discovery drew me not deeper into melancholy; rather, it lifted my heart, especially as I watched him gambol through the streets, finding wonder and adventure in a world that I had come to take for granted. As we approached the Castle gate, I started to produce my letter with the Lord Mayor's seal, but when the guards saw Tree, they opened the gate for us as if we followed the Lord Mayor himself rather than a skinny child.

"The guards know you well," I said.

"I run errands for them for a penny each. They usually send me for a whore or a pot of ale." He did not notice the look of horror that crossed my face at the nonchalance with which he described his tasks. What life was this for a boy?

We crossed the compound to the same tower that held Esther. Tree banged on the door and shouted, "Samuel! I brought Lady Hodgson!" Samuel Short's face appeared momentarily in the small window before it snapped shut. The bolt slid back, and Samuel beckoned us in before securing the door behind us.

"Welcome, my lady," the dwarf said with an ironic bow but a genuine smile. "If you make many more visits, I'll talk to the captain about renting you a room on the premises."

"It *would* save me a good bit of walking," I admitted. "And the Lord knows that Tree would benefit from a mother's influence. But where would I hang my pictures?" I examined the tower closely. "No, I don't think this is quite what I'm looking for. Do you have a tower room on the north side of the Castle? I would prefer having the winter sun." Samuel burst out laughing, and I found myself joining in. "To business, Samuel, who is the woman who has called for me?"

The dwarf turned serious. "She won't say, even though she hasn't been fed since she arrived. She's a stubborn creature, I'll give her that."

"You are denying her food?" I asked, shocked.

"The captain's orders," Samuel replied. "He's afraid she might be a spy trying to take information to the rebels. She'll eat when she talks."

"Well, let me see her. I'll see what I can do."

Samuel and I started down the stairs, but when Will began to follow, Samuel stopped him. "I beg your pardon, sir. The prisoner only wants to see Lady Hodgson. She refused to see anyone else."

Will started to object, but I intervened. "It's probably women's business." He nodded and returned to the entry room.

Samuel stopped at the door opposite Esther's and unlocked it. I tried to catch a glimpse of Esther through the barred window but saw only a figure lying on the bed. Samuel opened the door, and to my surprise I found Anne Goodwin sitting on a straw pallet inside.

"Lady Hodgson!" she cried as she leapt to her feet.

"I'll be upstairs," Samuel said, and shut the door behind me.

"Anne," I said. "What in heaven are you doing here? You tried to escape the city? What has happened?"

"Please help me," she said, and tears began to stream down her cheeks. "They killed my baby, and I'm sure they will kill me as well."

I put my arms around her as she collapsed into my chest, sobbing. "What do you mean?" I asked. "Who killed your baby? Who is going to kill you?" I knew the answer, of course, and at the same time my heart wept with Anne, a part of me thrilled that I had found a witness against the Hookes.

"I don't know," she said. "One of the Hookes. James said he loved me, but my baby's gone. One of the Hookes killed him. My mother told me." Anne's words came out in a rush and caught me off guard. I had suspected the child in Coneystreet had been Anne's and that the Hookes were involved in his death. But James hardly seemed to be cruel enough to murder a child. And he had told Anne that he loved her?

"Calm yourself, Anne. Tell me what happened from the beginning." I eased her down onto the edge of her bed.

"You know I was servant to Mrs. Hooke," she said, trying to

regain control of herself. "She is a hard mistress, and I tried to do my work without attracting overmuch notice. After a few months, James began to court me."

"Court you," I repeated. It seemed unlikely that a wealthy young man would court a maid in earnest. It was far more likely that he intended to seduce her and then move on to another maidservant. Then again, James had never been known for his judgment.

"He told me I was beautiful and gave me presents," she said. "He wanted to have knowledge of my body, but I denied him. He said he loved me and promised to marry me, so I let him." I found yet another reason to pity Anne, for this part of her story was far too common. Countless maidens bore bastards after a man broke his promise of marriage, and for this they lived lives on the poor rolls. "When I discovered I was with child, I told him."

"And he turned you away?"

"No, my lady!" she said, apparently horrified that I held James Hooke in such low esteem. "He swore he loved me, and that he would marry me. He took me to his mother and told her of our plans." I admit this surprised me. At the same time I wondered at James's silliness—promising to marry his maidservant?—I admired his loyalty. He was a dull boy, to be sure, but not so cruel as his mother.

"I imagine she objected."

"Mrs. Hooke's fury was something to behold, my lady." Anne's eyes grew wide at the memory. "I have never been called such horrible names. I had never even *heard* such language. She screamed and screamed. James had the worst of it. She broke his nose with a Bible." As much as I regretted Anne's fate, I had to suppress a smile at the scene she described.

"What happened then?" I asked.

"I continued my work," she said. "She could not dismiss me, for she knew I would say her son was the father of my child. She promised that she would give me five pounds after the baby was born, but only if I swore never to lay the child on James. She told me to pick another servant from the neighborhood, and father the child on him." Such arrangements were not uncommon, of course. Only the Lord knew how many bastard-bearers fathered their children on innocent men in exchange for a few pounds.

"When did you have the baby?"

"Mrs. Hooke and one of the other servants delivered me the night you saw me in the Pavement. I wanted to call for my mother and for a midwife, but she would not allow it. She said she was as good a midwife as any in the city, but in truth, my lady, she was hard and cruel." I nodded. I had seen the bitter fruit of her labors. "Once I was delivered, James was very loving towards me. He said he would convince his mother to let us marry. He even brought a present for the baby." Her chest heaved as she sobbed into my shoulder for a time. I stroked her hair and tried to contain my own tears. Once she had regained her breath, she continued. "On Thursday, James brought me supper and bid me sleep. When I awoke, James and the baby were gone. I haven't seen him since. They locked the door to my chamber and the other servants only opened it to bring me food and empty my chamber pot. I begged them to bring me my baby, but they refused. Then Mrs. Hooke came to me and told me that he was dead. Oh, my lady, it was horrible!"

Anne dissolved into tears again and I held her as she cried. For a time I mourned with Anne, but soon my wrath at Rebecca Hooke overcame my grief at Anne's loss. Now I had no doubt that Rebecca had killed the child, perhaps even with her own hands. But I also saw how difficult it would be to obtain justice for Anne's son, and this realization infuriated me all the more.

After a hitching sob, Anne looked up at me. "My lady, are you unwell?"

I realized that my face betrayed my anger and tried to compose myself. My first priority had to be helping Anne, not bringing down Rebecca. "I am sorry, Anne. Yes, I'm fine. Tell me how you came to the Castle."

"I knew that they had murdered my baby, and feared they would kill me as well, so I decided to escape. The window of my chamber opened onto the roof next door. Last night I climbed out and jumped to the street. I went home—I had to see my mother. But I knew the Hookes would try to find me, so I fled."

"And that's when you decided to escape the city?"

"I was going to London. They would never have found me there," she said wistfully. "But the guards captured me, and sent me here."

I puzzled for a time over what I should do next. I could probably arrange for Anne's release from the Castle, but to what end? I didn't know if Rebecca Hooke really planned to kill her, nor did I want to find out. Until the siege lifted, the safest place she could be was in her cell.

"Anne," I said, "I know these are not the most comfortable quarters, but you are safe here, and for the time being you should stay. I will speak to the jailor and he will treat you well. For a start, he will provide you with a blanket and food immediately. I will see what I can do to secure your safe passage to London, but it will take time."

"Thank you, my lady." She wiped her cheeks with her sleeve.

I knocked on the door, and Samuel opened it and let me out. "You may tell your captain that she is not a spy," I said.

"He's unlikely to take your word for it," he replied. "Who is she?"

"She is a maid who hoped to go to London. Nothing more."

"So you will ask the captain to release her?"

"Er, no," I said. "It would be better if she stayed here for the present."

"If she's just an innocent maid, why do you want her to stay here?" he asked. He was suspicious but clearly sensed an opportunity to make some money.

"I am not at liberty to say." I handed him a small purse full of coins. "But I know her well, and give you my word that she is no spy."

"Would you put that in writing? For the captain, I mean? If I tell him, he'll laugh, but if it comes from a gentlewoman like yourself, it's a different matter."

"Give me some paper. I'll write to him immediately. That money also should pay for a blanket. If she calls for me, do not hesitate to send Tree."

When we reached the top of the stairs, we found Will and Tree playing at dice, with Will clearly coming off the worse. While they played, I wrote a letter to the captain, assuring him that Anne posed no threat to the city and guaranteeing her good conduct. After Tree had pocketed all of Will's pennies (he wisely declined the boy's offer to play for shillings), I gave him the letter and sent him to the captain. With that business taken care of, Will and I left the Castle and started home.

"Do you realize that the boy was cozening you?" I asked.

"Of course. But for the life of me I could not figure out how. I still don't know. So who was the woman who summoned you?"

"Anne Goodwin, of all people."

"The Hookes' servant? She was trying to flee the city to escape the Hookes?"

I related Anne's story of her delivery, imprisonment, and

escape. "She's safe for the moment," I said. "But I don't know what to do next." We reached my house, and even as we settled in the parlor Martha joined us. I filled her in on what I'd learned from Anne, and together we considered our options.

"We could go to Alderman Hodgson," Martha suggested. "He trusts you and might begin a formal investigation."

"You know that's not how the law works," I said. "Edward would not order the arrest of *any* citizen based only on the word of a bastard-bearing maidservant who was caught trying to flee the city."

"But if you talked to him . . . he trusts you."

"I am still a woman and Anne is nothing but a girl. The Hookes would cast her as a disorderly servant and a wench of lewd character. Edward would not believe a word she said."

"What then?" she asked angrily. "Will you let them escape unpunished?"

"What would you have me do?" I snapped back. "If Anne is the only witness, there is nothing we can do! The Lord Mayor and Aldermen are rushing to burn Esther Cooper for murdering her husband. They are not going to pull down another respectable household on the word of a maidservant. The Hookes would destroy her."

"Then we find someone else," she said angrily. "Someone must have seen something. One of the servants, perhaps. We can't just give up."

I thought for a moment, an idea slowly dawning on me. "The servants would never testify. But James might."

"Why in God's name would he do that?"

"Murdering a child brings with it a heavy burden, one that few people can bear alone. Even if he didn't kill the child himself, he knows what happened and is responsible, at least in part. If we can confront James without his mother nearby, he may tell us the truth."

"If he did, he would send himself or his mother to the gallows," Will said. "Why would he do that?"

"Out of guilt. I've seen it too often in mothers. They deny everything at first, but all men seek forgiveness in this world, no matter what their fate might be in the next. Bacca was right: Papists have their priests for confession—we Protestants are not so fortunate. We must confess to each other, or live and die with the burden of our sins. James is unaccustomed to living with a guilty conscience. If we give him the chance to unburden his soul, he may confess."

"I must assume you have some idea how to do this," Will said.

"I do, and you are the key player. We'll need Tree as well." I laid out my ideas, and shortly after supper Will left the house to set the plan in motion.

After Will had been gone for nearly two hours, there came a knock at the door. Martha opened it to admit Tree. "They've been in the alehouse since four," he reported. "Mr. Hodgson has had two pints, but the other man has doubled that, and drunk some liquor as well."

"Well done, Tree," I said. "Do you remember the rest of your job?"

"Of course," he said tartly.

Martha, Tree, and I walked swiftly up Stonegate to an alehouse not far from the Minster. Martha and I waited out of sight, while Tree ducked inside to signal Will. A few moments later, Will and the boy exited the alehouse and crossed to the alley where Martha and I had hidden.

"He's inside. I told him I had to go to the jakes."

"Good man," I said, and turned to Tree. "Here's the three pennies we agreed upon, and another for doing such a fine job."

"Thank you," he said, his eyes widening at the sum. I looked at him hard, withholding the coins. "Thank you, my lady," he said.

I smiled and gave him the coins. "We'll civilize you yet. Now, be off with you." Tree scampered off toward the Castle, reveling in his newfound wealth.

I set my sights on the alehouse and the serious business that lay before us. "Will, I hope you will stay close and watch the door. I'd like to avoid any unpleasant surprises." He nodded.

Martha and I entered the alehouse and saw James Hooke sitting at a small corner table, staring sullenly into a mug of ale. We crossed the room and sat on either side of him. If he wanted to leave, he'd have to climb over us or across the table. James glanced up and then back at his ale.

"Hello, James," I said. At this he looked more closely at me, squinting slightly as he tried to clear his vision. He was extremely drunk—Will had done his job well. "We're here for Anne Goodwin," I continued. "She asked us to come see you." To my surprise, at the mention of Anne's name, James's bloodshot eyes filled with tears, and he reached over and clutched my hand.

"You've seen Anne?" he asked. "She is alive?"

"She is alive, and she sent us to you," Martha said. "She hopes you are well."

"She did? Anne said that?" he asked eagerly. "Where is she? Will she see me?"

"She will," Martha said. "But not now."

"No, of course not," James said hastily. "What would my mother do if she knew?" Tears overflowed his eyes an ran down his cheeks. "She is in good spirits?" My heart went out to the lad, and

I briefly wondered whether he was about to put his life in my hands. If he had a role in his son's death, he would have to die.

"James," I said, "before she sees you, she wants you to tell us about the baby." The guilt and shame that filled James's face told me that he knew what I meant. He gazed into my eyes, and I watched impassively as his face crumpled and he began to sob. Other customers looked over at us, but if he noticed, he didn't care. He buried his face in his hands and continued to cry.

"Tell me, James," I said gently. "Tell me." I put my arm around his shoulders, and he leaned into me, his body shaking. I doubted Rebecca had ever offered him even this much consolation.

"I didn't know," he said. His eyes were bright from crying. "I didn't know what she was going to do. I thought I could change her mind."

"What happened, James? Anne went to sleep, and when she awoke the baby was gone. What happened?"

"I thought if I brought the baby to my mother, she might not hate Anne so much. She might not hate me." Here is a man who does not know his own mother, I thought.

"Did she change her mind?" I asked, knowing the answer before he gave it. The only remaining question was how the child had died.

"I thought she did. She asked to hold him, and when she looked into his eyes, I thought she saw her grandson. I thought holding him had softened her heart." Martha started to speak, but I shook my head to silence her. James would tell us everything in his own time. "She asked me to go to a wine shop and bring back the finest bottle I could find, so that we could welcome her grandson properly. When I returned I gave my mother the wine, and she called for two glasses. I asked if she had given the baby back to Anne. She looked at me as if I were an idiot. She said, 'Never you mind what has become of the bastard. I've cleaned up your mess.' Then she poured the wine and made me drink."

"Your mother murdered her own grandson?" Martha said. It was as much a statement as a question. James nodded. "What should we do?" she asked me.

"I'll tell you what to do, you pocky-arsed whore. Move away from my son!"

I looked up and saw Rebecca Hooke striding across the room, eyes fixed on James. I wondered how she had gotten past Will. Then I saw her footman following close behind. He bore all the marks of a fight, so I knew that Will had not given up easily. I prayed that he had not been hurt. Heart pounding, I stood up and stepped forward to confront Rebecca. Without breaking stride, she planted her hand in the middle of my chest and shoved me backward. I tripped on the bench behind me and tumbled to the floor. Rebecca ignored me, instead fixing her baleful stare on James, who steadfastly refused to meet her eyes. Rebecca turned to her footman. "Take him back to the house and keep him there." The footman stepped past Martha, grabbed James roughly by the arm, and jerked him to his feet.

"Come on, Mr. Hooke," he said, dragging him toward the door.

Rebecca looked down at me with a baleful gaze. "Stay away from my son," she hissed before starting for the door.

Martha looked at me, desperate for guidance. Fearing that our last chance to obtain justice for Anne's son was slipping away, I scrambled to my feet and charged after Rebecca. When I reached the door, it opened before me, and Will appeared. He leaned unsteadily against the frame, bleeding profusely from the nose.

"Stay with him," I said to Martha, and started up the street. Rebecca had caught up to James and her footman, but her son's stumbling gait slowed them, and I was able to draw within ear-shot. Just before they reached Davygate, I cried out, "You're a mur-dering bitch, Rebecca Hooke." The words had their intended effect. She stopped and turned slowly to face me.

Without taking her eyes off me, she called to her footman, "Take him home. I will be there shortly." She walked toward me, staring at me with a mixture of hatred and disdain. I could feel my heart racing as she approached. "A murdering bitch? I'm a murder-ing bitch?"

"Your son thinks so. He told me what you did."

"My son," she spat. "I will tell him what to think. He's no better than his father. But I don't need to tell you about weak and useless husbands." By now she stood with her face just a few inches from mine. From a distance you might have thought we were good friends having a talk.

"You murdered your own grandchild," I said softly. "You threw him into a privy and left him there to die."

"I protected my family. Do you really think I would allow my son to marry our washing-maid? I raised my family up from nothing, and I will not see it brought low by that silly boy and his whore. I will choose his wife, and by God she will be a woman of means and honor. You, of all women, should understand that. She will guide him the way I have guided Richard and you guided your useless husband." I started to speak, but she gave me no chance. "Would *you* have let your son marry a washing-maid? Do you think that stupid girl could protect my fortune from the vain fancies of a profligate boy like James? She knows nothing save housewifery, nothing of business or government. In her hands my estate would waste away to nothing. I could no more allow James to marry a girl like that than you could allow your daughter to marry the penny-man who comes to kill your hog."

"And for this you murdered your own grandson?"

"That bastard, born of a whore? He was no more my grandson than he was King Jesus Himself. Who knows where else that whore raised her skirts? That child could be my husband's, my footman's, or any other man's. I did what I did in order to look after my family. If you say you wouldn't have done the same, you're a liar or a fool. In truth I did her a favor. Now she's free to find a husband closer to her own station—perhaps a rag-picker."

I stood in silence, amazed by her malice. "I'll go to my brother," I whispered. "And tell him."

"And tell him what?" she said with a cruel laugh. "That I confessed to murdering an infant? Tell me, Bridget, who has heard me confess? You've hated me for years, and none will believe you. I'd sue you for defamation, and I'd win." A thin smile spread across her face. "Perhaps I'll sue you anyway. If women think you spread malicious gossip, they'll find another midwife soon enough. We shall see." She started to walk away but stopped after a few steps. "I have heard that you think I murdered that penny-pinching Jew Stephen Cooper. Remember two things, Bridget Hodgson. You'll never prove that I killed Stephen Cooper, and if you continue to meddle in my business, I swear that I'll have my revenge." She smiled at me before turning away.

Once she disappeared into her house, my body began to shake and I worried I might collapse on the spot. I stumbled out of the street and leaned heavily on the wall surrounding St. Helen's churchyard. Without warning my stomach clenched, and I vomited over the wall into the graveyard. Keeping one hand on the wall, I walked slowly back to the alehouse to see how Will and Martha fared.

# Chapter 22

I found Will and Martha inside the alehouse, at the table James and I had just left. Will held a cloth to his nose to stem the bleeding, but he removed it periodically so he could drink his ale. He would bear the marks of his fight for days to come. They looked relieved when I entered, and I quickly crossed the room to their table.

"How are you, Will?" I asked.

"The blackguard hit me without a word of warning. He just walked up and started swinging," he said morosely. He hated losing a fight under any circumstances, and I knew that this loss felt worse than most.

"I saw the footman's face. It looked like you gave as good as you got," I said, trying to comfort him.

"Not good enough," he said, signaling the barmaid for another ale.

"Did you catch them?" asked Martha.

"Yes. She all but admitted throwing the child in the privy herself. She came close to *bragging* that she had done it. She wanted to protect her family from the shame of a bastard and prevent James and Anne from marrying. She sacrificed the child for that."

"James wanted to marry her?" Will asked. "What did he *think* his parents would say to that?"

"He still cannot see his mother for what she is. He thought he could change his mother's mind if she saw the child."

"What do we do now?" Martha asked.

"I don't know," I said. "She won't give James the opportunity to make that mistake again. From the look on her face, she may cut out his tongue just to be sure." Martha looked despondent, and I put my hand on her shoulder. "Justice can be slow in coming," I said. I almost added that the Lord would see that justice was done, but I knew she would find cold comfort in such a suggestion.

"I know. I just hoped that this time the rich might be subject to the same laws as the poor." I could say nothing to this. She knew that was not the world in which we lived.

"She also brought up Stephen Cooper's murder," I said.

"I don't imagine she took the opportunity to confess," Martha said.

"It was a weak denial at best, and she coupled it with a threat. She said that if I continue to pursue her for Stephen's murder, she will take her revenge."

Will suppressed a laugh and winced in pain. "I seem to remember similar threats when you saw her banned from practicing midwifery."

"Perhaps, but if she really did kill Stephen Cooper, her threats won't be so empty. All I did then was take her license, and the stakes are much higher now. If she killed Stephen to protect her fortune, she would not hesitate to kill me to protect her life. As you said, she cannot be hanged twice."

"Where does this leave our search for Mr. Cooper's murderer?" Martha asked. "The bottle led us to Penrose, but the killer snipped that loose end and tried to do you in as well."

"I don't know," I said. "We have to do something, but I cannot imagine what."

Will smiled ruefully. "We could wait for him to try to kill you again. That would be a pretty sure sign of guilt."

"That might work, but why don't we come up with another plan as well," I suggested.

"We should return to Penrose's shop," said Martha. "It's where the killer bought the ratsbane, so it's our best hope. Perhaps there is another account book we missed, or something hidden in Mr. Penrose's room."

"It's possible," I said, but without much hope. "We can talk more about it in the morning. Right now it's time to sleep."

Will finished his ale, and we left together. He saw us home and disappeared into the darkening night. I dismissed Martha and had Hannah help me dress for bed. As was my custom, I tried to pray, but this time I found myself unable to do so. I knew I should put my faith in God, but He seemed less interested than ever in earthly justice. With a sigh I climbed into bed, knowing that sleep would be a long time coming.

I don't know how long I had been asleep when Hannah shook me awake.

"Lady Hodgson, there is a messenger at the door. Dorothy Mann sent him. She needs your help." Dorothy was another of the city's midwives, and a good one. If she called for my help, the situation must be dire indeed. I dressed quickly and collected my valise. "Shall I wake Martha?" Hannah asked.

"No, let her sleep," I said. I did not want to involve her in a difficult birth so soon after the death of Elizabeth Wood's child. The chances of a second tragedy were too great.

I descended the stairs and found a lad waiting just inside the front door. One of the guards stood there as well, eyeing him suspiciously. "Where is the birth?" I asked the boy.

"It is near St. Martin's church," he said. "My mistress is Elizabeth Woodall."

I looked over the boy. He seemed stout enough but was unarmed. I turned to the guard. "I need you to accompany me to this labor." He nodded and the three of us set out.

We arrived at Elizabeth's home in short order, and I asked the guard to wait at the door until I completed my work. A servant ushered me in and took my cloak. "Her room is at the top of the stairs, on the right," she said.

I hurried up but paused when I reached the door, for I heard laughter coming from within. I opened the door and saw why. Elizabeth lay in bed, nursing her newborn child. She saw me and waved me over. The child's face bore the bruises of a difficult delivery but seemed no worse for all that, thank the Lord.

"Thank you for coming at such a late hour, Lady Hodgson," she said. "The baby came just minutes after we sent for you. He gave us a scare, but all is well."

I congratulated Elizabeth and searched the room for Dorothy Mann. She sat on a couch, holding a glass of wine. I sat beside her. I recognized the mixture of exhaustion and relief on her face—she knew how close the night had come to ending in tragedy.

"A difficult case," I said. Dorothy nodded and sipped her wine. "Elizabeth doesn't know how bad it was, does she."

"I didn't want to worry her while she was in travail, and now that the child is safe there is no reason to frighten her. The child came with his shoulders first. Every time I tried to turn him, he seemed to fight me. Soon he lodged himself so tight I feared for both mother and child."

"How did you save him?"

"I remembered something you talked about once," she said with a faint smile. "I put her on her hands and knees, so the baby might work back up to the matrix. That gave me enough room to work. He took a beating, but I turned him."

I could hear the pride in her voice. She had performed a miracle and knew it. A servant brought me a glass of wine, and I gladly accepted. Dorothy and I drank and talked of the news of the town, of births and deaths.

"I don't know if you have seen her yet, but I sent a client your way last week," I said.

"Really? Who was it?"

"In truth, I don't know. I heard talk of a pregnant serving-maid in All Saints parish. I told them to report it to you."

"Oh, yes, Ellen Hutton. I visited her yesterday. She refuses to name the father, but I haven't started to press her yet. She will tell me soon enough. She doesn't seem brave enough to deliver a child alone."

"Ellen Hutton?" I asked, my mind racing. "Stephen Cooper's servant? *She* is the pregnant maid?"

"She didn't deny it, just refused to say anything. But I felt her belly and breasts. In my judgment she is pregnant." She paused. "Aren't you caring for her mistress while she is in the Castle?"

I sat in silence, trying desperately to make sense of this piece of news. I knew that Ellen's pregnancy could be vital to solving Stephen Cooper's murder, but between the wine and the late hour, my addled mind could not see the picture clearly.

"Lady Bridget, are you all right?" Dorothy asked.

"Yes, I'm fine. How long has she been pregnant?" I asked urgently.

"It's hard to say—five months, perhaps. What is going on? When did you become interested in ordinary bastardy cases?"

"It is nothing," I said. "I must go."

I paid my respects to Elizabeth and walked home as quickly as I could. The rising sun transformed the Minster's walls into towering columns of flame. As I gazed at their majesty, my mind raced over the facts of the case. In the fresh air, my head cleared and I began to understand the importance of what I'd learned.

When I arrived home, I pulled Martha into the parlor. "Ellen Hutton has been pregnant since February," I blurted out. She looked at me sharply and I saw her mind begin to work its way through the implications of my discovery.

"Who is the father?" she asked. "Could it be a suitor? She told us Mr. Cooper chased her suitor away even though he was an apprentice nearing his freedom."

I furrowed my brow, trying to get the final pieces to fit together. "Who did Cawton the tailor say Richard was courting?" I nearly shouted in excitement when I remembered. "The tailor said Richard was courting a girl named Helen. But it wasn't Helen, it was *Ellen*! It must have been! And it can't be a coincidence that both their masters were murdered. Richard and Ellen killed them both."

"But why would they kill Mr. Cooper to begin with?" Martha asked. "What did they have to gain from murder?" Her question brought me up short.

"I don't know. Perhaps they hoped to rob him?" I wondered.

"But they didn't rob him. They deliberately killed him."

I shook my head and continued to think. While some of the

pieces fit, Martha was right—Ellen and Richard had no obvious reason to kill Stephen.

A dark look crossed Martha's face. "They killed him for revenge."

"Revenge for what? Because he tried to keep them from courting? That's hardly the worst thing that Stephen did."

"When we saw Ellen at the apothecary shop, what herbs was Richard using?"

I closed my eyes, picturing the scene in my mind. "Thyme ... hyssop ... Oh, God!" I cried, my eyes flying open. "Dittany. Ellen wasn't there getting herbs for Esther's cough. She was getting them for herself to end the pregnancy. They wanted to kill her child before he was born. But why?"

"Because it's not Richard's child," Martha said softly. "It's Stephen Cooper's. Ellen said he beat Mrs. Cooper, but never hit her. But what man strikes his wife but not his maidservant? She was hiding something, and now we know what. He raped her and left her pregnant. No doubt he threatened to have her whipped if she fathered the child on him. Richard and Ellen sent him the letter demanding the money, and after he paid, they took their revenge. And once Cooper was dead, they tried to get rid of the child as well."

Martha retreated into her thoughts, and we sat in silence as I considered what she had said. "If you're right, when we questioned Richard about the ratsbane we signed Penrose's death warrant," I said. "Penrose would have denied selling the poison, and we would have returned to Richard. They had to keep him from talking to us. *Ellen* was the whore who lured Penrose upstairs at the Black Swan, and Richard beat him to death."

"With all he had suffered, Richard would have taken as much satisfaction in murdering Penrose as Ellen did in killing Cooper."

"Esther isn't guilty of treason. Ellen and Richard are."

"You can't be serious," Martha cried. "Ellen and Richard might be murderers, but traitors?"

"That is what the law says," I answered, taken aback by her tone. "It's the order of things."

"Why? Because they rose against their *natural* lords? Such shit! By that thinking, I'm a traitor, too, am I not? I had a hand in my master's death; shouldn't you charge me as well? Stephen Cooper and Thomas Penrose were tyrants. They deserved no better."

I stared at Martha, recalling the abuse she had suffered before coming to my home. I wondered for a moment if she, rather than Tom, had murdered her master. I chased that thought away and tried to mollify her.

"Your situation is different, and you know it," I said. "You did not intend to kill your master. And while I do not mourn Mr. Cooper and Mr. Penrose, justice must be done. Ellen and Richard are murderers, and it was probably Richard who tried to kill me and Will. We have to stop them before they kill anyone else."

Martha nodded. "But what do we do?" she asked softly. "We've no evidence of their guilt, and Mrs. Cooper still stands convicted."

"I will ask my brother to question Ellen. She will confess soon enough."

"Perhaps," Martha replied. "But I'm not so sure."

"I've questioned murderesses before," I reminded her. "Few women have the stomach to lie when pressed."

"I don't think Ellen will confess so easily."

"Why do you say that? Even Rebecca Hooke confessed."

"Yet she is free," Martha replied archly. "I know Ellen seems like a harmless maidservant, but look at what she's done. She planned her master's murder carefully, and when threatened with discovery, she planted—*and then discovered*—the ratsbane in Mrs.

Cooper's cabinet. She intended for Mrs. Cooper, *who had done her no wrong*, to be burned in her place. Then, when we began to close in on her and Richard, she led Penrose into a trap and watched as Richard dashed out his brains. A woman who has done all this can endure a few hard words without bursting into tears and confessing her crimes."

I considered her point, and my heart sank when I realized that she was right. The murderesses I'd questioned had killed on the spur of the moment and been racked by guilt. Ellen had murdered two men in cold blood and connived in the death of her mistress. How sure could I be that she would confess? And if she did not, what then?

"What do you think we should do?" I asked.

"They won't try to leave the city until the siege is lifted. Richard is too careful for that." I nodded. "We can search his quarters again. Perhaps there is something there. And then we find them and question them separately. We can lie, and turn each against the other. If we drive a wedge between them, one or the other will confess. The constables tried to do that with Tom and me once. If either of us had confessed, we'd both have hanged."

"Let's hope Ellen and Richard trust each other less than you two did." I didn't know if the plan would work, but I had no alternative to offer. "I'll have one of the guards escort us to the shop." Neither of us had forgotten that a killer still might be lurking in the city's alleys, hoping for another chance to attack.

We arrived at Penrose's shop and found it locked. I wasn't sure that the guard would appreciate our plan to break in, so I posted him at the end of the block closest to the Black Swan. "Hurry," I told Martha as she began to work on the lock. "Our guard thinks we have a key." Luckily the lock proved more cooperative than on her first attempt, and a few seconds later we stepped in. "Secure it behind us," I said. "If someone tries to enter the shop, I would like to have some kind of warning." Martha nodded, and I heard the lock click.

"It doesn't look like Richard has been back," Martha said.

"If there's any evidence, it will be in his chamber." We crept upstairs and found Richard's room exactly as we'd left it.

"What are we looking for?" Martha asked.

Despite the tension, I laughed out loud. "I don't know. Remember, this was your idea. You check the bookshelf, I'll search his desk." When I saw Richard's journal, I realized that it was our best hope. I found the early entries detailing his abuse at Penrose's hands and read quickly until I found his first mention of Ellen. She had come into the shop to buy nutmeg. "We were right," I said. "He started courting Ellen in March."

"She was already pregnant by then, wasn't she?"

"Dorothy thought so. It seems that Stephen was the father of her child. Have you found anything?"

"Not yet," I said. "He's got lovely handwriting, though."

I read through the diary as Richard detailed both Penrose's outrageous abuse and his growing love for Ellen. As their courtship progressed, his entries began to include poems about Ellen, often comparing her to the flowers and herbs that heralded the coming of spring. It was overly elaborate, of course, and I could not help marveling that the same hand that wrote these poems beat a man to death with an iron bar. After a long description of a kiss he stole from Ellen on the Ouse Bridge, the entries suddenly stopped. I checked the date of the last entry—May 28. I called Martha over.

"Look," I said, pointing to the date and the diary's sudden end.

"You think that's when they decided to murder Mr. Cooper," she said.

"The timing is close enough," I said grimly. "Once they started planning, he could either create false entries or stop writing altogether. They are the murderers."

"But is having the diary enough? Will your brother order their arrest?"

"He might. We could also use it against Ellen. I'll tell her that in the diary Richard blamed both murders on her. If she thinks Richard betrayed her, she might tell us about his role."

I handed the notebook to Martha and she started toward the door. A loud creak came from the stairs. I froze and looked desperately at Martha. The alarm on her face told me that she had heard the sound as well. Another stair creaked, and I scanned the room in desperate hope of finding some sort of weapon. Martha and I stood as still as we could, though we knew that we were as good as caught.

"Mr. Penrose asked me to fix that stair some months ago," Richard Baker said as he climbed the last steps and entered his chamber. "I suppose I should have listened to him, at least on that occasion." He held a short cudgel in his right hand and slapped it softly in the palm of his left.

I tried to speak but found that my mouth had gone dry and only a croak emerged from my throat. I tried again. "Richard . . . please." I found myself at a loss.

"Why did you come back?" he asked. "You know what kind of man Penrose was. Why couldn't you just accept his fate? I heard that Alderman telling you it was God's justice. Why didn't you listen?"

"Richard, put down the club and let us go," I said. "This doesn't have to happen."

"Really?" he asked with a harsh laugh. "If I let you go, you'll forget you were here? You'll let a murderer escape? Are you going to ask me to believe that? Do I seem so stupid?"

"No," I whispered.

"Thank you for that. Penrose had no idea how much smarter I was than him. Even as an apprentice I was ten times the apothecary he could ever hope to be. The man killed far more patients than he ever helped."

He gazed at me for what seemed like hours but could only have been a few seconds. "How did you figure it out?" he asked. "I thought that with Penrose dead we were safe."

"I found out that Ellen is with child," I said, playing for time. "Martha realized Stephen Cooper must have been the father. We just came here to search for evidence."

Richard looked at Martha closely. "Once again we see that the world has no use for thoughtful servants, does it? It did me no good. See where it got you? Give me the notebook."

"Richard," I said, "please, you don't have to do this."

"Of course I do," he said softly. "If I don't, Ellen and I both will hang. I'm sorry, Lady Hodgson, but I *do* have to do this."

Richard stepped forward and swung the cudgel at Martha's head.

# Chapter 23

Martha ducked as best she could, but Richard's club hit the side of her head with a thump. She cried out and tumbled backward onto Richard's small bed. Richard stepped forward and stood over Martha. I watched in horror as he raised his cudgel to deal the finishing blow. Desperate, I picked up the stool that sat before his desk and hurled it with all my strength. Just before Richard could swing his club, the stool struck the back of his head and he gasped in pain and surprise. He glanced at me before turning back to Martha. When he raised the club again, Martha's eyes snapped open and she landed a vicious kick between his legs. Richard bellowed in pain and brought the club down with terrifying force. Martha rolled to her left, barely escaping the blow.

By now, Richard seemed more beast than human. His face was purple with rage, and spittle flew from his lips as he roared at Martha. He threw himself on top of her and began to choke her with his left hand. Once again he lifted the club over his head. This time he would not miss. With no other weapons at hand, I hurled myself at Richard, breaking his grip on Martha's throat and knocking him to the floor. As he fell, he pulled his bookshelf from the wall and I had a weapon. I seized the plank and swung it at his head. The board struck his face with a loud *crack*. I heard a sob escape my throat when the dry wood splintered into a dozen pieces. I had knocked him off balance, but that was all, and it was not going to be enough to save us.

I dropped the splinters I still held and raced for the door. If I made it to the street, I could call for help. I clattered down the stairs, nearly tripping over the hem of my skirts. Even over the thundering of my own heart, I could hear Richard's heavy footsteps behind me, gaining with every step. By the time I reached the bottom, I knew I would never make it to the street—the counter blocked my way and Richard was too close. I dashed into the workshop and realized with a sickening feeling that I'd made a mistake. The only door out of the shop led to a small, high-walled courtyard. I was trapped.

I turned to face Richard. He saw that I could not escape and stopped in the doorway. He was breathing heavily, and a thin line of blood ran from his nose where I'd hit him. His hands were now empty—he had lost the club when I hit him—and I thanked God for small mercies. He spat on the floor and wiped the blood on his sleeve. "No more running," he said. "You've nowhere to go."

My eyes darted around the shop as I searched desperately for a weapon. I spied a knife among the shop's tools and scooped it up. I turned to face Richard, but he was too fast. He threw his weight against me and we crashed to the ground. I watched aghast as the knife skittered across the floor. I clawed at his neck and fought with all my strength to push him off. He sought a grip on my throat, and for a moment I feared he'd found it, but I slipped from his grasp. As we struggled, I looked up into his face, twisted in rage, and knew that this was the last sight that Mr. Penrose had seen. With one hand I pushed up on his throat, and with the other I thrashed about, hoping to find some kind of weapon. My hand closed around the neck of a bottle and I swung. I landed only a glancing blow to his temple, but it was enough to knock him off balance. I scrambled from beneath him and leapt to my feet. I saw the knife and scooped it up, but he was already upon me. Once again he knocked me to the floor and landed on top of me. For a moment we lay on the ground looking into each other's eyes, in a horrid parody of a lover's embrace. I could feel his breath on my face as he struggled to wrap his hands around my throat.

I was sure that my luck had run its course and only hoped that Martha would be able to escape. I pushed his hands away and somehow escaped his grasp. Kicking at his face, I crawled away from him, then stood and searched desperately for the knife. It was nowhere to be found. Richard staggered to his feet and grasped my shoulder from behind. I turned to face my death and saw the knife protruding from his chest. He looked down at the knife, then up at me. I stretched out a trembling hand and pulled the knife free. A plume of bright red blood spread rapidly across his chest, and he fell to his knees. He stared into my face for an eternity before falling forward. He died before he hit the ground.

I dropped the bloody knife and raced upstairs to find Martha, terrified that Richard had paused long enough to dash out her brains before pursuing me. Relief flooded my body when I found her standing in the doorway. She had a lump on her forehead and her throat was bright red from where Richard had tried to choke her. "Martha, are you all right?" I asked.

She nodded. "I'll be all right," she croaked. "Where is Richard? Did he escape?"

"He's downstairs. Dead."

"My God," she gasped. "What happened?"

"I killed him. I don't know how it happened, but the Lord watched over me today." I took her arm to help her downstairs and we went into the workshop. Martha and I gazed at Richard's body. "It still doesn't seem real. Last year I bought medicine from him, and today I killed him."

"And you'll likely dream about it for some time," Martha said. "Most nights I dream about the soldier I killed."

"Martha, I had no idea," I cried. "How awful."

"I tell myself it's better that I'm having the nightmares than he is." She quickly changed the subject. "How did he get in? I locked the door behind us."

"He didn't use the front door." I pointed to the back door of the shop, which still stood ajar. We stepped into the rear court-yard and looked about. Richard had set up a makeshift camp against one of the high walls surrounding the yard. Blankets lay under a canvas sheet, and a crust of bread sat on a plate, the remnants of his last meal.

"He's probably been hiding back here since he murdered Penrose," I said. "Most likely, he and Ellen were just waiting for the opportunity to escape."

"What should we do now?" she asked.

"Send for the constable, I suppose. He will order Ellen's arrest."

"We still have no evidence against her."

"That won't matter now. Richard as good as admitted his guilt when he attacked us. And with him dead Ellen will put up little resistance. Or am I wrong about her again?"

"Without him, she will break," she agreed. "But let's wait to call the constable. We started this, and we found the truth. I want to see this through to the end. We should bring her here and show her his body. She will answer our questions then."

I considered her suggestion before nodding in agreement. I had no desire to turn over an unfinished case to the same officials who had made such a mess of it in the first place. If we could prove Ellen's guilt, we would. I found a basin to wash the blood from my hands, and we went outside. We waved to the guard and he crossed the street to meet us.

"Where now, my lady?" he asked. He looked warily at the marks on Martha's face and the spots of blood on my dress but held his tongue.

"Martha and I are going to Stephen Cooper's home," I said. "I need you to summon the constable and tell him to bring two or three of his men back here."

"Yes, my lady. You don't need an escort?"

"It is midday, and the streets are busy enough. Besides, we have no time to waste." The lad nodded and disappeared up St. Saviorgate. It took only a few minutes for us to reach the Coopers' home. We knocked on the door, and after a moment Ellen cracked the door and peered out.

"Lady Hodgson, what a surprise!" she said. I looked at her closely, trying in vain to find some sign of the murderess that lay within.

"Hello, Ellen," I said. "Could you come with us, please?"

She looked at me suspiciously for a moment. "I should stay here, my lady. I have much work to do." She was not going to make this easy.

"I must insist. It is very important business, touching on your mistress's fate." I knew she could hardly refuse this request.

She peered up and down the street, as if some passerby might tell her what to do. She furrowed her brow when she saw Martha's bruises but said nothing. "Now, Ellen."

"What happened to you?" she asked Martha with a tremor in her voice.

"I fell," Martha said flatly.

Ellen stepped outside and locked the door behind her. The three of us started toward the Pavement, and Ellen looked around nervously. "Where are we going, my lady?" she asked.

"Just up here," I said, "to Mr. Penrose's shop." She swallowed hard and nodded. She must have known that her plans had gone terribly wrong, but her face remained impassive.

"Why have we come here?" Ellen asked.

"We are meeting some people," I said evasively.

"I'm afraid I cannot spend the day like this," she said. "I must return to my mistress's home." She started to go, but Martha seized her wrist.

"There is something inside you should see," she said. "We have discovered evidence that Mrs. Cooper is innocent."

Ellen gazed at Martha a moment before answering. "She cannot be. She had the poison. She hated Mr. Cooper. He was an evil man."

"I'll grant you that he was," Martha replied. "But that does not make Mrs. Cooper a murderess. Come inside."

I opened the door and gestured for Ellen to enter. She stepped into the shop and looked around nervously. She likely knew of Richard's hiding place in the courtyard and worried we had found it. "Let us go into the workshop," I said.

Ellen walked around the counter and stepped through the doorway. When she saw Richard's body and his dead eyes, she cried out and fell to her knees. Martha stood over her, watching impassively as her scream turned to a keening wail. "You killed him? Why did you kill him?" she cried.

"I had no choice," I said. "He was trying to kill me, just as he killed his master."

A harsh laugh escaped Ellen's lips. "His master? Do you know how ill Penrose used Richard?"

"I saw the bruises," I said softly. "Mr. Penrose was not a kind master, but——"

"The bruises?" Ellen interrupted. "You have no idea, do you? The bruises weren't the half of it. *Mr.* Penrose was a cursed sodomite, and used Richard's body most unnaturally." Tears began to stream down her cheeks. "He would come home from the alehouse drunk as a lord, and throw himself on Richard. He swore that if Richard ever complained, he would dismiss him, have him whipped, and ensure he never gained his freedom. *That* was Richard's master."

"And Stephen Cooper raped you," Martha said. "He's the father of your child, and you poisoned him."

At the mention of Stephen's name, Ellen's face hardened and her tears stopped. "He pretended to be the godliest of men. Family prayer, Bible reading, gadding to sermons. But under it all, he was no less rotten than Penrose."

"Did Mrs. Cooper know?" I asked.

"No. He was careful. He only summoned me when she was out. He told me that he would deny it if I told her, and then cast me out for lying. I knew he was right—Mrs. Cooper would never believe me. What could I do except submit?"

"And he got you with child," Martha said.

"It's funny. Once I was with child, I had proof of his sin, and he lost his power over me."

"So you demanded money."

"Richard thought it would be enough to open his own shop. He has relatives in Norfolk. We were going to go there." She looked down at his body, and once again the tears began to flow. My heart softened, for I knew that her fate was sealed, and she would end her days at the stake.

"Why did you kill him?" I asked. "Why not just take the money?"

She turned to me with a puzzled look on her face. "He drove away Richard, he raped me, threatened me, got me with child … what would you have had me do? The last night he pulled me from my bed while I slept and raped me in the parlor. After he finished he sent me for a glass of milk. 'I need to cool my blood,' he said. We hadn't planned to kill him until after the siege ended, but I had the poison at hand and could not stop myself. I chose to rise up against my master rather than serve him another day."

"After you killed him, you stole the money and changed the lock," I said.

She nodded. "We wanted to confuse things until the siege ended." She looked down at Richard again. "And you ruined it. You ruined it."

"Then you told Richard we were interested in Lorenzo Bacca."

"When you said that you would never believe that Mrs. Cooper was guilty, we decided to help you find other suspects. I knew from your reaction when I told you about the Italian's visit that you suspected him. Richard just led you where you wanted to go. If you'd chased him just a few more days, we would have escaped."

"The constable will be here soon," I said. "It is almost time to go."

"Time to go?" Ellen whispered as if to herself. "Yes, I suppose it is." Without warning, she seized a large brass pestle from the counter, and as a guttural cry roared from her throat, she swung it at my head. I took a step back, but the blow struck me on the cheek. A bright light flashed before me and I fell to the ground, dazed. "I'll kill you, you bitch!" she screamed, and stepped toward me with murder in her eyes. "You ruined everything!" I watched the pestle begin its arc toward my head. As it reflected the afternoon sunlight, I could not help admiring its beauty. Just before the pestle would have ended my life, Martha hurled herself between us. I heard a sickening crack as the pestle struck her forearm. She cried out and fell against the counter. Ellen ignored Martha and took another step toward me, her face twisted in rage. She raised the pestle and swung. I rolled to the side and heard the dull thud of the pestle striking the floor next to my head.

As she prepared to strike again, I heard the sound of heavy footsteps and a man shout, "Stop!"

"Will!" I cried as he raced into the room, sword drawn.

For an instant, Will took his eyes off Ellen to look at me and nearly paid for his mistake with his life. Without a moment's hesitation, Ellen swung the pestle at his head. Will stepped back, but not far enough, as the blow found its mark and sent him crashing to the ground. Ellen turned back to me, but I had already scrambled to my feet. I launched myself across the room, knocking her to the floor next to Richard's corpse. I leapt up, found Will's sword, and placed its tip on her throat. "Stay right there," I said. "I don't want any more blood on my hands today." Ellen lay still for a few seconds and then turned to look into Richard's face. Tears streamed from her eyes as she silently mourned her beloved.

I risked a glance at Will as he pulled himself to his feet. Blood ran down his forehead, but his eyes were clear. I said a prayer of thanks that the blow had not done serious damage. "My God, where did you come from?" I cried.

"I came to your house and Hannah told me where you had gone. I thought you might need some help, but I didn't expect this."

At that moment, Henry Thompson strode in and surveyed the scene. I can only imagine what he thought. By now, the once orderly workshop had been thoroughly destroyed. Richard lay dead in a pool of blood, and I stood next to him, holding a sword to Ellen's throat. Blood continued to run down Will's face, and Martha stood in the doorway, her arm hanging uselessly by her side.

"Hello, Lady Bridget," Henry said dryly. "Might I ask why you sent for me? Everything seems to be under control."

That night I dreamed of Richard Baker. In the dream we were back in the apothecary's workshop. He entered the room, just as he had that afternoon, and attacked me. When he reached me, I stabbed him in the heart with a knife that had appeared in my hand. He fell to the floor, screaming in pain and rage. After I stabbed him, he lay on the floor for a moment before standing up. When he did, the knife reappeared in my hand, and he attacked again. And again. Sometimes he carried his club, sometimes a bottle of ratsbane, sometimes an iron bar. Sometimes he screamed with Ellen's voice.

I must have killed him a thousand times that night before I finally pulled myself awake at dawn. I climbed from bed and sought refuge in the Gospels. When I heard Martha rise, I followed her downstairs and found her in the kitchen doing what work she could with her arm wrapped in bandages. It had taken the bonesetter three tries to get her arm in place, and she had nearly bitten through a leather belt while he worked, but she'd survived and he predicted a swift recovery.

"How did you sleep?" I asked, gesturing at her arm.

"It ached something fierce," she said. "But from the circles under your eyes, I would guess that I slept better than you."

"The dreams were as you said. I kept stabbing Richard, but he refused to stay dead."

"In mine the soldier is chasing me through a maze of alleys and streets. No matter how fast I run, I can never escape him. Sometimes it's Tom, but usually the soldier." She paused for a moment. "What is going to happen to Ellen?"

"Nothing good," I replied. "I imagine she'll be tried shortly. If she's with child, she won't be executed yet, but there's no escaping what she did." We lapsed into a melancholy silence.

"You were right about Mrs. Cooper," she said. "You saved her life."

I smiled at her efforts to lift my mood. "Yes," I said. "I suppose we did." I knew what she said was true, but I felt neither triumph nor vindication. I was relieved that Esther had escaped execution, but I got no satisfaction from Richard's death or the prospect of Ellen's burning. I knew that blood cried out for blood, that treason could not go unpunished, but I also knew that Stephen Cooper's and Thomas Penrose's tyrannies had driven their servants into rebellion. The Lord Mayor would try to rebuild the natural order on top of the ashes of those who challenged it, but I could no longer see that as an end in itself. It seemed to me that God demanded justice, not merely order. And if Richard and Ellen were to be burned for their crimes, why could Rebecca Hooke escape unpunished for hers? The order of things had never seemed so unnatural.

A few hours later, my brother-in-law, Edward, appeared at the door. I met him in the parlor and asked Martha to join us.

"How is your arm?" Edward asked, glancing at Martha.

"Very well, sir, thank you."

"Martha," I said, "I don't think my brother has ever acknowledged one of my servants before. He knows perfectly well that you saved my life. Take his question as the compliment it is." Edward ignored me, of course, but Martha blushed and curtsied.

Edward got right to business. "The Lord Mayor has convened another special court to deal with the murders of Stephen Cooper and Thomas Penrose. He reversed the conviction of Esther Cooper and oversaw the trial of the maidservant."

"I imagine that went as smoothly as Esther's trial," I remarked dryly.

"She confessed to both murders. The constable found the money she extorted from Stephen in her clothes chest. The Lord Mayor sentenced her to be burned to death for the murder of her master." He paused, clearly uncomfortable with what he had to say next. "The Lord Mayor also ordered that Richard Baker be hanged and his body burned as a warning to all who would rise up against their masters. A gibbet has been built in front of the Black Swan." He looked up at my clock. "The ceremony will begin shortly."

"Surely you are joking," Martha said. "You are going to hang and burn a dead man?"

Edward glanced at her but ignored the question. "Stephen Cooper's maidservant has pleaded the belly. Dorothy Mann has confirmed that she is with child. She will burn in the fall, after the child is born."

"Did the Lord Mayor admit his error to Esther?" I asked.

"He did not think it seemly for her to be in court. But she has been released from the Castle."

"He's a fountain of justice, he is," murmured Martha. I shot her a look, but in truth I could not have agreed more.

"Lady Bridget," Edward said, "may I have a word with you in private?" I nodded to Martha, and she slipped out of the room. "It has come to my attention that a member of the King's garrison who was wounded in the fighting has been speaking of you and members of your household in most unsettling terms."

"I—I do not know what you mean," I stammered, trying to control the sinking feeling in my stomach.

"His name is Tom Hawkins. Isn't Hawkins your maidservant's name? He mentioned her as well. He says she is a murderess."

# Chapter 24

"There must be some kind of mistake," I said. "Where is this man?"

"He is in the garrison's hospital at Peasholme Green. He's been swearing the vilest oaths against you and your servant. The surgeons are convinced he suffers from delirium caused by his wounds. They could be right, but in light of your recent adventures, I thought I should speak to you."

"Martha has no kin here in the city, so he can't mean her." At that moment, I wished I had Martha's ability to lie convincingly—I felt sure Edward could see the truth. "It is possible he overheard our names at the Black Swan, and in his delirium confused us with someone he knows, perhaps someone from before he came to York."

"It is possible," he said, but I did not think he believed it. "If you wish to see him, you should not wait. He will not live much longer."

"The wounds are that serious?"

"A nasty cut on his leg. It should not have been fatal, but for some reason he waited several days before seeking treatment. Now it is badly infected." I wondered if Martha would want to see her brother one last time before he died. I knew I should at least give her the choice.

"Thank you, Edward. Perhaps I will visit him. Even though he is a stranger, I may be able to put his mind at ease in his final hours." I didn't imagine for a moment that he believed so unconvincing a lie, but he left without challenging me. I called for Martha.

"Edward says that they've found Tom."

"Is he alive?" she asked. I could not tell what answer she hoped for, but I could only imagine her anxiety. If he was alive, her new life in York would be in jeopardy; if he was dead, she would have lost her nearest kin.

"For now. Edward said he is in one of the garrison's hospitals. He must have been the one who attacked me after the christening. Will wounded him, and now he is dying of the infection." Martha's eyes filled with tears, and I took her hand.

"How did Mr. Hodgson know to come to us?" she asked, wiping her cheeks.

"Tom's been cursing us both by name." Martha's eyes widened with fear. "I think you're safe," I said. "Nobody takes such nonsensical accusations seriously. The doctors say it is the infection."

"What should we do?"

"Edward suggested a visit," I said cautiously.

"I want to see him before he dies," she whispered.

The walk to St. Anthony's Hall took longer than usual, because we took a roundabout route. Neither Martha nor I had any desire to pass by Penrose's shop. I did not know when I would return to that neighborhood, but it would not be soon. There was no way to avoid the Black Swan, however—it lay directly across the street from the hospital entrance. From the outside, one would never have guessed that a murder had taken place there just a few days before. I wondered if the room where Penrose died had already been put back in use by the alehouse whores. The gibbet still stood in the street, but Richard's body had been cut down, thank God. I averted my eyes as best I could until we reached the gate to St. Anthony's.

"What is your business here?" barked the guard.

"We're here to visit one of the wounded soldiers," I said. "To give him comfort in his final hours."

The guard looked us over, decided we posed no threat, and opened the gate. We climbed a set of narrow stairs to the main hall. Before the war, poor children had been taught to knit here, in the hope that they would not become a burden on the city. Now beds filled the hall, each one holding one of the garrison's sick or wounded. When we entered, a young man in a blood-covered smock came over to greet us. I could smell the liquor on his breath long before he opened his mouth.

"Good morning, my lady," he said. "I am Mr. Stevens, the surgeon here. How can I be of service?"

"We are here to see a wounded soldier, Sergeant Hawkins. We have heard he is delirious."

"Yes, a regrettable case," he said, shaking his head. "The wound itself would not have been serious if he had come to me immediately. For some reason, he tried to treat it himself. His bed is in the far corner. We moved him there because his yelling disturbed the other patients. It's stopped now, though. He's too weak."

"How long will he live?" Martha asked.

"Not long, I don't think. With infections it is hard to say, but he'll be dead tomorrow." I was appalled by his blunt language, but Martha nodded her thanks. I looked closely at her face, but I could not tell how she felt about her brother's impending death. Perhaps she did not know, either.

We thanked Stevens again, and he wandered off to check on other patients, God help them. Martha and I went to the corner that he had indicated. We reached the last bed, and for a moment I thought we had come too late. Tom lay in the bed, but he was little more than a husk of the man I'd met at the Black Swan. His sallow complexion and sunken cheeks made his face the very mirror of death—only the slight movement of the sheet covering his chest indicated that he still lived. Even from the foot of the bed, I could smell the infected wound and knew that the surgeon's prediction was likely on the mark. I did not regret his death, of course, but I knew that Martha's reaction would be much more complicated, and I felt for her.

Martha pulled a stool from a neighboring bed and sat next to her brother. "Tom . . . Tom, can you hear me?" She reached out with her good hand and caressed his cheek. He took a deep, hitching breath and opened his eyes. He saw Martha and his features hardened. "Oh, Tom," she whispered, "what have you done now?"

"Hello, sister," he croaked. From the foot of his bed I could barely hear him. "Have you come to dance on my grave? Was betraying me in Hereford not enough?"

"Why did you do it, Tom? Why couldn't you let me be?"

He started to laugh but dissolved into a coughing fit. "Let you be? After what you did? I'd kill you now if I could."

"Tom, please!"

"What is your plan now, Martha? Will you spend your life as a servant?" Even in his weakened state, his voice dripped with scorn. "Didn't you have enough of that life back home? Wasn't

Mr. Holdsworth's cruelty enough? You could have been free of all that if you'd stayed with me."

"For how long? Until I met my fate at the end of a rope?"

"That's better than the life you've chosen. You'll find out soon enough how ill suited you are for service." He looked up at me. "Do you think she'll carry your shit and wash your clothes forever? She'll turn on you, just as she did me. It's in her blood. She can't bear to be ruled by another. A natural-born rebel she is."

"You will die soon, Tom Hawkins," I said. "You should repent for the things you've done. I can have the surgeon summon a minister."

"The only thing I regret is that I didn't cut your throat. If it weren't for that cripple of yours, you would be the one lying on your deathbed, not me." He turned back to look at Martha for the last time. "You'll hang yet, sister, you'll hang yet." Then he turned his head and closed his eyes.

Martha looked impassively at her brother. Without a word, she stood and walked out of the hall. I hurried after her and caught her at the gate. I searched desperately for words to comfort her, but none came. Neither of us spoke as we walked back to my house. That afternoon, Edward sent word that Tom had died. I told Martha and she nodded but said nothing.

From that day, life in my household returned to something like normal. With Tom safely in the ground, I dismissed the guards. Esther sent profuse thanks by letter but kept to her house and refused all visitors. I understood her reluctance to see anyone. The Lord Mayor had made much of her conviction but said nary a word about her exoneration. Her friends and neighbors knew that she had escaped burning, but few could say why. As a result, rumors spread far and fast. Some said she had bewitched the Aldermen, while others claimed she had bribed or even seduced the Lord Mayor. I did not think she could stay in York for long. Better she should go to London and start anew. With the money left to her by Stephen, she would have no trouble finding another husband.

The siege continued for another week, but without hardship, even for the city's poor. Martha and I attended two or three births and talked about many things, but not her brother. During the day, I sometimes forgot that I had killed a man with my own hands. But Richard Baker continued to haunt my dreams.

The return to normalcy also gave me the chance to plan Anne Goodwin's escape from York. I knew that Rebecca would not rest until she had protected herself from Anne, so she would never be safe in the city. For Anne's sake, I wanted to wait until the siege ended, so I sent a few shillings to Samuel Short to ensure her comfort. A week later, word came that Prince Rupert's forces would soon arrive at York, and the city rejoiced to see the rebels breaking camp. As the rebels fled and Rupert's men came into sight, the Lord Mayor ordered the city's church bells be rung to celebrate the city's miraculous deliverance. I did not know how long our reprieve would last, so I hastened to the Castle. When I arrived, the gate was wide open as the garrison celebrated the end of the siege. A guard took me straight to Samuel's tower, and Tree met me at the door.

"Hello, lady," he said brightly, and to my surprise and pleasure he threw his arms around my legs, gave me a hug, and began to chatter on about the doings in the Castle. "There's a pregnant lady in one of the other towers," he said. "They'll execute her after she has the child. If you're her midwife, you can visit me and Samuel all the time!"

"I'm not her midwife," I said, forcing a smile. "But I'll tell

Samuel that you can visit me as often as you want." And I'll wash you every time you do, I thought.

"Welcome, Lady Hodgson," a voice called out, and Samuel Short appeared at the top of the stairs that led to the cells. "I've only got one guest of yours now, and she is doing well. You can go down to see her on your own. Since she's staying voluntarily, I stopped locking the door." He thought for a moment. "Perhaps I'll start renting out the rest of the rooms as well," he said with an impish grin. "I could advertise the healing properties of the Ouse. You could invite your friends from the countryside! What do you say?"

"With the end of the siege, business would be quite brisk," I said. "I'll summon my relatives from Hereford. They'd much prefer this to one of the inns. It has a lovely view of the moat and river."

"Excellent news! We'll be rich!"

"I am rich, Samuel."

"True enough," he said with a laugh. "But then we'd *both* be rich. I could be knighted, perhaps even become a lord!"

When I reached Anne's cell, I found that it now held many of the comforts Esther had left behind. Anne sat on the bed, reading a cheap pamphlet. I glanced at the title and saw that it detailed the horrid murder of Thomas Penrose by his rebellious apprentice and a whore. I supposed that description of the crime came nearer the truth than the one about Stephen Cooper's murder.

Anne rose when I entered and curtsied deeply. "My lady, thank you again for arranging my stay here."

I could not help laughing. "Any time you would like to stay in a prison cell, I think I will be able to find you a spot." Her smile gladdened my heart, and I knew that all would be well with her. "Anne," I said, "I think now is the time for you to leave."

"But what about the Hookes? They can't have given up already, can they?"

"No, they haven't. But I don't mean that you should leave the Castle. You still need to leave York. London would be best, and I have purchased a seat on a carriage leaving this afternoon. It is unlikely the Hookes would follow you so far, and they would have a devil of a time finding you if they did. They say it is growing by the thousands every year. I have already sent letters on your behalf to my friends in the city. They will see that you find a good position." I gave her a packet with the names of my London friends, and a few coins to help her until she found a position.

"What of my family?" she asked. "Surely I will see them again, won't I?"

"They will meet us at the carriage to bid you farewell, but you must remember that your life here is over, and your new one lies in London. Gather your belongings, for we must leave immediately. If the King's men lose their advantage, the rebels may renew their siege of the city."

Anne nodded and began to put her meager possessions in a canvas bag. She followed me to Coneystreet, where a southbound carriage prepared for its departure. Her seat had cost me a pretty penny, but after all she had suffered, it seemed the least I could do for her. As we approached the inn, I could see Margaret and Daniel Goodwin peering anxiously into the crowd in search of Anne's face. The smiles that lit up their faces when they caught sight of her will stay with me for the rest of my days. I saw joy and love, of course, but also a trace of sadness, for they knew that they might never see their daughter again. I stood back while they embraced, and when they started to cry, I swallowed my own tears. To say farewell to one's child is a terrible thing. All too soon, the driver shouted for his passengers. Anne clambered aboard and found a seat by the window. As the carriage pulled into the street and started toward the Ouse Bridge, Anne spied me and raised her hand in thanks and farewell. I looked for Margaret and Daniel in the crowd but could not find them. After the carriage turned out of sight, I went home.

The hope provided by Prince Rupert's arrival proved short-lived. Two days later, the rebels, assisted by the upstart Cromwell, defeated the King's men at Marston Moor, and the siege began anew. But this time nobody believed that the garrison would resist for more than a few weeks, for with the defeat of the King's army, the city's fall became inevitable.

A few days after the battle, I sat in my parlor reading when Hannah appeared in the doorway. "My lady, there is a gentleman here to see you. He says he comes from the Lord Mayor." She paused for a moment. "He is *Italian!*" she whispered in a conspiratorial tone.

I could not imagine why Bacca had come to see me, but it seemed unlikely that he would announce himself if he intended to do me harm, and with Richard's death, he had no reason to do so. I told Hannah to see him in.

"Lady Hodgson, how are you?" Bacca said. "I am happy to see that you survived your recent troubles." I instinctively brought my hand to my cheek and felt the plaster covering the wound I'd received from Ellen. "Ah, do not worry about a scar on the cheek," he said, running his finger along his own. "It will make you all the more alluring."

I smiled despite myself. "What can I do for you, Mr. Bacca?"

"Always to business. You English are so serious," he said, pouting. "I came to tell you that the Lord Mayor has decided not to pursue you for defying his will. He has sent a letter to the

Minster asking that you be allowed to keep your license to practice midwifery."

"And I presume you will no longer threaten me?"

"Oh, Lady Hodgson . . ." He laughed. "I hope you did not believe that the Lord Mayor would have hurt you. You are the daughter of his predecessor! These rebels may not know the meaning of honor and loyalty, but the Lord Mayor certainly does. He apologizes, and sincerely regrets any misunderstanding on your part."

"On my part?" I asked in disbelief.

"I am simply delivering the message," he said. "Whether you believe it is up to you."

"Does his apology have anything to do with the fact that the rebels will soon take the city?"

"He did not say this to me, but I think it would be a reasonable conclusion." He paused for a moment. "I must commend you on freeing your friend from the Castle. The Lord Mayor is pleased that justice has been done."

"Did you ever believe that Mrs. Cooper killed her husband?"

"You seem to have confused me with the constable, my lady," he said. "I have more important concerns than a single murder. In truth, I don't much care whether Mr. Cooper was killed by Mrs. Cooper, Charles Yeoman, or your brother Edward."

"Edward?" I cried. "What do you mean?"

Bacca stared at me for a few moments and then began to laugh. "You have many commendable qualities, but are quite blind to those closest to you."

"You suspected Edward?"

"I did from the start, and so should you. If the maidservant hadn't killed Mr. Cooper, Mr. Yeoman might have. And if he hadn't, I imagine your brother would have paid him one final visit.

Mr. Cooper seemed quite intent on the destruction of the city, and your brother is not nearly fanatical enough to stand by and let it happen."

"And if the Lord Mayor had demanded it, you would have killed him?"

"Are we not at war, my lady? If we count the apothecary's apprentice, you have slain more rebels than most of the soldiers in the King's army. If I had killed Mr. Cooper, it would have been no different.

"I also came to bid you farewell," he said, rising to his feet. "I will leave the city after it falls into the rebels' hands. I look forward to going home, but I found your case interesting, to say the least. I've not met many midwives who can kill with their bare hands—it was a job well done."

An image of Richard's lifeless eyes came to mind and I looked away from Bacca. "I am very lucky to be alive."

In the end, predictions about the city's fall proved accurate. Thankfully, the garrison held out long enough to negotiate favorable terms of surrender. The city's leaders insisted that none of the Scottish barbarians be garrisoned in the city. Once the rebel generals agreed, the Royalist garrison retreated to the south. With the loss of York, the rebels now held all of the north, and the King's cause seemed in greater danger than ever.

The ensuing weeks heralded great changes for the city. The King's men, including the Lord Mayor and his retinue, fled the city, and the godly seized control of the city's government. This meant even more authority for Edward and also those around him, including me. I disagreed with Edward on all manner of political and religious questions and lamented what he had done to Will, but I was not fool enough to cut him off when he was at the height of his power. Ironically, even as the city saw its political life turned upside down, my own home found peace. I delivered as many women as would have me, and Martha proved an able assistant. Our physical wounds healed as well. The bonesetter had done such a fine job that by the fall none could tell that her arm had ever been broken. In this I was less fortunate, for Ellen's blow left me with an inch-long scar on my cheek, a token by which to remember her. To my great surprise and pleasure, Tree took me up on my invitation to visit, and he soon got in the habit of stopping by several times each week. At first he came for the food—and resisted the scrubbing I gave his face—but after a time he made himself a second home in Birdy's old room. Hannah, Martha, and I took turns teaching him to read, and I even dragged him to church whenever he slept at my house on a Saturday night.

Ellen's pregnancy continued without incident, and in the fall, Dorothy Mann delivered her of a stillborn girl. Once the child had been born, preparations began for Ellen's execution. Edward had pressured me to attend, saying that I was the woman responsible for her capture, but I denied him. A few weeks after Ellen's death, I made a decision that would prove the most consequential since I agreed to marry Phineas and come to York. Martha and I had just returned from delivering a woman in Goodramgate parish, and once again Martha had proven herself useful. I found her in the kitchen.

"Martha, please come to the parlor with me." She was a bit taken aback but followed. "You have acquitted yourself well since coming to my house. You kept your head and acted quickly when you had to. Let me see your hands." At this she hesitated, but she held them out, palms up. They were rough, of course, thanks to the work she did. Her fingers were long and thin, not as gnarled as they would become with years as a maidservant and then a lifetime as wife to a blacksmith or clothier. I put my hands into hers. "Squeeze."

"My lady?" This was not what she had expected.

"Squeeze my hands," I repeated, and she did, with a firm grip. "Good. You need a quick mind and strong hands, and clearly have both. I can teach you the rest."

"The rest?" she asked, wiping her hands on her apron, looking nervous.

"Martha, I want you to be my deputy," I said. "I will teach you the mysteries of my profession, and in due time you will become a midwife yourself." For the first time since we'd met, Martha seemed unsure of herself.

"My lady," she said, "I don't know what to say. What would I do?"

"Well, you'd still be my servant, and you will assist Hannah as you have until today. You will assist me in the delivery room as you have these last few months. Over time I will ask much of you and teach you more. You'll learn how to care for women when they are with child, in travail, and after they deliver. Once you gain a reputation as a skillful midwife, women will start to seek you out on their own. If you are good at it, you will have more respect and earn far more money than you ever would otherwise."

"I would be honored to do this, my lady."

"Good," I said, taking her hands in mine. "I think we will work well together."

# *Author's Note*

This book has its origin in the serendipitous discovery of a will written in 1683, for it was there I first met a York midwife named Bridget Hodgson, who provided a model for the fictional midwife in *The Midwife's Tale*. These two Bridget Hodgsons have much in common: they were both wealthy gentlewomen; both lived in the parish of St. Helen's, Stonegate; and both practiced midwifery. What attracted me to Bridget in the first place was that in her will, she defined herself by her profession, "midwife," rather than her martial status, "widow." I have read hundreds, if not thousands, of wills, and she is the only woman I found who did this. The historical Bridget also seems to have had a strength of character not often visible in the historical record, as she named her daughter and at least four of her godchildren after herself (Bridget Swain, Bridget Ascough, Bridget Morris, Bridget Wilberfoss).

In addition to Bridget, I have included fictionalized versions of other historical figures in *The Midwife's Tale*. She did, in fact, have a deputy midwife named Martha, and was friends with Sir Henry Thompson, who was one of the pallbearers at her funeral. The historical Bridget was married twice and widowed twice, the second time to Phineas Hodgson. Phineas appears to have been a bit of a spendthrift, for while his father's will left large sums to Phineas's brothers, Phineas did not do so well: "I give unto my son Phineas Hodgson in full satisfaction of his filial child's part and portion the sum of ten pounds of lawful English money . . . in regard he hath been so chargable to me."

I have, of course, taken a few liberties with the historical Bridget—this is a novel, after all. The historical Bridget had better luck with her children, with two daughters still living at the time of her death. One of these (named Bridget, naturally) received two hundred pounds as well as, "my coral necklace and bracelets, my large ring with two and twenty stones in it . . . and also a sealed ring of gold with my late husband's coat of arms and my own engraven on the same." Bridget's other daughter (or her husband) seems to have been as profligate as Phineas, for Bridget left her entire branch of the family just over ten pounds, "in regard they have been chargeable unto me in an extraordinary measure." (There are also tantalizing rumors of two sons hanged as highwaymen, but I could find no evidence to support this claim.)

I have done my best to portray Bridget's work as a midwife as accurately as possible. The techniques she used to bring forth a child or strengthen an infant who was born weak are described in contemporary midwifery manuals. I also have done my best to capture the sociability inherent in early modern childbirth, when a mother was attended by her friends and neighbors.

For more on the historical Bridget Hodgson and the history of midwifery, visit my Web site at http://www.samthomasbooks .com.